The Second Question

By James Arendorf

Inspired by true events and real people

Will it be difficult? … Yes

Will it be painful? … Yes

Will it be worth the effort? ... The Excelbox smiles.

Contents

Chapter 1

The Excelbox

A strange little box. Made of a shiny and solid metal. On one side, a small rectangular opening is permanently unlocked. Suddenly, the top side of the box opens, a transparent and luminous oval glass cage, slowly straightens up. The cage is soldered by four yellow gold cylinders, forged in a shape of a vine plant.

A round clock rises inside the transparent cage. The time is not about hours and minutes, but days and months. A small needle is focused on a very specific date:

December 12th, 1891

The big needle indicates a date 12 months earlier, between the nights of 04th to 05th January 1891.

This strange box gave out a small piece of paper that changed the fate of a little girl ... forever.

5 clues when requested will be granted

The challenge will be as followed:

Before midnight of each December 12th, one question will be asked.

I permit you continuity, if I am answered without a fault

When all the 7 lessons will be assimilated

The challenge will be completed

And the Heir will be proclaimed.

Chapter 2

2 cents

Monday, January 05th, 1891.

Mr. Ernest Laszlo, the famous Lawyer of Georgetown city, was standing and observing the winter landscape through the windows of his luxurious living room. The sky was gray, trees didn't have any leaves, a thin layer of Snow covered the ground, winter promised to be peaceful and quiet. Yet, Mr. Ernest Laszlo was concerned and worried. In his entire career, never a legal case did upset him that much.

A tormented voice interrupted his thoughts:

- But what is happening?

Mr. Ernest Laszlo turned toward a man sitting on a big chair in the luxurious living room. Leaning on a wood cane with an anxious attitude, Mr. Ferdinand Edelmen repeated his question:

- What is happening, Ernest?!

Mr. Ernest Laszlo, his Lawyer and longtime friend, had no answer to this question; he himself couldn't understand the strange turn of events. Mr. Ferdinand Edelmen was the nephew of the late Governor of Washington State, Mr. Iskander Balthazar. After his Uncle passed away just few months ago, Mr. Ferdinand Edelmen was the legitimate Heir of his Uncle's colossal fortune. Sole and legitimate Heir. A simple inheritance transition. However …

The little girl knew the way to the Lawyer's office, Mr. Ernest Laszlo. She had taken this corridor several times in recent months. But when she arrived at the Secretary's office, she didn't find the woman in her usual place. She searched for the Secretary left and right, but no trace of her. After few minutes, the little girl couldn't wait any longer, if she didn't want to be late for her classes at school, that morning. She had an important message to deliver to Mr. Ernest Laszlo. And it had to be transmitted today.

The little girl then decided to enter the Lawyer's office, without waiting for the Secretary. She knocked twice on the big luxurious wood door, and she stepped inside.

Mr. Ernest Laszlo's office was vast. A luxurious black wood desk occupied the room; the floor was cold black, a large chandelier illuminated cold lights. On the left, a long meeting table was placed. Twenty people were sitting around it, and at the head of the long table, there was Mr. Ernest Laszlo. The Lawyer seemed very surprised to see the little girl in his office, interrupting a work meeting.

- What are you doing here? He asked with an arrogant and angry voice.

All the heads and eyes turned around to observe the little girl. She wore her best clothes that day; denim overalls, a white shirt yellowed and over washed, small worn out black shoes, and a large cap that covered most of her hair. The little girl replied in a shy voice:

- Good morning, Mr. Ernest. I came to give you back your money.

The Lawyer seemed confused:

- What money? What are you talking about?

The little girl came close to the Lawyer, and she put in front of him on the long meeting table, 2 cents. Mr. Ernest Laszlo still couldn't understand what she handed him:

- A little beggar like you, interrupting me in the middle of a work meeting, to give me 2 cents? What does that mean?!

Employees around the long meeting table didn't dare to move. They all observed the little girl with the poor appearance. Some had recognized her, others doubted who she was. Only Mr. Sloan Wilfrid, the Lawyer's right-hand man and Lyor Laszlo, Mr. Ernest's son, were sure of the poor little girl's identity.

In front of the Lawyer's confusion, the little girl explained in a spontaneous voice:

- These are the 2 cents you gave me, Mr. Ernest Laszlo. Before the first challenge, on my last visit to your office, you offered me these 2 cents for me and my family, when we would leave the Annex house of the grand Mansion. And since we are still in ... I thought to give you back … your 2 cents ... Monsieur.

Mr. Sloan Wilfrid didn't hold his amused smile. Mr. Lyor Laszlo looked shocked. And the Lawyer, Mr. Ernest Laszlo became red angry, unable to answer and find his words. The other employees sitting around the long meeting table, were whispering and exclaiming, all surprised to see a little girl making their employer speechless and angry.

When she turned around to leave the Lawyer's office, the little girl was unaware that her spontaneous move, returning back the 2 cents, will leave everyone present in this meeting, astonished.

You see, that little girl, born into a poor family, was designated and chosen by Late Mr. Governor to be his Heiress ... after she would have succeeded the challenges, each December 12th, on her birthday.

This 13 years old little girl who defied all bets, she was Dalya Kartal Bouvard.

Chapter 3

Finally, like the others

Wednesday, January 07th, 1891. 7:50 AM, at the Royal Georgetown College.

During the last 6 months, Dalya studied in private courses with Professor Canfield. After passing three evaluation tests, the little girl was still not allowed to join the other students in classes. Dalya didn't complain of this situation, on the contrary, it was the first time in her life that the little girl was learning and attending school. And not just any school; the prestigious Royal Georgetown College. Professor Canfield was an excellent teacher and mentor for her, he was always encouraging, patient and kind.

That day, Dalya paused for a minute to observe the splendor of the College; an enormous red brick building, hundreds of large square windows, a black iron front door. It was an intimidating and a majestic place.

Walking few steps toward the entrance, Dalya met a familiar figure; the new recruited school Concierge; Dadès. Wearing a large coat and winter boots, the new employee had a multicolor crochet slouch hat on the head. And while he sprinkled hard salt on the stairs to help dissolve the ice, Dalya passed near him and she said a discreet hello. The worker looked up and smiled at her.

Dalya waited quietly on the bench in front of the Director's Secretary Desk; Miss Uplerine Amana. The woman was writing names on a big register. Dalya could clearly notice the frequent glances and the proud smiles of Miss Uplerine toward her.

When the School Director, Mr. Darkfett called Dalya to come in, her heart tightened up.

- You're back again!! Said a cold voice behind a large desk.
- Good morning Headmaster. Dalya replied politely.

Director Darkfett looked up to the little girl, examining her clothes.

- And how do you expect me to have a good day, while a veggy seller studies in my prestigious school, among students of the most distinguished families in our country?!!

Dalya lowered her head and she stared at her old shoes. Director Darkfett got up and came close to her. The old man turned around her, thinking aloud, not caring that his words may be hurtful:

- But ... the real question is ... how is it possible? ... How an ignorant veggy seller was able to answer the Will challenge? ... it's weird ... it's unusual ... it must surely be beginner's luck ...

Director Darkfett paused, before continuing:

- And I'm certainly not the only one thinking that it is pure madness to hand over his entire fortune to a girl without a social status or Nobility and even less an education ...

Director Darkfett stared at Dalya and he said:

- But ... I admit ... What concerns me the most is how long you will remain in my school? ... Am I not getting rid of a beggar like you?

Facing the degrading and humiliating remarks of the Headmaster, Dalya didn't dare to raise her head, even less say a word. And although the Headmaster spoke in a soft voice, his words were venom:

- You will not stay with us much longer. You have my word. Don't be delighted so fast and don't get used to this school!! ... I need you to understand something girl; you do not belong to this school, you do not belong to this social status, and you will never be!! ... No matter how much you try, you were born a veggy seller at the market, living in a rat hole, and you will always remain that!!

Dalya's throat tightened up, her cheeks became all red, and she felt her legs trembling. Dalya couldn't understand the insolent and crushing attitude of the Headmaster toward her. She couldn't understand what wrong could there be for someone like her, to attend school and follow courses, just like the other students.

- You will join Professor Canfield in his usual classroom. He will tell you the new schedule that you will follow ... for the next few months.

Dalya was eager and happy to leave Director Darkfett's office. She immediately turned toward the door, before the Headmaster's yell stopped her abruptly:

- ONE MINUTE LITTLE VERMIN!!

Dalya turned to Director Darkfett who screamed menaces:

- I SHALL NOT CATCH YOU TRYING TO MAKE FRIENDS!! YOU ARE FORBIDDEN TO TALK TO ALL STUDENTS!! ALL THE STAFF!! ALL THE TEACHERS!! ALL THE EMPLOYEES!! YOU ARE FORBIDDEN TO TALK TO ANYONE IN THIS SCHOOL!! IS IT CLEAR ENOUGH?
- Yes, Sir. Dalya replied in an intimidated voice.

And what a relief Dalya felt when she finally left Director Darkfett's office, and walked the school hallway. She hoped that the cold and crushing behavior of the Headmaster, would have changed when she would have succeeded the first challenge. Unfortunately, the little girl's achievement has enraged even more Director Darkfett. But it is to admit that despite the indecent remarks of the Headmaster, the little Dalya Bouvard was so happy to go back to school and continue her learning.

Before, when she worked with her father, selling vegetables on their carriage and in the kiosk in the Saturday's market, Dalya gathered most of her knowledge from newspapers that her friends Alfie Jaq and Maurice Gus brought to her, in exchange for vegetables and fruits basket. Dalya often visited her Uncle Giorgi Bouvard in his funny home full of objects and gadgets, her Uncle always explained to her how things worked.

But now, for the first time in her life, Dalya Bouvard was learning things in a school. A real school! And thanks to the late Governor Mr. Iskander Balthazar who insisted in his Will to sign her up in this school for her education.

A woman's scream startled Dalya when she turned left on a hallway:

- HOW WONDERFUL TO SEE YOU HERE MADEMOISELLE!!

It was Miss Guendolyn, a young woman with ruby red hair, the Library assistant of the Royal Georgetown College. The Library was Dalya's most favorite place. The little girl would spend hours and hours, discovering millions of books of all kinds, types and subjects. And Miss Guendolyn was the nicest and caring woman that Dalya knew. Since her first day at school, Miss Guendolyn had always helped and encouraged the new student, without judging her poor clothes, or her origins.

- Hello Miss Guendolyn!! ... It a nice pleasure to see you too!!

Miss Guendolyn was not embarrassed to hug Dalya in her arms. The young woman couldn't hide her happiness:

- Is it your first day this semester?
- Yes, I have just come out of the Director's office. He didn't seem happy to see me, like you are.
- Don't you worry about him ... So then? Will you study with the other students in a class? Have you had your schedule yet?
- Director Darkfett asked me to join Professor Canfield in his classroom. I know nothing more about my status or my schedule.

Miss Guendolyn came close to Dalya and she whispered:

- On your free time, come visit me at the Library. We have received hundreds of new books and stories. Since I know you like them, I have them arranged on the lower shelves ... to be more accessible for you, on your return.

Dalya observed Miss Guendolyn in a surprised look:

- But ... how did you know I will come back?

Miss Guendolyn smiled innocently:

- I hoped for it.

Professor Canfield was at his desk, arranging his papers and lessons for his next class, as usual. And he was elegant as always in his checked suit and brown bow tie. When Dalya entered the classroom, Professor Canfield stood up to greet her with his big welcoming smile:

- I am delighted to see you with us again, Mademoiselle Dalya Bouvard.
- Thank you Professor, I am glad to be back too.

Professor Canfield came near her and he whispered softly:

- You have achieved a triumph, Mademoiselle. Nobody believed you could answer the first question.
- I myself didn't believe that I could, Professor. But when I followed your instructions on our last class, I was able to focus and see things a little clearer. Thank you, Professor.
- I am pleased to have been a good help to you, Mademoiselle. Anyway, I congratulate you. You can be proud of this success!! ... But you still have several steps to go. And from now on, everyone will be watching you. So don't lose your courage!

Dalya appreciated all Professor Canfield's encouragements. His comments were very different from those of Director Darkfett. Professor Canfield returned to his office to take a paper, and he gave it to Dalya:

- Now that your school admission has been confirmed for this semester, Director Darkfett allowed you to ...

Professor Canfield couldn't hold his innocent little laugh:

- ... Well, actually, Director Darkfett was forced to allow you to follow classes with the other students! ... I will provide you all the books and notebooks needed for your next courses ... they will be ready in my office tomorrow. And ... here's the new schedule for your courses. Classrooms numbers are below. This semester you will take classes of Mathematics, Music, History and Geography.

  You have made good progress during the last 6 months of your accelerated private courses. Which is the reason why you were placed in the advanced class, with 14 years' students. And although you will be younger than the students of your class, I think you are perfectly ready to follow some classes with them.

Dalya couldn't believe what she had just heard; she will finally attend classes with other students. Professor Canfield smiled:

- Congratulations Mademoiselle! You're officially admitted as a student in this school!
- Thank you Professor ... Thank you very much!!! Dalya repeated, shocked and overjoyed.
- It is due to your hard work and your own merit. Professor Canfield smiled, before continuing:
- Now, follow me please. I will take you to your first Mathematics course. Your teacher will be Mr. Wyatt.

8:30 AM. Class N°060, Mathematics course.

When Professor Canfield entered a room, Dalya followed him. The classroom was immerged in a warm light coming in through the huge windows; the smell of chalk filled the air. Twenty wood tables were placed symmetrically one behind the other, a huge blackboard was installed along a wall.

Except that this room was full of students and another teacher was standing near the big blackboard. The Professor was short, very chubby, with a large pepper mustache and a bald head, which gave him a friendly look.

Professor Wyatt interrupted his course and he greeted the new comer:

- Good morning Professor Canfield. How can I help you?
- Good morning Professor Wyatt. I wanted to introduce you to your new student. Mademoiselle Dalya Bouvard.

Dalya was intimidated by all the stares that have turned toward her, at that moment. All the students have interrupted their writing and were watching the new schoolgirl. Professor Wyatt spoke to Dalya in a formal and friendly tone:

- Welcome among us, Mademoiselle. Please, join the empty chair on the right. I will provide you in a moment, the documentation of this course.

Dalya walked toward the place indicated in slow steps, under the whispers and the gazes of the other students. Professor Canfield retired after greeting Professor Wyatt. And the course went on.

When Dalya sat in her chair in the back of the classroom, among other students, feelings of anxiety, but also of great joy, filled the little 13 years old girl. When she was selling vegetables and fruits in the kiosk on the Saturday market, Dalya never thought that one day she will be sitting in a classroom, finally like the other students, in the most prestigious College in the country!

Chapter 4

Strange attitudes

Friday, January 09th, 1891.

Dalya woke up early this morning. She was delighted to be in her first History class. She wore her poor usual clothes and went to join her parents in the kitchen to have breakfast.

- I AM TIRED OF COOKING FOR EVERYONE!!

Dalya's mother, Mrs. Augustine Bouvard yelled angrily, dropping the milk jug with such a sudden move, that half the milk dispersed quickly on the table. Mrs. Augustine continued:

- I CAN'T CONTINUE DOING THIS!! I CAN'T WAIT TO GET RID OF ALL OF YOU!! COOKING ... CLEANING ... GROCERIES ... LAUNDRY ... IT IS TOO MUCH FOR ME!! I SHOULDN'T BE DOING THIS!!

In the kitchen, the little twins were placed on their usual chairs. They were eating their oatmeal with milk, not caring or understanding what their mother was saying. Mrs. Augustine put on the table a heated bread plate, so brutally that the pieces flew off and landed on the table with crumbs everywhere. Dalya sat on the kitchen table, without even daring to greet her mother.

- I DREAM OF THE DAY WHEN I WON'T BE COOKING FOR YOU!! I AM TIRED OF SERVING MEALS MORNING AND NIGHT!! THIS IS AN AWFUL LABOR FOR ME!!

The jam jar didn't escape Mrs. Augustine's mood this morning. The good marmalade found itself also dispersed on the table. Dalya's mother removed the butter knives from a drawer; she crushed the drawer to its place. Then, she threw the butter knives on the table, making a crushing noise.

Dalya's mother was always in a violent and aggressive temperament, even at 7:00 AM. And one must admit that it was not the best day start we can hope for. Mrs. Augustine always made her family feel that they were a burden to her; it was a real chore to take care of her own family. And she never shied away to let them know they were a burden, all the time, and always so violently.

Dalya remained silent; she ate her bread and milk as quickly as she could. Then, Dalya slipped away from the kitchen to the exit.

Dalya's father was in the little garden of the Annex house. He was preparing his carriage to join his delivery work at the Toscana restaurant.

- Good morning father.

Mr. Antman Bouvard didn't reply to his daughter, but he stared at her in an angry and aggressive look. It has been many days now since Antman Bouvard no longer answered his daughter; either he completely ignores her, or he looks at her with a strange stare.

Dalya noticed that her parents' attitude was unusual and bizarre, since she answered the first question. The little girl had managed to succeed well at the challenge, which allowed her parents and her younger sisters, to remain in the Annex house of the grand Mansion, for one more year until the date of the next challenge. Dalya was one step closer to reach the colossal fortune of Mr. Governor Iskander Balthazar. Yet, Dalya's parents behaved strangely toward her. Her mother was becoming increasingly violent, and her father stared at her with threatening looks.

Was it because Dalya reminded her father that the card game made him lose the money his family needed? Was it because Dalya finally replied to the critics and cruelty of her mother?

Dalya didn't know the exact reason for their strange behavior. Yet, she didn't dare to ask them.

Heading to the grand Mansion's exit, Dalya noticed the presence of a familiar silhouette; the Snow Panther, Mr. Iskander Balthazar's pet. A great allure, a light gray fur with tattooed patterns, large paws. The Panther was laying down on the garden wall, and when she noticed the little girl, the animal straightened its small head and its long tail swung up.

Since their first meeting, Dalya always felt the stare of the Snow Panther on her. It was a very different stare than her parents'. The animal observed Dalya with a serene look. For several months now, Séraphine always waited for the little girl at the entrance of the grand Mansion, every morning and every afternoon, before and after school. You would have thought that the animal was watching over the little girl.

7:45 AM. The Royal Georgetown College. Classroom N°309. History class.

When Dalya crossed the school door, most of students were also heading to their classrooms. The Concierge Dadès was carrying small pots filled with earth, to the school yard. Dalya passed close to him and she said:

- Good morning!

Dadès looked cheerfully and he replied with a strange accent:

- Hello Lalla!!

Dalya didn't understand the last word spoken by the worker. She smiled at him and went on her way to her classroom.

The History lesson was held in a vast class at the end of the corridor. Despite the large windows, gray light covered the room in a weighty cold. The students' tables were in shiny black wood, arranged in perfect symmetry.

Dalya arrived few minutes early. The classroom was already full of students. Dalya immediately noticed a very particular disposal; a crowd of students gathering around a girl and a boy in particular. The girl was tall and strong, a slightly tanned skin, long blond curly hair, and big light brown eyes. The boy was almost the same size, marble white skin and blond platinum hair. All eyes and faces were focused on both students, who seemed to be very popular.

Once Dalya appeared in the classroom, the conversations and the laughs stopped. The students stared curiously at her. When Dalya sat down on an empty chair at the back of the classroom, whispers were clearly heard:

- But ... what is she doing here?
- From what world does she come from?
- Wasn't she supposed to be in another school, for people of her kind?
- Will she be following our classes? Until the end of the year?
- So I have been told, but I did not believe it!
- Look at what she is wearing ...
- Can she at least read or write?

Dalya didn't know what to do or say, to respond the students' remarks on her. After a moment, Dalya preferred to remain silent.

Seconds later, a girl with two long braids entered the classroom. Dalya recognized her at once. She had met her few months ago, at the Headmaster's Office. Dalya remembered her name, Amira Mounier. The girl was the same age as Dalya; she was the youngest in her class too. The girl wore her chestnut hair in two long braids with pink silk butterfly ties on each end. She was small, a little plump and with chubby cheeks. She put her backpack on a chair, and then walked toward the group of students gathered near the window. The girl said timidly:

- G ... Good morning!

But none of the students heard her. They were laughing and talking, without paying any attention to Amira Mounier. Yet, she was clearly present. She repeated in a slightly higher voice:

- Good morning ... b ... beautiful day, is ... isn't it?

Dalya, who was watching the scene, didn't understand what was really happening. The students were well aware of Amira Mounier standing in front of them, and they heard her well. Except that all the students ignored her, none of them replied. Amira remained motionless all alone in front of the students' group, while they were laughing and talking to each other.

When an old man entered the classroom, all the students quickly joined their chairs. Professor Ajanar had white hair, he was tall and slim, and he wore a dark refined suit. He put his big briefcase on his desk. With a firm and dominant voice, the Professor addressed the students:

- Good morning everyone. I hope you're all ready to start your second semester!

Professor Ajanar took a few steps forward and he continued in a strange voice:

- I was informed this morning ... that a new student will be joining my class ...

All the students turned around to observe Dalya Bouvard; as if she was the strangest thing they had ever seen in their lives. Dalya didn't understand this sudden curiosity and the scrutinizing looks of the students.

- I never have taught that I would be giving History lessons to a ... veggy seller.

Bursts of laughs invaded the classroom. Dalya didn't understand the Professor's remark, she asked, in a spontaneous voice:

- Why not?

The students' laughs stopped immediately, replaced by a shocked expression on their faces. Knowing very well their teacher's character, the students held their breath and no one dared to move. Professor Ajanar walked toward Dalya, and he explained with a mean and vicious smile:

- Because you are worth nothing ... Mademoiselle.

He continued with such arrogance:

- The fact that you're sitting on this chair, in my class, doesn't mean that you are of the same social status as these students coming from Noble families ... and I'm curious to know how History can help a little girl like you ...

The popular boy with platinum blond hair answered:

- To better sell vegetables to passersby in the street ...

The students laughed. Even Professor Ajanar smiled at his student's comment. Dalya went silent and didn't dare to add a word. She did not expect this welcome. Professor Ajanar continued to address Dalya, in a threatening tone:

- Let it be very clear, little one!! During the next 6 months of the semester, I do not want to hear you, or see you participate, and much less educate you on anything in History. You have succeeded in getting a place in this school ... but don't dream that I teach you something in my class!! ... Sit down and shut up!! ... Is that clear enough for you?

Dalya answered in a shy voice:

- Yes, Sir.

Professor Ajanar went back to his desk, under the proud and satisfied look of his students, and Dalya's humiliation. He continued:

- Now ... I would like to remind the students who deserve to be in my class ... that the renowned essay contest of this year will take place on 5th December. The winner will receive the prestigious award of the dissertation of the Royal Georgetown College.
  And it will be with the attendance of parents, students, and teachers of this school. Just like the previous years; a distinguished person will honor us with his presence to this contest. So I suggest you start your preparations. You have several months to participate.
- Professor Ajanar ... will you be among the contest jury, this year too? Asked the popular girl with curly blond hair.
- Certainly yes. Said Professor Ajanar before continuing in a proud tone:
- And ... since you have won the award for the last 3 previous years ... I am assured that you will be the winner this time again, Miss Eriem Eyelord!

Dalya noticed that the popular girl with curly blond hair, answered with an arrogant confidence:

- Certainly, Professor.

Professor Ajanar took out of his briefcase a book and some files. And he addressed the students:

- And now ... open your History books of the Roman Empire ... page 22 ... Amira Mounier ... start reading the first chapter.

Amira Mounier, the girl with long light brown braids, tied with a pretty pink ribbon in the end, was sitting a few chairs away from Dalya. Suddenly, Amira became all red and confused. She opened her book with a trembling hand, and pronounced her words in a shaking voice:

- The rom ... roman em ... empire ... from -509 B.C. to 27 B.C ... the rom ... roman rep ... rep ... republic ... const ... const ...

Dalya noticed a strange thing in Amira's pronunciation. Professor Ajanar shouted:

- LOUDER!!

Dalya could feel Amira Mounier jump up from her chair. Amira doubled her efforts to raise her voice, but without succeeding to be heard by the entire class. Dalya noticed that she was struggling to get the words out of her mouth. Yet, Amira Mounier continued her efforts, whiel trembling:

- Constitute progressively ... a vast empire ... its conquests are ... ma ... ma ... made ... po ... po ... possible ... becau ...becau... becau...

Professor Ajanar exclaimed in an amused tone:

- Anyway, Amira Mounier ... we cannot count on a snail like you to win the essay contest this year!!

A wave of laughter filled the classroom. Dalya stared at Amira Mounier for a moment. And although she didn't know her, Dalya had a feeling that Amira was not like the other students of the class. In the middle of the laughs on her, Amira buried her head inside her book; her cheeks went even pinker than before.

At the end of the History class, Dalya went to her favorite place; the Library of Royal Georgetown College. As soon as she entered, Miss Guendolyn, the Library's assistant, greeted her with a bright smile:

- Dzień dobry, Mademoiselle Dalya!!
- Good morning, Miss Guendolyn. Dalya replied.
- So ... how are your new classes? I hope you like your courses with the other students!

Dalya hesitated a few seconds to answer. She always dreamed of being admitted to a school and study like the other students, but she didn't imagine it would be so stressful and intimidating.

- I had a History class with Professor Ajanar today ...

Miss Guendolyn exclaimed:

- Ah yes!! I know him. He is a little tough and ruthless. But hold on strong, Mademoiselle!! You can succeed in his course, I'm sure of that!!

Miss Guendolyn has always been supportive and kind to Dalya, since the first day the little girl entered the school. The young woman continued:

- A collection of French fairy tales arrived, two days ago. And I know you'll like them. Check the left aisle, section 5!!

Dalya thanked her with a smile, and walked to the recommended section. The Library was a magical heaven for the little girl who loved to read all kinds of books, and spend hours without getting bored in this place.

When Dalya approached Section 5 to seek the French tales, she heard a strange noise. Dalya turned on the aisle, to discover a familiar face. Her classmate Amira Mounier sitting on the floor, legs crossed, her face buried in her hands and she was crying.

Dalya was well aware that Director Darkfett banned her from speaking to any student of this school. But in front of Amira Mounier's crushed attitude, Dalya couldn't ignore it. Dalya came near her and she said in a kind voice:

- Hello.

Amira raised her head, all curious to know who was addressing her. Her cheeks were pink, her eyes full of tears. Amira stared at Dalya in confusion, not knowing what was happening.

- Is everything alright? Dalya asked with a compassionate smile.

Amira stood up rapidly, and she answered in a trembling voice:

- Do … don't … co … come near me!!

Dalya didn't understand Amira's reaction, she insisted:

- You were crying ... because of Professor Ajanar's remarks?

Amira stepped back and she ordered Dalya in a serious tone:

- Don't ta … ta … talk to me!! Don't … co … come near me!! I don't w … want them ... to see me w… with you!!

Dalya didn't dare to add a word. Amira dried her cheeks and she left the Library, leaving her classmate Dalya behind, all confused with so many questions.

Why did Amira refuse that Dalya speak to her? Who was she afraid of? The other students or the teachers? Why was she afraid to be seen with Dalya?

While returning to the Annex house, Dalya couldn't stop thinking about what had happened during Professor Ajanar's class, and Amira Mounier's reaction in the Library. When Dalya finished drying the dinner dishes, she retired to her bedroom to get some rest after her eventful day.

Chapter 5

A door closes

Saturday, January 24th, 1891.

Mrs. Marianne Poirier was a great beautiful woman of French origin. Her silver hair and big emerald green eyes made her even more magnificent, despite her advanced age. She had an imposing and serene allure. She lived in a luxurious house, near the grand Mansion of Late Mr. Governor Iskander Balthazar. Suffering from a complicated disease that prevented her from going outside, since several years now, Mrs. Marianne spent all her days in her bedroom.

The great woman had Mrs. Glorina for help, a domestic worker in charge of the household. Mrs. Glorina had a warm allure, always a welcoming smile, and a chatty character, agile and very cheerful. And having tasted her cakes, Dalya could confirm that Mrs. Glorina was the best pastry Cook of all Georgetown city. The French family was on Dalya's road path at Dumbarton Oaks Park, so she often visited them while returning back from school.

One cold gray afternoon of January, Dalya knocked on the Poirier's kitchen door. Mrs. Glorina greeted her with her usual sunny smile:

- But what a pleasure to see you, Mademoiselle Dalya!! Come in, please!!
- Thank you, Mrs. Glorina. How is Madame doing today?

Mrs. Glorina closed the kitchen door and invited Dalya to sit near the kitchen table. She told her while serving her a cup of hot and sweet tea:

- Mrs. Marianne is better since few days now. That's nice of you to ask about her. The cold season is the most difficult for Mrs. Marianne; her pain intensifies because of the cold. And even if we take all necessary precautions to heat her bedroom and avoid wind draught, there are always cold leaks that she can feel from hundreds of meters.

Dalya tasted her delicious tea and replied:

- Yes, I understand that it is not easy on her ...
- No ... it is a terrible disease. Sighed Mrs. Glorina.

Suddenly, a young man interrupted Mrs. Glorina and Dalya's conversation in the kitchen. It was Mr. Richard Poirier, Mrs. Marianne's son. He had the same bright green eyes as his mother. Peaceful and attractive face features, blond well-ordered hair, his dark suit and black tie made him look older and serious than his twenty-one years old. In a discreet attitude, Richard Poirier appeared on the kitchen door and he spoke to the housekeeper in a respectful tone:

- Mrs. Glorina ... I've asked the driver to pick me up tomorrow early morning. So it would be unnecessary to prepare me breakfast. I will take it out.
- Understood, Mr. Richard. replied Mrs. Glorina
- And ... I've instructed Mr. Eastman to come and visit you regularly; he will be in charge for the expenses during my trip. If you need anything, please let him know and he will take care of it.
- Yes, Monsieur.

Before Mr. Richard would close the door, he realized Dalya Bouvard's presence in the kitchen of his house. From little contact they have had together, Dalya felt that Mr. Richard was very intimidating, she never dared to speak or move in his presence. Richard greeted Dalya, bowing his head and saying:

- I know that mother will be in good hands and good care, during my absence.

Mrs. Glorina assured him:

- Certainly, Monsieur.

Dalya greeted him with a shy smile. And as strange as it was, Dalya was sure that the last words of Mr. Richard Poirier were addressed to her. After he left the kitchen, Dalya all curious, asked Mrs. Glorina:

- Is he travelling?

Mrs. Glorina continued to fold the tablecloths and she replied:

- Yes ... Mr. Richard will be traveling for a few months abroad, because of an important training he must undergo for the Government.

Mrs. Glorina had a sip of tea and she continued:

- It's a charming boy ... he works so hard, day and night ... and he is very caring toward his mother.

Dalya said to Mrs. Glorina without hesitation:

- Since I live quite nearby, I can come see you more often, if you need any help. I will be happy to assist you Mrs. Glorina!

Mrs. Glorina smiled tenderly at the little girl and said:

- You are always very helpful and kind, Mademoiselle, thank you very much!!

In an instant, Mrs. Glorina lost her smile when she thought of something else:

- May God help me endure his sister Francine Poirier in this house, during his absence!!
- Will Miss Francine ... stay here ... full time? Dalya asked hesitantly.
- Isn't it a punishment? Mrs. Glorina laughed ironically.

Sunday, January 25th, 1891.

The next day, coming back from the groceries in downtown, Dalya thought to pass by Mrs. Glorina, to bring her some pears, she was sure that Madame will like them on this season.

- What a great coincidence!! I thought about making some jam, just this morning!! Thank you Mademoiselle!! Mrs. Glorina exclaimed joyfully.
- They are very fresh. Said Dalya proudly
- Fresh and delicious!! Mrs. Marianne will love Pears jam!! Mrs. Glorina giggled.

Mrs. Glorina served Dalya a piece of her tasty pie:

- Here you go, Mademoiselle ... a pie like nothing you have ever tasted before!

Dalya didn't need any invite to taste it, and it was true that the pie was exquisite! Mrs. Glorina walked around the kitchen and she picked up in a small basket every kitchen towel, while thinking aloud:

- I better wash these towels, to hang them out in the sun today ... as it's still shiny and hot!
- I can help you with that, Mrs. Glorina.

Dalya got up from her chair, before the woman stopped her from taking a further step:

- No no Mademoiselle!! Finish your pie!! I'll be back in a few minutes, and after that I will escort you to Mrs. Marianne's bedroom.

Mrs. Glorina could never understand the humble and natural ways of the new Heiress, but she got used to it. And Dalya wasn't about to change her habits and kindness, whether appointed Heiress or not.

Dalya sat down to finish her pie. The Poirier kitchen was well organized and warm; Mrs. Glorina carefully arranged the kitchen tools, in a way to make them visible and easier to dispose of. Dalya admired the perfect storage of white porcelain plates and shining glasses settled in perfect arrangement. When all of a sudden, Dalya heard a cold voice from behind her:

- Should we count you among the residents of this house, now?

Dalya turned around to be in front of Miss Francine Poirier, Madame's daughter. And although Dalya haven't seen her for a long time, Francine Poirier had not lost her obese size nor her icy black stare. Miss Francine didn't inherit the physical beauty of her mother, even less her kindness. Dalya had the strange feeling that Miss Francine Poirier didn't like her, but Dalya couldn't understand why.

Yet, Dalya did her best to remain always polite, facing criticism and rude comments from Miss Francine:

- Hello Miss Francine. How are you today?

- How does it concern you to know how I am doing? Miss Francine replied harshly, before continuing:
- What are you doing here?
- I came to bring some good pears to Madam, your mother. I am waiting for Mrs. Glorina who is washing out towels outside, to walk up with her and visit Mada...

Miss Francine noticed the plate filled with a piece of pie:

- And ... you don't have enough food at your home, you get served here?

Confused by the aggressive attitude of Miss Francine, Dalya didn't know what to respond to that comment. Miss Francine came close to Dalya and she ordered her abruptly:

- Mother is not willing to see anyone today.
- But ... Mrs. Glorina told me that I can visi...
- Mother asked me to let no one in. She wishes to rest alone in her room! How many languages do I have to translate that for you?

Dalya refrained from disrespecting and upsetting Madame's daughter, she preferred to withdraw immediately, without waiting for Mrs. Glorina, or even finish eating her pie.

Chapter 6

Numbers

Tuesday, February 03rd, 1891. The Royal Georgetown College. Class N°48. Geography Course.

In the classroom, Dalya sat on an empty chair, she opened her notebook, waiting for the Geography course to start. Dalya's head was buried in her book, not only to read her notes, but also to avoid the scrutinizing looks of the other students. However, and unfortunately, Dalya couldn't help but hear their comments on her.

- I wonder how a school education can be useful to her ...
- Excellent question ... she has neither a social status nor a Nobility title to manage ...
- And even less a fortune ... my father assured me that she will not be an Heiress!
- Why do you think the Governor chose her?
- That is true!! he could have chosen anyone ... at least someone of an equal Nobility status ... more distinguished ...

Amira Mounier was the last student to join the classroom. She put her backpack on a chair, and then she walked toward the group of the other students, displaying her bravest smile:

- Hello Eriem, ho ... how ... how are you?

Gael Benoble, the popular boy, turned around toward Amira Mounier and he asked curiously:

- Say ... have you heard anything?

Amira Mounier repeated in a shy voice:

- He ... hello ...

Gael said while staring at Amira Mounier:

- That's funny. I had the impression of hearing a noise ...

The other students laughed. Eriem Eyelord replied in a serious voice:

- I heard nothing. It must be your imagination, Gael.

Eriem Eyelord let out a crushing laugh, while observing Amira Mounier with a contemptuous stare. All the other students turned toward Amira Mounier, laughing and staring at her from head to toe.

Dalya followed the scene with interest. She finally understood what the other students were playing at. They amused themselves by making Amira Mounier invisible. They completely ignored her. They were delighted in standing in front of her, and saying that they heard nothing and saw no one. Dalya thought it was a really cruel game. And she didn't understand why Amira persisted on trying to greet them and stand near them.

When a man came into the classroom, all the students joined their seats. Dalya thought that the History teacher, Professor Ajanar was the hardest and strictest, but she was wrong. Professor Felozi was more intimidating than him. He was a man in his early sixties, large size, with a pale almost transparent white hair, a large nose and small piercing black eyes.

In a rigid and strong voice, Professor Felozi addressed the class as soon as he put the documents on his desk:

- Good morning. This semester we will study the coastlines. Can anyone tell us a little about this geographical aspect?

Eriem Eyelord raised her hand to answer in a confident voice:

- It is a more or less wide band of territory between 15 and 20 km, between land and sea.

Professor Felozi said proudly:

- Very well said Miss Eriem. Always studious. Mr. Gael, any other information about the coastlines subject?

Gael answered without hesitation:

- About 20% of the world population lives in these areas.
- Right ... that's right, Mr. Gael. Professor Felozi replied, before turning to a student with long braids, he asked in a strangely cheerful voice:
- And Amira Mounier ... Would you like to enlighten us by your knowledge on this subject?

Amira jumped up from her chair, she replied a yes with great struggle. The Professor asked:

- So, what can you tell us about the forms of the coastline?

Amira blushed, she whispered with difficulty:

- The coas ... coas ... coastline are ... var ... var ... var ...

Professor Felozi pressed her:

- Are what?
- Are varied spaces. There are gu ... gu ... gulfs and bays, ver ... ver ... very rel ... rel ... reliable to install po ... po ... po ...

Professor Felozi yelled:

- RELIABLE TO INSTALL PORTS!!! PORTS!!! ARE YOU THAT UNABLE TO SPEAK A SIMPLE WORD?!!

Professor Felozi screamed in an enraged tone. All the students had their eyes on the girl who stuttered. They all seemed to become used to see Amira being tortured and humiliated by teachers because of her stuttering. Eriem Eyelord and Gael Benoble didn't hold their laughs. Amira straightened up in her chair, and it seemed that she had real trouble in getting words out of her throat. She tightened up and put a great effort to get out a few more words; her cheeks became redder and about to explode. Dalya sitting near her, could almost see the sweat on Amira's forehead:

- Ports ... islands and ar ... ar ... ar ...

Professor Felozi lost his patience and self-control, he came close to her and yelled:

- ARCHIPELS ... YOU IDIOT!!! HOW MANY YEARS DO YOU NEED TO DELIVER A CORRECT SENTENCE?!!!

Amira Mounier choked, her throat tightened and no word could come out of her mouth. Professor Felozi turned around and walked toward his office:

- SILLY GIRL WHO STUTTERS!! I WONDER WHAT WERE THEY THINKING WHEN THEY ADMITTED HER IN THIS SCHOOL!!

Dalya Bouvard was perhaps the only person in this class who watched Amira in a compassionate look. Dalya has never known anyone who struggled that much to speak.

When the course went on, all students turned toward the Professor. And he resumed his lesson with a satisfied and proud tone, after humiliating a student. Except that Amira Mounier didn't raise her head, and she kept her eyes lowered for the rest of the class.

At the end of the Geography lesson, and before leaving the classroom, Dalya was held by Professor Felozi's voice:

- Dalya Bouvard. Come over here!

Dalya came close to the old man:

- I was informed that Professor Canfield has provided you some courses in different subjects during the previous semester ... except that it is your first lesson in Geography, isn't it?
- Yes, Professor.

Professor Felozi stared at her, from head to toe, in a curious and haughty look, before continuing:

- So ... from what I understand ... I must not expect that you'll be at the same level of the students of this class ...

Even though she was intimidated by the Professor's very tough personality, Dalya answered anyway:

- I ... I will study harder to catch up and be at the same level, Professor.

Professor Felozi had an amused smile:

- How touching ... and you seriously think you can succeed?

Dalya answered all naturally:

- I passed the admission exams of this school ... Professor.

Professor Felozi forgot this slight little detail, yet so important. And the audacity of the new little student didn't please him much. Dalya could feel that Professor Felozi didn't like her for some reason she didn't know. She forced herself to be polite anyway:

- Can I leave the classroom now ... Professor Felozi?

After being released from her Geography Professor, Dalya thought to consult some books at the Library before going back home. When turning on a hall, Dalya was busy in her thoughts, she didn't see the person coming in front of her. Dalya crashed the person and they both fell to the ground. When Dalya raised her head, she found herself in front of Amira Mounier who was carrying books. Dalya stood up immediately and she held out a hand to Amira:

- Sorry ... I didn't see you coming.

Amira refused Dalya's hands, and she replied coldly:

- I don't ne ... ne ... need your help!

Yet Amira struggled to get up. Meanwhile Dalya knelt to pick up Amira's books that fell down. Suddenly, Amira exclaimed:

- Stop that!! Don ... don ... don ... don't touch that!!

Dalya froze in her place, confused by Amira's reaction. Dalya explained:

- I ... I would like to help you pick up the books. After all, it was I who made you fall.

At that moment, a group of students passed upon the corridor. And they couldn't appear in a much worse time; it was Eriem Eyelord and her court. After they noticed Dalya and Amira's scene, Eriem Eyelord let out a crushing laugh:

- A veggy seller and an accountant's daughter ... friends!!

Another student continued:

- But what are they doing?

Gael replied, while looking at them with a scrutinizing glance:

- Probably discussing how to set up a veggy selling business in the market!

Eriem turned to Gael:

- It is true that these two make a very good team!!
- Because they are from the same social level ...
- Likes attracts!!

A wave of mean laughs invaded the students, who pursued their way on to another corridor. Amira turned red and upset, she yelled at Dalya:

- I don ... don ... don't want ... you to come near me!! I don ... don ... don't ... want to be linked to you!!

Dalya didn't understand neither Eriem and her court's mockery, nor Amira's anger. Dalya wanted only to help. She didn't dare to upset Amira anymore than that. Dalya stepped back and she watched Amira pick up her own books from the floor, before disappearing at the end of the corridor.

Heading out of the college, Dalya thought it would be wiser not to approach Amira Mounier in the upcoming days, or any other student in the school. Not because the Headmaster banned her from it. But because Dalya realized that it would be difficult to make friends in this place. She who has dreamed of studying in a school!

The Concierge Dadès was painting the iron fences of the school. A black paint container in one hand and a brush on the other hand, he was focused not to spill drops of paint on the floor. Dalya greeted him with a hand wave:

- Have a good day.

The Concierge Dadès paused and smiled:

- Good day Lalla!!

On the road of Dumbarton Oaks Park, Dalya met the housekeeper of the French neighbors, Mrs. Glorina. The woman was walking in fast steps. And when she noticed Dalya, Mrs. Glorina stopped:

- Hello Mademoiselle Dalya!! Are you coming back from school?
- Yes, Mrs. Glorina. And you?

Mrs. Glorina said breathlessly:

- I am coming back from the market. I had some groceries to do. I am so overworked these days!! I have work chores all day long!!

Dalya replied without hesitation:

- I can help you Mrs. Glorina ... if you need groceries, or anything ...

Mrs. Glorina smiled:

- You are always so polite, Mademoiselle. Thank you for offering. But you need to focus on your classes at school, to get good grades!!

As the two continued their common road, Dalya noticed that Mrs. Glorina had a newspaper in her grocery bag, she dared to ask:

- Do you read newspapers, Mrs. Glorina?

In an instant, an innocent smile appeared on Mrs. Glorina lips and her cheeks turned pink. She answered Dalya in a whisper:

- In the evening, I enjoy completing the guessing words game.

Dalya was curious:

- The guessing words game? ... What is it?
- It's a new game of words they publish in the newspaper. And the results appear few days later. They give clues, and you have to guess the correct words. It's incredibly fun!! I just love it!! ... I can't afford the newspaper as often as I want, to complete the game and check the results. But sometimes ... I admit, I cannot help it!!

Dalya and Mrs. Glorina both giggled. When suddenly, Dalya remembered something:

- Mrs. Glorina ... my friend, Alfie Jaq, he sells newspapers ... I can ask him to lend me the newspaper to only copy the guessing words game, and the results. And I can bring them to you ...

Mrs. Glorina stopped walking:

- Oh!!! But that is so kind of you, Mademoiselle!! I must say it will please me so much!!

When they arrived at the French family house, Mrs. Glorina insisted:

- Come inside please, it's been many days since you have visited us.

Dalya followed her to the inside of the house. When Mrs. Glorina put down her grocery bag on the kitchen table, she turned to Dalya:

- So? Tell me! How are your classes? How are your teachers? Have you made new friends? Do you like being at school with the other students?

Dalya had always dreamed of being in a class to learn. She used to watch with envy the students walking down in the streets toward their schools. She had always dreamed having friends, learning new things, having kind and encouraging teachers, spending a good time studying and reviewing her lessons. But reality was different from what Dalya had imagined in her mind. Yet, she answered Mrs. Glorina's questions in a little voice:

- The school is ... interesting. I learn so many things. And there are many students.

- Oh!! But I'm sure everyone likes you, Mademoiselle Dalya!! Exclaimed Mrs. Glorina.

Dalya smiled, she didn't dare to contradict the woman. Dalya asked:

- Is Madame free to receive me? I haven't seen her since long ago. I would like to just say a hello.
- But certainly, Mademoiselle!! Mrs. Glorina replied. You can go join her in her bedroom. I'll warm some bread for her, and I'll bring her dinner in a few minutes.

Dalya got up and left the kitchen. Having visited Mrs. Marianne Poirier several times, the little girl knew the path to the upstairs floor, to Madam's bedroom. Except that before she could walk up the first stair step, Dalya was called by a rigid, cold voice:

- But where do you think you are going?

When Dalya turned around, she noticed Madam's daughter in the living room. Miss Francine Poirier was sitting alone on a big divan. On a little table in front of her, there was a tea cup and a big plate full of various pastries, only for her. Politely, Dalya turned around and greeted her:

- Hello Miss Francine. How are you today?
- Can't you ever answer a question properly? And what are you doing here again? Asked Miss Francine in an annoyed tone, before picking up a large piece of raspberry pie, that she swallowed in a single bite.

Dalya knew no one as fat and obese as Miss Francine. All her dresses stuck to her skin, and her clothes appeared to rip in any movement. Yet, Miss Francine didn't worry about her weight, she enjoyed all to herself, the big plate full of pastries.

In front of the curiously cold and harsh attitude of Miss Francine, Dalya forced herself to remain polite and respectful to Madam's daughter:

- I met Mrs. Glorina on the way back from school. I wanted to say just a quick hello to Madame your mother ...

With raspberry tart crumbs around her mouth, Miss Francine ordered Dalya, in a softer voice:

- Come over here, a moment!

Dalya came close to her, inside the living room, with hesitant steps. Miss Francine continued in a sweet strangely tone:

- I feel it is my duty to inform you of some things ... how am I going to say it? ... well, some delicate things ...

Dalya, still standing in front of Miss Francine, didn't understand her words, yet she didn't dare to interrupt her. Miss Francine continued with an oddly kind tone, for once:

- Well, you see, mother is a very refined person ... we come from a very Noble family of French origin. I don't expect a little veggy seller like you to know our Nobility status, even less our lifestyles and distinguished manners.

Dalya still couldn't understand what Miss Francine was meaning.

- Some manners are wrong and offensive ... like visiting someone without asking permission in advance, at least a day before ... coming into people at any time, it's offensive to mother.

Dalya replied all confused:

- But ... Mrs. Glorina never told me that my visits offended Mada...

Miss Francine laughed sarcastically:

- And does Glorina come from a Noble family? How could Glorina know the distinguished manners of the French high society? ... And besides, Glorina didn't want to make you feel bad and hurt you.

Dalya thought about it a few seconds in silence, and then she said:

- I'm sorry, Miss Francine. I had never intended to offend Madam, nor force her to receive me. I just wanted to visit her, and check on her.

Miss Francine smiled, and it was a strange smile:

- But of course ... I understand that a little veggy seller like you knows nothing of our refined manners. Don't worry about that. I hope you understand that mother cannot frequently receive you, like before. There are specific good manners you should follow.
- Yes, Miss Francine, I understand.

Miss Francine continued, always in a calm and soft voice:

- And ... there's something else too ... I don't know how to tell you that ... but I hope you will not be offended ...

Dalya listened with all her attention. Miss Francine spoke in a serious tone:

- Glorina is nice and soft; she didn't want to tell you that, she feared that you would be embarrassed. But ... you see ... Glorina told me that you disrupt her many time, while she is busy in her housework. And since your visits, she is always late. Her work accumulates because she spends time with you, instead of doing her job properly in time.

Miss Francine Poirier was right. Dalya remembered that on the way back to Dumbarton Oaks Park, Mrs. Glorina complained of the lack of time and all the housework she had to do. Miss Francine whispered:

- My brother even thought to fire her ...

Dalya jumped:

- Fire Mrs. Glorina!

Miss Francine calmed her down:

- Yes ... that's what my brother was planning to do. It was I who begged and begged him for hours, to not do it. Glorina wouldn't be in this house without my help.

Dalya was shocked by what she has just learned from Miss Francine, she didn't believe her ears. Miss Francine stared at Dalya for a moment, with a proud look, before continuing with a soft kind voice:

- I think it's best if you don't bother Glorina very often ... so that she won't be late in her housework ... and not to be fired by my brother ... Do you understand what I've just told you?
- Yes, Miss Francine.

When Dalya left the Poirier house, she was pale and trembling. She never had the intention to create worries for Mrs. Glorina. And she never wanted to disturb Madame. Yet Dalya didn't understand why her visits offended Madam, she didn't understand why Mrs. Glorina had never stopped her and corrected her, and she didn't understand the sudden kindness of Miss Francine Poirier.

Returning to the Annex house of the grand Mansion, Dalya's mind was busy because of an eventful day. While washing the dinner dishes, Dalya couldn't help thinking not only of Miss Francine's words, but Amira Mounier's words too. Her little head was full of questions without answers:

- Why is everyone shutting me down? Why did Amira reject my help? Why are Madame and Mrs. Glorina bothered by my visits? What have I done wrong? All I have ever wanted was to help.

That night, sleep didn't come easily. The little girl turned around and around right and left, on her bed, for hours. When she got tired of waiting for sleep, Dalya lit her lamp and got up from her bed. She took a storybook from her backpack, and went back to her bed. Except that before opening her book, a little box on her desk caught her eye.

A strange box ... the Excelbox ... a small rectangular opening was always opened on one side. The cage made of transparent glass was illuminated discreetly to recharge under the moonlight. The golden clock inside the glass cage was clearly visible. The small needle was still focused on 12th December 1891. The big needle wavered between the night of February 03rd and 04th.

Dalya stood up again from her bed, and she sat in front of her desk.

Since some time now, no one could understand how a poor little vegetable seller, has been able to uncover the mystery of the strange box and correctly answer the first challenge. Dalya herself didn't know how she managed to succeed. But if there's one thing Dalya was now so certain of and convinced about, is that the Excelbox always provided answers to her doubts and confusions.

And like all previous times, Dalya took a piece of paper and she wrote on it:

What is the 1st clue?

As soon as she placed it on the rectangular opening of the Excelbox, the piece of paper disappeared inside the box. The glass cage lit up in an instant, and seconds later, a little paper appeared on the board. Dalya removed it and she read:

Windows and doors can close in,

Forbid air and goodness to come in!

In JV-20-89, breath will be found,

In 17-HR-08, by a small key, fear will be released,

Between 69th and 59th, many things can be prepared,

In 1703, the pressure will be displaced,

In AV-07-90, the mirror will reveal a forgotten kind.

As dark and disturbing as the fog may appear,

It's only a weak cloud when we continue to walk.

The Excelbox shut down, its luminous cage transformed back into a gray colored glass. And the night silence came back to the bedroom. It is true that the Excelbox had always given enigmatic answers. Except that this time, the Excelbox exceeded itself. Dalya exclaimed in a shocked tone:

- Numbers?! ... I have enough trouble understanding the words of the clue!! ... It gives me numbers this time?! ... JV- 20 - 89 ... 17- HR- 08 ... But what is that?! ... 1703 ... how will I find the meaning of these numbers? … It can be anything and everything!! … AV - 07 - 90 ... what is this supposed to mean?!

Chapter 7

Dare to enter

Tuesday, February 10th, 1891.

Dalya had strict orders to inform the Lawyer, Mr. Ernest Laszlo, of all the messages that came from the Excelbox. And although it was his son, Lyor Laszlo, who was Dalya's legal guardian, according to the Will of the Late Mr. Governor Iskander Balthazar, Mr. Ernest Laszlo excluded his son, and he took charge of this case, himself. After all, this strange box caused him to fail the simple transfer of the biggest fortune in the United States of America.

Dalya stopped at the desk of Mr. Ernest's Secretary. The woman didn't notice Dalya's presence; she was busy organizing some papers.

- Good morning. Can I meet Mr. Ernest Laszlo, please?

The Secretary looked up to Dalya and she replied in a cold voice:

- Mr. Ernest is absent today. Talk to Mr. Lyor.

Dalya asked in a polite tone:

- Is Mr. Wilfrid present at the offi...

The Secretary interrupted her:

- Mr. Lyor!

Dalya didn't want to meet Lyor Laszlo. He was forced to be her legal guardian, and since he was nominated despite himself in the Will, Lyor made it clear that he didn't stand Dalya at all. And one must admit that Dalya didn't like him either. Each time, their meeting ended in a quarrel.

Reluctantly, Dalya turned around and she looked for Lyor Laszlo's office in the hallway. After few minutes and indications of an employee, Dalya knocked on a door. Having heard no voice, she decided to enter Lyor's office.

The February sun has invited itself into this room. The desk was buried under a mass of files, papers and office supplies everywhere. Books and folders were piled on the couch, in the small Library, and even on the floor. Dalya smiled:

- It reflects very well the chaos Lyor has in his head!

Yet, Dalya couldn't stop but enjoy the sweet smell that infused the room. When she walked up toward the desk, she noticed near the big window, a large pot of beautiful little flowers with blue purple petals, an orange interior, and fresh green stems and leaves. Dalya had never seen such splendid flowers. She was surprised to know that Lyor Laszlo, her legal guardian, who is always a provocative and rude temper ... he could take care of fragile and beautiful flowers.

When suddenly, the office door opened brutally and Dalya turned around to be in front of Lyor Laszlo himself. He was as much surprised as she was, to meet her in his own office.

- What are you doing here?

Dalya didn't expect good manners from Lyor Laszlo. She answered him as politely as she could:

- I wanted to meet Mr. Ernest Laszlo, your father, but the Secretary said he is abs...
- Absent, yes.

Lyor interrupted her, while bypassing her and placing his files on the desk:

- So, what do you want?

Dalya gave him a piece of paper:

- The first clue ... of the Second Challenge.

Lyor took the piece of paper without even reading its contents; he placed it inside a file:

- I will give it to him when he returns. Goodbye.

Lyor turned around toward his Library to search for a book, ignoring Dalya's presence. She immediately left his office without even greeting him. After all, the fewer words Dalya and Lyor used, the better it was to avoid confrontations.

Friday, February 13th, 1981. Room N°18. Music Course.

Dalya entered the Music classroom, indicated on her schedule paper. It was one of the largest rooms of the school. Huge transparent windows stood at the entire length and width of the wall, illuminating the room with a soft light. The classroom was divided in two. In one part, tables and chairs were placed symmetrically, like in the other classrooms. A large blackboard was hanged on the wall. In the other part of the room, Musical instruments of all types and genres were placed; pianos, violins, harps, clarinets, trumpets ... and several other instruments that Dalya had never seen before.

The other students were already all present, and gathered as usual around Eriem Eyelord and Gael Benoble. When Dalya came inside discreetly, one of the students said in a loud voice:

- They admit anyone in this school now ...

Dalya guessed that the conversation would be on her. And yet, she pretended not to hear them, and as usual, she sat on a chair and took out her notebook.

Eriem Eyelord laughed with a confident voice:

- Be sure that next year, you shall see studying with you in the same courses, the son of your driver and the girl of your Cook ...

A wave of wicked and arrogant laughs filled the place, just when Mounier Amira entered the classroom. Gael continued his friend's sentence:

- And the accountant's daughter ...

The other students continued to laugh. Amira was carrying books, she put them on her desk and she addressed the students with a cheerful tone:

- He ... he … hello!

No one looked at her, and barely even heard her. Amira came close to the students' group, and she dared to say:

- I ad ... I admire your talent on the p ... p ... p ... piano Eriem … nobody can play as well as you ... doing so well ... I would like to ... p … play … like you … d … do …

All the students ignored Amira; they were laughing and talking as if she did not exist. Yet, the poor Amira tried and tried with all her might, to please and be accepted by this group:

- I wonder who will b ... be ... our new Music teacher this year ... it is a pity that Mr. Leblanc ... left us because of his ret ... ret ... retirement ...

Gael asked the group, with a serious voice:

- It's strange ... do you hear that noise? ... It doesn't stop bothering me!

Eriem Eyelord replied, staring at Amira with a mocking look:

- The wind maybe ...

Gael Benoble laughed:

- A bit like the sound of a bee!

Eriem Eyelord finished his sentence:

- A stuttering bee!!

All the students looked at Amira and laughed at her, while she was standing right in front of them. Amira's cheeks became red, and she let out an embarrassed nervous smile. Dalya watched curiously, the same scene was repeated each time. It was clear that Amira wanted to make friends and be accepted by the group of the popular students, but they all had fun making Amira invisible. They ignored her in a cruel and evil way. A vulgar game.

At this moment, an adult entered the Music classroom. And Dalya was surprised to see a familiar face.

Miss Haîyang was a young woman with Asian features. She was wearing a short dark blue silk tunic and black pants. Her long straight black hair was tied in a ponytail, waving with her every movement. Miss Haîyang was a beautiful woman, with gentle but steady allure.

Dalya had met Miss Haîyang on several occasions during the previous semester. Since arriving to this school, Dalya frequently had the strange feeling that this young woman was watching her from afar.

Miss Haîyang moved toward the large desk, while the students took their places. In a kind but strict voice, the young woman addressed the students:

- Good morning everyone. My name is Miss Haîyang. I will be your Music teacher this semester. I am replacing your previous Professor, Mr. Leblanc.

Miss Haîyang took out of her briefcase some papers, and she distributed them herself, to the students, one by one:

- I will make you pass a quick test ... to recognize the Music level of each one of you ... and then, we can start with the standard program of this semester.

When Miss Haîyang arrived at Dalya's desk, she paused and looked at the little 13 years old girl. It was not a scornful and rude stare like the other people used to, but rather a curious look. Dalya took her test paper and Miss Haîyang continued her way.

- You have 1 hour to complete the test.

Dalya read carefully the content the paper:

Question 1: What origin was the Musician Antonio Vivaldi?

Question 2: What are the 5 most famous piano compositions of the Musician Johann Sebastian Bach?

Question 3: Describe the anatomy of a Musical note of your choice

...

Dalya looked up; all the students were busy answering the questions. Professor Haîyang was busy checking the effectiveness of some Musical instruments, in the other part of the classroom. Besides her name at the top of the page, Dalya didn't write a single word on her Music test paper.

At the end of the test, all the students put down their copies on the Professor's office. Miss Haîyang reread for a few minutes all their copies, and then she began a small review of the previous semester lessons. Professor Haîyang was different from the hard character of the History and Geography teachers. She explained and spoke in a firm and strict voice, yet without humiliating or diminishing any student.

When the Music class ended, all the students left the room. Dalya was called by Professor Haîyang:

- Mademoiselle Dalya Bouvard ... I've noticed that you have not answered the test I gave you. May I know why?

Dalya hesitated to give an answer. When finally, she decided to stay uncomfortably silent. Professor Haîyang continued in a kind voice:

- In my next class, try to participate a little more ...
- Yes, Professor. Dalya replied before leaving the classroom.

Miss Guendolyn, the Library assistant of the Royal Georgetown College, was sitting at her desk, updating the list of borrowed books of the week. When she noticed Dalya come in to the Library, the young woman greeted her with a wide smile:

- Hello mademoiselle!!

Dalya politely replied:

- Hello Miss Guendolyn.
- Have you finished the book you borrowed, few days ago?
- No ... not yet Miss Guendolyn. The classes' rhythm is accelerated; I need more days to finish this novel.
- Take your time, Mademoiselle Dalya!! And good luck on your classes!! Miss Guendolyn encouraged her.
- Thank you, I will need it. Dalya sighed.

The young woman noticed that Dalya's smile was less enlightened than usual, she asked her all curious:

- Is everything alright, Mademoiselle?
- Yes ... Yes ...
- What course did you have today?

Dalya replied in a small voice:

- The ... Music class.

Miss Guendolyn guessed in an instant and without one more word, what was bothering the little girl. The woman put down her pen and she asked Dalya in a compassionate voice:

- You've never touched an instrument ... or learned something in Music, Mademoiselle?

Dalya answered with a head sign, not daring to pronounce a word. Before being admitted to this school, Dalya was selling vegetables and fruits with her father, and helping her mother in housework. Dalya Bouvard never had a normal childhood or an education like the other children. Her parents were too poor and not interested to offer their daughter any learning. The only idea that the Bouvard had for their little girl was that she would work for them and serve them, at the market and at home, for the rest of her life. And day by day, the more she grew up, the more Dalya realized she was different from the other children of her age, she missed many things to learn, and Dalya was ashamed of that.

Given the long silence of the little girl, Miss Guendolyn addressed Dalya in an admiring tone:

- Mademoiselle Dalya Bouvard ... you have answered the first challenge of the Will, and no one ... seriously; no one thought that you would make it!! ... So then, you have to believe that you will succeed whatever you undertake. You are as smart and talented as any student in this school ... and I can confirm that!!

The encouraging words of Miss Guendolyn made Dalya smile in an instant. The young woman continued with a confident voice:

- The willingness to learn at any age, is a pride!

Miss Guendolyn was well right. She came close to Dalya and whispered:

- Aisle 5, section 68, 3rd shelf ... you will find Music books of beginners' class, for 5-6 years old children. It will be easier for you. And it will help you to catch up quickly.

Dalya was touched by her kindness and her help:

- Thank you, Miss Guendolyn. Thank you very much!

The little girl quickly walked toward the book place indicated by the Library assistant. Dalya pulled out the books she needed and she joined an empty desk to work.

After a few minutes of reading, Dalya thought aloud:

- So ... a note is a symbol that represents ... a sound. Okay. There are 4 main features ... the pitch, length, intensity and tone ... the little dot is the head of the note ... and the small sign on the line is the length ...

Dalya started to understand a little more clearly. After all, Miss Guendolyn was right. Although Dalya had never learned Music before, her lag wasn't impossible to catch up.

Focused on reading, Dalya was interrupted by a little voice sitting some chairs away from her; it was her classmate Amira Mounier. The History book opened in front of her, Amira was trying to read a paragraph, as slowly and clearly as she could. But she couldn't take out of her mind the frightening face of the History teacher and his cruel words. After each 2 words, her voice was blocked, her throat tightened, her cheeks swelled and reddened. After several attempts, Amira lay back on her chair, she hid her face in her hands and she cried:

- I can't d ... I can't do it ... I will n ... not succeed ...

Dalya watched her classmate crying silently for several minutes. She had pity on Amira. It seemed that Amira Mounier was smart and hardworking, just like any student of this school. Her only handicap, the stuttering, was blocking her and made her the laughing stock of everyone, students and teachers.

Dalya didn't dare to interrupt Amira, nor talk to her. She was afraid of being rejected by Amira, just like the last time she tried.

- If only there was a way to encourage her. Dalya thought.

When suddenly, Dalya straightened up from her chair. Since the very first message issued by the strange box, many months ago, Dalya could only understand the Excelbox words in the most unlikely times. And at that moment, in the school Library, sitting a few chairs away from a crushed Amira Mounier, Dalya remembered some strange words she read a few days ago.

With its mysterious clues, the Excelbox was making the little girl's neurons, work harder. Dalya had a little idea, she was not sure about it, but she wrote a few words on a piece of paper. A few seconds of reflection later, Dalya stood up from her chair in a quick brusque move, and he exclaimed in a voice loud enough to be well heard:

- How dizzy I am!! I forgot to go home early to help my parents!! I am very late!!

With tearful eyes and pink cheeks, Amira Mounier turned right, to finally notice Dalya's presence few chairs away from her. Dalya gathered her books in a hurry, and she ran toward the Library exit. Amira stared for a moment at her classmate Dalya, but something else caught her eye; a little piece of paper forgotten by Dalya on her desk.

When Dalya stopped at the Library exit and turned around, she was glad to discover that her idea has well succeeded. Amira stretched out her hand to take the little piece of paper forgotten by Dalya, and she read:

As dark and disturbing as the fog may appear,
It's only a weak cloud when we continue to walk.

Dalya left school in unhurried steps. Amira Mounier reread these words several times, and despite the tears still present on her cheeks, a smile appeared not only on her face, but also in her heavy heart.

It seems that the Excelbox was cooking something...

Saturday, February 21st, 1981.

The sky was all covered with gray white clouds. Winter was soon to leave the city of Georgetown. The trees have survived the Snow, standing still firmly and obstinate. The air was sweet and fresh.

On his 12 years old, small size and chubby allure, Alfie Jaq was arranging his red scarlet tie. A backpack filled with newspapers placed down on his feet. It was the market day, and so a great day to earn money!

The same age as him, Maurice Gus, his business partner joined him a few minutes later. For several years now, Maurice has been shining the passerby's shoes, and Alfie offered customers to buy and read newspapers while their shoes were cleaned.

- Why are you dressed like an onion? Asked Alfie, all curious.

Maurice Gus could barely walk properly. He was wearing several sweaters, a large coat that came down to his knees, large pants floating with his every movement, Snow boots, a shawl around his face, far too big gloves, a large green cap covered his head. Maurice replied in a trembling voice:

- I am hiding from the sun.

Alfie Jaq was wearing a half-sleeve shirt, simple pants and he had not yet put on his jacket. Alfie looked up at the sky, curious and confused:

- But ... there's no sun today?

Suddenly, Maurice exploded with rage:

- OF COURSE THERE IS NO SUN!! ARE YOU KIDDING ME?! WE ARE ON FEBRUARY AND YOU WEAR HALF SLEEVE SHIRT?! I NO LONGER FEEL MY TOES AND I AM THE ONE YOU TREAT AS AN ONION!!

Alfie didn't have time to answer, Dalya interrupted them:

- Hello Maurice! Hello Alfie!

Alfie and Maurice greeted her with a smile. Dalya settled on an empty vegetables box near them.

- Do you need something from the market? Asked Alfie.
- Yes, I have some groceries to do for my parents. How is business going?

Alfie explained to Dalya in a cheerful tone:

- Not bad, we maintain the goal of 5 dollars per month. We will be able to open our store in about ...
- 128 YEARS!! Said Maurice, shaking.

Dalya and Alfie exchanged a confused look, before she whispered to Alfie:

- What is happening to him? Why is he so upset?

Alfie replied in a low voice too:

- He needs warmth.

Immediately, Dalya and Alfie had the same idea in their minds, and at the exact same time. Swiftly, Dalya and Alfie both jumped and surrounded with their arms their trembling friend Maurice, squeezing him as strongly as they could. Maurice was crushed in the middle like a shrimp, he yelled upset anyway:

- WARMTH OF THE SUN!! THAT IS WHAT I NEED!! NOT HUMAN WARMTH!!
- Human warmth ... it's even better!! Exclaimed Alfie laughing.
- Do you feel a little better, Maurice? Dalya asked barely holding her giggle.

Maurice felt a little warmer, surrounded by his friends' arms. After a few seconds, Maurice Gus smiled, he found his voice and his usual calm mood:

- Yes ... feeling better. Thank you.

Dalya returned to sit on the empty box, while Alfie organized his newspaper backpack, and Maurice arranged the inside of his shoeshine box.

- Alfie ... can I borrow today's newspaper for a minute? ... To copy something.
- Of course!

Alfie gave the newspaper to Dalya. And while her friends were preparing to start their work day, she copied a drawing and few words on a little paper, and then she returned back the newspaper, and greeted her friends:

- Good luck today, guys!!

After grocery shopping, and on the way back to the grand Mansion, Dalya passed near the French neighbors' house, les Poirier. Not daring to enter, Dalya stayed outside the forged door of the small garden. She looked for Mrs. Glorina, the housekeeper. But the woman didn't appear anywhere outside; Dalya thought that she must be busy inside the house, cooking dinner or doing housework. Dalya knew that Miss Francine was inside. She didn't dare to disturb Madame or Mrs. Glorina, especially after what Miss Francine told her on their last conversation.

Without a trace of Mrs. Glorina, Dalya thought to leave her a little piece of paper anyway. She quietly opened the garden gate and she walked hesitantly. Dalya searched right and left for a safe place to leave her message to Mrs. Glorina. When she noticed the bird's nest, Dalya had an idea. She crossed half the large garden with hurried steps; she wrapped the little piece of paper and placed it inside the bird's nest. Dalya was sure that Mrs. Glorina will find her message, as the women regularly cleans the bird's nest and fills it with wheat grains.

Hello Mrs. Glorina.

I will leave you the guessing words game in this bird's nest, each week start.

And I will bring you the answer at the end of the week, at the same place. As often as I can.

Have a good day.

Dalya made a swift U-turn and she left the garden by closing the forged iron door without any noise. Dalya knew that Mrs. Glorina would be happy to receive the guessing words game and its answers.

When the little girl continued her way back home, she didn't realize that from the beginning, a silhouette was watching her from a window of the second floor in the Poirier's house.

As firmly closed as the windows and doors can be ... as impossible as it may seem ... as sure as the rejections may be … air and goodness can still come in. And nobody can stop it...

Chapter 8

How to protect her?

Sunday, February 22nd, 1981.

Calm reigned on this dark and narrow street in the South of Georgetown city. Miss Haîyang opened the front door of the house. The hall was a large square garden with an open roof. Dozens of candles with exquisite scent, were lit in every corner of the garden, cradling with their soft light all the plants and trees. Fresh air breezes discreetly touched flowers and branches.

An old man was sitting on a thin mat on the floor; he was admiring the full moon and the thousands stars. Miss Haîyang approached him and she bowed respectfully. The old man still staring at the moon, asked in a calm voice:

- Tā zěnme Yang? *(How is she?)*
- She is alright, Master. She is in my Music class at school.
- Dàn yǒuxiē Shiqing Ling nǐ Danxin *(but something worries you).*

Miss Haîyang sat on the thin mat on the floor, near Master Fong Ka-Ho. She hesitated to answer for a few seconds and she finally said:

- It's just that ... I don't understand why and how she has been chosen. It's so unusual ...

Master Fong Ka-Ho smiled:

- Sometimes ... there is no point to ask the why and the how of things ... sometimes, some questions have simply no answers.

Miss Haîyang retained her silence and confusion. Master Fong Ka-Ho continued in a convinced tone:

- Rest assured, Miss Haîyang ... nature never does things by coincidence ... the Snow Panther has always well-chosen its picks.
- But ... she is just a little child, Master.

Master Fong Ka-Ho let out an innocent laugh:

- Only for now ...

Miss Haîyang dared to ask:

- Master ... Do you think she will be capable enough to meet the challenges ahead of her?

After a few seconds of reflection, the old man smiled, without removing his eyes from the sparkling sky:

- The biggest challenges are destined only for the strongest people.

Miss Haîyang had trouble understanding the Panther's choices. The young woman was well aware that the upcoming challenges will be enormous and difficult to conquer:

- Master ... what can we do to help her?

And for the first time since her arrival, Master Fong Ka-Ho turned toward Miss Haîyang, and he looked at her. He replied in a determined and clear tone:

- The best way to protect her ... is to prepare her.

There was no need for more words; Miss Haîyang understood exactly what she had to do.

Chapter 9

Lalla

Monday, February 23rd, 1981.

Dalya got up early that morning. Her sisters were still asleep, and her mother had prepared breakfast before going outside to wash some towels. Dalya had some books to give back to the Library before her class; she thought about going to school earlier. She then quickly ate her breakfast, and left the house. When a voice called her:

- Hey you!! Take a shovel and come fill these boxes!!

Dalya turned around and walked toward her father, who was near the garage. Mr. Antman had put twenty large empty boxes on the floor, in front of his carriage that was filled with a mountain of wood residues. Dalya wondered:

- You want me to empty the carriage, and fill all these boxes? Now?

Mr. Antman replied with an icy tone:

- Yes ... empty the carriage ... now!!

Dalya hesitated for a moment:

- It's just that ... I ... I ... have ...
- What? What's the matter?!

Dalya dared to answer:

- I can't do it now ...

Mr. Antman stopped, putting down the last empty boxes and he stared at Dalya in a curious and upset look:

- You have something better to do, this morning?

Dalya was surprised of her father's question. He was well aware that his daughter had to attend classes at school, and that since several months now. Yet, Dalya gathered her courage and she answered as naturally as possible:

- The History class starts in less than an hour, and I thought I'd return some books to the libr...

On that moment, Mr. Antman came close to his daughter in a fast and angry steps. He removed her backpack with such a sudden move, that Dalya vacillated around, and he threw the backpack in the garden with a strong move. Notebooks, books and Dalya's pens, spread all over the grass. Mr. Antman held his daughter's arm in a tight grip, and he said with a threatening voice:

- LISTEN TO ME VERY WELL LITTLE WITLESS!! I DON'T CARE A SHIT OF YOUR DAMN COURSES!! YOU DO EXACTLY WHAT I ASK YOU TO DO!! YOUR LIFE GOAL IS ONLY TO SERVE US, ME AND YOUR MOTHER, FOR THE REST OF YOUR LIFE!! YOU DON'T HAVE ANY RIGHT FOR A LIFE OR FREEDOM, EVEN LESS AN OPINION!!

Dalya ran until the entry door of the school. She had no explanation to give to her History teacher for being late. When she walked the steps of the school entrance, it seemed to Dalya that she heard someone call her name. Except that she was so late for class, Dalya didn't turn around and she continued running toward the History class. When she arrived, Dalya could hear the voice of Professor Ajanar from outside the classroom. She opened the door carefully and quietly. Immediately, silence settled in, and all eyes were turned toward her. Professor Ajanar came close to her, with slow steps:

- You're late ... well well, we are becoming lazy, aren't we?
- I am very sorry, Professor. I was retained by someth...

Professor Ajanar interrupted Dalya, in an icy voice:

- Silence!! ... You're in detention after this class!! ... You will learn that in this school, there is no room for laziness!!
- Yes, Professor.

Coming closer to Dalya, Professor Ajanar asked her with a mocking laugh:

- And ... did you spend the night in a farm? Sleeping near the horses?

Dalya didn't understand the teacher's comment. She noticed that all the students were laughing and pointing at her. When Dalya looked at herself, she discovered that her clothes were all covered with the wood residues that she moved from her father's carriage to the empty boxes. Her hair was full of tangled wood residues, her black shoes were gray with dirt, and her backpack was not well arranged. Being late to class, Dalya forgot to return back home to clean herself.

Dalya didn't dare to add a word, nor explain to the History Professor, the reasons for her delay. She walked between the chairs, among the laughing and mocking looks of the other students, and she settled on an empty chair.

At the end of the school day, and after spending one more hour detention in History class, writing 300 times: I will never be late again, Dalya finally walked to the school exit door, to go back home. However, as soon as she walked down the stairs to the main door, a voice and a strange accent retained her:

- Lalla Dalya ... Lalla Dalya ...

It was the Concierge, Dadès. He approached Dalya with quick steps. She was curious to know what he could possible want from her. When the worker came close, he smiled, leaning his head:

- Hello Lalla Dalya.

Dalya all confused, politely replied:

- Hello

Dadès the Concierge pulled an object from his pocket and he handed it to her.

- But ... it's my hat!! ... I didn't even know that I had lost it! Exclaimed Dalya all surprised.

The Concierge Dadès said some words in a different accent:

- Lalla Dalya runs ... this on floor ... this morning.
- I dropped it this morning when I was running ... because I was late for class!!

Dalya understood his words. She thanked him with a smile:

- Thank you very much, Mr. Dadès.

The Concierge Dadès greeted her by bowing his head. But before he could leave to continue sweeping the floor, Dalya asked him a question that preoccupied her for a while:

- Why are you calling me Lalla Dalya? What does Lalla mean?

The Concierge turned around and he didn't seem to understand. Dalya repeated her question:

- Why Lalla Dalya? ... I'm just Dalya Bouvard.

The Concierge was silent for a long moment, with an innocent confusion on his face. Dalya was well aware that Dadès was a new stranger in this country, and he didn't master yet the language perfectly. So then, she simplified her question:

- Me ... my name is Dalya ... Dalya Bouvard ...

The Concierge was following her with his full attention. Dalya continued:

- I ... Dalya ... why Lalla Dalya? ... explain to me Lalla ...

The Concierge laughed, and he seemed to have finally understood the little girl's question. He replied in a serious tone, trying to find the words in this new language:

- Here in America, Lady ... in my country, Lalla ... Lady ... Lalla ... And because you, in all this school, only you always say hello to me ... so Lalla Dalya!

Dalya Bouvard finally understood why the school Concierge has been calling her Lalla and the meaning of the word. She didn't think that a simple hello would please the poor man, and get her to be called a great title. At that moment, Dalya forgot her long tough day, her father's chores, the teacher's humiliation and the students' mockery. One word changed her mood in a second. Dalya smiled, touched by the courtesy of a stranger toward her.

And by the simple fact that this stranger called her Lalla, Dalya certainly will not forget this gesture.

Chapter 10

Underwater

Friday, February 27th, 1981.

At the end of her classes that day, Dalya decided to visit her Uncle Giorgi in his workshop before returning to the Annex house. When she opened the workshop door, Dalya found her Uncle perched on the top of a ladder, trying to remove some books from a top shelf. His peppered curly hair was of the same mess as the bazaar. He was wearing as usual a long apron with several pockets, filled with craft and manufacturing tools, his passion since ever. When he noticed his niece, the man greeted her with an enthusiastic tone:

- Hello Biggo!!
- How are you, Uncle Giorgi?
- As usual, creating and building!! He laughed. I am looking for some old plans to build a cutting wood machine.

When he came down the ladder, Giorgi Bouvard put the books on a large table in the middle of his workshop. Dalya sat on an empty chair, near him, and she handed him a piece of paper:

- Uncle Giorgi ... I got a clue ... for the Second Question.
- Ah!! That famous box is always fascinating!! Exclaimed Uncle Giorgi before taking the paper and reading it with his full attention.
- This time the Excelbox provided me with numbers. I was wondering if you could help me. Do you know what these numbers are about?

Giorgi Bouvard sat on an armchair, shabby but comfortable, he thought aloud:

- JV-20-89 ... 17- HR - 08 ... 69th, 59th ... 1703 ... AV-07-90 ...

After a long reflection moment, Giorgi exhaled:

- For now, I have no clue what these numbers could possibly mean. But ... I'll keep this paper; I will do some more research to find out what these numbers refer to ...

Dalya thanked him with a smile. She spent the rest of the day in her Uncle's workshop, trying to understand the construction plans of a cutting wood machine.

Monday, March 02nd, 1981. Room N°48, Geography class.

Before her Geography course, Dalya arrived earlier than expected. She headed toward the Library before joining her class. Miss Guendolyn had just finished arranging some books in her chariot to sort them later.

- Hello mademoiselle!! You are early today!!
- Hello Miss Guendolyn. Yes, I arrived a little earlier. I wanted to give back the book I borrowed a few days ago. I've finished it.

Miss Guendolyn exclaimed delighted:

- Nobody in this school reads as faster as you do, Mademoiselle!!

When Miss Guendolyn took the book from the little girl, she couldn't help but notice a small note written on the back of a notebook that Dalya was holding. Miss Guendolyn couldn't hold her amused laugh:

- I understand that our modest Library is no longer enough for you, Mademoiselle.

Dalya didn't understand Miss Guendolyn's comment.

- Why do you say that?
- Because you are borrowing books from the National Georgetown Library.

Dalya was confused:

- The National Library? ... No, I've never set foot in there, Miss Guendolyn. What makes you say that?

Miss Guendolyn pointed out the number written on the back of Dalya's notebook.

- JV - 20 - 89 ... that's the coding books number of the National Georgetown Library. It is a well-known classification.

Dalya began to see things a little clearer. Miss Guendolyn continued to explain:

- JV is the aisle ... 20 is the row... and 89 is the exact location on the shelf. But ... if you have never visited the National Library, then how did you get this number, Mademoiselle?
- The Excelbox!! ... This number was included in the first clue of the Excelbox!! Dalya replied, surprised by her discovery, before continuing:
- So then, Miss Guendolyn ... these are the indications of a book? Are you sure? From the National Library?
- Yes ... yes ... certainly!!

Dalya thought aloud for a minute:

- But ... I don't know how to get inside the National Library. I have never set foot in there ... and I don't know if they will allow me to search and borrow this book ...

Miss Guendolyn came close to her and replied joyfully:

- I can be useful, Mademoiselle! ... At the end of your classes today, join me at the school exit. And I can get you inside the National Library, and even borrow the book for you. I will ask someone to replace me here for a few hours.

Dalya thanked her with a smile and she joined her Geography class. When Dalya entered the classroom, and as usual, the same group of students surrounded Eriem Eyelord and Gael Benoble. They laughed and talked about the latest rumors at school. Amira Mounier was already present and sitting alone in her chair without anyone approaching her. Dalya slipped quietly into her usual place. And a few seconds later, Professor Felozi entered the classroom. His arrival was abrupt, and he didn't seem in a good mood that day.

- Amira Mounier!! To the blackboard!!

While the other students returned to their seats, Amira got up and walked to the chalkboard hesitantly. Professor Felozi handed her a book before sitting in his office:

- Page 35! Read!

Amira faced the students; she opened the book, she took a long breath and she began to read:

- Threats and vul ... vulnerabilities of the coastlines. Various fac ... factors contribute to ... mak ... mak ... mak ...
- FASTER! exclaimed Professor Felozi
- Make the coastlines vulnerable. The natural sensitivity to mar ... mar ... mar ... marine erosion. The coastline dec ... dec ... decline or the sil ... sil ... silting, natu ... natu ...
- HURRY UP!
- Natural or intensified by ri ... rising of sea level and the cli ... cli ... climate change phen ... phen ... phenomenon serious ...
- STRONGER!

During the 3 hours' Geography course, Professor Felozi made Amira read the whole chapter, fifteen pages, standing in front of the entire class, yelling at her between every 2 words. The other students were watching Amira in annoyance; some were even sleeping because of the slow speed of her reading.

Amira had become very pale, a sweaty forehead, her cheeks puffy and swollen, her eyes all red, her exhausted legs have been standing for too long. At the end of the class, Professor Felozi displayed a smirk and peaceful smile, after discharging his mood on his student. Never Dalya thought to witness anyone capable of such cruelty, just for the pleasure of humiliating someone.

When the class was over, Dalya met Miss Guendolyn at the school exit. And they both made their way toward the National Georgetown Library.

The building was enormous, in white and gray marble. The stairs were about fifty steps toward the gigantic door. After passing a few offices, Miss Guendolyn and Dalya reached the inside. As overflowing as her imagination could be, Dalya could have never imagined that such a place existed. Aisles and floors of books, beyond the eye's sight. In the middle of the massive room, long wood tables and thin chairs were installed symmetrically. Luxurious lamps were placed on each corner of the tables, and giant chandeliers hung up from the ceiling. The place irradiated sunlight and knowledge.

Miss Guendolyn seemed to undoubtedly know her way, Dalya followed her.

- So ... the aisle JV ... here we are ... row 17 ... 18 ... 20! There it is ... and shelf 87 ... 88 ... shelf 89!

When Miss Guendolyn removed a book and gave it to Dalya, she smiled, very proud that she was able to help:

- Here it is, Mademoiselle. This is the book that is indicated by the numbers you were given.

Dalya was surprised to discover the book's title:

The memoirs of Edmond Halley,
Specialist marine diving researcher.

- Marine diving? Dalya wondered.
- It is about staying underwater to explore the marine landscape. Miss Guendolyn explained.
- Staying underwater ... Miss Guendolyn, are you sure this is the book that is indicated by these numbers? asked Dalya
- Yes, Mademoiselle. Certain! ... We are in the JV section of Marine Research. Everything related to the sea studies. Row 20, and shelf 89! … That's the book indicated for you.

Dalya was confused:

- But ... it's just that ... it's strange … how can marine diving be useful to me?

Miss Guendolyn was surprised by this discovery, as much as the little girl.

- I don't know, Mademoiselle. But, I will borrow this book for you, for a couple of days. Maybe after reading it, you may find an answer …

That night, after the last stored dried dinner dish, Dalya went to her bedroom. And although she didn't understand the Excelbox's pick for this book, still Dalya decided to read it anyway. The first chapters were not very revealing, the author described the different oceans and countries he had visited, various fish and marine creatures met...

Dalya was feeling the fatigue of a long day catching her up, she decided to quickly flip through the last pages of the book, in order to return it the very next day to Miss Guendolyn.

Maybe Miss Guendolyn was mistaking about these numbers. Perhaps the numbers indicated something other than the coordinates of a book of the National Georgetown Library, and maybe the Excelbox was mistaking for once...

When suddenly, two words retained Dalya's attention:

Respiratory reflexes

Dalya straightened up on her bed, and she re-read the paragraph from the beginning:

"... Underwater, the respiratory reflexes are modified: on the surface, the inhalation and exhalation are automatisms. Underwater, the breathing work is more difficult because the pressure increases and it becomes voluntary. The complex mechanism that takes place within the cell is changed. Carbon dioxide becomes more difficult to get rid of; the risk of breathlessness becomes important ..."

Dalya thought aloud:

- Breathing is more difficult because of the pressure underwater ... the risk of breathlessness becomes important ... breathlessness ... pressure ... this is exactly what happens to her ...

"... according to my research on the best methods to breathe underwater, I state 5 tricks: the first, stretching before each dive, it evacuates tension related to the stress and it is to better prepare the body for immersion. Second, if you are nervous and your heart rate is abnormally high, you can incline your face down before the dive and stare at your feet a few moments, this method is called immersion reflex, it improves breathing and helps to bett.... "

Dalya jumped out of her bed and she looked astonished at the Excelbox placed on her desk:

- Oh ... but ... so, this is what needs to be done?!

Wednesday, March 04th, 1981. Room N° 060. Mathematics class.

Throughout the previous night, Dalya searched for a way to send a piece of paper to Amira Mounier, her classmate. After their last conversation, Dalya didn't dare to approach or talk to her. But on that day, Dalya was determined to make her plan work!

After she arrived early, Dalya was delighted to be the first to enter the classroom for once. Dalya loved the Mathematics course and also its classroom. She got used to the chalk floating smell, and the golden light that graced the room. This classroom was the warmest and the most welcoming in the school. And Professor Wyatt was a kind and caring teacher.

Dalya settled in her chair, waiting for the slightest opportunity that would present itself that day. Eriem and Gael entered the classroom, followed by their usual court of students. They all settled near the large windows that offered a view of the school garden. And as always, the students' court surrounded the two popular students of the class. Immediately, laughs and whispers were heard. Dalya stayed silent and discreet, sitting alone, the Mathematics notebook opened in front of her, but her mind was preoccupied at finding a way to act.

A few moments later, Amira Mounier came into the classroom; she placed her backpack and books on her desk and chair, and then she walked to the students' group.

- Be ... be ... beautiful ... d ... day ... isn't it?

None of the students turned around to answer her, they completely ignored her presence. Amira Mounier continued:

- Is any ... anyone going to ... t ... t ... the win ... win ... winter party at the ... n ... new Gov ... Gov ... Governor's house?

Eriem laughed at a student's joke, some students laughed at how Gael mimicked the walking of the Mathematics Professor, other students were telling the latest rumors from other classes. No one seemed to see or hear a student standing in front of them, trying to fit in.

With a crushed and excluded feeling, Amira decided to return back to her chair. When she sat down, she noticed a little paper on her desk. Amira didn't know where this paper came from, and she was surprised to read its content:

Tips for better breathing and talking:

1 - Stretch the legs and arms before speaking

2 - Incline the face down, and stare at your feet for a few moments

3 - Do not move too much, stay as calm as possible

4 - Inhale slowly. You should feel your lungs stretched, and the muscle down filled with air. Hold your breath and count to 10 on your fingers.

5 - Exhale slowly, at once, to feel your lungs emptied

Amira looked up; she searched right and left at who could have placed this little paper on her desk. Students around Eriem and Gael were far from her desk, some students were sitting in their chairs, some busy reading their textbooks, and others were busy talking. Nobody noticed Amira's presence. And she had no idea who gave her this little paper of tips.

The arrival of Professor Wyatt to the classroom, announced the beginning of the Mathematics course. Professor Wyatt placed his briefcase on his desk, before starting a review of the previous course. Half an hour later, Professor Wyatt announced:

- We will now study a new form of Mathematics: the fractions. Can someone tell us this word's definition? ... Miss Amira Mounier?

Amira stood up from her chair with a slow movement. The Mathematics course was Amira's favorite subject, and it was well known that Amira excelled in all the paper Mathematics tests, better than all the students, including Dalya herself. Amira knew perfectly well the definition of the word fraction, but to pronounce it clearly, now that was a real challenge for her.

Professor Wyatt was encouraging, he smiled at her:

- Definition of the word fraction ... only in a short sentence, Miss Amira.

Amira gathered all her energy, and she began:

- In mat ... mat ... Mathematics, a fr ... fr ... fraction is a cert ... cert ... certain ... number of pa ... pa ... pa ...

Barely 6 words spoken and Amira had puffy cheeks and she turned all red. Professor Wyatt reassured her in a compassionate tone:

- Take your time, Miss Amira ... breathe well ... slowly ...

At this moment, Amira remembered something strange. She pulled a little paper from below her book, and she read it briefly. Dalya was sitting one table away from her classmate; she straightened up to get a better look at her. Dalya noticed that Amira stretched her arms and legs in a discreet movement. Then, Amira inclined her head down and she looked at her feet a few seconds. Amira looked up at Professor Wyatt, and then she said in a calm and slow voice:

- In Mathematics ... a fraction is a certain number of parts considered after the division of an integer number in equal parts.

Amira slowly breathed a long inhalation. She paused. Dalya noticed Amira's fingers counting up to 10 ... then; Amira exhaled gradually and she emptied her lungs. Amira continued slowly:

- For example ... the fraction 56 of 8 means the quotient of 56 by 8. It is equal 7, because 7 times 8 equal 56. In this fraction, 56 is called the numerator and 8 ... the denominator.

When Amira finished her explanation, Professor Wyatt was frozen up, surprised by what had just happened before his eyes. All the students had turned around toward Amira; they looked at her astonished and shocked. Amira fall back on her chair, confused by what she had just done. For the first time in her life, Amira spoke several sentences slowly and clearly ... and most importantly without any stuttering!!

- Well said, Miss Amira!! ... Very very well said!! Exclaimed Professor Wyatt, proud of his student.

Professor Wyatt, Eriem, Gael, the other students, and Amira Mounier herself ... they were all surprised by her clear speech without any stuttering. All were surprised. Except one student. She continued to write a fraction's definition on her notebook, giggling quietly:

- Underwater diving ... really?!

Chapter 11

Cleaning the windows

Thursday, March 05th, 1981. Royal Georgetown College. Room N°18. Music class.

The Music course became a little clearer for Dalya. She could now understand the vocabulary, and she had spent hours and hours to amass as much knowledge as possible about Artists and Musicians. Dalya came close to the other students' level in that course.

Two months since the beginning of the class, the theoretical part of the Music course was over. Now, the work on Musical instruments was about to begin. Professor Haîyang assigned to each student, the Musical instrument according to his choice and abilities. The rule of the Royal Georgetown College was that students should excel in at least 4 Musical instruments. Eriem Eyelord sat down at the piano. Gael Benoble took a trumpet. Amira Mounier was glad not to have to use her voice in a course, she prepared her violin. All the other students were trying on their instruments.

The moment that Dalya feared, has finally come. She had never touched an instrument before. And even after she could catch up in theory, thanks to the beginner's books that Miss Guendolyn provided her, Dalya doubted that the practice on an instrument would be as simple. While other students were already familiar with the use of Musical instruments since years, Dalya knew absolutely nothing about it!

- Mademoiselle Dalya Bouvard, follow me.

Dalya followed Professor Haîyang to a side of the Music classroom. Dalya was curious about the Musical instrument she will have to try. When Professor Haîyang stopped, she pointed at 2 pieces of rags and she said in a calm natural voice:

- You will clean all these windows.

Although her words were few and simple, Dalya didn't understand what Professor Haîyang wanted her to do. The Professor explained:

- Your occupation in my Music lessons will be to clean the windows of this classroom. You will start with these at the bottom, from left to right. Then you will use the ladder to clean the upper windows. And when you're done, you will restart again from bottom to the top.

Dalya thought the History and Geography Professors were the cruelest and humiliating ones, but she was mistaking. Dalya was living a nightmare, her throat tightened and the fever overwhelmed her. The other students watching the scene were hardly retaining their laughs. And yet, Dalya dared to ask:

- But Professor ... isn't there already a person to do this job? The Cleaner?

Professor Haîyang smiled:

- Yes, there is.
- But then ... you ... I ... but, I thought I should practice a Musical instrument, like the other students of this class ...

Professor Haîyang explained to Dalya in a calm but serious voice:

- Mademoiselle Dalya Bouvard, this is my Music class, and I decide who does what. I will repeat it to you once again; your occupation in my class will be to clean the windows.

The other students, although surprised by the situation, didn't hesitate to laugh. Gael Benoble laughed:

- Cleaning the windows ... it's a good occupation that matches her social status!!

Immediately, Professor Haîyang replied with a much firm cold tone:

- It is not for you to judge the social status of someone, Mr. Gael Benoble!! ... And unless you wish to clean the windows with her, I recommend you focus on your instrument, and be quiet!

Gael, Eriem, and all the other students stifled their laughs and didn't dare to add a word. Amira Mounier looked at Dalya from afar, without laughing like the other students.

Professor Haîyang handed 2 pieces of rags to Dalya, who took them with a heavy heart. She has never been so much humiliated and crushed in her life. Professor Haîyang came near the window, and she explained how to clean it, always in a strangely soft and calm voice:

- I want you to clean the windows, precisely like this. Make a half circle with your left hand and stretch your right hand in front.

Dalya was accustomed to all sorts of household chores in her home, but it was the first time she was asked to clean the windows in such a bizarre hand movement.

- Professor ... it would be easier to clean with a wave of up-and-down ...
- Yes, indeed. But I want you to clean the windows of my classroom, the way that I recommend!

Dalya looked confused and stunned. With a heavy heart, Dalya started cleaning the windows with this strange movement: a half-circle with her left hand and stretch her right hand in front. Professor Haîyang corrected Dalya's moves twice before returning to the other students who were trying on their instruments.

After a few moments, the sounds of Musical instruments, floated in the air. All the students continued their learning of Music ... all except one; she was cleaning the windows of the classroom.

Chapter 12

A small key

Friday, March 06th, 1981.

Winter was slow to leave Georgetown city. Tree's greenery appeared timidly, some Snowfall was still present on the ground, the cold was felt in some sudden wind breezes, and gray skies presaged a dark time.

Dalya quickly ate her breakfast, she put some books in her backpack, and she left the house, toward school. Antman Bouvard was carrying boxes in the garage. When he noticed his daughter, he asked:

- On the way to school?
- Yes, for the History course today.

Mr. Antman looked at his daughter for a moment, and then he ordered her:

- Arrange these tools crates in the carriage, and then sweep the garage!!

Dalya was paralyzed for a moment. Her father was well aware that the tasks he was asking her to do, will get her late for her classes at school. Dalya didn't understand her father's attitude toward her. Why was he acting like that? Why was he forcing her to work without worrying about her classes at school? Why must her father's work be a priority than her classes?

Yet, Dalya couldn't dare to disobey. She put her backpack on the floor and she started to organize the tools in the carriage. After many minutes, Dalya swept the garage as fast as she could. Then, she took her backpack and ran at full speed toward her school. Dalya was very late to her History class.

As soon as she opened the classroom door, Dalya found herself confronted alone against all the eyes of the other students, and the cold and icy voice of the History Professor was soon to be heard:

- Well ... it has become a habit of being lazy ...

Dalya tried to explain:

- I'm sorry, Professor. My father needed help wit...
- GO TO YOUR PLACE!!

Without daring to add a word, Dalya complied. She walked to the back of the classroom, she sat down on a chair and she opened her History book. Professor Ajanar continued to tour the tables, while the other students were copying the lesson of the day, written on the blackboard.

After a few minutes, Professor Ajanar asked the students to open the pages of their book to a new Chapter.

- Miss Eriem ... please read the 1st paragraph, page 3, please.

Eriem got up and read:

- Birth and education of Caesar. Born in 100 B.C, Caius Julius had a nickname Caesar ... ... as is customary among the Noble families. The father of Julius Caesar is a politician, Senator and magistrate, who participated in the Government of the Republic.

Professor Ajanar said:

- Thank you for this excellent reading, Miss Eriem. It's always a pleasure for the ears to hear you. Mr. Gael Benoble, continue the second paragraph, please.

Gael stood up and read:

- It is the mother of Julius Caesar, Aurelia, who watches over the education of her son, until the age of 7 years. And because he was born into a Noble family, the child had special courses, which took place in his own home.

Professor Ajanar announced:

- Very well Mr. Gael ... very good reading. Amira Mounier, continue the rest of the Chapter.

The student stood up and she took the book in her hands. Since several weeks now, and thanks to a mysterious little paper she found on her desk before the Mathematics class, Amira Mounier stuttered much less and she could even read complete sentences. Amira took a deep breath, she inclined her head down for seconds, and then she read the paragraph slowly and clearly:

- A litterator ... teaches Julius Caesar ... to read and write and count ... at the age of 12 years ... a Grammaticus teaches ... Julius César ... Latin and Greek literature.

Dalya was happy to know that Amira didn't stutter, not once. She spoke slowly and clearly, without repeating or having trouble pronouncing a word. Yet, Dalya couldn't help but notice that Professor Ajanar became strangely upset in an instant. Dalya wondered; shouldn't he be proud that his student's elocution is improving?

Professor Ajanar came near Amira and he interrupted her:

- Your father is an accountant, isn't he?

By hearing this question, Amira immediately blushed and her voice choked. Professor Ajanar continued in a falsely sweet tone:

- I've always wondered ... how could a poor accountant manage to register his daughter in this prestigious school ...

Students' laughs could be heard; all the eyes turned around to watch Amira. Dalya didn't understand why Professor Ajanar was speaking of Amira's father. His comment was within the privacy of his student. What was he getting at?

- I guess that your father works day and night to pay for your tuition in the college ...

Amira was paralyzed standing, holding the History book in her hands, not daring to raise her head, her cheeks turned all red.

- A poor little accountant who signed up his daughter in the same college as his Noble employer's son ... he dreams of becoming of the same social status as the rich people ...

Sitting a few chairs away from her, Dalya could clearly see the sweat on Amira's forehead. The other students laughed and whispered. Professor Ajanar thought aloud:

- A poor little accountant ... an incompetent little girl ... and a silly dream ...

Professor Ajanar went back to his desk before ordering Amira, in a calm voice:

- Keep reading ...

Amira pulled herself together. She inhaled and exhaled a long breath, she stretched her hands and legs, and then she continued:

- A by ... by ... by ... 16 years ... ol ... old ... young ce ... ce ... ce ... Cesar ... st ... st ... stud ...

Dalya finally understood the vicious game of the History teacher. All the students laughed. Professor Ajanar sat on the chair in his office, observing his triumph with a joyful smile, he seemed proud to have demeaned his student.

Because when they look down on you, when they crush you because of your poverty and your social status, when they ignore you because you're not as rich and as Noble ... it's a feeling of shame and inferiority, that no one deserves to feel.

Midday. In the canteen of the Royal Georgetown College.

When time for the lunch break rang, all the students got together in the immense lunchroom. Nearly one hundred round tables, surrounded by a dozen chairs for each table, were installed in the room. A long counter dominated one wall, where trays, forks and spoon, plates and glasses were placed. Students used trays, and followed the horizontal line to get served their meal. Many aid cooks were standing behind the counter to refill the food, clean or help serve lunches.

Since the beginning of her second semester in January, Dalya have been authorized by Director Darkfett to have lunch in the canteen, with strict orders to sit alone and speak no word to anyone. The menus were always delicious and complete; salads, soups, vegetables and meat ... worthy menus of the prestigious Royal Georgetown College.

On that day, Dalya got her lunch served on a tray, and she looked for an empty table. She noticed that Amira was sitting alone as usual in her place. After a hard morning in History course, Dalya had pity on her classmate. Professor Ajanar has indeed managed to humiliate Amira Mounier. In a matter of seconds, Professor Ajanar made her lose all her previous efforts to better and clearly speak.

When she moved to a nearby table, Dalya pulled out a book of her backpack and she decided to finish her Geography homework, due the next day while eating her lunch.

Focused on her reading, Dalya was interrupted by a wave of laughter from the students' table in front of her. When she raised her head, Dalya couldn't believe what she had just seen; Gael Benoble poured an apple juice drink on Amira Mounier's head. Her light brown hair was all soaked in apple juice. Eriem Eyelord and her court laughed loudly and didn't bother to hide it.

- It's alright ... it's nothing. Amira repeated, wiping her head with a napkin and trying to display a normal smile.

Gael Benoble returned to his place, and the laughter diminished, while Amira dried her hair. Dalya couldn't understand the students' attitude and what fun they had in humiliating and ridiculing their classmate. Nobody deserved this treatment. Dalya got back to her homework and to finish her lunch.

Moments later, another wave of laughter broke out. Dalya watched Gael Benoble empty a glass filled with apple juice on Amira's head, for the 2nd time!!

Her entire face was soaked in apple juice; Amira didn't dare to move, while the other students laughed so much and so loud. Gael returned to his seat and he stared proudly at the success of his joke. Amira took a second napkin and she wiped her face, repeating:

- It's just an accident ... it happens ... just an accident ...

Everyone was aware that it was not an accident. Yet, the students were amused watching Amira drying her face.

Dalya was struggling to witness this scene, unable to intervene. Director Darkfett was very strict, ordering her no interaction with any student. Dalya had a hard time to keep her focus on her Geography homework. She read the same question three times, before finally understanding its meaning. And the homework was due tomorrow morning in the first hour. Dalya could have finished it before, if not because of her mother's housework ... The students burst out laughing for the 3rd time!! And Dalya didn't believe what she was seeing again!!

As slowly as he could, Gael was pouring the apple juice on Amira's hair. She didn't have any courage to move away. All Amira could do was to whisper in a crushed voice:

- But ... w ... w ... why?

After Gael emptied the entire apple juice on her hair, he returned to his court and he imitated her in a small stuttering voice:

- W ... w ... w ... why? ... be ... be ... be ... because you ... you ... you ... are an ... an ... an ... idiot ...

Eriem and her court were so much amused by this scene. They warmly applauded Gael. Dalya felt anger invading her, not only because of Gael's joke, but because she couldn't intervene and prevent it. Director Darkfett had threatened her not to talk or approach the students. And Dalya couldn't be expelled from school.

After several minutes of silence, Dalya could finally finish her Geography homework. She didn't touch her lunch, having lost her appetite. When she was placing back her books in her backpack and she was about to leave the canteen, Dalya heard a noisy laughs invading the room.

For the 4th time, Gael was pouring apple juice on Amira's already soaked hair. The students had a good laugh during this lunch; many had a stomach ache from too much laughing. Amira remained motionless, paralyzed, receiving apple juice on her hair, on her forehead, on her nose, on her neck; on her ears ... all her school uniform was soaked. Except this 4th time, Amira's tears mingled and joined with the apple juice she received. And Dalya could clearly see her tears.

The day ended without any further incident. Amira skipped the History course this afternoon. Dalya thought that after such a difficult day, Amira must have returned home to dry her hair and get some rest. Dalya was upset and angry against Professor Ajanar, against Eriem and her court, against Gael ... and against herself too! Dalya couldn't help her classmate Amira.

At the end of classes, Dalya walked toward the school exit. Her mind was fully preoccupied because of this long difficult day. When a brutal blast of wind made her spin, Dalya lost her balance and she fell.

- Lalla Dalya ... Lalla Dalya ... is okay? ... is okay?

The Concierge Dadès rushed to help up Dalya. She replied while standing up:

- Yes, thank you Dadès. I don't know how I fell because of a sudden blas ...

All of a sudden, Dalya Bouvard froze in her place. Something strange happened right at this second; when the Concierge Dadès was picking up Dalya's backpack from the floor, a small key fell from the man's pocket, and it landed on Dalya's shoes. A small gray key.

Dadès handed her the backpack, after cleaning it from dust. Except that, Dalya had her eyes focused on the key she picked up from the floor. Dalya remembered some mysterious words:

In 17-HR-08, by a small key, fear will be released,

While holding the key in her hand, Dalya thought aloud:

- A small key … a small key … fear will be released, by a small key … but the numbers 17-HR-08 …what do they mean?

And as strange as it may seem, on that moment, Dalya looked up at the big clock above the main entrance of the Royal College. The time indicated 17:08. Dalya thought aloud:

- 17-HR-08 ... 17:08 ... 17-HOUR-08 …17:08 ... so then, the numbers were about a specific time? … In 17:08 time, the key that I am holding will release fear! …how?

Firmly holding the small key, Dalya turned toward the Concierge and she asked him:

- Dadès … this key ... which door does it open?

The Concierge explained immediately:

- Tower key!!

Dalya didn't understand what he meant. The Concierge pointed his finger to a big tower on the top floor, in the College left wing. Dalya had never been in this side of the school. She heard from Miss Guendolyn that this section was empty and unused since decades. Dadès continued:

- Missio Director say ... me clean tower … me cleaned tower last week!!

Dalya dared to ask him:

- Dadès ... can I visit this tower?

A few minutes later, when Dadès opened the door of the tower room, Dalya followed him inside. Dadès had previously cleaned and arranged the room. It was a large place with 3 small windows that illuminated the room with a bright light, a huge triangular ceiling, parquet flooring. There was a big old wood office table. Dadès explained to Dalya, while he walked toward the room windows:

- This tower empty... no one comes here ...

And the strangest thing was when Dadès spoke; his voice was intensified because of the echo produced by the immense triangular ceiling. Dalya repeated, while looking up:

- Hello … hello … hello …

Dadès laughed. The echo had an odd effect on the voice. Dalya laughed too. Not only because of the intensified voice ... but because she finally understood what the Excelbox meant…

Monday, March 09th, 1891.

All the weekend, Dalya thought about this isolated and empty tower at the Royal Georgetown College.

On that day, Dalya followed from afar her classmate Amira Mounier, who immediately went to the Library, at the end of classes. Dalya had an idea in her mind, but she didn't know how to pass it on to Amira, without speaking to her and being rejected. When a female voice interrupted her:

- Is everything alright, Mademoiselle?

When Dalya turned toward the young woman, an idea appeared in her mind:

- Miss Guendolyn ... I need your help!

The young woman leaned toward Dalya and she replied:

- Of course, Mademoiselle!! What can I do for you?

Dalya explained to Miss Guendolyn in a whispered voice, so that no one can hear them. When she finished, Miss Guendolyn's eyes were happily illuminated, her cheeks became rosy, and a wide smile displayed on her face:

- It's understood Mademoiselle!!

Dalya knew that she could count on Miss Guendolyn's help to make her plan work. Dalya walked inside the Library. And although all the desks and chairs were empty, Dalya settled on a desk near Amira. Her classmate was busy reading quietly, her head inside her big book; Amira didn't care or realize who sat near her.

Dalya pulled a notebook from her backpack, she wrote something on a piece of paper, she wrapped it around an object, and then she waited.

A few seconds later, Miss Guendolyn passed by with her book carriage near Amira, and she exclaimed with an angry voice:

- Miss Amira!! You must not read aloud!! You are disturbing the others!!

Amira Mounier was confused; she turned around and looked up at Miss Guendolyn in surprise tone:

- But ... I haven't ... talked ...

Miss Guendolyn exclaimed with a shocked voice:

- Miss Amira!! You are not allowed to read this book!!

Amira Mounier replied, astonished at this remark:

- All the books in the Library ... are allowed ... since when there are ... restrictions on books?

Miss Guendolyn immediately protested:

- Since yesterday!!

Amira Mounier stared at the young woman with a puzzled look:

- Miss Guendolyn ... yesterday was Sunday ...

Amira was about to turn around to her desk. But a hand was still inside Amira Mounier's backpack. At this sight, Miss Guendolyn trembled and yelled suddenly:

- MISS AMIRA!! THIS BOOK IS NOT ALLOWED TO YOU!! IT IS ONLY FOR THE 9TH GRADE STUDENTS!!

Amira looked back at the young woman with confused eyes:

- But ... I'm a 9th grade student!!

Miss Guendolyn turned all red; she was out of ideas at this point:

- Oh I see ... I remember ... yes ...
- Is everything well ... Miss Guendolyn? Asked Amira, concerned about the strange state of the young woman.

All of a sudden, Miss Guendolyn flashed a satisfied wide smile:

- Oh yes ... Everything will be fine, Miss Amira!! ... Everything will be fine!!

The young woman pushed her book carriage and greeted the student:

- I'll let you get back to your work ... Good day, Miss Amira!!

Amira turned around back to her desk, thinking aloud:

- But what is it with her? What is happening to her?

It was only at this moment that Amira Mounier realized the presence of Dalya Bouvard sitting in the desk near her. Dalya looked focused on her book; she seemed to have heard nothing of the strange conversation between Miss Guendolyn and Amira. And it was true, Dalya heard nothing of their talk, she was busy executing her plan...

The next day. Tuesday, March 10th, 1891.

The Mathematics class of Professor Wyatt ended earlier than expected. The students got up to leave the classroom. Amira rushed toward Eriem and her court:

- It was an ... ea ... ea ... easy ...course ... was ... wasn't it?

None of the students answered. Amira continued:

- Are y ... you ... heading to th ... th ... the Library ... to study?

Eriem Eyelord looked at Amira in the eyes and then she said with an amused voice:

- I think I need to see a Doctor ... I still hear this strange voice speaking ...
- And especially stuttering!! Gael laughed.

The students left the classroom with laughs and giggles. Amira watched them for a moment, and then she returned to her chair, looking disappointed once again, because she has failed to join in the group of the popular students.

When Amira was putting her books in her backpack, and about to leave the classroom, she suddenly remembered something. Last night at her home, Amira found a piece of paper and a key in her backpack. She didn't know who put these items in her bag, nor why nor how. The little paper had a lovely handwriting:

With a small key, fear will be released

In the highest tower of the College

- The highest tower? ... It's in the other side of school ... no one goes there. And why do I have this key? ... What can it be for?

Curious and confused, Amira decided to visit the place indicated in the little paper. After some minutes, Amira reached the other side of the school. The corridor was long and empty. The windows to the left along the corridor, allowed the last lights of the day. A small door stood at the end of the hall.

- This might be the key to open that door. Amira thought.

She stepped forward hesitantly. When she arrived at the door, Amira took the key from her pocket and she opened it. Amira couldn't contain her surprise and she didn't believe her eyes. She never thought that such a place could exist.

A large wood table desk and chair stood in the middle of the room, an old vase filled with beautiful flowers and several books were placed on the table desk, an old yet comfortable couch was set a few steps away, the windows let inside the beautiful rays of the day. The huge triangular ceiling was spectacular. The room appeared to be cleaned and well prepared.

Amira Mounier came inside timidly. There was no one in this room. She reread once again the piece of paper in her hands, trying to understand why it had brought her to this place.

- It said that with a small ke...

Amira stopped suddenly. She realized that her voice has changed. It was as if her voice was amplified ... and even stronger. She continued reading the small paper:

- With a small key ... fear will be released ... in the highest tower ...

Amira ended the sentence with few breaks and without stuttering. A smile lit up her face instantly.

- But ... How is this even possible?

Amira looked up at the massive ceiling. She didn't understand exactly how the echo helped her to speak better and with less stuttering, she didn't know who indicated her this place, and how the small paper and the key landed in her backpack.

But what is certain and for sure ... is that a little trembling fearing voice ... was about to be released !

And what is even more sure ... is that a little silhouette was observing Amira Mounier through the small opening of the tower door... and this little silhouette, she never gave up!

The Excelbox had some strange ways to unlock the best from you.

Chapter 13

Cruelty

Saturday, April 04th, 1891.

The first Saturday of April was an ordinary day like any other. The sun was shining and glowing, the trees were covered with a thin layer of green, and spring appeared to be joyful.

On that day, Dalya had some grocery shopping to do at the Saturday market, in front of the Toscana restaurant. There, she met her friends Alfie and Maurice, and she copied the guessing words game from the newspaper, before heading back to the grand Mansion.

Passing by the house of les Poirier, Dalya looked for Mrs. Glorina, the housekeeper taking care of the French family home. But she couldn't be found, Dalya tiptoed quietly toward the bird's nest in the garden, and she put a small folded paper inside of the bird's nest.

In the evening at the Annex house, Dalya took care of the dinner dishes, while her mother put the little twins to bed. Dalya had almost finished washing all dishes, when her mother came into the kitchen, holding two milk bottles:

- Here ... wash these two.

But, before Dalya could dry her hands and turn around to take the two bottles of her mother's hands, Mrs. Augustine dropped the two bottles, they fell to the ground and they broke into several pieces. Mrs. Augustine transformed in a second:

- LOOK AT WHAT YOU HAVE DONE, YOU IDIOT!!! WHY DID YOU BREAK THE BOTTLES??!!

Dalya jumped, not only because of the bottles' crash sound, but also because of her mother's scream. Dalya dared to answer anyway:

- I didn't do anything ...
- STUPID WITLESS!! INCAPABLE IDIOT!!
- But ... you dropped them before I could even touch them ...

Mrs. Augustine's anger increased. She has never accepted to be wrong, even less being told that in her face. And the only thing that Mrs. Augustine did best in her life, was to blame others for everything, including her own mistakes. Mrs. Augustine continued to scream with all her might, while Dalya knelt down to pick up the broken pieces of the bottles:

- YOU LET THOSE BOTTLES FALL, LITTLE WITLESS!! WHEN WILL YOU EVER LEARN TO PROPERLY SERVE US??!! YOU ARE JUST AN INCAPABLE IDIOT

AND YOU WILL ALWAYS BE!! LOOK AT WHAT YOU HAVE DONE NOW!! WHY DID YOU BREAK THEM?? EXPLAIN IT TO ME!! YOU IGNORANT IDIOT!!

Dalya could never understand her mother's thinking. Kneeling on the ground, still picking up pieces of the bottles, Dalya wondered aloud:

- What is the point of screaming? The bottles are already broken; the yells will not fix them back.

And if there's one thing Mrs. Augustine cannot stand, it is that you defend yourself while she abuses you, insults you and mistreats you. On that moment, Mrs. Augustine came close to her daughter and she pinched her ear so hard, that Dalya turned all red. Mrs. Augustine pulled up her daughter, and she dragged her by the ear in a brutal move, toward the house exit. And they both disappeared in the garage.

Monday, April 06th, 1891. Room N°48. Geography class.

Dalya arrived earlier to the Geography class; she quickly sat on her chair. And as usual, the other students were all surrounding Eriem Eyelord and Gael Benoble; some were sitting, others were standing by the window. When one of the students turned around and exclaimed sarcastically:

- Pretty outfit, Mademoiselle the Heiress!!

Dalya didn't turn toward the other students; she lowered her head down, looking at her hands wrapped in thick and crumpled gloves. Dalya clasped her hands buried in her gloves; she slowly opened her backpack and pulled out her notebook.

- Why are you wearing gloves in class? asked a boy
- It's hot today ...
- Isn't she aware that we are in April month?
- Or probably because she is used to wearing them when she sold vegetables at the market!
- Are you taking back your old job?
- Maybe she finally understood that her place isn't here ...
- Finally!!
- Her place is in the Calinours world!!
- Certainly ... the Calinours world!! Well said!!

All the students laughed and mocked Dalya. Except Amira Mounier. She was sitting a few chairs from Dalya, and she didn't dare to interfere. But Amira Mounier felt that something was wrong with Dalya, that day. And although they were not friends, Amira suspected something unusual, while Dalya was watching her thick gloves and everyone was laughing at her.

When Professor Felozi entered the classroom, the students sat on their usual places. The teacher put some files on his desk, and then he ordered in a strict tone:

- Dalya Bouvard!! To the blackboard!!

By hearing her name, Dalya jumped. She stood up and walked to the blackboard. Professor Felozi handed her a paper:

- Write these words on the board.

The list contained about 15 words of Geography vocabulary. Dalya had only to write them on the board. A very simple task. However, this move seemed to be so hard to do, while keeping her gloves. Still, Dalya took the chalk and she started writing.

Several minutes later, Dalya barely managed to write one single word on the board. Professor Felozi hurried her:

- ARE WE SPENDING THE NIGHT IN IT? HURRY UP!!
- Yes, Professor.

Dalya pressed the chalk between her fingers and she continued. Except that the slightest move of her fingers, was very difficult.

- BUT WHAT IS WRONG WITH YOU?! ARE YOU BECOMING INCAPABLE TO WRITE!

Although she could hear the students' laughs behind her, Dalya focused and she finished the second word, letting out a long effort sigh. Professor Felozi yelled:

- AND WHAT ARE THESE DAMN GLOVES?! YOU LOOK LIKE HAVING A POLAR BEAR'S HANDS!!

Dalya undertook to write the third word, but she couldn't finish it. Professor Felozi lost his patience:

- Miss Eriem ... please take the list and write these words on the board.

When Dalya gave the paper to Eriem, and returned to her chair, Professor Felozi thought aloud:

- They admit really anyone in this school!! Such a waste!!

At the end of classes, Dalya returned back home. And after a hard day, she was happy to see a familiar face waiting for her at the garden gate of the grand Mansion; the Snow Panther. Séraphine was laying down on the green grass in the garden, playing to catch a butterfly that was spinning around her. And when she noticed Dalya, Séraphine paused and stared at the little girl, just like usual. Dalya smiled at the Snow Panther, before continuing her way home.

Before Dalya could go up the few steps of the Annex house entrance, her father called her out to the garage:

- Come over here, you!!

Dalya put her backpack on the house steps, and then she joined her father:

- Good eveni...
- I want you to organize these tacks by size in these boxes. Her father ordered her without replying to her greeting.

There were at least a thousand tacks of all sizes and types. Because of Dalya's silence, her father asked her in an annoyed tone:

- What's the matter?
- It's just that ... I've had a long day at school ... I can do it tomorrow afternoo...

Mr. Antman came near his daughter, he grabbed her arm hard and he yelled:

- WHEN I ASK YOU TO DO SOMETHING, YOU EXECUTE IT IMMEDIATELY! I DON'T CARE IF YOU'RE TIRED OR BUSY ... IMMEDIATELY! ... IS THAT CLEAR ENOUGH?

Dalya bowed her head without daring to answer.

- I'll be out at the grocery store in town. When I come back, the work must be done!

When her father left the workshop, Dalya knelt down and she sorted the tacks in the different boxes that her father ordered her.

After 2 hours of work, Dalya finished her task, and she joined her mother in the kitchen; the dinner table was already served. Dalya didn't dare to say good evening. Her mother seemed to be in an angry mood. Dalya sat on her place at the table, silent and immobile. Her little sisters were eating the pea soup alone, they loved this soup. Mrs. Augustine put down on the table the pea soup container and a bread plate, with her usual brutal moves, sighing in exasperation:

- I'm tired of cooking!! Morning and evening!! Every day!!

Dalya didn't dare to raise her head, even less say a word. She served herself some soup and bread, and she ate in silence. When her father came in, he greeted cheerfully his little twins and kissed them:

- Good evening Ari and Adi!!

The twins continued to eat their pea soup, all by themselves. Mr. Antman spoke to his wife in an amused voice:

- Good evening Augustine!! What did you cook for us tonig...

Mrs. Augustine interrupted him in a snap:

- Oh because I shouldn't be tired of cooking! You think I'm going to serve you every day great dishes like at the restaurant?!

- Didn't I tell you that the Toscana restaurant have a new Cook? Said Mr. Antman, while ignoring his wife usual criticism, he asked her:
- And guess who that is?
- Who? Questioned Mrs. Augustine, all curious.
- You remember the man who always asked me the best apples? The manic man who examined them one by one for minutes before putting them in the basket of his assistant? Mr. Antman said, proud of his news.
- I knew he was a strange man!! Exclaimed Mrs. Augustine in an awed voice. He works as a Cook at the restaurant now? Are you sure?
- Yes!! I saw him this morning with his cap before dropping off my groceries delivery!!
- And how is he at work? He must be crazy!

The conversation between Mr. Antman and his wife took a normal tone. Both parents ignored the presence of their daughter Dalya on the dinner table. And it was better that way, Dalya didn't want any more attention after this hard long day.

In fact, it has been several months now that Antman have been ordering his daughter to do chores and work, every day, morning and evening. He spoke to her very little, he doesn't even look at her, and he just orders her heavy work, ignoring her class schedule, her fatigue or her time to do her homework. Dalya didn't understand why her father was treating her that way. And it made her sad. Besides being harassed and mocked at school, the tension at home was only increasing.

When she finished washing, drying and storing the dishes, Dalya retired to her bedroom, while her father was playing with her little sisters in the living room and her mother was sewing her husband's shirt. Before walking up the stairs, Dalya looked discreetly at her parents and her sisters. Why were her parents so hard on her? Why did her parents treat her differently than her little sisters? What did Dalya do to deserve their severity? Why does her father charge her with heavy work? Why does her father seem upset and angry about her? Why does her mother hate her even more than before their arrival in the Annex house?

So many questions that Dalya couldn't find an answer to. She went back to her bedroom, alone, crushed from a long hard day.

It was a long night. Questions didn't stop appearing in the little girl's mind. And the cruel behavior of her parents didn't stop either.

Friday, April 10th, 1891.

Dalya came home from school in the late afternoon. She met the Snow Panther Séraphine at the entrance wall of the grand Mansion. Séraphine stared at the little girl until she disappeared into the woods that separated the grand Mansion from the Annex house.

When Dalya opened the front door, a delicious fruit scent came away from inside the house. Dalya walked toward the kitchen. Her little sisters were placed on their chairs around the dining table. They tasted the fruit jam, and they had some of it on their faces and hands.

- Good evening. Said Dalya.

Mrs. Augustine didn't reply. She was busy filling glass jars of fruit jam, while a potato soup for dinner was cooking in a pot. Dalya kissed her little twin sisters, and she hurried to her room to change her clothes. When Dalya came down a few minutes later in the kitchen, the little twins had finished their jams, and Mrs. Augustine was closing her jam jars, pressing the cover firmly.

Dalya started to wash the dishes and clean the counter. And since the fruit jam quickly stuck on the plates almost like glue, Dalya hurried to clean the dishes, her little sisters' plates, the wood spoons on the dining table, and the large containers that her mother used to mix the jam. Suddenly, a scream shacked the kitchen:

- WHAT IS THAT!!! WHAT IS THIS HORROR!!

Dalya's mother stood in front of the stove and she watched the pot of potatoes soup with a horrified look. Dalya moved toward the pot of soup, to understand what was happening. And Dalya was also shocked by discovering a soup of potatoes ... pink!

- BUT ... IT IS ... THE FRUIT JAM IS IN THE POTATO SOUP!!! ... WHO DID IT?!

Mrs. Augustine exclaimed angrily, turning toward her daughter:

- YOU IDIOT!!

Dalya immediately replied:

- I didn't do anything!
- AND WHO ELSE COULD HAVE DONE THAT!! YOU WITLESS!!
- But ... I didn't come close to the pot!!
- AND ABOVE ALL YOU LIE!! YOU ARE THE ONE WHO PUT JAM IN THIS SOUP!! LITTLE VERMIN!!
- I am not lying! I just got in the kitchen ... when will I have had the time to pour the jam into the soup!! And besides ... why will I do it?

Dalya defended herself as best as she could. But in front of the logical arguments of her daughter, Mrs. Augustine insisted on calling her guilty.

- I didn't do it!
- YOU DARE TO TALK WHEN I SPEAK TO YOU!!
- What should I do then to defend myself?
- SHUT UP! THAT'S WHAT YOU NEED TO DO WHEN I SPEAK TO YOU!! SHUT UP!!

Because yes, Mrs. Augustine didn't like to be corrected or answered to when she attacks you. You should be silent when she falsely accuses you of something you have not done.

When suddenly, Dalya noticed something very strange. A long fruit jam wood spoon was placed near a long potatoes soup wood spoon. Dalya pointed to her mother:

- Look!! ... You have put the two spoons; one near the other ... you surely must have confused them when you have spun the potatoes soup!

Mrs. Augustine froze for a moment, not knowing what to say. But one thing is certain, Mrs. Augustine never apologized ... never for her mistakes, even though she was fully aware of being unfair to you. The feeling of oppression, the little Dalya Bouvard knew it very well, thanks to her mother.

At that moment, Mrs. Augustine had only one idea on what to do, as usual. She came close to her daughter, she grabbed her in a sudden movement by squeezing her neck, and she led her outside of the kitchen. Toward the garage.

Chapter 14

Lace beige gloves

Tuesday, May 05th, 1891. 7:05 AM. In the Annex house of the grand Mansion.

Awake since very early, Dalya was sitting at the breakfast table; she was reviewing for the last time a homework. Her little sisters were still asleep upstairs. Dalya's mother, Mrs. Augustine was warming some bread. When suddenly, Dalya felt the presence of a silhouette behind her.

- What are you doing?

Dalya looked up at her father, who came into the kitchen, without her noticing. Antman Bouvard stared at Dalya's notebook in confusion, and he repeated his question:

- What are you doing?
- I am checking my homework of Music class. Dalya replied.

Dalya's father burst out laughing:

- What? ... Music?! ... Really?! ... That's the most stupid thing that ever existed!!

Dalya didn't understand what was funny, she asked all curious:

- Why is Music a stupid thing?

Many parents would be proud of the curiosity and the intelligence of their children. But certainly not the Bouvard parents. Mr. Antman never liked his daughter's questions. He took out the jam jar from a closet, and he answered in a mocking voice:

- Music is useless!! That's why it's stupid!!

Dalya was not convinced by her father's answer. After a few seconds of reflection, she said:

- Anyway, in Music class, it's beautiful to hear the instruments play. When Miss Haîyang played for us the violin once, it was magnif...

Her father interrupted her brutally:

- Your goal is to study to answer the next challenge and give me this fortune!! Music will not help you in anything, you little idiot!!

Dalya didn't dare to add a word. Mr. Antman sat in his usual chair and he laughed arrogantly:

- Music is useless; it doesn't put food on the table!!

Dalya's father didn't care about Music or any form of Art. The only thing that mattered to Antman Bouvard was money. And the only opinion that mattered to him was his.

A few hours later. At 9:05 AM. Room N°18. Music class.

The Music class went on just like the previous ones. Professor Haîyang was touring the class, correcting the moves and notes of each student. While Dalya was standing up on a ladder, cleaning the windows of the Music classroom. Professor Haîyang made sure that Dalya cleaned the windows with the same strange and complicated hand movement she ordered her.

Professor Haîyang left the classroom for a few minutes, to pick up some papers from the Headmaster Secretary's office. All the students continued their work. All but one.

Gael Benoble stopped playing his trumpet, and he decided, as usual, to make everyone laugh by imitating the teachers. Dalya didn't like this kind of game, and she didn't think it was that funny. Dalya focused on her work and she continued cleaning the upper windows of the Music classroom.

When all of a sudden, Dalya felt that the ladder was moving. When she looked down, Dalya was surprised to find her classmate Gael Benoble holding the ladder with both hands and he tried to move it. Dalya immediately exclaimed, terrified of falling:

- Hey!! ... What are you doing?! ... Stop!! ... You'll make me fall!!

Gael replied while shaking the ladder:

- Exactly!! That's my goal!!

Eriem and her court were all laughing, amused in front of this scene. Dalya had no time to think or say a word; the ladder fell to the ground so abruptly. And luckily, Dalya had a quicker reflex to hold on to the window handle, she placed her feet on a thin brick on the wall. Under the amused stares of Eriem, of Gael and the other students, Dalya stood still hanging on the window.

- She is a monkey now!!
- She is gifted to hang on the windows!!
- I guess she learned it when she lived in her world ...
- The Calinours world!!
- She is much more fun than I thought ...
- I admit this little veggy seller amuses us very well...

Under the laughs and mockery of the other students, Dalya stood motionless, hanging tightly to the window handle, for many long hard seconds. Except that Dalya was wearing thick and crumpled gloves, she felt that her hands would soon let go, Dalya then decided to jump to the ground, before losing her balance. When she landed on the floor, Dalya let out a painful scream because she fell on her shoulder. While Dalya was immobile and in pain, laying down on the floor, the other students were laughing aloud.

All of a sudden, a firm and strict voice exclaimed:

- WHAT IS HAPPENING HERE?

All the laughs stopped immediately. Professor Haîyang stepped forward and she rushed toward Dalya, she helped her get up slowly and painfully.

- What happened to you? Asked Professor Haîyang in a worried voice.

On that moment, all the students' eyes stared at Dalya. Eriem and Gael watched her in a serious and tense look. None of the students dared to laugh, they all waited for Dalya's answer.

- I ... I lost my balance on the ladder ... and ... and I fell, Professor.

It was the only answer Dalya could provide. Yet, Professor Haîyang didn't seem very convinced of this simple reply. Professor Haîyang turned around and she examined the students one by one, with a strangely menacing look.

- Are you sure ... Mademoiselle Bouvard?

Dalya didn't need more trouble at school. So she tried her best to answer clearly:

- Yes, Professor. I just lost my balance on the ladder.

Professor Haîyang forced herself to accept Dalya's answer. She asked her to sit and relax for the rest of the Music class. Professor Haîyang turned toward the other students, and the class continued on normally.

Later in the afternoon, all the students were busy in their reviews and studies. The college Library was fully occupied with students of all levels, and yet the place was quiet and calm.

Dalya settled in her usual seat next to the Library windows. She had lots of homework and catch up to do. The exams were approaching, and Dalya was determined to get good grades and be at the same level as her classmates. She put on her desk several books piled one over the other. Dalya consulted them to solve the Mathematics equations. Her mind busy and focused, Dalya's head was buried in books.

Out of the blue, a hand sent to the floor, in one move, Dalya's books. When she jumped and looked up, Dalya found herself surrounded by Eriem and Gael, followed by several students. Eriem pulled down the rest of Dalya's books to the floor, looking at her in a defiant stare:

- You better go back to your world ... the Calinours land!!

Dalya couldn't get up nor say a word to defend herself from these students. Any reaction would expel her from this school. Eriem, Gael and their court, they stared at Dalya in a contemptuous and mocking gaze for long seconds, before continuing on their way toward their usual study desks.

After they went, Dalya got up from her chair and she knelt down to pick up her books dispersed all over the floor. Dalya didn't understand the pleasure procured by humiliating and belittling people. She didn't understand the reason of this free nastiness. Dalya wondered:

- What have I done to them? ... I don't even know them! ... How long must I endure their attitudes? ... Why are they so mea...

Suddenly, an item got Dalya's attention. Between 2 books, there was a piece of cloth. Dalya took it and she discovered with amazement what it was; lace beige gloves!!

- But ... how ... who dropped it off?

Immediately, Dalya got up to search for who could have put these gloves on the ground among her books. The study desks were occupied with focused and busy students, all from a different level and class.

Dalya put her books back on her desk. Then, she lay back on her chair, admiring the magnificent pair of lace beige gloves. On that moment, even though Dalya didn't know who gave her these gloves, she felt the empathy and the kindness of someone toward her. Dalya put on her new gloves. Her eyes filled with tears, her cheeks became rosy. And despite the cruel attitudes that Dalya Bouvard was suffering from her parents and from her classmates, a hopeful smile appeared on the little girl's lips...

Chapter 15

A place, a recipe

Wednesday, May 13th, 1891. At the Annex house of the grand Mansion.

That day, Dalya finished her classes a little earlier than usual. When she returned to the Annex house, her little sisters welcomed her by waving their little boots in their hands, and yelling simultaneously:

- Garden!!! Garden!!! Garden!!!

The weather was warm; the sun was increasingly present. The May month announced a close summer. Dalya put her backpack on the stairs and she led her little sisters to the large garden of the grand Mansion. The Gardener, Mr. Rosenwald, was planting some beautiful flowers of purple and blue color, around the large windows of the grand Mansion. The Snow Panther was taking a nap nearby, lying down on the grass; the sunlight warmed her beautiful white tattooed fur.

- Hello Mr. Rosenwald!! Dalya greeted him.

The old man turned and replied:

- Hello Lady Dalya.

Mr. Rosenwald was the first and only one to call her Lady Dalya. In all her life, never someone had ever called her that way. And although she knew the Gardener since several months now, Dalya never dared to ask him why he calls her Lady.

Ari and Adi ran into the garden, chasing a big butterfly. They screamed:

- Looky Dindin!! Looky Dindin!! Zoli butterfly!!
- Yes ... sure it's pretty. Dalya replied, while sitting near the Gardener.

Mr. Rosenwald asked her, while removing a flower off a pot before planting it in a hole:

- You've finish school early today?
- Yes, the History Professor preferred to start the new chapter next week, and he set us free earlier.
- Dindin!! Dindin!! Looky!! Zoli squirrel!! Looky he jumps!!

Ari and Adi were jumping in front of a tree, while pointing out with their little fingers at a squirrel moving from one branch to another.

- Yes ... he jumps very fast ... it's nice to see ... but stay away and watch only. Dalya replied to her little sisters.

Dalya turned to the Gardener:

- These are very different flowers than what you usually use.
- Yes, I've found them some time ago in a flower shop in downtown. I planted some of them in the front door ... and I noticed that it grows quickly and it lasts longer, so I thought of planting them also here, near the windows.
- What are they called?

But before the Gardener could speak a word, screams rose up suddenly:

- Dindin!! Dindin!! Looky Looky!! A little bird!! On tree ... Looky Looky!!

Without even turning around to see, Dalya answered them:

- Yes ... the bird is very lovely!!

The Gardener emptied a second flower pot and he placed it in a hole:

- This flower is called agapanthe.

Dalya caressed the flower gently; she came close to smell it. And it is true that the perfume was very exquisite.

- Dindin!! Dindin!! Looky Looky!! Little snake!! Little snake!!

Dalya handed a 3rd flower pot to the Gardener, responding to her sisters in a spontaneous tone:

- Yes ... it's a pretty snake!! ... very pretty sna... SNAKE!

When suddenly, Dalya and the Gardener turned around right away, and they noticed that the little twins Adi and Ari, both were holding from each side a 1-meter-long snake. They had fun stretching the snake, each in an opposite direction. Dalya and the Gardener got up abruptly. But before they could do one more step, a white arrow surpassed them and speeded toward the little twins. The Snow Panther snatched the snake from the twins' hands and she disappeared in the woods just outside the grand Mansion.

Dalya ran toward her little twin sisters and she caught their hands. After flirting with disaster, Dalya's heart was beating fast and her face went pale:

- BUT WHAT IS WRONG WITH YOU TWO??!! LOOKING FOR TROUBLES EVERYWHERE AND EVERYDAY!!

Ari and Adi didn't understand the worried and anxious behavior of their sister Dalya. They murmured spontaneously:

- Zoli snake ... Zentil snake ...

Dalya knelt down, and she looked at them in the eye:

- No no!! Snake is not pretty!! Snake is dangerous!! You must not play with it!!

The Gardener Mr. Rosenwald joined Dalya:

- I've searched for that snake for many days ... I even laid some traps in the garden to catch it ... we are lucky that the Snow Panther Séraphine was present here today.

The Gardener knelt down, in front of the little twins, and he spoke to them in a kind but serious voice:

- Mesdemoiselles Ari and Adi, you must not play with all the animals in the garden ... some are nice and pretty, yes ... but other animals can be very dangerous for you ... so do not touch any other animal except Séraphine ... you knows you by now, she is harmful … you can play only with Séraphine, alright?

Ari and Adi exchanged a serious look, and they both answered:

- Yes ... only Séraphine ...

The Gardener got up and he returned back to his work. Immediately, the little twins rushed toward the Snow Panther, who had returned back to its place. But before the little twins could take a further step, Dalya grabbed her little sisters by the back of their jackets and she retained them:

- Oh no!!! You won't get anywhere now!! Pests as you are, I'll bring you back home right now!!

Dalya hold firmly her little sisters by their hands and she walked them toward the Annex house. She had enough fear and anxiety for today. When suddenly, a familiar voice stopped Dalya:

- I'VE ... FOUND ... IT … BIGGO!!!

Dalya turned around to see her paternal Uncle Giorgi Bouvard coming inside the garden of the grand Mansion, and he was running toward her.

- Hello Uncle Giorgi!! How nice to see you he…
- I'VE … F… FOUND IT!! He screamed happily, with a breathless and barely comprehensible voice.
- What did you find? Dalya asked all curious.

Uncle Giorgi gave her a paper, and he forced himself to regain his normal breath, displaying a wide proud smile:

- The part of the 1st clue ... the 69th and 59th!!

Dalya read the paper that her Uncle gave her. She then looked at him, astonished and surprised:

- I would have never guessed that it was … an address! ... Uncle Giorgi, you are a genius!!

Uncle Giorgi blushed:

- I must admit that it took me some time to find out what this number meant.

Dalya was always fascinated by her Uncle's brain and cleverness:

- How did you find it out? ... I read this number at least a hundred times, and I didn't think it could be an addr... ARI!!!!! ADI!!!!! LET GO OF THAT SQUIRREL IMMEDIATLY!!!! THAT IS INSANE!!! 2 SECONDS WITHOUT FOOLERY IS TOO MUCH ASKED OF YOU TWO!! AAAARI LET GO OF THE SQUIRREL!! AAAADI STOP PULLING THE SQUIRREL'S TAIL!!!

Thursday, May 14th, 1891.

The bell announcing the end of the classes at the Royal Georgetown College rang. And instantly, the main exit of the school was invaded by students leaving to their homes. Eriem Eyelord stopped at the last step of the big stairs. She was followed by her usual court. Eriem took out of her backpack a little pink envelopes' stack, and she gave them to Lakita Fleuritel, a student who was part of her court.

- Here ... hand out these for me ... it is the invites for my birthday on Saturday ... for the people I would like to be present.

Lakita Fleuritel distributed the invites to each name. Amira Mounier joined the students group and she exclaimed cheerfully:

- It's yo ... your birth ... birthday on Saturday, isn't it?

Eriem Eyelord didn't stop her conversation with Gael, and she ignored Amira as usual. Amira remained standing; she watched the pink envelopes' stack decreasing in Lakita Fleuritel's hands. Amira hung to the hope of receiving an invitation to this party, but after the last envelope that Lakita handed to Gael, her hopes crashed.

Yet Amira Mounier didn't give up. She followed Eriem Eyelord and her court when they were about to cross the huge exit door. Amira exclaimed cheerfully, stuttering a bit, mostly begging:

- I'm sure ... your ... p ... p ... party will b ... be... successful Eriem!!

At that moment, Eriem Eyelord stopped and she turned around to Amira; she stared at her from head to foot with a calm look:

- Yes, you're right ... my party will surely be successful.

Then, Eriem Eyelord smiled at Amira Mounier. A nice smile. Something that has never happened before. Gael and all the students were surprised of Eriem's reaction. Amira herself didn't believe her eyes, Eriem Eyelord in person ... she talked to her and smiled at her!! Amira will be invited to the party!! After all her efforts to join the most popular group in this school ... Amira Mounier finally succeeded to have friends!!

After a few seconds of silence, Eriem came close to Amira, and she said in a soft voice, displaying her most sympathetic smile:

- And I must admit ... it is a shame that ghosts will not be invited to my birthday party.

Instantly, a wave of laughs erupted among all students surrounding Eriem Eyelord. Amira Mounier became pale and crushed, standing in front of their laughter and mean comments:

- Did she seriously think she will be invited?
- A real glue that one!! ... She never gives up!
- It becomes harassment ...
- I totally agree ... she's obsessed with this group ...
- She looks so hopeless ... for harassing us like that!

Amira gathered all her strength to justify herself, in a trembling voice:

- No it is not what I've me ... meant to ... harass ... harass ... harassment ... It's just that I ... just wanted to han ... han ... hang out w ... with y ... y ... you ...

Gael didn't shy away from imitating Amira's stuttering, in a serious voice:

- Han ... han ... hang out with you at ... at ... the ... bir ... birthday ... par ... party!

Eriem and her entire court laughed:

- An accountant's daughter who absolutely wants to fit in!!
- I have pity on her!!
- She is still unable to speak a single sentence correctly ...
- And she wants to be part of our group!! Imagine that!!

Amira Mounier watched Eriem Eyelord and her prestigious court, leaving through the school's exit door, laughing at Gael's stuttering imitations. Amira's throat tightened and tears ran down her cheeks.

It may seem futile and insignificant. But the only thing that Amira Mounier ever wanted more than anything in the world ... was to have friends. Because often, loneliness was crushing her. Amira hoped to have friends to spend time with, to laugh with, to study together. Friends who would accept her as she was, and encourage her to overcome her weakness. Friends. She just wanted friends.

Disappointed and crushed, Amira picked up her backpack and she left the school, heading in the opposite direction of the other students. All alone.

A little silhouette had witnessed the entire scene from its beginning. She watched Amira Mounier leaving to her house, looking crushed and humiliated by her classmates' mockery. Amira Mounier was tired of everything; trying to be accepted by Eriem and her court, trying to make friends, trying to overcome her weakness, trying to talk normally like all the others...

Amira was ready to give up. But this little silhouette observing her, thought: ... Not yet!

Friday, May 15th, 1891. At the Royal Library of Georgetown College.

- Did you understand what you should do? Dalya asked for the 2nd time.
- Yes, Mademoiselle!! Said Miss Guendolyn in a determined tone.
- It will take me about 2 minutes. Dalya insisted.
- I will get you these 2 minutes!! Count on me!! Miss Guendolyn said eagerly.

Dalya had no choice but to get help from Miss Guendolyn to make her plan work. The afternoon promised to be long and quiet. Amira Mounier spent 2 hours studying in the school Library, when she got tired and decided to go back home. When a voice stopped Amira at the Library exit door:

- Miss Amira Mounier!!

Amira turned toward Miss Guendolyn, the Library assistant. The young woman was sitting at her usual desk. Amira Mounier came close to her. Miss Guendolyn displayed a nice smile:

- Good evening, Miss Amira!! How are you today?

Amira was surprised by the unusual question of the young woman. Never someone had ever asked her this question before. Amira hesitated:

- Uh ... well ... thank you ...

Miss Guendolyn continued in a cheerful and warm voice:

- So? Have you finished your homework?
- Yes ...
- Are you going home now?
- Normally ... yes ...
- I hope this semester's classes aren't too difficult for you?

Amira looked at Miss Guendolyn, in a confused stare. The young woman's questions were very unusual to Amira. Never someone was ever interested in Amira or her classes.

- Uh ... some courses are easy ... and others ... are a little difficult ...

Miss Guendolyn hesitated a few seconds, and then she exclaimed:

- And ... did you borrow any books from the Library?
- Yes ... yesterday.

Miss Guendolyn jumped joyfully:

- Perfect!! I need to register them in the repertoire of borrowed books and write down the date. Tell me the books' titles...

Amira looked at the young woman, all confused:

- Miss Guendolyn ... you wrote them yesterday ... on the repertoire ...

Miss Guendolyn trembled for an instant. She exclaimed with a nervous tone:

- Well ... I have to do it again!!... Dizzy me!!

Amira Mounier didn't understand the young woman's strange behavior. Miss Guendolyn opened a large register, she took a pen and she asked Amira with a cheerful voice:

- So ... What's your name?

Amira stared at her for a moment, thinking it was surely a joke:

- Miss Guendolyn ... you already know my name … you've just said it a minute ago …

The young woman's cheeks turned pink. Miss Guendolyn knew all the students' names, since many years. But with Miss Guendolyn staring at her and waiting for an answer, Amira replied:

- Amira Moun...

At that moment, Amira felt a silhouette behind her, and the strange feeling of a hand getting into her backpack. But before Amira could turn around her head to see who it was, Miss Guendolyn screamed in a trembling and furious voice:

- HOW DARE YOU??!!

Amira turned back to Miss Guendolyn:

- Sorry?

Miss Guendolyn seemed terrified and pale. She exclaimed angrily:

- YOU DO NOT GET TO TALK TO ME ON THIS TONE!

Amira asked:

- What tone? ... What are you talking about? ... I was just telling you my name ... that you know perfectly well by the way...

At this point, Miss Guendolyn was short of ideas. Amira continued:

- Is everything alright ... Miss Guendolyn?

In a second, the young woman's face completely changed, illuminated by a wide joyful and satisfied smile. Miss Guendolyn answered:

- Yes ... yes ... all is well!

Confused, Amira stared at the young woman for a moment, and then she asked:

- And … Miss Guendolyn ... are you going to write down the books that I borrowed?

Miss Guendolyn replied in a natural voice:

- Why? I already did that yesterday ...

At that moment, Amira Mounier was convinced that something was wrong with the Library's assistant. The young woman was behaving in a very strange way. Amira greeted her and she left the school Library, puzzled and confused.

When Dalya came close to Miss Guendolyn, the young woman asked her curiously:

- So?

Dalya observed Amira walking down the long corridor leading to the school exit, and she replied:

- It's done.

Miss Guendolyn said proudly:

- We made it!! Luckily I have followed your plan Mademoiselle!!

Dalya looked at Miss Guendolyn, and she could hardly hold her giggle. They've succeeded, luckily. But the original plan was way far from what has been done.

Saturday, May 16th, 1891. The Market Day.

Dalya wasn't sure of what the words of the first clue meant. But, thanks to her Uncle Giorgi, she discovered that the 69th and 59th numbers referred to the intersection of two streets, where the Saturday market was hold, in front of the Toscana restaurant. And yet, Dalya didn't know what the market could be useful at...

The Merchants' kiosks and carriages were already installed. Almost all the kiosks had covers on top to protect their goods from the warm sunshine. All the Merchants were busy serving their customers. The work in the Saturday market was well advanced.

Dalya undertook to do the groceries for her mother that day. And in fact, it was the perfect good excuse for Dalya to be at the market.

When Dalya arrived to the place, she noticed her friends Alfie and Maurice near the Toscana restaurant. Coming close, Dalya noticed something strange about Alfie. The weather was hot, yet Alfie wore a large shawl covering all his neck up to his nose.

- Hello Alfie ... Hello Maurice!!

Alfie waved at her. And Maurice greeted her, while handing her a newspaper:

- Hello Dalya... we were waiting for you. Here is this morning's newspaper.
- Thank you. I have some groceries to do for mother.

Dalya took the newspaper from Maurice, wondering why her friend Alfie was strangely silent that day. Way too silent.

- All is well ... Alfie?

Her friend nodded to confirm, and he continued to arrange the newspapers in his backpack. Maurice noticed Dalya's confusion about the unusual silence of their friend. Maurice explained to her:

- He had an allergic reaction to a spice … the Macis.
- How?

Maurice giggled:

- I left him alone one minute in my father's store ... and Monsieur Alfie Jaq served himself a cake made of Macis, which my mother had prepared.
- And … do you feel better now?

Maurice seemed to be amused by his friend's state:

- It will take a few more days ...

At that moment, Alfie took off the shawl around his nose and Dalya understood what Maurice meant. Alfie's mouth was enlarged five times its normal size, his mouth was huge, all red and surrounded by many red buttons. Maurice didn't hold from teasing his friend:

- I told you not to touch this cake!! … But do you ever listen me? ... No no ... Monsieur Alfie must taste everything!!

Alfie seemed annoyed by his friend's comment, he yelled:

- Itch not myhe faulthe!!! You hadhe to puthe the cakehe in fronthe of mehe!!!

Dalya struggled to not laugh, watching the deformed face and hearing the incomprehensible words of Alfie. Nevertheless, Maurice enjoyed annoying his friend:

- What are you talking about? ... I don't understand this language!! ... A new invention of yours?

Alfie raised his tone:

- Nexcht time don'tch put the cakehe anywherehe!! How couldhe I have known thathe this cakehe was badhe for mehe!!

Dalya turned her back to Alfie, to release her laugh before it chokes her. Maurice came near his friend, and he helped him close his newspapers backpack:

- I couldn't understand you before your allergy ... and it's even worse now!!

Dalya gave back Alfie's newspaper after noting the guessing words game on a piece of paper.

- Did he take a remedy for his allergy?
- Yes ... the same day, we visited Lalla Fatim Fadl ... the old woman who sells flowers ... she gave him an herb mixture drink to remove the toxins ... his condition is improving ... he can speak words now ... more or less understandable ...

Dalya and Maurice exchanged a laugh, even though their friend Alfie's situation was unfortunate.

After buying some vegetables, Dalya sat on an empty box, near a kiosk. She watched the market's activity with a focused stare. Dalya was waiting for someone. She searched right and left, for a few minutes. The Market's activity was noisy and lively as usual.

Dalya waited many minutes, without seeing the person she was waiting for.

- Maybe she will not come. Dalya thought.

Dalya stood up, and greeted the salad salesman:

- Bye Mr. Dupont. See you next Saturday!

Busy serving a customer, Mr. Dupont replied with a smile:

- You are leaving us already? … Did you get everything you needed?
- Yes, and I have to go home to help my mother prepare din...

When suddenly, Dalya froze in her place. She noticed a familiar silhouette. The person she has been waiting for ... her classmate: Amira Mounier!

Amira Mounier could be distinguished from afar by her long braids. She gave up her school uniform for a casual outfit, a long spring dress, flowers printed patterns.

Amira was standing near the vegetables' kiosk, watching the movements of passersby and the market, without really daring to move further. She was holding a piece of paper in her hand. The day before, in her home, Amira discovered the address of this market in her backpack. She didn't know who put this paper in her bag, and even less for what reason. But curious as she was, Amira decided to come to the market to find out why...

Without losing sight of her classmate, Dalya thought aloud:

- The clue specified that something in this market could help Amira ... but, what is it? … What could it be? … Where exactly? ... And how can I find it?

After a few seconds of thinking, Dalya had only one idea; she decided to tour the market stands, one by one, until the solution manifests by itself!

Dalya had no time to lose. She walked toward the vegetables kiosk, where Amira was standing near it. When she got close, Dalya acted like she didn't see her classmate Amira. Dalya asked Mr. Pierre with a clearly loud voice:

- Hello again Mr. Pierre!! ... Can I have some onions, please?

- Sure! ... Do you need another grocery bag? Asked Mr. Pierre.
- No thank you, I still have some free place in my bag.

Dalya spoke aloud. Mr. Pierre didn't realize it, busy serving Dalya and simultaneously taking a new client's order. But Amira Mounier who was standing near the kiosk, she heard Dalya's voice. Amira stepped back and she hid in a corner, while watching Dalya. When she took Mr. Pierre's onions, Dalya thought in a loud voice:

- So I have fruits ... onions ... What did my mother need else? ... Some flowers! Yes!

Dalya walked toward Lalla Fatim Fadl kiosk, checking with discrete glances behind, that Amira was following her. Amira came out of her hiding and she walked a few steps behind Dalya. Lalla Fatim was busy preparing a mixture in a jar of wood. And when she noticed Dalya, Lalla Fatim Fadl exclaimed cheerfully:

- Moonlight!! Welcome!!
- Hello Lalla Fatim. How are you today? asked Dalya
- In a very good shape, my pretty. The old woman smiled

Dalya checked behind her discreetly to notice Amira's presence, a few steps away.

- Did you come for the groceries, today? Asked Lalla Fatim Fadl.
- Yes, mother needed some fruits and vegetables.

Dalya sat near the old woman who was mixing a liquid in a jar with a small wood spoon. After a few seconds of silence, the woman was still busy and Amira was still standing close to the flowers' kiosk, Dalya thought for a moment:

- And now ... What should I do? ... After the vegetables and flowers' kiosk... should I go to the fish kiosk... or maybe the herb Merchant? ... I'll go to the milk and cheese kiosk ... and then I will visit the fish kio...

When suddenly, a great man interrupted Dalya in her thoughts. It was Mr. Kenan Einsenberg. The Dean of Merchants was making his usual tour between the kiosks that day. He greeted the woman and Dalya with a respectful sign, taking off his hat:

- Lalla Fatim Fadl ... Demoiselle Dalya ... hello!

Dalya smiled back at him. The old woman greeted him joyfully:

- Hello Sir ... I understand from your voice that you feel better?

Mr. Kenan Einsenberg replied with a childlike laugh and a soft voice:

- Yes!! Thanks to you Lalla Fatim!! I took the remedy you've prepared for me and it has worked!! My voice is clearer; my throat is neat. I can speak better since I have been taking your remedy. Thank you very much!!

Lalla Fatim Fadl looked at him in a happy gaze:

- Glad I could help you ...
- And ... I admit, the remedy was well delicious too!! Exclaimed Mr. Kenan Einsenberg.

Lalla Fatim Fadl stood up, she put the liquid of the jar in a small bottle, and she offered it to him with a kind smile:

- This is another bottle for you, Mr. Kenan Einsenberg!
- Thank you, Lalla Fatim Fadl!! ... What could have we done without your remedies?!

When Mr. Kenan Einsenberg left, Dalya asked the old woman curiously:

- Was Mr. Einsenberg ill?

The old woman turned to Dalya and she explained:

- He had lost his voice for a few days because of a cold. And I knew an old remedy for that.

Dalya came close to see the content of the syrup in the wood jar; it was a strange mixture.

- What is it?
- This is a recipe based on 5 ingredients ... simple but very effective.
- How do you prepare it?
- You warm some honey, you mix it with a pinch of salt, a little hot water, some fresh lemon juice. Everything needs to be well mixed until it's consistent. You add seeds of the échinacée flower ... it is found at the spices Merchant, across the street. You crush the mixture in a jar, to release all the benefits of the seeds in the liquid mixture. And you quickly swallow a spoonful, every morning and evening. As long as it is needed.

On this moment, Dalya finally understood some strange words:

Between 69th and 59th, many things can be prepared,

The first clue indicated that in the Saturday market, one will discover Lalla Fatim Fadl's prepared recipe to relief the throat, and allow the person to clear its voice and intonation!!

Right away, Dalya turned back to search for Amira Mounier. Except that her classmate has already left the market place, in hurried steps. Dalya smiled while observing Amira disappearing around the corner.

The last days of spring announced their end. The air was soft and dense. The sun shined longer over the people of Georgetown city. The Saturday market was still noisy and active.

It is funny how on this Saturday, Amira Mounier has hoped to get invited to Eriem Eyelord's birthday party. And instead, Amira found herself in a new place, and she discovered a recipe to release her voice.

Because, as you can see, fate is always having fun ... it doesn't take you to the places you want ... but it takes you to the places that help you become the person you want.

Chapter 16

Darkness

Saturday, May 30th, 1891. The Toscana Restaurant.

At 3:30 PM, the Toscana restaurant activity decreased gradually. Most of the orders were now for desserts. The kitchen stoves cooled off. Waiters walked more slowly, as the latest menu dishes were served cold, not like the other hot dishes.

The famous Toscana restaurant was a place of luxury and elegance. The most distinguished customers of Georgetown city came there to savor the best Italian specialties. In a refined interior, the Toscana restaurant was decorated with beautiful big sparkling chandeliers in the ceiling, excessively white tablecloths, cutlery and shiny plates, and ample elegant armchairs.

The Lawyer, Mr. Ernest Laszlo and his son Lyor, were having lunch with 3 managers of BalthEnterprise. The Late Mr. Iskander Balthazar being busy in his work as a Governor, he had appointed a management board to handle BalthEnterprise in his absence. And after the death of the Governor since several months now, the Lawyer and his son met with the managers once a quarter terms, in order to discuss the state of the company and make the most appropriate decisions. BalthEnterprise was a Holding Company for several firms, in many different industries and sectors.

The Lawyer, Mr. Ernest Laszlo, was cutting his red meat with a strong move, while asking:

- And ... what about the results of the Gantt firm?

One manager put his fork down and explained:

- Since the increase of the workforce, the leather production has become faster. The sales' numbers have increased significantly compared to the previous period. We've detailed all the results in the quarterly report.
- Good ... good ... and did the problem of the goods' transportation have been resolved in the Ord business?

The second manager quickly swallowed his forkful of salad, and replied:

- Yes, Mr. Ernest. As it was agreed in the previous quarter term, we have acquired three large trucks added to our fleet, and we were able to catch up the delivery delay of wood to our clients.

While the three managers and the Lawyer discussed the results of BalthEnterprise around lunchtime, the Lawyer's son, Lyor Laszlo was quiet and invisible, listening to the conversations and eating his food in silence. His father, the Lawyer, was a very meticulous man:

- What is the current turnover for the concrete factory?

The third manager informed him:

- 173 500 dollars at the end of the quarter term, Mr. Ernest.

The Lawyer put down his fork and knife, and lay back on his chair, looking a little surprised:

- The turnover results of this factory have not improved since 3 quarters?!

One manager explained:

- It is obvious that the construction industry is in difficulty right now. The sector is facing great competition from new imports of Canadian concrete. That is why, the Board recommends to renovate the fa ...
- To sale it would be more profitable. Mr. Ernest interrupted him, before taking his knife to cut his red meat.

The 3 managers exchanged a confused and puzzled look. One of them declared his disagreement with the Lawyer's opinion:

- But ... Late Mr. Iskander Balthazar would have never sold a factory in difficulty. That's the reason itself of BalthEnterprise! ... The Holding buys companies in financial or managerial complications; we ensure their renovation in order to make them more efficient and profitable. Mr. Iskander Balthazar has always clearly stated that we use this approach to follo...

Mr. Ernest Laszlo interrupted him in an arrogant voice:

- From what I know ... Iskander Balthazar is not sitting with us in this restaurant ... he is 7 feet underground at this moment. I am the one in charge of BalthEnterprise now.

The 3 managers were astonished and shocked by the Lawyer's insolence for the memory of their former boss, the Late Mr. Governor. Except that one manager seemed confused about one thing:

- But ... according to the Will, we understood that it is Mr. Lyor Laszlo who was in charge of BalthEnterp...

Mr. Ernest Laszlo gave a strong fist on the table, that all the cutlery and plates jumped, and he yelled:

- I AM THE ONE IN CHARGE OF BALTHENTERPRISE!!! IF IT DOESN'T PLEASE YOU, YOU CAN LOOK FOR WORK ELSEWHERE!!!

Lunch ended sooner than expected. The 3 managers retired within minutes, even before finishing their dishes. Mr. Ernest Laszlo was never embarrassed by his rude and authoritarian temper. The Lawyer took on to read the BalthEnterprise quarterly report that the managers presented him, while waiting for the chocolate mousse he had ordered.

Lyor Laszlo, who had remained silent throughout the entire meal, dared to address his father, in a courteous voice:

- The concrete factory is located in Baltimore City ... near the new industrial zone ...

Mr. Ernest didn't answer, focused in his reading. So then, Lyor continued:

- I heard that it was Late Mr. Iskander Balthazar himself who supervised the reform of the concrete factory ...

Without lifting his eyes from the report, Mr. Ernest replied:

- And...?

After finally getting his father's attention, Lyor Laszlo explained his idea:

- I think if the factory is renovated with new machines, the managers can contact the new businesses built in the industrial zone, near the port of Baltimore. Manufacturers may be encouraged with discounts of the concrete price, and shorter delivery time, than the concrete coming from Canada. The money that will be invested in the machines can be returned in less than a year, if we take advantage from the strategic location of the factory, near this new industrial area.

Mr. Ernest finally looked toward his son. He asked in a calm and cold voice:

- And ... who asked for your opinion?

Lyor Laszlo froze in his chair, surprised by his father's question. Mr. Ernest stared at his son, with an arrogant look, and he continued on an icy tone:

- Let it be clear, Lyor ... I will not permit the greatest fortune of this country, to be managed by an inexperienced apprentice like you! ... I don't know why Iskander has appointed you, and I really don't care what his Will dictate on us. I know the management of BalthEnterprise better than you do ... I am the only one who can manage it well ... so then, hold yourself from giving your opinion on it!

The dessert that the Lawyer had ordered finally arrived. Mr. Ernest Laszlo put down the report, and he rejoiced in eating his chocolate mousse. While his son, Lyor Laszlo became silent and immobile again.

Tuesday, June 16th, 1891. At the Royal Georgetown College.

At the end of the Music class, Dalya headed toward the Library, to borrow some books for her studies. At the end of a corridor, Dalya was called by a familiar cold voice that she recognized and she tried her best to avoid:

- Dalya Bouvard ... When shall we definitely get rid of you?!

Dalya turned around to Director Darkfett. Dalya tried to be as polite as she could:

- Good evening, Headmaster.

Director Darkfett stared at her, from head to toe, in a scornful look and he replied in a haughty and cold tone:

- I admire your will ... although you will never belong to this social status ... you still try to fit in.

Dalya didn't say a word, but she hoped from the bottom of her heart, that this meeting with Director Darkfett would be brief. Yet, he continued in a calm cold voice, while coming close to her:

- I'll explain something very important ... that you probably didn't know, kid. You see, the Nobility and the social status are hereditary titles since decades. Whether you are rich or educated, it will not contribute in the slightest way, to place you in a higher social status...

Dalya dared to tell her opinion, for once:

- But, I am not trying to have a Noble status, Headmaster.

Director Darkfett let out a mean laugh:

- Obviously ... Because you'll never make it, kid! ... you will never succeed to be part of the Nobility ... and this is not your fault, it is because of your grandparents ...

Dalya turned all pale in an instant. And Director Darkfett realized that he had just touched a sensitive chord. So then, he continued to turn on the knife in the wound:

- From what I've heard, your grandfather was a vegetables and fruits Merchant, wasn't he? ... A poor miserable veggy seller ...

Dalya felt her throat tightened, her cheeks redden and her blood burned. Although Dalya had known him only for a short time, her grandfather, Idriss Bouvard was the dearest man to her heart. He was the first and only one who taught her how to read and to count. Being his first granddaughter, Idriss Bouvard cuddled and loved Dalya so tenderly. That's something Dalya's own parents never did. And to hear the Headmaster demean her grandfather, Dalya refrained herself with great difficulty. The Director enjoyed humiliating and crushing her:

- Your grandfather was unable to achieve anything in life; you are doomed to be like him ... a poor miserable veggy seller. Never forget that!

Dalya was standing paralyzed, not believing her ears. She lost her words. Proud of his achievement, Director Darkfett turned around and he left the hall, displaying a joyous and victorious smile.

Dalya could never understand the nastiness of the Director or his cruelty toward her. Yet, of all the times the Director has spoken to her, this time, he exceeded the limits. Dalya had tears in her eyes, and her throat tightened. Why so much hate and cruelty toward her? What did she do to him? Why do the Noble people feel the need and the pleasure of despising the poor, who are less fortunate? ... Just why?

After her meeting with the Headmaster, Dalya walked directly to the Mathematics classroom, skipping the Library. She needed to sit down and gather herself.

The Mathematics Professor was a few minutes late than the usual time. This allowed Dalya to take out her books and review her homework. Eriem and her court arrived and they settled on their usual chairs. The final exams of the year were close, Eriem and her court spent less time laughing and chatting before class. Currently, everyone was busy studying for the exams.

Amira Mounier was the last student to come in the classroom. When she sat down in her chair, Dalya noticed that Amira displayed a calm and cheerful face.

It is to be said that since many weeks now, Amira stuttered less during her interventions in class. Before the beginning of each course, Amira would drink a few sips of a small bottle. It was a recipe she had prepared at home, based on five simple ingredients. This juice appeased the heat rising in her throat and it softened her voice, thus smoothing the release of her words.

And that was not all. Thanks to the secret place in the high tower of the school, which she alone had its key; Amira was training almost every day in this room, at the end of her classes. The huge high triangular ceiling helped to amplify her voice, and it allowed her to speak more clearly and quickly. Because of all her efforts, Amira Mounier slowly improved every day. And Dalya was secretly happy about it!

At the end of the current Mathematics class, everyone got up to leave the classroom. The end of the day was announced, and Dalya thought to return back home quickly; she had a lot of homework to do. While packing her backpack, Dalya heard Gael Benoble emitting a strange sound:

- To ... to ... to ... mul ... mul ... multiply ... a ... a ... a ... frac ... frac ... fraction ...

Gael walked toward Amira Mounier's desk, and he stuttered:

- By ... by ... by ... a ... a ... num ... num ... number ...

Dalya didn't understand Gael's attitude. After all, Amira's speaking has much improved in the last days, the result of her efforts and her work was obvious when she spoke now. Amira pronounced her words slowly, but much more clearly than before. The Mathematics Professor was very happy and delighted by his student's efforts. Even the History and Geography teachers didn't address Amira anymore, because she mastered her stress and her voice now. Both teachers had no reason to humiliate her. So Dalya thought that the students would also forget about Amira's stuttering. Except that ... not everyone was pleased with Amira's progress...

Dalya put her books and papers in her backpack, as slowly as she could. She was curious to know what Gael and his friends were up to, this time.

Amira remained seated in her chair, immobile and silent, while the other students laughed and surrounded her. Amira didn't understand why the students mistreated her and laughed at her again. It had been several weeks now since Amira didn't speak or tried to approach the popular group of students.

Gael didn't stop imitating Amira's stutter, adding ugly frowns on his face. The other students had uncontrollable laughs, which became even louder. Dalya wanted to interfere, but she didn't know what to say and what to do. And after Amira had pushed her away and asked her not to come close to her, Dalya was afraid to create her more mockery from the other students.

When Eriem Eyelord came close to Amira, all the students went silent; Gael also stopped his imitative game. Amira was sitting immobile on her chair, her head down. That's when Eriem Eyelord said in a calm cold voice:

- Your mother certainly died because she was not able to make you talk properly.

Gael continued his friend's sentence:

- Her mother is surely dead of shame!!

And Gael spoke with a female voice this time; everyone guessed it to be Amira's mother:

- Oh goodness!!! ... What have I done to deserve a girl who stutters!! How will I fix her?

The laughs became more overwhelming and less human. Eriem Eyelord said to Amira, in an arrogant voice:

- Don't think because you have less stuttered these last weeks, that you are cured forever ... don't fool yourself ... you will always be the most famous stuttering student of this school!!

Gael confirmed the idea of his classmate, with a mean laugh:

- And I'm sure your mother would be so proud of you, now ... the most famous stutterer of the entire school!!

Amira Mounier didn't move. She was paralyzed in her chair, surrounded by her classmates who made fun of her. After some long tense minutes, Eriem turned around and she left the classroom, followed by Gael Benoble and the other students, laughing loudly.

Dalya never thought that she would witness such cruelty. Dalya didn't know that her classmate Amira Mounier was a mother orphan. Since her first day in this class, Dalya couldn't understand why the other students were so hard and mean with Amira, sometimes ignoring her and sometimes having fun humiliating and ridiculing her. But on that day, their cruelty has exceeded by far the limits. Amira's deceased mother shouldn't have been a mockery subject.

The Mathematics classroom emptied. Only Dalya and Amira remained there. After several seconds of a heavy silence, Amira still didn't move from her chair. Dalya then decided to get up and she walked toward Amira, in slow steps.

After this scene of mockery and cruelty, Dalya expected Amira Mounier to be crying as usual. Except that this time, Dalya was surprised by Amira's reaction. She was calm, a cold face, without tears or rosy cheeks. Dalya came close to her, and she dared to ask her with a compassionate voice:

- Are you alright?

Amira didn't move, she stayed motionless and calm. But for the first time ever, Dalya noticed something strange in Amira Mounier's eyes.

Because when the people you dream to be friends with, when the people you try to please, when the people you admire ... when these people make fun of you, humiliate you and demean you ... it really really hurts.

And on that day, for the first time ever, Amira Mounier was angry. Very ... very ... angry.

After Amira packed her books in total silence and left the classroom, Dalya decided to go back home too. But at the school exit door, Dalya noticed her classmates; Eriem Eyelord, Gael Benoble and their court, some were sitting on the steps, others were standing leaning on the wall. And it seemed that, Amira Mounier wasn't their only mocked person. Dalya was surprised to hear Eriem Eyelord talk to the school Concierge in a serious voice:

- You're a moron, Dadès.

The man was sweeping the stairs of the school entrance; he was wearing a long work apron, large gardening boots and his usual crochet hat of several colors. Dadès was always cheerful and smiling. He seemed to be pleased of having a conversation with the students of this prestigious school. Each time he heard his name, he replied with a smile:

- Thank you Mam'selle ... Thank you Mam'selle ...

And immediately a wave of laughs invaded the students who surrounded Eriem. Without losing her serious voice, Eriem continued her conversation with the Concierge:

- But ... really ... you are very inane, Dadès.
- Thank you Mam'selle ... Thank you Mam'selle ...

Gael Benoble joined the joke too:

- You're an inept Dadès!

The Concierge turned around to him and he smiled:

- Thank you missio... Thank you missio ...

Dalya watched the scene for a few seconds, she understood what was happening. In fact, the Concierge didn't understand what Eriem and Gael were saying to him. The students used insults in an advanced vocabulary, which the poor Concierge couldn't understand. Since several months now, Dalya knew that the Concierge was a new immigrant in this country. His accent was weird and different. He understood only a few words of the new language, but not all the words, even less an advanced vocabulary. Yet, the poor man answered Eriem and Gael, with a smile and a thank you.

Never Dalya could have suspected that the students' insolence would reach the point of making fun of a poor man without even his knowledge, and in such a cruel way.

Dalya couldn't understand why some people needed to humiliate you, laugh at you, and bring you down. Dalya couldn't understand the pleasure of being cruel, arrogant and mean.

It was a long and a difficult day. Dalya couldn't defend the Concierge Dadès, nor her classmate Amira Mounier, from the student's jokes and mockery. Dalya couldn't even defend herself from Director Darkfett's comments on her grandfather.

Her throat choked, her cheeks turned all red, her breathing accelerated, an overheating sensation filled her body. Dalya had never been so angry before today. She was furious against the humiliation and the free cruelty.

When leaving the school, Dalya walked with slow steps. But the more anger invaded her, the more her steps became faster. And the only way to let out her anger was to run. At the end of the day, the sky was darkened and filled with many obscure clouds. The trees were moving because of the windy air. When she arrived at the gardens of Dumbarton Oaks Park, Dalya ran with all her might. And despite the wind that blew harder and harder, Dalya ran against the current, against the wind.

When she arrived at the big entry of the grand Mansion, Dalya paused, out of breath. The Snow Panther straightened up swiftly when she noticed the little girl coming. Its long tail raised to the sky, her gray tattooed fur was noticed from afar. Séraphine came down of the garden wall, and she hurried toward the little girl, staring at her with sapphire blue eyes. You would have thought that the animal understood and felt the little girl's anger.

A few moments after regaining her normal breath, Dalya walked slowly toward the Annex house, under the worried stares of the Snow Panther Séraphine. The run did Dalya some good. However, something didn't cool down within her, something still burned inside of her.

Her father had not yet returned from work, her mother was picking up the clothes before the rain falls, and her little twin sisters were playing near their mother outside. Dalya immediately went straight to her bedroom. She put her backpack on the bed, she sat down in front of her small desk, and she stared at the strange box for a long while.

The Excelbox was a mysterious box, with strange words. Dalya could never understand the clues from the first try; she always needed several days, even weeks to discover what the clues meant. But the Excelbox always seemed to have the exact answers to Dalya's impossible questions and difficult situations.

And on that day, Dalya couldn't be silent about cruelty. No one should be silent about cruelty.

So then, the little girl did the only thing she knew, she asked for the second clue:

26 lights illuminate our mind
From darkness to dawn
The blind comes out
No failure is infinite
When will and continuity are picked
Knowledge is, against cruelty, an ally
Knowledge is, against insolence, a dignity.

After reading this clue, Dalya lay back on her chair. And this time, as strange as it may seem, the Excelbox provided a pretty clear clue. When she read the clue only once, Dalya's cheeks turned pink, her blue sapphire eyes lightened up, and a determined smile displayed on her lips.

For the first time, the Excelbox and Dalya understood each other, on the first round.

Chapter 17

Zeros

Wednesday, July 01st, 1891.

On the first morning rays, Dalya left her bed. She couldn't stay asleep anymore. It was a very important and crucial day for her. Dalya wore her best clothes; overalls and a white shirt. She had polished her shoes the night before. She put her large cap on, and then she went down to the kitchen.

No one was awake at 6:30 AM. Therefore, Dalya prepared the breakfast table herself, she heated the milk and bread, placed the butter and some jam on the table. Dalya was very happy not to endure her mother's usual angry mood, nor her father's cold attitude. She spread butter on her toast and ate breakfast alone that morning, in a silent calm kitchen.

At 7:00 AM, Dalya decided to leave the house to join the school. A small silhouette was waiting for her as usual, at the entry of the grand Mansion. Séraphine was sitting on top of the garden wall, watching Dalya with her intense sapphire eyes.

- You are early today, Séraphine! Dalya smiled at her.

And apparently, the Snow Panther understood the little girl's comment. Séraphine wagged her long tail up to the sky with a joyful gesture.

A few minutes later, Dalya arrived at school. She stopped for a moment to admire the Royal Georgetown College. An immense red brick building, hundreds of large square windows, a splendid main iron gate, and green trees planted around the building. The Royal College was still intimidating and magnificent as always.

Although it was early for classes to start, many students were present, they were all holding their books and focused in reading. It was the exam's week. All the students, of all levels, will be passing their tests in all the subjects. And Dalya too, had exams to pass in History, Geography, Mathematics and Music.

Several weeks before, Dalya studied every day for long hours in the school Library. And at home, after washing and drying the dishes, Dalya would lock herself in her bedroom and study a few more hours before falling asleep.

Making her way among the students, Dalya walked to the classroom N°060, to pass the Mathematics exam. She sat in her usual chair, and opened her notebook for a last quick review. Several minutes later, the Mathematics Professor entered the classroom, and all the students took their places at once.

- Hello ... Hello!! Professor Wyatt greeted them, in his usual cheerful tone.

The teacher took out several papers out of his briefcase, and he announced:

- I will give you copies of your year final exam in Mathematics. You have 2 hours to answer all the questions. Please write clearly your answers. Think carefully and do your best!

Professor Wyatt walked between the desks, handing over the exam copies to each student:

- Ladies ... gentlemen ... Good luck!

Dalya observed her exam paper for a while. Then, she raised her head and looked at the classroom. All her classmates had their head bent down and focused on their exam's paper. Professor Wyatt sat on his desk chair; he opened a book to read, while regularly looking at his students.

At that moment, Dalya Bouvard looked around and she smiled. Not because she knew the answer to the first question of the exam's paper ... Not because the Mathematics course was her favorite ... She was smiling because the little girl who was selling vegetables and handmade potato bags in the Saturday market ... the little girl who was sleeping in a corner on the floor of the kitchen ... that little girl, today, she was sitting in a classroom, among students almost her age, and she was passing her final exams in the most prestigious school of the country ... this little girl was living a dream that she never dared to think of.

Several days later. Friday, July 10th, 1891.

During the last week of classes, all the Professors gave students their homework for the summer vacation and their exam results. Dalya Bouvard, being a different student than the others, she had to get her results from Director Darkfett, the school's Headmaster himself. The idea of this meeting didn't enchant Dalya. She hesitated for several minutes to go to the Headmaster's office, before finally giving in.

The Director's Secretary, Miss Uplerine Amana was among the few people that Dalya liked in this college. This great woman had a beautiful caramel skin color; her long hair was freely released on her shoulders, despite the summer heat. And as always, Miss Uplerine Amana was very elegant in a long light green dress, bringing out her big almond eyes. And although Dalya spoke to her rarely, Dalya appreciated the courtesy and the kindness of the Executive Secretary toward her.

- Good morning, Miss Uplerine. I came to take my exam results from the Headmaster.

Miss Uplerine always greeted Dalya with a smile, happy to see her:

- Good morning to you Mademoiselle. The Headmaster had an urgent matter to deal with. He left school, only a few minutes ago.

The Executive Secretary pulled out a little paper, and she gave it to Dalya:

- Here is your Gradebook ... would you like to wait for the Director to hear his kind remarks? Or you can do without it?

Dalya could hardly hold a laugh at the Secretary's funny question. Dalya took the paper that Miss Uplerine handed her, and she thanked her with a smile, before leaving her office.

Eager to discover her exam results, Dalya opened her grades' report paper in the school hallway:

Gradebook of: Miss Dalya Bouvard

2nd semester of the school year 1891

History: 0/20	**Mathematics: 16/20**
Geography: 0/20	**Music: 14.5/20**

Dalya froze in her place, while holding the paper in her hands:

- 0 in History and 0 in Geography??!! ... But ... how is that even possible?! ... I answered all the questions ... not even one answer was correct? ... but, these are the subjects that I have studied the most in the recent weeks ...

Rereading her gradebook a dozen times, Dalya didn't understand her results. She didn't expect to have an excellent grade, well aware of having years of delays compared to the other students. But Dalya was sure she didn't deserve a zero. And there could not be an error on the gradebook; her name was indeed written on it. Shocked by her grades, Dalya ran to the school Library, in order to check her answers. She went immediately to the History section. She searched the shelves, she pulled out a book, and then flipped its pages:

- Where did Julius Caesar do his military service? ... I'm sure I have answered Minor Asia and the Greek islands ... yes ... that's right ... that's what is written in the manual!!

Dalya flipped a few more pages:

- And for the question ... when did Julius Caesar return back to Rome ... I wrote in 78 B.C ... yes, that's right too ... after the death of General and politician Cornelius Sulla in 78 B.C!! ... It's the exact date written in the manual ... but then, how did I get these grades?!

Dalya couldn't understand these Zeros. She closed the History book and walked toward the Geography section, when a familiar voice called her out:

- It is nice to know that the Library is still your favorite place, Mademoiselle Dalya Bouvard.

Professor Canfield was holding some books in his hands. And as usual, the Professor was wearing an elegant blue checked suit with a black bow tie. He displayed his great usual smile.

Dalya greeted him with a forced smile and a pale face that the Professor couldn't help but notice.

- Is everything alright, Mademoiselle?

Dalya immediately replied in a trembling voice:

- Yes ... Professor, all is well.

Professor Canfield asked kindly:

- I guess that you had received the results of your exams?
- Yes, Professor. It's just that ...

Dalya hesitated to finish her sentence. Professor Canfield felt that something was bothering the little girl; he came close to her and said in a thoughtful voice:

- You must understand that this is your first year at school ... If you do not have excellent grades; you have done your best, Mademoiselle. If you need extra hours to catch up, we can arrange it for you ...

After a few seconds of silence, Dalya dared to confess:

- It's just that ... Professor ... I thought I had answered correctly at some questions in History and Geography exams ... I don't know why did I receive Zeros in both subjects.

Dalya's response wiped out Professor Canfield's smile. He asked in a calm and serious tone:

- May I see your gradebook, Mademoiselle?

Dalya handed it to him immediately. Professor Canfield read it:

- Have you answered all the questions of these exams?
- Yes, Professor. I've answered all the questions!

Professor Canfield was confused between what Dalya was saying in a confident tone, and what was written on the gradebook. Dalya explained:

- Some questions were difficult, yes ... but other questions were easier. I have just checked the History book, and I remember writing the same answer as it is in the manual ... I think I may have given at least some good answers ... So I don't understand how did I manage to have Zeros, Professor.

Professor Canfield thought for a second, and then he reassured Dalya with a kind smile:

- I will try to clarify this situation. I will give you back your gradebook, as soon as I'm done.

Dalya greeted the Professor with a forced smile, and then she walked toward the Geography section in the Library. She really didn't expect these Zeros at all. Dalya searched a Geography book on the coastlines, to check her answers, because she was sure to have learned her lessons by heart.

Meanwhile, Professor Canfield observed Dalya. He was just as confused and surprised as she was.

The teachers' room was vast. Several comfortable chairs and luxurious wood desks were installed throughout the entire room. One wall was covered by a large Library with several shelves filled with textbooks and books to be used by the teachers. Large transparent windows illuminated the place.

Professor Canfield walked toward the History teacher, who was sitting in a corner of the room. Professor Ajanar was quietly reading a book. Professor Canfield greeted him with a respectful tone:

- Good morning Professor Ajanar!

Professor Ajanar didn't even look up at the speaker, he replied in a disinterested voice:

- Hello ...
- I have a request for you, Professor.

Professor Ajanar didn't answer a word, his eyes still focused on his book. Professor Canfield continued:

- May I see the exam's paper of Mademoiselle Dalya Bouvard?

At that moment, Professor Ajanar raised his head up, all curious:

- And by what authority are you asking for this exam paper?

Professor Canfield replied in a very calm voice:

- The authority that I have as a member of the College Board.

Professor Ajanar seemed angry, not only for being interrupted in his break moment, but also because he was forced to comply to the request and the authority of Professor Canfield. Furious, Professor Ajanar opened a folder near him, and he pulled out a paper. He handed it to Professor Canfield with an abrupt move, before continuing reading his book.

When Professor Canfield took the exam paper of Dalya Bouvard, he read it for a few minutes, then he asked all curious the History teacher:

- Professor Ajanar ... about the Question 4 ... give the definition of Cursus Honorum ... she wrote : all the functions that magistrates continuously perform in a government ... it seems to me that it's a right answer ... why did you write on it false?

Without taking his eyes off from his book, the only answer that the History Professor was able to provide was:

- A correction error ...

Professor Canfield didn't seem easily convinced by this answer, and yet he continued to read the exam paper:

- Question 7 ... who elects the magistrates and for how long ... she wrote: elected for one year by Roman citizens ... you have marked it false ... I guess it's a correction error, again?

The History teacher felt the anger getting hold of him:

- How can a good grade in History be useful to her?! She is only temporary in our school ... she will not be among us next year!!

There and now, Professor Canfield finally understood the History Professor's trick. Professor Canfield remained calm and he said with a defiant smile:

- Professor Ajanar ... I gladly inform you that it is not up to you to judge or state about the admission of Mademoiselle Dalya Bouvard into this school.

Professor Ajanar didn't believe his ears; he closed his book with a sudden move and jumped swiftly off his chair. But before he could say a word, Professor Canfield looked at him, with calm but menacing stares:

- Professor Ajanar … I will review myself the exam paper of Mademoiselle Dalya Bouvard. And I will let you know, the real grade, in a few minutes … so that you will correct her gradebook.

The History teacher raised his voice:

- ARE YOU CORRECTING MY WORK?!

Professor Canfield smiled at him, and he answered in a calm threatening voice:

- Yes, I am correcting your work. And ... if a similar incident was repeated again, I will make sure that you will assume the consequences.

When the Geography Professor was putting his books in his briefcase and about to leave the classroom N°48, he received a visit from Professor Canfield.

- Good morning, Professor Felozi.
- Good morning, Professor Canfield.
- I wanted to know the exam results of one of your students, if you don't mind.
- Who?
- Mademoiselle Dalya Bouvard.

- The veggy seller in the marke...
- The Heiress nominated by the Late Mr. Governor Iskander Balthazar. Professor Canfield interrupted him in a strong voice.

Professor Felozi didn't appreciate the correction. He closed his briefcase with a snap and replied:

- She had a zero!!

Professor Canfield respectfully asked:

- Yes, I'm well aware of that. However ... I would like to see her exam paper, please.
- Sorry? Professor Felozi was surprised by this unusual request.

Professor Canfield calmly and firmly repeated his request:

- The Geography exam paper of Mademoiselle Dalya Bouvard. Please.

In front of the persistence of Professor Canfield, Professor Felozi put down his briefcase in a rough move; he pulled out a large folder, he looked for a paper a few seconds and he handed it to Professor Canfield, who thanked him with a natural smile.

Except that, strangely, at the first glance of the exam paper, Professor Canfield's smile disappeared, and was replaced by a confused expression:

- But, Professor Felozi ... this exam paper has not been corrected ... you haven't even touched it ...
- Yes indeed! The old man replied in an arrogant and confidant tone.

Professor Canfield didn't believe his ears:

- Professor Felozi ... I don't understand ... you gave a zero to a student, without even correcting her exam paper?
- Obviously, yes!! ... It is my class, I teach only students from Noble status... She is just a veggy sell...
- SHE IS AN HEIRESS NOMINATED BY THE LATE MR GOVERNOR ISKANDER BALTHAZAR!!

This time, Professor Canfield interrupted him in a loud angry strong voice. The Geography Professor was astonished by this unusual attitude. For Professor Canfield to raise the tone of his voice and lose his composure, it had to be an insolent provocation he received. Professor Canfield pulled himself together at once; he came close to Professor Felozi and he explained to him in a calm but firm voice:

- Professor Felozi ... I remind you that our profession and our role in this College, is to educate students ... whatever their origins, affiliations and social status. And if you have a problem with this rule, Professor Felozi, I recommend another College for you.

Professor Felozi didn't appreciate this comment, he asked in a mocking and arrogant voice:

- Is it a warning, then?
- Yes, it is! Professor Canfield replied in a determined tone.

After the incidents with the History and the Geography teachers, Professor Canfield decided to check the other exam papers as well. And although he was assured by the integrity of the Mathematics Professor Mr. Wyatt, since always, Professor Canfield joined him in his classroom.

- Professor Wyatt ... How are you today?

The old man was cleaning his blackboard. He laughed joyfully:

- Swimming in a chalk cloud ... as usual!!

Professor Canfield smiled back, before asking him:

- Professor Wyatt ... I'd like to see an exam copy of one of your students, if you don't mind.

Professor Wyatt put down his brush, immediately:

- But of course ... which one?
- Mademoiselle Dalya Bouvard.

Professor Wyatt pulled out a paper from a folder, and he explained:

- 16 ... It's an excellent grade, given that she had a lot of lessons to catch up.

When Professor Canfield took the exam paper, he consulted it for a few moments in silence, before asking:

- How is she doing in class?
- She is quiet and studious. She gives back her homework on time. She is fast and smart. She lacks some concepts in Mathematics ... but I wouldn't worry about that. A few extra hours, and she will be at the same level as her classmates.

Professor Canfield was pleased to hear these comments.

- Thank you for these informations, Professor Wyatt. Good evening.

Leaving the Mathematics teacher, Professor Canfield walked toward the Music classroom. But before getting there, Professor Canfield noticed Professor Haîyang's silhouette in a corridor, leaving toward the school exit. When she heard her name, Professor Haîyang turned around:

- Hello, Professor Canfield.
- Forgive me for keeping you, few more minutes, Professor Haîyang. I need something.
- No worries at all. How can I help you?

- I wish to know the grade of one of your students ... Dalya Bouvard. May I see her exam copy, please?
- Certainly.

Professor Haîyang took out a paper from her bag and she gave it to Professor Canfield, who consulted it in a curious look. He asked a bit surprised:

- It's a good grade ... 14.5 ... most of her answers are correct ... however, she never studied Music before ... not that I know of, anyway ... so then, how did she manage to have this grade in your class?

Professor Haîyang smiled:

- You underestimate her, Professor Canfield. She is artful.

Professor Canfield seemed even more confused by the teacher's response. Professor Haîyang enlightened him:

- Since the first lesson of my class, Dalya Bouvard decided to study Music books of the beginner's level ... 5-6 years old. She learned the basic Musical notes from the beginning.

Professor Canfield laughed loudly:

- Artful ... very well artful!!

Chapter 18

What Séraphine Felt

Monday, July 13th, 1891.

Despite her school holidays, Dalya woke up very early that morning. She took her breakfast, washed the dishes and helped her mother hang the washed laundry outside. After finishing her housework, Dalya decided to clean her bedroom.

When suddenly, Dalya heard a loud noise downstairs. She dropped her pillow and blanket, and she ran downstairs. The sound was repeated again, Dalya realized that it came from the kitchen. She rushed into the kitchen to discover a weird scene. Mrs. Augustine looked furious and angry. The coulis sieve that was used to filter liquids, was broken into many pieces on the kitchen floor.

Dalya was curious to know what was going on:

- What happened?

Mrs. Augustine didn't reply to her daughter, but she took a large piece of the coulis sieve and crashed it to the floor for the 3rd time, screaming with all her voice:

- I DESTROYED THIS SIEVE, YOU IDIOT!!!

Dalya dared to ask:

- But why ... why did you destroy it?

Mrs. Augustine answered her daughter with a furious stare and an enraged voice:

- BECAUSE IT DIDN'T WORK!! YOU IDIOT!!

Dalya couldn't understand why her mother has destroyed the sieve. Dalya thought in a loud confused voice:

- You destroyed this sieve ... because it wasn't working?

Mrs. Augustine crashed a few pieces on the floor with her feet, screaming furiously:

- YES!! IT DIDN'T WORK!! SO I DESTROYED IT!! ISN'T IT CLEAR ENOUGH?! YOU ARE JUST AN IDIOT WHO UNDERSTANDS NOTHING!! A FOOLISH WITLESS!!

At that moment, Dalya asked her mother curiously:

- But ... if something doesn't work ... shouldn't we fix it and repair it, instead of destroying it?

Mrs. Augustine froze in her place, paralyzed by her daughter's comment. And on that moment, Mrs. Augustine realized how her act to destroy the coulis sieve was ... silly. And it wasn't the first or the last foolish act that she did. One could almost swear that Mrs. Augustine had no brain to think. Very often, she wasn't aware of her inabilities and her brainless attitudes. And when someone confronted her with her own mistakes, Mrs. Augustine never accepted it well.

Enraged by her daughter's comment, Mrs. Augustine came close to Dalya, she grabbed her arm with a sudden and violent move and she lead her outside ... into the garage.

Tuesday, July 14th, 1891.

Being busy with her studies and her final exams, Dalya haven't had time to inform the Lawyer, Mr. Ernest Laszlo about the 2nd clue. Dalya decided to visit the Lawyer's office on that day.

After her quick breakfast, Dalya left the Annex house and walked toward the grand Mansion. When she arrived at the big exit door, the Snow Panther came down from the branch of a tree.

- Hello Séraphine! Dalya greeted her with a little smile.

When Séraphine came close to Dalya, the Snow Panther made an unusual gesture, never done before. The Snow Panther caressed Dalya's hand, with her little head. And although her hands were wrapped in thin lace beige gloves, Dalya could feel the soft fur of Séraphine's head. The Snow Panther uttered a soft sad mewing, while licking the little girl's gloves. Séraphine didn't need any words to feel Dalya's heart.

When she arrived at the Lawyer Mr. Ernest Laszlo's office, Dalya pushed the door and stepped inside. It was terribly hot that day; the air was dense and heavy to breathe, although Georgetown city was coastal. The sun was shining with all its might, and whether you were outside or inside, you could feel the summer heat.

The office was occupied; all the staff seemed overwhelmed and busy. The folders and papers covered all the employees' offices. Dalya walked toward Mr. Ernest's office. And once arrived, the Secretary observed the little girl with the same arrogant look, as her employer. Dalya greeted her with a polite smile:

- Hello, Miss Javotte ... I would like to mee...

The Secretary interrupted her abruptly:

- Mr. Ernest is traveling. He is not here today. Come back later!

Dalya replied in a polite voice:

- When can I come ba...

The Secretary seemed irritated by Dalya's presence in front of her, the woman yelled in an arrogant loud tone:

- Mr. Ernest will be back in a few days. And besides, he has no time to waste with a little veggy sel...

A familiar voice appeared and interrupted the Secretary:

- Miss Javotte ... did you finish your conversation with Mademoiselle Dalya Bouvard, the Heiress of the Late Mr. Governor? I need her for a moment ...

Mr. Wilfrid was always calm and very elegant in his suit. He displayed a kind smile for Dalya, and a cold smile at the Secretary. The woman became pale, and she buried her head in her files, without daring to pronounce another word in the presence of Mr. Wilfrid.

- Please follow me, Mademoiselle Dalya Bouvard. Mr. Wilfrid asked politely.

When they entered in a closed office, Mr. Wilfrid invited Dalya to sit down. Mr. Wilfrid's office reflected perfectly his warm character. Dalya was dazzled by the light coming from the large windows that illuminated the entire room. The desk and chairs were in clear brown varnished wood. A large lamp stood in a corner. A big cupboard filled with well-ordered books, was installed next to the office. Dalya noticed many types of birds' figurines, beautifully colored and in many kinds, placed on a shelf of the cupboard.

Mr. Wilfrid sat down behind his desk and he asked, in his usual jovial tone:

- Well, Mademoiselle Dalya Bouvard ... How are you doing? ... How did your classes go this semester? If you don't mind me asking.

Dalya was delighted that Mr. Wilfrid was interested in her education:

- Very good, Sir. I passed the final exams a few days ago.
- I have no doubt that you have been a studious student!!

Dalya blushed a little because of Mr. Wilfrid's compliment, she continued:

- I had a big delay to catch up, in some courses. But I got good grades anyway. I had a 16/20 in Mathematics ... a 14.5 in Music ... a 17 in History... and 15.5 in Geography.

Mr. Wilfrid straightened up from in his chair; and he whispered:

- I've never had more than 11/20 in these four subjects ...

Dalya and Mr. Wilfrid giggled for a moment. He lay back on his chair, Mr. Wilfrid continued in a more serious tone:

- Well, these are excellent results ... Congratulations Mademoiselle!! Keep impressing us!!

Dalya smiled back. Mr. Wilfrid asked:

- So ... I guess you came today to inform us of a clue, Mademoiselle Dalya?
- Yes, Sir. Dalya gave him a small paper.

Mr. Wilfrid was a smart and a clever man, but also naturally very curious. When he took the paper that Dalya handed him, he asked spontaneously:

- You are wearing gloves, in the middle of a summer month ... in this heat?

Dalya hid her hands quickly; she murmured in a hesitant voice:

- It is to ... protect my hands ... of ... from ... the sun, Sir.

Mr. Wilfrid didn't question Dalya's answer; he read the 2nd clue immediately. After some long seconds of hard thinking, he looked up at Dalya, with an amused smile:

- Does this strange box, the Excelbox, always provide you incomprehensible enigmas?
- Yes, Sir. Dalya laughed. Sometimes it takes me days, even weeks to understand the clues!

Mr. Wilfrid observed Dalya in a fascinated stare, and he smiled:

- And yet, you have managed to answer the First Question. The Late Mr. Governor Iskander Balthazar sure didn't choose randomly his Heiress!

Dalya replied back with a smile. She greeted him, before leaving his office. A minute later, Sloan Wilfrid stood up and he looked through the windows of his office. And for a long moment, he watched the little girl walk down the street, until she disappeared.

Chapter 19

The summer holidays

Friday, August 07th, 1891. In the morning.

During August, the Royal Georgetown College remained open despite the holiday period. Some students had catch-up classes or were finalizing their school project. And this summer, Dalya attended school 3 days a week; she spent several hours in the empty school Library, to catch up on her lessons.

Dalya was not the only one spending her summer time at school, her classmate Amira Mounier practiced to improve her voice, in the upper tower of the school.

Despite the sweltering heat of the summer months, the city of Georgetown was full of energy and work. Even in the Annex house of the grand Mansion. Antman Bouvard was busy in his merchandise delivery work at the Toscana restaurant. This was the busiest period of the year, and the merchandise must always arrive on time. At the end of his work, Antman Bouvard got busy with crafts in the Annex home, for the rest of the day.

Mrs. Augustine Bouvard took care to wash the covers and curtains of the entire house. Obsessed with cleanliness, Mrs. Augustine took advantage of the bright summer sun, to clean the entire house, 2 to 3 times daily.

During her free days, Dalya stayed at home, to help her parents or to take care of her own crafts.

Dalya woke up much earlier, that day. In the kitchen downstairs, Dalya found her mother who was preparing breakfast.

- Good morning mother.

Mrs. Augustine seemed to be in a bad mood as always; Dalya didn't say another word, to avoid worsening her mother's mood. Dalya served herself some bread. The eggs were still warm, Dalya peeled one, and she poured herself milk.

A few moments later, when she had just finished eating breakfast; Dalya's father came into the kitchen. Antman Bouvard sat on the table, and he also served himself eggs and bread.

- You need to clean the garden this morning ... it's in a terrible state!
- Yes, father.

Dalya didn't need to be asked again. She put on her plastic boots and she went out to cut and clean the garden of the Annex house. It certainly was not a huge garden like the one of the grand Mansion. But it would still take her 2 to 3 hours to clean it.

Dalya pulled her gardening tools; scissors, shovels, watering can, gloves, fork spade, rake. And then, she started to cut the grass, remove the dead leaves, and water the garden...

After hours of work, Dalya was proud of the results. The garden looked beautiful, the little twins would certainly appreciate it even more now.

Dalya put away her gardening tools in a corner, and then she walked toward the Annex house to wash and change her clothes. When a voice called her out:

- You're done? ... Come over here!

Immediately, Dalya joined her father in the garage. He had lay on the floor several tools; saws, hammers, screwdrivers, tendrils, tongs, and nails. When Dalya appeared, her father handed her a little rag and a bottle:

- Clean all the tools with this oil. Then store them back, each in their place.

After her father left the garage, Dalya sat on the floor and she began cleaning the tools one by one, with a few drops of oil on the rag. The tools were small and somewhat blackened by the frequent use, so it took Dalya several minutes to shine each tool, and more than 2 hours to polish all of them.

It was noon now. And Dalya had just finished putting back the tools in their boxes in the garage. When she entered the Annex house, her little sisters were already awake since a long time. They were playing in the small living room with their two prefabricated plush rabbits. Her mother was busy preparing lunch; she didn't notice her daughter's presence. Dalya decided to go upstairs to her bedroom to wash and change her clothes. A voice stopped her on the stairs:

- Did you wash the carriage?

Dalya turned around and she froze on the 2nd step of the stairs:

- The ... carriage?

Her father came into the kitchen and he put down a large box of fresh vegetables.

- Yes, the carriage!! I need it cleaned for tomorrow. I have to make deliveries all day!!
- I can clean it this afterno...

Antman interrupted his daughter with a cold stare:

- Why this afternoon? ... Do you have something else important to do now?

Dalya didn't dare to answer, she wanted to change her clothes, clean herself up and relax a bit of all this morning's work. She remained motionless.

- Do it now!!

Her father ordered her, before disappearing outside to bring another box. Dalya turned around and went outside, with slow steps. She took a bucket filled with water, a sponge and she began to scrub and clean the carriage, all alone.

The August heat could be felt on this midday moment. The sun was shining with all its strength, the air was dense and the rare wind breezes were not sufficient to cool you off.

Dalya finished drying the carriage wheels with a dry cloth. It was 2:30 PM, and Dalya was very tired and hungry after a long morning housework. She returned back home just in time for lunch. Her little sisters were already placed on their chairs, and her mother served pasta with tomato sauce and chicken. Dalya sat next to her twin sisters.

- Cut the chicken into small pieces for your sisters. Her mother ordered.

Dalya took care to serve pasta to her little sisters and cut their meat. Ari and Adi were very hungry; they swallowed everything that their big sister put on their plates.

Dalya's father joined his family for lunch. Antman Bouvard exclaimed joyfully:

- Pasta with tomato sauce!! My favorite dish!! ... This is the best season for tomatoes by the way!!

When Dalya finished filling her sisters' plates, she served herself some pasta. Her mother joined them:

- The tomatoes are delicious this year. But with this heat, it ripens too fast. I am thinking of making compote out of it.

Between 2 bites, Antman said:

- Dalya ... take the tomato boxes inside the garage ... your mother is right, this heat will make them ripe too soon ... the garage is a cooler place; sheltered ... the boxes are near the entrance steps ... hurry up!

Dalya was about to eat her 3rd fork of pasta. She hesitated a moment. When her father's voice startled her from her chair:

- Hurry up!!

With tired legs and a heavy heart, Dalya put down her fork, and she left the kitchen. When she came outside, Dalya was surprised to find 8 large boxes filled with tomatoes. The garage was many steps afar at the back of the Annex house; this task would get Dalya busy for a while. She lifted the first tomato box, and she walked toward the garage, in slow steps.

Monday, August 10th, 1891. The afternoon.

While her sisters were taking their afternoon nap, Dalya was drying the lunch dishes. Her father was busy outside, while her mother was cleaning the living room.

- When you finish the dishes, hang the laundry that is outside in the basket ... as long as the sun is still shining ... I need the bed covers dried for tonight!!

After putting back the last plate in a closet, Dalya executed what her mother ordered her to do. She went outside, to the garden behind the Annex house. The basket was filled with several bed covers, pillows and white blankets. The elastic to hang on the laundry, was above her reach, Dalya had to stand on her toes to reach it. But before she could start to hang the laundry on the elastic, Dalya was interrupted by her father who was in the garage:

- I need you to put the full boxes into the carriage before I go ... I'll take care of some tools and I'll come back!

When her father disappeared inside the house, Dalya remained frozen in her place. Her mother and her father had asked her simultaneously to do housework. And Dalya was confused; she couldn't do both jobs at the same time. Yet, both tasks were urgent; the laundry should be hang before the sun's goes down, and the boxes were to be charged in the carriage before her father went out. So what to do first? To who obey first? Her father or her mother?

After several seconds of hesitation and reflection, Dalya decided to start with hanging the laundry that her mother asked her to do, and then take care of loading the boxes that her father ordered her. It was already 3:00 PM and the sun was only present for a few more hours. Dalya speeded up and put the laundry on the elastic, as quickly as she could. She quickly hangs the pillows one near the other, and then she run back to the basket to pick up more laundry, she stretched up with all her strength to reach the elastic, she hang the covers in a vertical way to make more space in the elastic, she run back toward the basket to pick up the white bed covers, she hang th...

- Why didn't you load the boxes in the carriage?

Dalya, breathless, turned around to her father:

- It's just ... the laundry should be hang ... before the sun disapp...

Antman Bouvard was furious, he didn't try to understand or listen to his daughter.

- Why didn't you load the boxes?

Dalya tried to explain to him:

- I was going to do it, father ... right after hanging the laundry ... because mother needed the bed covers dried for toni...

Her father yelled:

- FROM NOW ON, YOU DO EXACTLY WHAT I ASK YOU TO DO!! ... YOUR ONLY REASON FOR LIVING IS TO SERVE ME!! MORNING AND NIGHT!! SO WHEN I ORDER YOU TO DO SOMETHING, YOU EXECUTE IT IMMEDIATELY!! UNDERSTOOD??

Dalya was paralyzed, not daring to move or say a word. Because no matter how hard she worked, it's was never ever enough!

Wednesday, August 12th, 1891.

Dalya had a pretty busy day. Her mother ordered her to clean all the windows of the Annex house, from the inside and the outside. It was a small house, but with large windows. In the morning, Dalya took care of the windows of the second floor, she ate her lunch quickly to clean the windows of the first floor the afternoon. Dalya polished the windows as quickly and actively as she could. She hoped to be free in the afternoon to do her summer homework of Music lessons. If she was unable to play a Musical instrument like the other students, Dalya had borrowed some Music books from the Library, to be at least at the same level of knowledge than the others students.

The windows of the living room were the last to be cleaned. After she finished cleaning, Dalya washed her hands, and ran toward her bedroom. It was 6:00 PM; she had some time left to finish her Music homework, before setting the dinner table.

Dalya sat down on her bedroom floor, and she spread all the Music books in front of her, on the ground. Professor Haîyang gave them about 30 questions to answer during the summer holidays.

1- **Question 1: Describe the influence that the Musician Antonio Lucio Vivaldi had on his successors' Music.**
2- **Question 2: Who is the composer of the famous Concerto for 2 Violins in D minor?**
3- **Question 3: Quote in more details, the main works of the Musician Domenico Scarlatti.**

Dalya opened one of the books:

- The Composer of the Concerto for 2 Violins ... I read that somewhere in this book ... few months ago ...

A voice was heard from downstairs:

- Did you sweep the garage?

Dalya flipped the pages of the book slowly, while thinking aloud:

- I'm sure it was ... in the last pages of this book ... 2 Violins in D minor ...

The same voice called from downstairs:

- So? ... The garage is swept or not? ... I don't want the carriage getting dirty!

Dalya jumped happily, while holding the book in her hands:

- Found it!!! The composer of Concerto for 2 violins ... Johann Sebastian Bach!! ... or jean?

The voice from downstairs became closer:

- Have you become mute?

Dalya thought aloud:

- But ... Professor Haîyang asked to write the name of the composer... one composer ... was the melody created by two men?! ... in this book it says Johann Sebastian Bach ... and in that book there ... it is Jean Sebastian Bach ...

Some steps were heard at the end of the stairs:

- Why aren't you answering!!

Dalya was confused, she took another book on the floor and searched:

- So ... are these two different men ... or the same man with 2 different names ... Jean or Johann? ... Is it a misprint or jus...

Suddenly, a tall figure entered Dalya's bedroom. Mr. Antman didn't understand why his daughter was sitting on the floor, surrounded by a stack of books and notebooks. He asked in an angry voice:

- What are you doing?

Dalya didn't understand her father's furious mood. She explained to him spontaneously:

- I ... I was doing my summer homework for the Musi...
- I HAVE BEEN TALKING TO YOU FOR SEVERAL MINUTES AND YOU DIDN'T ANSWER ME!!
- I'm sorry, father. I didn't hear you. I was confused by a questi...
- DID YOU SWEEP THE GARAGE?

Dalya, still sitting on the ground, she froze in her place. She completely forgot to clean the garage like her father ordered her to do this morning. She hesitated to reply:

- I ... I'm sorry ... I forgot to do it. I will finish just a question of this homework, and I will immediately swe...

Her father stared at her for a moment, before asking in a strangely calm voice:

- Homework of what class exactly?

Dalya answered:

- The Music course. Professor Haîyang gave us 30 questions that we should answ...

Suddenly, Antman Bouvard walked toward his daughter, and in a violent and aggressive movement, he crushed with his big shoes full of mud, all the books and notebooks spread on the floor, in front of his daughter. Dalya jumped back several steps away, not daring to get up, she was shocked by her father's attitude. When all her books were crumpled, torn and damaged, Antman Bouvard knelt in front of his terrified daughter, and then he said in a calm but menacing voice:

- Get that inside your little brain ... that you attend this school, I really don't care a shit ... your priority is to obey me, your priority is to do the housework I order you and to serve your family for the rest of your miserable life ... you need to understand that you're not allowed to rest whenever you want, or do whatever you want ... you're not allowed to have a life to yourself... and you're not allowed to be free!!

Saturday, August 15th, 1891.

At the end of the day, Dalya was playing with her little sisters in the garden. When unexpectedly, the weather became gray, clouds hid the blue sky, and Dalya felt a drop of water falling over her forehead.

- Ari ... Adi ... I think we should go inside the house ... it might rain soon!!
- Play more little bit ... pease ... pease! The little twins begged.
- No no!! It is about to rain soon, we must go inside now.

Dalya and her little sisters ran to the Annex house. They arrived just in time before the rain could catch them up. When they entered the kitchen, Mrs. Augustine came inside holding a large basket filled with all wet black grapes; she was in a very bad mood:

- Stupid rain!! It had to rain today!! We are sick of this damn rain!!

Dalya helped her sisters to dry off and remove their garden boots, while talking to her mother:

- The Gardener Mr. Rosenwald told me that the best rain is on this period. It is beneficial in this season ... the soil cools down and the plants are refreshed from the hea...

Mrs. Augustine interrupted Dalya and screamed:

- YOU WITLESS!! WHY HAVEN'T YOU PICKED UP THE LAUNDRY HANG OUTSIDE BEFORE THE RAIN FALLS DOWN!!

Dalya laughed:

- It was beautiful sunny day, only a minute ago ... how can I predict that the weather will change?

And it was obvious. How can anyone foresee the rapid change of the weather? How could Mrs. Augustine possibly expect her daughter to guess the bad weather? And above all, why was Mrs. Augustine holding her daughter responsible for the weather? Isn't it insane to blame someone for an event beyond human control?

As silly as it may seem, Mrs. Augustine held her daughter responsible for the weather, and the wet laundry. And as usual, Mrs. Augustine never liked to be answered or proved she had a brainless thinking. So then, the mother did the only thing she mastered well in her entire life. Mrs. Augustine walked toward her daughter, she pinched her cheek so hard and so strong, and she led her daughter outside the house. Under the rain. Toward the garage.

The August month didn't flow the same for everyone. While the students of the prestigious Royal Georgetown College, were on holiday with their parents, having fun, resting, enjoying the beautiful weather and the free time. The little Dalya Bouvard was split between the housework her father ordered her to do the entire day, and between her mother's excessive anger and aggressive temper.

And every night, when she finish washing and drying the dinner dishes, Dalya would go back to her bedroom, exhausted and drained from a long day of hard work. After changing her clothes, she would take several small bags of thick fabric. Dalya collected these potato bags, from many farmers, at the start of summer vacation. She would take a big needle and a thread from her toolbox. And since some time now, Dalya wore more frequently her beige lace gloves. The little girl would sit on the floor, leaning on her bed, and facing the large window of her bedroom.

And despite the great difficulty and pain to move her fingers, despite tears coming down her cheeks, despite the long night summer heat, despite the fatigue of the incessant housework of her father, despite the insane cruelty of her mother, despite her parents' selfishness ... every night, the little Dalya Bouvard sew the edges of the potatoes fabric bags.

Chapter 20

An excellent health

Monday, August 24th, 1891.

Richard Poirier waited in the lounge, while the Doctor checked his mother, for her usual medical examination. Richard came back home a few days ago, from a long absence abroad because of his work.

Several minutes went by. When the Doctor left Mrs. Marianne's bedroom, Richard put down his newspaper immediately and he stood up to greet him. The Doctor looked pale and confused.

- Is everything alright Doctor? Richard asked, impatient and worried by the Doctor's face.

The Doctor was an old man. White Snow hair, golden round glasses, a prestigious and elegant black suit, and a briefcase carried at his hand. The Doctor murmured in a hesitant tone:

- It's just ... that ... it's ...

In front of the Doctor's confusion, Richard Poirier expected the worst. Since many years now, Richard was well aware of his mother's health condition, which was deteriorating day by day. Her illness was very rare and incurable, weakening her body, depressing her mind and holding her in her bedroom. Richard had called upon the greatest physicians and medical researchers of the country, in order to cure his mother. Besides tranquilizers, anesthetics, and warm compresses, nothing seemed to be useful to cure Mrs. Marianne Poirier.

Since long ago, Richard Poirier gave up all his hopes of healing his mother. With a heavy heart, he observed his mother lose her health, and he was unable to help her.

- It's just that ... your mother is ... she in excellent health, Mr. Richard.

Richard thought he mistakenly heard the Doctor's news:

- Sorry? You said ...

The Doctor looked at Richard, and a surprised smile appeared on the face of the old man:

- Your mother ... she is in excellent health.
- My mother? she is ...
- Yes ... Mrs. Marianne Poirier ... her health has very much improved.

Both the Doctor and Richard Poirier had a hard time to believe this news. The old man seemed even more confused than Richard. The Doctor sat down on one of the big armchairs in the lounge, and Richard followed him. The Doctor stared at Richard for a moment before saying:

- You are well aware that her disease is very rare and incurable.
- Yes, I understood that matter long ago.

The Doctor seemed lost. He thought aloud:

- Her illness prevented her from having a normal life rhythm. The slightest wind breeze or a hot sun ray, triggers in her excruciating pain. It forced her to stay in her bedroom, for many years. And as a consequence, her physical health deteriorated because of this isolation.

The Doctor looked at Richard:

- All the medical checkups that I have done before, were in decline ... except this time!
- Is it the tranquilizers that have become more effective? Richard asked.
- No ... the tranquilizers are prescribed to reduce the pain ... only 10% to 15% ... but they do not improve the physical health.

Richard seemed as lost as the Doctor. The old man continued to think aloud:

- Your mother is in better shape than the last checkup that I did. Her blood pressure is stable ... her heart's rate is excellent ... her reflexes are much better than before ... she can easily walk and at a much faster rate ... she even gained weight!!

Richard didn't know whether to laugh of joy at the good news or be worried by this surprise. The Doctor also tried to understand what was going on:

- Did something changed in her daily routine?
- No.
- Did you changed her meal's menu that was prescribed?
- No.
- Does she get out of her bedroom?
- No.
- Is there any new event that came into her life?
- No.

The Doctor relaxed on the chair, he repeated aloud and confused:

- I have never had such a case ... this is the first time in my career ... Despite her illness ... for years she has been immobile ... yet, she regained her physical health ...

Richard Poirier was also curious about this strange news:

- But ... how, Doctor? ... How did it happen?

The Doctor looked at Richard and he laughed. A surprised, amazed, and uncertain laugh:

- Monsieur Richard Poirier ... I don't have a slightest idea of how it happened.

The day after, Richard Poirier preferred to stay at home in his office to work, near his mother. The Doctor's news has certainly pleased him, but one question kept spinning in Richard's head: how did his mother regained her excellent health?

Sitting in his office, Richard Poirier consulted some important documents for his work. When suddenly, a noise made him lose his focus. The garden gate opened and a little silhouette crossed the garden. He leaned toward his office window to see who it could be. And he was surprised to see Dalya Bouvard, the Heiress of Late Mr. Governor.

- But ... what ... what is she doing?

Richard watched Dalya from his office window. The little girl crossed the Poirier's garden with hurried steps. She walked to the bird's nest installed at the other end of the garden. Richard noticed that Dalya put something inside the bird's nest. Then, Dalya quickly ran back toward the house exit, checking left and right, to make sure no one had seen her.

Except that Richard has been observing Dalya since her arrival, he thought in an amused tone:

- What is she doing in our garden? ... She fills the bird's nest with seeds? ... But why does she do it? ... Mrs. Glorina fills it frequently ... That girl is strange... coming a long way from her home, only to drop seeds in the bird's nest of our garden? ...

Richard finally came back to his desk, and he continued reading his important documents.

A moment later, Richard heard a creaking door. He thought that it surely must be Mrs. Glorina coming out of his mother's bedroom after serving her tea. He continued his work.

When several minutes went by, Richard heard a second door creaking. And this time, it was the veranda door, which was overlooking the garden. Exasperated by the slamming doors at every moment, Richard Poirier got up from his desk and he approached the windows.

And what he saw, shocked him! ... His mother, Mrs. Marianne Poirier, she was slowly walking through the garden. And despite the heat of the summer month, and to protect herself from the wind breeze and the sun rays, Mrs. Marianne wore her big velvet coat, a fur on her neck, and a shawl covering most of her face. She clung to a cane, and she walked slowly, with firm steps. Richard Poirier was bewildered of what he was looking at...

When his mother stopped at the bird's nest, she removed a small item from inside of it. Mrs. Marianne then turned around and she came back inside the house, going up the stairs and she locked herself in her bedroom.

Richard sat down at his desk, surprised of what he had just seen. His mother rarely left her bedroom, even less to walk in the garden. Confusion haunted Richard's mind about his mother, about the little Dalya Bouvard, and also about the bird's nest. For many minutes, Richard Poirier failed to understand, he sighed:

- What is happening in this house?!
-

Chapter 21

The Bird's Nest

Thursday, August 27th, 1891.

For many days now, many questions were bothering Richard Poirier. He wasn't a naturally curious person, but the unusual behavior of Dalya Bouvard and his mother, kept him concerned. Why and what was Dalya hiding in the bird's nest? What could possibly motivate his mother to leave the bedroom and go through the entire garden to get it? And above all ... why couldn't Dalya hand it over directly to his mother in her bedroom? ...

One evening in the last days of August, the heat was oppressive; the air was dense and heavy. Mrs. Glorina was peeling some pears for Mrs. Marianne's dinner. When Richard came into the kitchen, and he informed her:

- Mrs. Glorina ... I may come back late tonight; I have an important appointment. It would be unnecessary to prepare dinner for me.
- As you wish, Mr. Richard. Mrs. Glorina smiled.

Before closing the kitchen door, Richard hesitated to ask about something. After a few seconds, he dared:

- Did ... mother receive any visits ... lately? … During my absence abroad?
- No, Sir. Mrs. Glorina replied carelessly. Besides your sister, and Mr. Eastman that you ordered to handle our expenses, nobody else visited Mrs. Marianne, lately.

Mrs. Glorina continued to peel the pears. But when he was about to get out of the kitchen for his important appointment, Richard asked one last question to Mrs. Glorina:

- And ... Mademoiselle Dalya Bouvard ... did she visit mother, during my absence?

At this question, Mrs. Glorina stopped to peel the pears. Richard had finally caught the attention of Mrs. Glorina. The old woman thought aloud:

- No ... It's true that it's been a long time since Mademoiselle has visited us ...

Richard was also curious:

- So ... she hasn't come here lately? ... You haven't seen in a while?
- No Sir, neither I, nor your mother, have met Mademoiselle Dalya Bouvard lately ... she used to come visit us quite often before. But it's been several months now, that she didn't come to this house ... I wonder why ...

While closing the kitchen door, Richard Poirier was more confused by what he was learning, every day.

Saturday, August 29th, 1891.

After Mrs. Glorina had realized Dalya's long absence, she decided to visit the Saturday market in front of the Toscana restaurant, sure to find there the little girl who was often doing grocery shopping. And Mrs. Glorina was right. On Saturday, at the usual market, Dalya was filling her shopping bag with potatoes, when she was called by a familiar voice:

- Mademoiselle Dalya!! Here you are at last!!

Dalya haven't had time to answer a hello, Mrs. Glorina hugged the little girl in her arms.

- How are you doing Mrs. Glorina? Asked Dalya, glad to see the woman.
- Very well, thank you!! ... And you mademoiselle?
- Split between groceries for my mother and helping my father in his housework at the Annex house. Dalya laughed.
- You are always so kind and hardworking!!! exclaimed Mrs. Glorina, before continuing with a little more serious tone:
- In fact, Mademoiselle ... I came especially to the market today to see you!! ... And I admit that if I hadn't found you here today, I would have surely searched for you at the grand Mansion...
- You ... you were looking for me, Mrs. Glorina? Dalya asked all curious.
- Yes Mademoiselle!! It's been a long while since you have visited us!! Mrs. Marianne and I were worried about you!!

Dalya was astonished; she didn't know what to say. Mrs. Glorina asked in a kind voice:

- May I know why you stopped visiting us, Mademoiselle?

Dalya hesitated to pronounce her words, but she finally dared:

- It's just that ... I thought that I was disturbing you and Madame ...
- You? Disturbing us? Exclaimed Mrs. Glorina. But ... where did you get such an idea from? ... Mrs. Marianne and I never thought that!
- Because ... but ... it's ... it's what I have been told. Dalya replied, hesitant and surprised by Mrs. Glorina's reaction.
- Who told you that you were disturbing us? Asked Mrs. Glorina in a shocked tone.

The only thing that Dalya could remember afterwards, is that in a split of a second, Mrs. Glorina became bloody angry. The woman turned around and she left the market, in fast steps toward the Poirier house. Dalya had to run to catch her up. She never saw Mrs. Glorina so furious.

- Mrs. Glorina ... please ... it was to avoid you having worries ... please ... wait ... Mrs. Glorina ... just a minute ...

Dalya begged all the way of Dumbarton Oaks Park road, but Mrs. Glorina wouldn't listen to her. Her rage increased with every step, she walked without paying any attention to Dalya who had to run behind her. And during all the way, Mrs. Glorina threatened aloud:

- I'LL TEACH HER GOOD MANNERS!! TO SAY SUCH NONSENSE!! BUT IT'S AWFUL!! IT'S RIDICULOUS AT HER AGE!! BUT IT DOESN'T MATTER!! I'LL RE-EDUCATE HER MYSELF!! IT'S HER LUCKY DAY!! I WILL TEACH HER THE LESSON OF HER LIFE TODAY!! SINCE SO LONG I AM PATIENT OF HER ANNOYING CHARACTER!! I'LL TEACH HER GOOD MANNERS ONCE AND FOR ALL!!

When Mrs. Glorina arrived into the house of the French family les Poirier, she opened the kitchen door suddenly, she dropped her vegetables' basket with a sharp knock on the table, and then she walked to the living room. Dalya tried all her best to reason the woman, one last time:

- Mrs. Glorina ... I beg you ... calm down ... it's not that bad ... Mrs. Glorina ... I beg you ... please ...

Francine Poirier was quietly tasting her tea in the living room. When Mrs. Glorina stopped in front of her and she exclaimed in an angry tone:

- WHAT DID YOU TELL HER?

Dalya didn't dare to make a step forward; she remained motionless behind Mrs. Glorina. Francine Poirier sitting on a big chair, she put down her teacup and she looked at Mrs. Glorina with astonishment:

- How dare you speak to me like that?
- WHAT DID YOU TELL HER? Repeated Mrs. Glorina, without decreasing the tone of her voice even by a note.
- But what are you talking about? Francine didn't understand the unusual attitude of Mrs. Glorina.
- YOU LIED!! Mrs. Glorina yelled.

At this point, Miss Francine Poirier got up from her chair. And as heavy and fat as she was, she stood up with great difficulty:

- You dare to call me a liar?
- YOU DARE TO LIE AND CREATE NONSENSE!! Screamed Mrs. Glorina enraged.
- You forget who you are, I suppose! Have you lost your mind talking to me like that! Exclaimed Francine, troubled by what was happening.
- NO I HAVE NOT LOST MY MIND!! BUT YOU HAVE CLEARLY LOST THE SENSE OF GOOD MANNERS!!

The tone of Mrs. Glorina's voice continued to increase. Dalya who had refrained to intervene until that moment, she decided to surpass Mrs. Glorina and place herself between the two women, before things get worse. Dalya has never seen Mrs. Glorina as furious and out of control, she insisted to reason her:

- Mrs. Glorina ... I beg you ... it's not so bad ...

But Mrs. Glorina completely ignored Dalya's pleading and she continued to address Francine:

- WHAT DID SHE DO TO YOU?? WHY DID YOU LIE TO MADEMOISELLE DALYA?? WHY DID YOU STOP HER FROM VISITING US BY CREATING A LIE?? WHY DID YOU CONVINCE HER THAT SHE DISTURBED ME AND MRS MARIANNE?? YOUR MOTHER ENJOYS SO MUCH HER PRESENCE!! EXPLAIN TO ME WHY YOU DI...

Francine Poirier interrupted Mrs. Glorina sharply:

- BECAUSE SHE IS NOT HER DAUGHTER!! I AM!!

Mrs. Glorina was overthrown by this answer. And she was not the only one, Dalya turned around toward Miss Francine, unsure of what she had just heard. Mrs. Glorina and Dalya looked at Francine in a stunned gaze, not believing what their ears had just heard. Mrs. Glorina asked in a surprised voice:

- You are jealous? ... Of the attention that your mother holds to Mademoiselle Dalya?

Francine Poirier was ashamed of being exposed. She didn't dare to answer. But Mrs. Glorina dared to clarify, in a calm but icy tone:

- Certainly ... Mademoiselle Dalya Bouvard is not her daughter ... But this little girl is better than Mrs. Marianne's own daughter!!

Francine Poirier didn't digest Mrs. Glorina's words. She exclaimed in an arrogant way, despite a trembling voice:

- But ... anyway, I did not lie ... she keeps you from doing your job properly ... all I did was explain to her that she disturbs you and makes you often late behind the housewor...

Mrs. Glorina lost her patience and her tolerance. She screamed with all her strength, while advancing a step closer toward Francine:

- THE ONLY REASON I'M OFTEN LATE BEHIND THE HOUSEWORK ... IT'S BECAUSE OF YOUR LAZINESS AND IDLENESS FRANCINE!! I HAVE TO WASH YOUR CLOTHES, MAKE YOUR FOOD, ARRANGE YOUR BRIDGE PARTIES AND EVEN MAKE YOUR BED!!

Dalya that stood between the two women, she tried to hold back Mrs. Glorina, and prevent her from moving toward Francine. Except that Francine didn't make it easy on Dalya, she didn't stop provoking Mrs. Glorina, with a mocking and arrogant tone:

- Really?! ... My dear brother was about to dismiss you because of your delay in the housework ... If it wasn't I who restrained him by mercy for your many years of services ...

Mrs. Glorina stepped forward again, and Dalya pushed her back hard with all her strength, while the woman screamed:

- OH!!! BUT LET ME CORRECT YOU, YOUR HIGHNESS FRANCINE!!! BEFORE HIS TRIP ABOARD, MR RICHARD POLITELY APOLOGIZED FOR ALL THE EXTRA NEW CHORES THAT I WILL HAVE BECAUSE OF YOU!! HE EVEN GAVE ME THE FREE CHOICE OF RECRUITING HELP IF I EVER NEEDED IT!!! BECAUSE HE IS WELL EDUCATED AND HONEST!!

Francine Poirier couldn't bear to hear this answer. She replied in a provocative way:

- You forget one thing ... I am your employer!!

This time, Mrs. Glorina finally realized that she was bothered by the little Dalya Bouvard that was pushing her and keeping her from stepping toward Francine, to give her a good lesson.

Out of herself, Mrs. Glorina took both Dalya's hands that were blocking her, and she swung away the little girl with a move so rapid that Dalya found herself behind Mrs. Glorina in a split of a second. But before Mrs. Glorina could take a step toward Francine, Dalya pulled herself together; she clung to the back of Mrs. Glorina's coat, and she pulled the woman with all her strength, to prevent her from moving forward. Even being held from behind, Mrs. Glorina could still scream:

- OH NO!! MY EMPLOYERS ARE MR. RICHARD AND MRS. MARIANNE!! AND NO OTHERS!! CERTAINLY NOT A LAZY PERSON LIKE YOU!!

When suddenly, someone entered the living room. Neither Mrs. Glorina nor Dalya nor Francine had to explain anything. Richard Poirier had heard everything since the beginning of the scene. Never Richard Poirier did seem so intimidating, without even saying a word. In his presence, Francine became all pale; she trembled from head to toe. Richard looked at her with a cold serious stare. Mrs. Glorina regained consciousness and her normal breath. Dalya let go of Mrs. Glorina's coat from behind.

Without a spoken word, Francine retired from the living room, in hurried steps. Instantly, Richard Poirier walked toward Mrs. Glorina and he addressed her in a calm voice:

- Is everything alright, Mrs. Glorina?
- Yes, Mr. Richard. Replied Mrs. Glorina in a calmer tone, but still upset, before continuing:
- Forgive me, Mr. Richard ... I couldn't hold back my anger when I found out the reason of Mademoiselle Dalya's absence.

Standing near Mrs. Glorina, Dalya murmured timidly:

- I ... I'm so sorry for causing this incident.

Dalya was embarrassed to have created worries between Mrs. Glorina and Francine Poirier. Disturbing the peace of the French neighbor's house, this was obviously not Dalya's intention. Yet, worries invited themselves to the French family home, since Dalya's visits.

Richard Poirier looked at the strange little girl in a curious stare, for several long seconds. Before he said in a calm voice:

- It's not up to you to apologize. I'm sorry for the misunderstanding that my sister may have caused.

Dalya didn't expect at all this answer, and she could even see that Richard Poirier smiled at her! The young man continued, in his courteous tone:

- You are always welcomed in this house, Mademoiselle Dalya Bouvard.

Dalya thanked him with a shy smile. Richard Poirier dared to ask:

- However ... I'm curious about what you have placed inside the bird's nest of our garden, few days ago?

Dalya naturally replied to Richard Poirier:

- I copy the guessing words game from the newspaper, that my friend Alfie lends me ... it's for Mrs. Glorina, she likes this game ... and since I couldn't visit her, I deliver her the paper ...
- In the bird's nest of our garden? Richard continued.
- Yes ... it was the only place I could find to deliver the guessing words game paper to Mrs. Glorina ...

At this moment, Mrs. Glorina observed Dalya, in a confused stare:

- The guessing words game? ... For me? ... But Mademoiselle, I didn't know that you were leaving a paper for me ... I've never found a paper in the bird's nest when I clean it ...

Dalya was confused, too:

- Really? ... but ... how ... yet, the bird's nest was always empty, whenever I placed the paper inside of it and its response a few days after ... you haven't received anything? ... But ... it's been months now, that I have been delivering these papers, Mrs. Glorina!!
- I am sorry mademoiselle ... but I have not received anything from you ... this is strange ... for months you say? ... Is it possible that your papers get lost ... or fall elsewhere? ...
- I don't think so ... I fold the paper on 4 and I put it inside the bird's nest ... you never found any paper inside the bird's nest, Mrs. Glorina? ... Are you sure?

But where did the guessing words game papers disappear? Dalya and Mrs. Glorina couldn't understand what had happened during all these past months.

Except that one person seemed to finally understand what happened. At that moment, and as unpredictable as it may seem, Richard Poirier laughed aloud:

- And suddenly, she is in excellent physical health ... because she walks outside, every time to collect the guessing words game ... from the bird's nest ...

Dalya and Mrs. Glorina exchanged a confused look, overtaken by the strange words and the unexpected laugh of Richard Poirier.

Because you see, windows and doors can close in ... certainly ... but the Excelbox challenge you anyway, to forbid air and goodness from coming in...

Chapter 22

A school supply kit

Tuesday, September 01st, 1891.

The back to school at the Royal College of Georgetown was in the next few days. Dalya had never set foot in a school supplies store before. And with the new semester starting shortly, Dalya needed a school supply kit; which included pens and study materials.

Professor Canfield was very nice to provide her with all the books and notebooks she needed. But she didn't dare to ask him for a school supply kit.

When Dalya opened the door, she was overwhelmed by the smell of wood and ink inside the store. The interior of the shop was luxurious. All the walls were well organized in shelves filled with labeled boxes stored impeccably. Dalya had never seen so many school supplies all in one place; hundreds of thousands of books, notebooks, all kinds of pens, pencils, erasers ... and many other tools that Dalya didn't even recognize. Behind the counter, employees were serving the customers as quickly as they could; they wore light blue jackets over flawless white shirts and blue ties.

Immediately, an employee appeared in front of Dalya. Long and thin, the employee had a big nose and a serious look. And with a quick movement, the employee led Dalya toward the exit door:

- We don't let in beggars in our shop!! Go and beg elsewhere!!
- But ... I'm not b... wait ...

Dalya had no time to answer, she found herself outside the shop, in the street, without understanding the strange behavior of the employee. Dalya needed this supply kit, so she opened the shop door for the second time.

- We do not accept the beggars here!! The employee exclaimed heading toward Dalya for the second time, trying to get her out.

Except that Dalya spoke in a clear determined voice:

- I am not a beggar, monsieur...

The employee froze in front of her, confused by her answer. He scanned the girl from head to toe, with an astonished stare. Dalya Bouvard didn't look rich. She was wearing her usual clothes; blue overalls, an over washed shirt, worn black shoes and a big cap. After a few seconds of silence, the employee asked, in an annoyed tone:

- And so, what do you want then?

Dalya politely replied:

- I would like a school supply kit, please.

The employee seemed thunderstruck by this request:

- What for?

Dalya naturally replied:

- Because I need it.

The employee didn't seem to understand:

- Why does a poor girl like you, need a school supply kit for?

Dalya didn't understand the bizarre question of the employee:

- It's for school.
- Because you go to school? ... You? Exclaimed the employee in a loud astonished voice, that the other customers turned around and observed the scene.
- Yes, monsieur. Dalya answered.

The employee was shocked. He crossed his arms and he asked in a mocking voice:

- And what school do you attend?

Dalya ignored the employee's arrogant tone, and she answered anyway:

- The Royal Georgetown College.

The employee laughed aloud, and the other customers also followed the funny scene.

- A girl like you? ... At the Royal Georgetown College? ... That's funny! Really funny!

Dalya went silent; she didn't know why the employees and the other customers were laughing about. The employee led her toward the exit door for the 3rd time:

- Come on!! We've had enough fun!! Go play elsewhere!! Let us work!!

Dalya protested in a firm voice:

- I came to buy a school supply kit!!

Given her stubbornness, the employee lost his smirk and he replied coldly:

- We have no more kits to sell to you.

Dalya didn't understand the employee's insolence. She pointed her finger:

- And what's behind you, there, on these shelves?

At least hundreds boxes of school supply kits were placed on several shelves along the wall of the store. The employee turned all red with rage. He pulled out a black kit with a sudden move, and he placed it on the counter in front of Dalya. She forced herself to remain polite despite the employee's rude manners:

- How much for this kit, please?
- 15 cents!! The employee yelled in a cold tone.

Dalya took out of her overalls' pocket a small purse full of silver coins, and she emptied its contents on the counter.

- Here's twen...

The employee interrupted her abruptly:

- The kit is too expensive for you!! Go buy elsewhere!!

Dalya looked surprised:

- But ... I have twen...
- We do not sell our supplies to the poor!! The employee yelled.

Dalya felt intimidated and humiliated by this situation. She didn't know what to say. Her throat choked, and anger overcame her. When all of a sudden, a familiar voice appeared out of nowhere:

- Really? You do not sell your supplies to the poor ... and why is that?

Mr. Sloan Wilfrid walked toward the counter. And as always, the young Lawyer was very elegant in his dark blue suit, impeccably ironed and tailored. His little round glasses reflected his gray eyes. And he displayed his usual amused smile.

Mr. Wilfrid heard the entire conversation between Dalya and the employee of the store, from its beginning. The employee hesitated to answer for a few seconds:

- She ... she doesn't have enough money, to buy this supply kit!

Mr. Wilfrid turned toward Dalya and he smiled kindly:

- Mademoiselle ... how much money do you have?

Without hesitation, Dalya replied proudly:

- I have … 20 cents, Mr. Wilfrid.

With a defying calm smile, Sloan Wilfrid addressed the employee:

- Mademoiselle has enough money to purchase the item.

The employee was forced to repress his rage. He took a small shopping bag, and he packed a black supply kit inside of it, with a brutal move. Dalya interrupted in a spontaneous voice:

- I would like a blue supply kit, please ... I don't like black.

Mr. Wilfrid had a mean pleasure repeating the little girl's request to the employee, again with a defiant and amused smile:

- Mademoiselle would like a blue supply kit, please ... she doesn't like black.

After several minutes, at the store exit, Dalya bought all the things she needed for the new school year; a full supply kit and notebooks, thanks to the help and the presence of Mr. Wilfrid. The Lawyer had also bought some office supplies that he needed. On the street, Mr. Wilfrid turned to the little girl and he asked her:

- Forgive my curiosity, Mademoiselle ... but may I know where did you get the money from, to buy your school supplies?

Dalya explained in a proud voice:

- Well ... during the school summer vacation, I've sewed and made many bags to carry the groceries ... I gave them all to the vegetables and the salad Merchants, so they can sell my bags with their goods ... I took 50% of the bags' earnings and the Merchants kept the other 50%.

Mr. Wilfrid was surprised:

- So then, you worked all summer, in order to buy your school supply kit?
- Yes, Sir! Dalya replied proudly.

Before leaving, Mr. Wilfrid asked Dalya to visit him at Mr. Ernest Laszlo's office, the very next day. Dalya thanked him for his help inside the supply store, and she immediately ran back to her house. Dalya was happy and proud to have managed to buy a school supply kit, just like the other students at school. While Mr. Wilfrid observed the little girl running down the street, he laughed:

- Fascinating ... simply fascinating!!

Wednesday, September 02nd, 1891.

The next day, Dalya entered the Lawyer's office. Mr. Wilfrid greeted her with a cheerful smile:

- Good morning, Mademoiselle!!
- Good morning, Mr. Wilfrid.
- You are right on time!

Mr. Wilfrid stood up and he put his coat on, before continuing:

- We'll go on a little ride. Please follow me, Mademoiselle.

Sloan Wilfrid left his office, he knocked the door of another office twice, and Lyor Laszlo came out. Wilfrid ordered him:

- Get your coat!! We have a ride to do!!

Lyor Laszlo didn't seem happy to be disturbed in the middle of his work, and he was even more upset when he noticed Dalya Bouvard. Lyor protested:

- I don't have time for he...

Mr. Wilfrid interrupted him in an amused tone:

- Yes you have time for the Heiress of Late Mr. Governor!! Come on!! Hurry up!!

In the car, Mr. Wilfrid continued reading his morning newspaper. Lyor crossed his arms and ignored Dalya who was sitting right in front of him. Dalya looked outside the car that was passing quickly, and she wondered where Mr. Wilfrid was taking her and Lyor. When the car stopped in front of a shop, Mr. Wilfrid entered first. Inside the shop, there was a much older woman, quite chubby, with a long elegant lilac purple dress, her clear brown hair was arranged in a perfect chignon, and a beautiful white pearl necklace covered her neck. The woman greeted them in a cheerful and loud voice:

- Good morning, Master Wilfrid! What a pleasure to see you here!

When Dalya stepped inside the shop, she was stunned by what her eyes were seeing. The place was very luxurious. Several wood mannequins were dressed in beautiful outfits. Refined chairs were installed in a corner of the room. A large wardrobe was open, displaying soft and expensive fabrics. A huge chandelier shined and irradiated the entire place. Dozens of large mirrors reflected the slightest movements. It was a couture shop ... and it was the first time in her life that Dalya Bouvard entered such a place.

Mr. Wilfrid replied with a smile and a respectful head sign:

- And it's a pleasure to be here, as well, Mrs. Lancel.
- What can I do for you today, Master?

Mr. Wilfrid introduced the two young people, to the woman:

- Mrs. Lancel, I present to you Mademoiselle Dalya Bouvard ... and this is Mr. Lyor Laszlo, her legal guardian.
- Dalya Bouvard? ... is she ...
- Yes, exactly! She is the Heiress of the late Governor Mr. Iskander Balthazar!!

The woman looked at Dalya from head to toe, not in a arrogant stare like the other people used to do, but an admiring and a delighted look. She approached the little girl and bowed in a breathless and happy voice:

- It is a ... it is a great honor to see you in my couture shop ... Mademoiselle!!

Dalya shyly replied:

- It's nice to meet you too, ma'am.

The woman seemed a bit surprised and overwhelmed by Dalya Bouvard's politeness. Mr. Wilfrid addressed the woman:

- Since it is the back to school in a few days, Mademoiselle needs a school uniform, please.
- But of course!! With great pleasure!! Immediately, Master Wilfrid!! I will take her measurements myself ... it will take only a few minutes!!

Mrs. Lancel asked her employees to bring her kit and measures notebook, before continuing:

- Master Wilfrid, Mr. Lyor ... please do sit down.

When the woman was busy with one of her employees, Dalya approached Mr. Wilfrid. She hardly dared to pronounce her words, in a shy and a whispered voice:

- Mr. Wilfrid ... I ... I can't ... I can't pay for this outfit.

The Lawyer answered her kindly:

- It will be on me ... Mademoiselle Dalya Bouvard.

Dalya didn't expect this gift from Mr. Wilfrid. She asked with a hesitant tone:

- But ... it must be very expensive, Monsieur.

The Lawyer couldn't hold an amused laugh. He whispered to the little girl:

- Don't worry about that, Mademoiselle. Mr. Ernest Laszlo pays me well enough to make up for his difficult temper!!

Dalya laughed too. Yet, something worried Dalya:

- It's just that ... the date of the Second Challenge is in 3 months ... and I don't know if I will succeed ... I don't know if I will stay in this school ... this uniform will be wasted, if I can't answer the Secon…

Mr. Wilfrid interrupted her politely:

- Mademoiselle ... we all have the right to live our dreams, as short as they can be!

Dalya smiled, she was touched by his kind gestures toward her:

- Thank you Mr. Wilfrid … thank you very much …

The Lawyer bowed his head respectfully:

- Mademoiselle, it is a great honor to be useful to you.

Mrs. Lancel interrupted their conversation by asking Dalya to come close to a mirror:

- Well ... First, we will take your measurements ... then I will let you wear a uniform ... and then, we will adjust it to your size. Mademoiselle, stand straight and raise your arms, please.

This was the first time in her life that Dalya entered a couture shop, and she will have an outfits made on her size.

Dalya never chose her clothes before. She usually wore boy's clothes; worn overalls, washed-out shirts, old black shoes, a large cap, and used clothes ... the boy's clothes that her father gave her. And because she had to work with him in the market, the boy's clothes were the most practical for work.

Since her first day at school, Dalya couldn't help but admire the other students wearing nice uniforms. The girls wore long black skirts, white blouses and marine blue jackets. The boys were in white shirts, dark blue jackets and long pants.

Even when she worked at the market with her father, she would frequently observe the girls of her age wearing pretty clean dresses, small elegant hats, and shining shoes. Dalya was well aware that she wasn't like the other children of her age. Although, sometimes she hoped to be like them...

And while Mrs. Lancel took the measurements for her new school uniform ... Dalya had joyful tears in her eyes.

A few minutes later, Mrs. Lancel came out from the workshop holding an outfit in her hands.

- Mademoiselle... follow me to the fitting room, please.

A moment later, Dalya appeared in front of the Lawyers Mr. Sloan Wilfrid and Lyor Laszlo. Mrs. Lancel made her wear a long black skirt, a white shirt, and a navy blue jacket.

Being skinny, Dalya floated in her navy blue jacket. And yet, Dalya was so happy to wear clean, new clothes, although too big for her. Dalya asked joyfully like any normal 13 years old girl:

- So? What do you think? It's so clean and soft and very beautif...
- It's ridiculous!! You look like a bear!! Lyor said in a bored tone, half asleep on his chair.

Mrs. Lancel hurried to clarify:

- This is only a fitting, Monsieur. We still have to do the necessary retouchi...

Dalya was offended by Lyor's comment:

- I wasn't talking to you, Ostrich!

Lyor straightened up on his chair rapidly:

- Sorry?
- I don't remember asking for your opinion! repeated Dalya

Lyor replied with an angry tone:

- I should be in the office, working on my files and on my law exams, instead of watching you trying outfits!!
- No one is forcing you to be here!!
- Because you think it makes me happy? Lyor exclaimed.

Mr. Wilfrid tried to intervene:

- Lyor should be here, he is your legal guar...

Dalya interrupted him with an angry voice:

- The Governor should have chosen someone sane as guardian!

Lyor asked in a shock:

- Wait ... did you just call me an idiot?

Mrs. Lancel felt the tension rising in the couture shop:

- Mademoiselle ... Monsieur ... please calm d...

Dalya naturally replied:

- It was you who said it this time!

Lyor lost his calm:

- ARE YOU PLANNING ON TREATING ME AS AN IDIOT FOR LONG?

And Dalya also lost her calm:

- AS LONG AS YOU NEED TO HAVE GOOD MANNERS!!!

Mrs. Lancel was worried:

- No Monsieur... this is not what Mademoiselle wanted to sa....

Dalya exploded:

- BUT HE STARTED IT!!!

Lyor couldn't restrain his temper:

- BECAUSE YOU NEVER STOP PROVOKING ME!!

A server came close to Mr. Wilfrid and he asked with a hesitant whisper, in front of the unusual scene unfolding in the couture shop:

- M ... Monsieur ... would you like something to drink? Tea? Coffee?

Lyor yelled:

- CAN'T YOU THINK BEFORE YOU SPEAK?!

Dalya also had a loud voice:

- HARD TO DO THAT WHEN I'M FACING AN IDIOT!!!

Mr. Wilfrid turned back toward the server and he sighed:

- 2 aspirins, please.

Chapter 23

A hand movement

Monday, September 07th, 1891. At the Royal Georgetown College.

The air became cooler, wind blew out a little more often, and trees around the school blemished in brown and yellow leaves, clouds filled the sky. The city of Georgetown was getting prepared to host the fall season.

It was the busiest time of the year for the Concierge, to clean the dead fallen leaves was not an easy task. While he was sweeping the stairs of the College entrance, the bell rang the end of classes and all the students were leaving the school.

Eriem Eyelord and Gael Benoble headed toward the exit, leading their court of students. Suddenly, Eriem Eyelord stopped and turned around to the Concierge. She said in a strangely nice voice:

- Good evening, Dadès.

The Concierge continued to sweep the fallen leaves from the ground, and without raising his head, he replied in a cheerful voice:

- Good evening Mam'selle ...

Eriem Eyelord continued in a serious voice, barely holding her laugh:

- Still inane, Dadès?

The students surrounding her giggled and laughed at the scene that will follow. They approved and admired all the jokes and the attitudes of Eriem Eyelord and Gael Benoble. As cruel and insolent as they can be.

The school Concierge turned toward Eriem, Gael and their court. Holding his broom proudly, Dadès raised his head and he looked at them for a moment, with an innocent smile. And then, Dadès replied in a calm and a confident voice:

- Less inane than before ... Mam'selle Eriem Eyelord!

The student's laughter stopped immediately. Eriem Eyelord and Gael Benoble exchanged a confused look, unsure of what they had just heard. Everyone thought they heard the Concierge answer something other than what they expected him to do. Yet, Eriem Eyelord continued on her joke, always in a serious and arrogant voice:

- It's fun to have a moron Concierge in our school!

Dadès looked her straight in the eyes, and he replied immediately with a different accent but quite clear words:

- Not moron for long ... Mam'selle Eriem Eyelord ... not moron for long!

This time, all the students froze in their places. No one dared to laugh, or say a word or make a move. Eriem Eyelord and Gael Benoble exchanged a well shocked look this time, but neither said a word. The Concierge Dadès perfectly spoke the language, and he understood all the words!

After long seconds of a heavy silence, the Concierge Dadès moved closer to Eriem Eyelord and her court, holding firmly his broom in his hands. Dadès said in a confident voice, displaying a natural smile:

- If your parents did not teach you good manners ... to respect all people ... to not mock ignorant people ... Mam'selle Eriem Eyelord ... I volunteer to do it.

In a second, Eriem Eyelord exploded in anger, even if she couldn't hide her trembling voice:

- How dare a Concierge like you give me lessons of good conduct?
- You need it Mam'selle ... you all need it!

The Concierge stared with a threatening look, at all the students among Eriem Eyelord's court. Her classmate, Gael Benoble was also stunned by the turn of the situation, yet Gael dared to say:

- But, you are just a Concierge! ... You don't have the right to speak to us on that tone!

And immediately, without any hesitation, Dadès replied with a loud strong angry voice:

- Really? ... And you have the right to laugh at me and call me moron and inane?

Gael Benoble swallowed his pride, and fell silent once and for all. Dadès continued in a calm and menacing voice:

- The Concierge is honorable profession. Fortunately, there are well-educated and honest people in this school ... but none of you is one of them!

Dadès smiled proudly. Then, he turned back to sweep the stairs of the school entrance.

Several weeks before, a strange little box helped the Concierge, out of the darkness into the dawn ... being illuminated by 26 lights of alphabets and letters...

Whether we like it or not ... the Excelbox made its choice ... deciding that knowledge is, against cruelty, an ally ... reminding that knowledge is, against insolence, a dignity...

Eriem Eyelord was petrified and she turned all pale, Gael Benoble was furious, all the students were afraid to speak or to move. Never someone had put into their place Eriem

Eyelord or Gael Benoble, not even the school Headmaster. Eriem and Gael were well famous; their families were among the richest and most distinguished of the Noble class in Georgetown city. Nobody ever dared to confront them ... until now.

Gael Benoble came close to Eriem Eyelord and he asked her:

- What just happened? ... How the hell could he have learned our language?

At that moment, a student stepped out from Eriem's court. Her name was Lakita Fleuritel, she had a big nose and a small mouth, and she wore her long straight black hair in a ponytail. Lakita Fleuritel said proudly:

- I saw her talk to him ... during the summer vacation, she often came to the Library for her catch-up courses ... I saw her talk to him several times at the entrance stairs ... she's probably in for something ...

Gael Benoble asked in a mixed and puzzled look:

- Who is she? Who are you talking about? Who did this?

And he wasn't the only student confused at this moment. The rest of the court were whispering and wondering who had the idea of teaching the language to the school Concierge. All were shocked and confused, except one person; Eriem Eyelord. She seemed less surprised, but more enraged by her discovery, she whispered in a threatening tone:

- So ... just like that ... she thinks she is smart defying me?

Gael Benoble insisted:

- Who are you talking about? Who could have taught him? Who is she?

With a burning angry look, Eriem Eyelord turned toward her friend Gael Benoble:

- She ... The little veggy seller...

Two days later. Wednesday, September 09th, 1891. Classroom N° 48. Geography Course.

The end of the class was announced. Dalya gathered her things and prepared to leave the classroom, following Professor Felozi and the other students. When she stood up from her chair, a hand from behind restrained her and sat her down back on her chair in a brutal move. Dalya turned around to find out who hold her on her chair; it was Gael Benoble.

He displayed a strangely amused smile. Immediately, the other students surrounded Dalya, who was still sitting in her chair. Professor Felozi had already left the classroom with some students, but Amira Mounier remained in the classroom, and she seemed surprised to see what was happening.

Seconds later, Eriem Eyelord appeared in front of Dalya, and she asked her in a calm cold voice:

- So just like that, you wish to re-educate us?

Dalya didn't know what was happening and what the students could possibly want from her. She replied naturally:

- I don't know what you're talking about.

Eriem Eyelord continued:

- And you also lie!

Dalya insisted:

- I can't lie about something I don't know about!

Gael Benoble was still standing behind Dalya, he exclaimed in a mocking tone:

- And she thinks she is smart!

Bursts of laughs invaded the classroom. All the students surrounding Dalya were laughing. Except Amira Mounier, she remained seated a few chairs away, surprised and confused at what she was witnessing, not daring to move or speak.

And although the situation didn't announce to end well, yet Dalya dared to ask the reason for the strange attitude of Eriem and her court toward her:

- What is happening? What do you want from me?

At this moment, Lakita Fleuritel came out among the students surrounding Dalya, and she exclaimed:

- Don't try to lie to us!!!
- Lying about what? Dalya asked in exasperation.

Lakita Fleuritel announced in a proud voice:

- I saw you several times talking to him ... the school Concierge ... during the summer holidays ... I told them that it was you who taught him our language!! ... I saw you and I uncovered you to Eriem and everyone else!!

Lakita Fleuritel seemed so proud to have reported what she had seen, and especially to have uncovered Dalya. Lakita smiled triumphantly, as if she had just succeeded an achievement.

Eriem Eyelord asked Dalya in a calm voice:

- I'm curious to know, why did you teach him our language?

At that moment, Dalya understood what provoked the students of her class. And to get out of this situation, she had to be smarter than the others, so as not to undergo the consequences of their anger. Dalya replied as naturally as possible:

- I thought it would be useful for him ... to do well his job. He had troubles to understand Director Darkfett's instructions and orders.

The other students were somehow convinced by Dalya's answer, but not Eriem Eyelord. She let out a cold laugh that resounded throughout the walls of the classroom:

- To help him do well his job? … Just that? ... And you think that by being kind and helpful, you will have friends in this school? ... But really, you live in the Calinours world!!

All the students laughed. Suddenly, Eriem looked at Dalya with a menacing stare, and she gave a strong and sudden knock on Dalya's desk:

- Listen to me carefully!! ... You're only a veggy seller and you will never belong to our social status no matter what your fortune can be!! Understand well your place in society ... we are at the top, you're at the bottom of the rat hole. So don't ever think to defy us again! Otherwise …

Under the threatening looks of all the students around her, Dalya expected the worst. She was not strong or big enough to defend herself against all these students.

At this moment, Eriem stepped back slowly, displaying a strange smile. And what came afterwards happened so quickly. Gael Benoble appeared in front of Dalya, and he moved his right hand fist toward Dalya's face!!

Instinctively ... without a second to think ... Dalya got up at once and she blocked the hand fist coming toward her. Dalya pushed away Gael's hand, forming a semi-circle with her left hand, and then she stretched her right hand forward and hit Gael's chest!!

Dalya's strange strong hand movement didn't just block Gael Benoble's attack. Despite the boy's big size, Gael Benoble lost his balance and he fell to the floor.

All the students stepped back immediately, shocked and surprised. Eriem Eyelord's smile disappeared at once. Everyone looked at Dalya in a petrified stare.

The students weren't the only ones astonished by what happened. Dalya herself was surprised that she dodged the attack, and she hit Gael Benoble down to the floor ... and mostly Dalya was shocked of her hand movement. Instantly, thousand questions invaded her mind:

- How did she do that? Why did her hands behaved like that? All in one second? Spontaneously? Gael is stronger and bigger than she is ... How did she manage to put him down to the floor?

No one, not even Dalya had an idea about what had just happened. After several long seconds of tense silence, Eriem Eyelord decided to turn around and walk out of the classroom, followed by her court and Gael Benoble who stood up in a jump, without anyone saying one more word.

After the students left the classroom, Dalya could finally breathe normally and recover from this incident. Dalya became aware of Amira's presence, only when Amira stood up from her chair and left the classroom, too. On her way out, Amira Mounier observed Dalya with discreet and curious stares. As long as she could remember, never Amira has seen anyone stand up and confront Eriem and her court ... even less block a fist punch and hit down Gael Benoble to the floor!

Throughout the night, in her bedroom at the Annex house of the grand Mansion, Dalya couldn't sleep. A whirlwind of unanswered questions was running at full speed in her mind. And the night was long. When Dalya turned around for the 100th time in her bed, she came in front of her desk, where the Excelbox was placed. And for several minutes, the little girl observed the strange box. Under the moonlight, the Excelbox seemed serene and peaceful, recharging itself on the nightlight; its glass cage was gray.

The first rays of dawn were approaching, Dalya then decided to get up from her bed; she lit her small lamp and sat down in front of her desk. Dalya asked the Excelbox, in a confused voice:

- I don't understand this free cruelty. I didn't do anything wrong ... I've teached a man a foreign language; I helped him ... So why did Lakita uncover me to the others? ... Couldn't she refrain from exposing my actions? ... Why was Lakita so proud of her achievement? ... Why is she so villain?

Dalya lay back on her chair. And after a few seconds, Dalya interrogated the strange box:

- And the other students, why did they surround me? ... Were they planning to laugh at the Concierge forever? ... But it's cruel and despicable ... They should help that poor man, or at least don't make fun of him ... I haven't deserved to be threatened by Eriem ... I didn't deserve Gael attacking me ...

Remembering her hand movement, Dalya continued to talk to the Excelbox:

- And the hand movement that I did ... how could I defend myself? ... How did I dodge his attack? ... Why did my hands act like that, instinctively? ... Without a second to think? ... But how do I know this hand movement?

Despite all the questions that were addressed to it, the Excelbox didn't move, remaining still and serene. Except that Dalya couldn't calm down. And something forced the little girl to write a question, on a small paper:

What is the 3rd clue?

Dalya placed it on the opening of the Excelbox. And as always, the cage of the strange box lightened up. A ray of shining light crossed the 4 iron vines plants, holding the cage. And this time, the Excelbox answered the little girl's question:

For those who laugh
The calinours will giggle too
For those who demean down
The determination will rise up
For those who terrorize
Never will their cowardice overcome
For those who unjustly expose
Their wickedness will pay back
Facing up the mocker, the cruel and the rude
Stubborn, will continue our way up.

Dalya read the paper several times. And as usual, she didn't understand well what the clue meant. And another thing remained in the little girl's mind. She stood up and repeated a hand movement many times. Dalya made a semi-circle with her left hand, and then she stretched her right hand forward. It's because of this strange hand movement that she could block Gael's attack. But ... how was she able to defend herself this way?

Tired of thinking about this question, Dalya returned back to her bed for a few more hours to sleep and rest from a hectic day.

Except that ... what the little girl completely forgot, is that this hand movement wasn't as unfamiliar as it seemed. Dalya had made this move hundreds and hundreds of times ... when she was cleaning the big windows of the classroom N°18 ... while the other students played Musical instruments.

Chapter 24

A tiny ball

Saturday, September 12th, 1891. At the Annex house of the grand Mansion.

That morning, Dalya went back into the kitchen, she had just finished cleaning her bedroom and her little sisters' room too. It was 9:30 AM; the twins were placed on their usual chairs, ready for their breakfast. Mrs. Augustine served them oatmeal with milk and honey. And before leaving the kitchen, Mrs. Augustine ordered Dalya:

- Wash the dishes and dry them. I have to take care of the laundry today ... and make sure your sisters finish their meals!

Dalya washed the plates and cutlery, while checking on her little sisters, with a quick look. Ari and Adi quietly ate the oatmeal with their little wood spoons. Since the twins have learned to eat by themselves, Dalya and her mother were free to do other work.

While washing the dishes, Dalya had her mind elsewhere. She was thinking about an equation in her Mathematics course, which was particularly difficult to solve. Dalya spent several hours last night trying to figure it out, without succeeding.

A few minutes later, Dalya heard her little sisters laugh. She put down her last washed plate on the counter to dry, and then she turned around toward her sisters:

- So ... did you finish your mea...

Dalya froze in her place, she didn't believe her eyes.

- But ... what ... why ...

The twin sisters beat the record of the most unimaginable foolery!

Ari was laughing out loud and Adi ... well Adi had her breakfast plate reversed on her head. Honey was dripping from her curly blond hair. Oatmeal flakes fell on her nose and her cheeks ... and Adi was laughing all happy and proud of herself. Dalya rushed to her little sister Adi.

- What were you thinking? Why did you spill your plate on your head! Look at your hair!! You're all wet in oatmeal!! Mother will be very upset!!

The little twins were giggling aloud, they were amused while observing their big sister Dalya all confused and upset.

Having no other choice, Dalya lifted Adi and she walked toward the bathroom. Dalya placed Adi in the tub, and she cleaned her up from the oatmeal and honey. She washed her sister's hair, dried it quickly and changed her sister's clothes. Then, Dalya came down to the kitchen and she placed Adi back on her chair, next to Ari who had almost finished her oatmeal dish.

Dalya had to prepare the rest of breakfast for her twin sisters. Compote of apricots and a few pieces of apples cut into cubes. Dalya served her sisters their small dessert plates, and then she took on to dry the dishes and put them away in the closets.

Suddenly, Ari let out a loud laugh. And when Dalya turned around to find out why, she exclaimed:

- ADI!!!!

Adi had fruit compote on her hair, apple pieces on her clothes, and her dessert plate on the head. It seems that Adi got used to reverse her meals on her head. Ari encouraged her twin sister with applauses, and the two little sisters giggled.

- No it's not funny!! ... Stop applauding Ari!! ... What is the matter with you both! ... The foolery never ends for you two? ... Not even a day break!

For the second time in less than an hour, Dalya washed apricot compote off her sister Adi's hair, under the applauses and laughs of her twin Ari. And for the second time, Dalya placed her sister Adi back on her chair, around the kitchen table.

Except that this time, Dalya used a little trick to prevent her sister to repeat the same foolery as earlier. So then, before placing the plate of apricot compote in front of Adi, Dalya took a small tube, and she emptied a few drops of gel liquid, in front of Adi's table before fixing her dessert plate above it.

- And here is your breakfast served! Dalya announced very proud.

Dalya used her father's temporary glue to fix Adi's plate on the table to prevent the compote from ending up on Adi's head. While the little twins ate their food quietly, Dalya placed back the dishes in the cupboards. After few minutes, Dalya turned around. And her heart stopped beating.

Ari laughed aloud. And Adi had once again the breakfast plate reversed on her head for the 3rd time! Her curly blond hair was covered by a layer of apricot compote, and she laughed innocently. Dalya wondered:

- But ... how?!

Dalya thought that she was smarter than her sisters, sticking Adi's plate on the table. Except that she had underestimated the little twins and their clever mind. In fact, when Adi was unable to take her plate off the table, Ari lent her own plate to her sister Adi ... and Adi proudly reversed it on her head.

As clever as Dalya could ever be, she was always surpassed by the fooleries of Ari and Adi.

After cleaning her sister for the 3rd time, Dalya decided to walk her little twin sisters outside to the garden. She helped them wear their little boots and hats. Then, all three of them left to the grand Mansion. It was a beautiful weather that day, fresh and sunny.

Instantly, Ari and Adi ran to the Snow Panther, who welcomed them by lowering her head. The little twins went up on Séraphine's back, they hang to her and exclaimed joyfully:

- Ooh!! Zolie kitten!! Zolie Kitten!!

The Snow Panther walked around the garden, sometimes speeding up and sometimes walking slowly, all to the delight of the little twins on her back who laughed happily. The Gardener, Mr. Rosenwald was pulling a little garden carriage, filled with earth soil. Dalya joined him.

- Good morning Mr. Gardener!

The old man greeted her with a head sign:

- Lady Dalya.
- You seem busy today.

The Gardener replied, while continuing to pull his little carriage toward a side of the garden:

- Yes ... and this entire week too. It's almost the rain season; we must plant the seeds before it rains, if we want to have them grown on time. And I have Séraphine to bring to the Doctor, and the car to clean and the grass cutting, and the trees on the left side to cu...

Dalya interrupted him:

- Bring Séraphine to the Doctor? … Is she sick?
- No. But once a year, I take her to the vet for her regular vaccine. Her checkup is next Saturday.

When the Gardener stopped his small carriage near a large clay vase, Dalya asked:

- I can cut the grass, if you want? ... I know how to do it! ... I cut the Annex house grass myself, once a month! ... And I can also wash the car after I finish…

The Gardener observed the little girl, for a long minute. The old man still had trouble to understand and accept the little girl's spontaneous manners. She participated in all the garden work and the cleaning ... yet, she was the future Heiress of the biggest fortune of the United States of America.

- As you wish, Lady Dalya. Replied the Gardener, with a discreet smile.

Sunday, September 13th, 1891.

Cristelle, the household maid of the grand Mansion, was cleaning the window frames of the living room. Fortunately, the grand Mansion was uninhabited. To clean all the rooms and living rooms, in a single day would have been an impossible chore to Cristelle. Since joining the grand Mansion, Cristelle cleaned the rooms of this huge house by following a diligent and organized schedule. Every day, she had specific rooms and places to clean.

When she noticed the little Dalya Bouvard walking outside toward the exit, Cristelle knocked on the window and she made a hand sign to Dalya to come inside. By the garden door, Dalya entered the living room of the Mansion.

- Good morning Cristelle. How are you today?

The maid Cristelle has always admired the politeness and natural manners of the little Heiress.

- Good, mademoiselle, thank you for asking. Are you heading to the city?
- Yes. I was going to meet some friends at the market in front of the Toscana restaurant.

The maid Cristelle exclaimed:

- It is a great market ... Anything you want can be found there!! And the products are always fresh!!

Dalya asked:

- Do you still have some cleaning to do in this living room? Do you need any help?

The maid Cristelle laughed:

- You are the only Heiress who loves doing housework!!

Dalya laughed too:

- Not yet Heiress ...

The maid Cristelle smiled:

- I have just finished cleaning this living room's windows. I still have to clean the windows of the room above. And I admit, just thinking about the endless stairs leading to this room, I already feel aches in the legs.

Besides the living room and the Library of the grand Mansion, Dalya had never visited the huge Mansion. The Lawyer Mr. Ernest Laszlo had formally banned her from entering the grand Mansion. However, the maid Cristelle allowed Dalya to sit in the Library as long as she wanted.

- I can help you carry up the brooms and the buckets to the top floor. Dalya proposed.

Cristelle agreed. They both came out of the living room, checking left and right that no one was following them. When they arrived to the upper floor, Cristelle walked toward the vast corridor. Dark and long, the corridor was decorated with several paintings, tables and empty vases. Huge luxurious chandeliers in the ceiling reflected no light.

When Cristelle opened the door of a room, Dalya followed her inside. The room was invaded by darkness. A huge bed was placed in the center, long velvet curtains prohibited light from coming inside, a wood desk was placed in a corner, and a carpet was on the floor. Dalya wondered aloud:

- Is this ...

Cristelle understood the little girl's question. She replied:

- Yes. This is the bedroom of the Late Mr. Governor.

Instantly, Cristelle pulled the curtains away, which illuminated the bedroom in a second. The covers and pillows of the huge bed were in a prestigious and soft fabric, a large fireplace appeared from darkness all suddenly, the wood desk was clearer and luxurious, and the carpet on the floor displayed beautiful colors. The bedroom brightened.

- And even if he passed away, I make sure to clean his room, regularly. Cristelle affirmed.

Dalya smiled at Cristelle kind gesture toward her late employer. When Cristelle took a wet sponge to clean the window, Dalya helped her clean the edges, with a dry cloth. After they finished cleaning the windows, Cristelle knelt in front of the large fireplace in the room, and she cleaned off the dust.

And the little girl couldn't help but observe the bedroom with a curious eye; Dalya walked around in the luxurious room, watching the prestigious furniture and the refined fabrics. When suddenly, Dalya noticed a strange item on top of the desk. There was a small clear glass vase filled with tiny balls, in many colors.

- What is this? Dalya asked all curious.
- Oh ... these are the pressure tiny balls of Mr. Iskander Balthazar. Cristelle replied spontaneously.
- Pressure ... tiny balls? Dalya still didn't know what she meant.

Cristelle stood up and approached Dalya; she took a ball from the vase, and she explained:

- During his last years, Mr. Iskander Balthazar was suffering from a back pain. Despite the prescribed medications, he would feel hard pain in the most unlikely times, during important meetings and work sessions. So then, to endure and handle the pain a few more hours, one of the Doctors advised him to use these tiny pressure balls.
- How does it work, Cristelle?

The young woman went on to explain, holding the ball in her hand:

- Apparently ... when you squeeze the tiny ball in your hand ... the pressure of your body focuses on the hand holding the ball ... and you feel less pain elsewhere ...

Never Dalya had heard such a thing. A ball to ease the pressure of back pain:

- Is it possible?
- Yes ... Mr. Iskander was complaining less from his back pain ... it is as if the pain in his back was reduced ... and there is more pressure on his hand holding the ball, that he no longer feels the back pain ... a bit as if the pain is displaced from his back to his hand ...

When suddenly, Dalya remembered some specific words:

In 1703, the pressure will be displaced,

Dalya squeezed the tiny ball in her own hand, and she thought aloud:

- Pain is displaced from his back to his hand ... pain is displaced … pain … the pressure on her throat … the pressure on her throat ... so the pressure on her throat can be displaced … the pressure can be displaced, yes! That's what the clue said ... pressure will be displaced from her throat to her hand … but the number, what does it mean?

After a few seconds of hard thinking, Dalya approached Cristelle who was cleaning the chimney.

- Cristelle ... does the number 1703 mean anything to you?

Without looking at her, or even stopping her work, Cristelle naturally replied:

- 1703 ... it's the postcode of the grand Mansion, Mademoiselle.

Dalya was thunderstruck. She finally understood what the clue meant. Dalya asked:

- Cristelle, can I have a tiny pressure ball? Only one ... it's for someone else who needs it ... if you don't mind, of course!
- Certainly, Mademoiselle ... I don't see why not ... after all, you are the Heiress of Mr. Iskander Balthazar.

Dalya thanked Cristelle with a smile, and then she left Mr. Iskander Balthazar's bedroom. The little girl went down the big stairs in a hurry. Dalya knew exactly what to do now. She left the grand Mansion and ran toward the Annex house.

Tuesday, September 15th, 1891. Course of Geography, room N° 48.

The Geography Professor wasn't yet in the classroom. Amira came in and noticed that almost all the other students had already arrived before her. She sat on her usual chair, without daring to join Eriem and her court.

- No bee sounds today, Amira? Gael asked in a mocking tone.

Amira Mounier took out her Geography book, and she focused on her reading, to avoid listening to the students' laughs.

- She understood that she doesn't belong in our world. Eriem replied.
- Finally!! It took her some time!! Salman added.
- We are well entertained in this year's class. Eriem said, observing Dalya sitting on her chair, with an arrogant stare, before continuing:
- One who lives in the Calinours world ... and the other who wants to join a much higher world than hers!!

While all the students burst out laughing, Amira sat still on her chair, intimidated by the other students' comments on her. When Professor Felozi entered the classroom, the Geography lesson began.

- Good morning. Please open your books to page 45!

Professor Felozi faced the students and he explained in a loud and strong voice:

- In today's class, we will study one of the geographer's tools ... the maps and the plans. Gael, please read us the definition of the plan.

Gael stood up and read aloud:

- The plan is a simplified representation of a space. On the plan, the street pattern is indicated, as well as roads, parks and marine borders.

Professor Felozi said:

- Good. Lakita Fleuritel, continue. What other information is contained in the plans?

Lakita Fleuritel stood up and she spoke in a clear voice:

- On the plans, there are street names, the locations of major government departments such as town halls. As well as schools, churches ...
- Well ... well. Eriem, read the definition of the map.

Eriem too stood up and she read:

- The map can transmit information by locating them in a space. The map represents a larger space than the one shown in the plan.
- Excellent. Amira, continue ... what are the different types of maps?

Amira jumped up from her seat, she stood up, she took the book in her hand, and then she read as loud as she could, in a slow but clear voice:

- There ... are several types ... of maps ...

- Faster!! Yelled the Professor.
- The p ... p ... political ... maps ... the them ... them ... thematic ... maps ...

Professor Felozi thought aloud:

- I have in my 14 years' olds class, a student who don't know how to read!!

A wave of laughs invaded the classroom. All the students turned around, watching Amira Mounier and laughing aloud.

- Salman Elpacha ... Please take on this paragraph.

The young boy stood up proudly and he read quickly:

- There are several types of maps, political maps, thematic maps, topographic maps ...

Amira Mounier sat back on her chair, with a crushed feeling. You would think that Amira Mounier got used to the students and teachers' mockery, since the first day she came to this school. Except that Amira wasn't getting used to any of it, every mockery hurt her even more than before, and it confirmed her inability to succeed like the other students. And although she was as smart and studious as everyone else, although she knew all the answers to the teachers' questions, Amira was unable to overcome her weakness, a normal clear allocution.

At the end of her classes and her day, Amira Mounier went back home. The weather presaged a cold night, a gray sky and a cool wind. A usual September day.

The road to the house was filled with shops and passersby. To the right of a street, Amira turned and took a few steps more, then she stopped at a house somewhat strange. The house was distinct from all the others. The entire street was of gray brick houses, except that one. The strange house was painted in blue wood. Although small and narrow, the house was in two levels, with two large windows in each level, a roof that let out 2 fireplace outputs, and 4 steps before a little entrance door in the middle. The house seemed modest, but it was well maintained.

When she opened the door, Amira was surprised with a terrible smell. She dropped her backpack on the stairs in front of her, and then she turned left into the small kitchen. The space was neat; a stove, an oven and a countertop were installed in one side of the kitchen, a small table and two chairs were placed in front of the large window.

- Good evening, my champion!!

Mr. Jacob Mounier was a man in his mid-thirties, with a little belly and filled cheeks. He wore a white shirt, a suit and a brown tie, beneath a large pink apron, which amplified his chubby size and gave him a funny look. Amira approached him and she asked hesitantly:

- Hello papa ... what ... are you cooking?

Mr. Mounier proudly turned to his daughter and he showed her a pot:

- A ratatouille!!

Amira looked at the pot, but she couldn't clearly see a ratatouille recipe. All the food was way too cooked and they all turned into a brown color. Mr. Mounier was far from being a good Cook, yet, he tried all his best to take care of his only daughter. Given the confused face expression of his daughter while looking at the pot, Mr. Mounier giggled:

- I think I've missed the recipe for tonight!

Amira smiled sweetly:

- I'll take care of dinner, papa. Let me handle it. I will change my clothes and I'll cook us some good pasta.

Mr. Mounier tenderly kissed his daughter on her head, he placed back the pot, took off his pink apron and then he walked toward the living room in front of the kitchen. Two big red chairs were installed in front of the small fireplace. A round coffee table in the middle. Several books and files were piled on the floor, forming columns. Mr. Mounier settled on a small desk in dark wood, placed in front of the large window overlooking at the street.

- You'll never guess what happened today!!

The house was so small and tiny; Amira could be in her bedroom on the 2nd floor and have a conversation with her father who was in the living room on the 1st floor. While she was changing from her school uniform, Amira asked:

- Where, papa? In your work?
- Yes!! In the office!! Mr. Bankster reviewed the previous month accounts and he found an error!!

Amira walked to the only bathroom in the house, which was separating the two bedrooms. She undid her long braids; she brought her hair together in a large chignon, before wearing a large night cap on her head to hold her bun:

- How much was missing, papa?
- 4 000 $!!
- What?! But it is a huge sum!!

Mr. Mounier turned the pages of a register and he also exclaimed:

- Yes it is!! Mr. Bankster became all pale, he almost fainted!!

Amira went down to the kitchen and she wore her own apron, shorter and smaller than her father's. She laughed:

- I can imagine that!! If he loses one single dollar, Mr. Bankster would go crazy!! But 4 000 $ ... I would have loved to see his face, papa!!

Amira and her father laughed out loud for several minutes. Without any hesitation, Amira threw all the contents of the pot that her father had cooked. She put the pasta to boil in a pot, and then twirled the diced tomatoes, garlic and onions in a pan. Mr. Mounier, busy calculating the numbers on a large register in the opposite room, he continued to explain:

- We eventually found the missing 4 000 $.

Amira was stirring the sauce slowly, when she jumped:

- How?

Mr. Mounier replied proudly:

- I recalculated several times ... when I realized that Mr. Bankster forgot to declare the amount he had taken from the cash register, to organize his little boy's birthday party!!

Amira froze, holding the wood spoon:

- The birthday party of his lazy son cost 4 000 $?!
- Oh yes ... apparently, Mr. Bankster is stingy for everyone, except on his son. I even heard from the Secretary, that at this party, there were clowns, games, and even inflatable toys.

Amira put the cooked pasta in two plates, and she was about to pour the tomato sauce and chopped herbs on top:

- Well, papa ... you surely saved his life today. If you haven't found the missing 4 000 $...
- Mr. Bankster would have not slept tonight!!

Amira and her father sat on the small dining table in the kitchen, in front of the large window. They giggled all through dinner on this story.

Mr. Jacob Mounier was well aware of his daughter's difficulty to speak and pronounce her words. The young father tried by all means to comfort his daughter, from her long hard days at school. Mr. Mounier told her every night around the dinner table, funny and amusing stories. She was his only daughter, and he loved her so dearly.

At the end of dinner, Amira took care of the dishes, while her father arranged his large folder. When suddenly, Mr. Mounier noticed through the window in front of his small desk, that the sign of the mail box was filled.

- Well ... this is weird ... I thought the postman comes only the morning and not at night ...

Busy putting back the dishes as quickly as she could, in order to do her homework, Amira didn't pay attention to what her father said. Mr. Jacob Mounier left the house; he opened the letter box and he pulled out a small package. Amira was about to go up to her bedroom, when her father closed the entrance door of the house and he gave her a small package:

- I believe this is for you, my champion.

Amira and her father were both confused. Amira had never received packages or letters from anyone.

- For me? ... Are you sure, papa? ... But who could have sent me that?

Being both curious, Amira took the little package from her father's hands.

- Who is the sender?

Amira turned the package in every angle:

- There is no name ... who could have sent me this?!

Both eager to discover what there was inside, Amira immediately opened the package in front of her father. Inside, there was a small sponge tiny ball. The father and the daughter exchanged a surprised look. Mr. Jacob Mounier asked:

- Is there any note inside of it?

Amira pulled out a little paper from the package and she read aloud:

Press the ball, the pressure will be displaced.

Amira and her father didn't understand what the sentence meant. Mr. Mounier returned to his small desk in the living room, thinking aloud carelessly:

- It may be a package that arrived by mistake ... it happens all the time!

Except that it was not a mistake. Since some time now, Amira would find little papers in her backpack or on her desk table, strange and bizarre messages. And that night, Amira was convinced that this package didn't arrive by mistake, like her father was thinking.

In her little bedroom, Amira sat on her bed. Although her father was a modest accountant in a company, he took care to give his daughter the best life. Amira's room had a small cozy bed with blankets and pillows in pink covers, a small desk in front of the large window, with some shelves for her books, a small wardrobe with a mirror above and a large closet for her clothes and shoes. Mr. Mounier made sure that his unique daughter lacked of nothing.

For a few minutes, Amira read the message she had received, at least fifteen times. She returned the package several times in all the angles, but there was no clue of the mysterious sender.

- Press the ball ... the pressure displaced ... but, it doesn't make any sense ... when we press the ball, nothing happens ... how can we move the pressure? ... The pressure cannot be displaced?! ... it is illogical ...

While thinking aloud, Amira was squeezing the ball in her hand. And suddenly, in an instant ... Amira understood!!

When Amira firmly pressed the ball in her hand ... the pressure on her throat moved to her hand, which released her throat's vocal cords, and it allowed her to better breath and talk!!

The little girl jumped out of her bed and she screamed with all her strength:

- PAPA!!! PAPA!!! IT WORKS!!! I DON'T KNOW HOW ... BUT IT WORKS!!

Mr. Jacob Mounier jumped and he instantly found himself on the 2nd floor in his daughter's bedroom:

- What happened?! ... What's wrong?! ... Is everything alright?!

Amira immediately showed him the tiny ball:

- Look papa!! Look!! ... When I press the ball ... I don't feel the pressure on my throat!! ... I don't understand how exactly it works ... It's just easier to talk when I squeeze the ball!

Mr. Mounier seemed confused but happy, all at the same time:

- It's ... how it ... but it's great!! ... Only with this tiny ball? Are you sure? ... But who ... it's amazing!! ... Your throat is really relaxed? ... It's incredible!!

Although the father and his daughter didn't know how the tiny pressure ball worked and who sent the package to their home, Mr. Jacob Mounier and Amira jumped, danced and laughed aloud, happy about their discovery.

In fact, the unknown sender was standing immobile outside, in the street right in front of the Mounier's house. Watching the father and his daughter jumping joyfully, through the window of the 2nd floor bedroom ... The unknown sender smiled, sincerely.

Because no failure is infinite ... when will and continuity are picked. This is what the Excelbox affirmed since a while ... and this is what should be believed since now.

Chapter 25

A slap swallowed

Saturday, September 19th, 1891. In the Grand Mansion.

Dalya returned earlier from her grocery shopping at the market, that day. Usually, Séraphine waits for her near the main gate of the grand Mansion, and sometimes the Snow Panther even walks with her to the Annex house. Except that day, Dalya noticed the absence of Séraphine. She remembered that the Gardener told her about the Panther's annual medical checkup.

As soon as Dalya entered the big garden, she was called by the head of the grand Mansion, Mr. Bûchebois.

- Mademoiselle ... Mr. Ernest Laszlo request your presence at the living room.

Surprised by this request, Dalya followed the head of the grand Mansion, inside the house. Many people were present in the living room. The Lawyer, Mr. Ernest was sitting on one of the big chairs, and all the employees of the grand Mansion were standing in a straight line. The maid Cristelle, the help Cook Océanie, the Cook Mr. Ferrero, the server Igor. The head of the Mansion stood alongside the other employees.

Dalya noticed that there was some tension in the air. Mr. Ernest Laszlo seemed in an angry mood. The employees of the grand Mansion were all silent; they seemed very intimidated by the Lawyer's presence. Mr. Ernest Laszlo observed Dalya for many long tense seconds, no one dared to move or say a word. The Lawyer finally spoke in a calm cold voice:

- I thought I have been clear ...

Dalya was standing in front of Mr. Ernest Laszlo; she didn't understand what the Lawyer meant. Yet, she did not dare to ask him. Mr. Ernest Laszlo continued:

- You disobeyed me ...

This time, Dalya was forced to ask, to know what he was talking about.

- I don't understand what you mean, Mr. Ernest.

The Lawyer was always shocked by the audacity of the little girl. It was something that he didn't like much, while everyone else trembled at his presence. Mr. Ernest explained calmly:

- You dared to enter the grand Mansion ... even though I have forbidden you from coming inside. It seems to me, that a poor little vermin like you, doesn't know how to obey to rules and orders.

Dalya's heart speeded and her throat tightened. She didn't know how Mr. Ernest Laszlo knew she got inside the grand Mansion. And she didn't dare to look at Cristelle at that moment; she feared that could reveal her. Dalya gathered all her courage and she said in a natural voice:

- I don't know what you are talking about Monsi...
- Needless to lie, kid!! Ernest interrupted her.

The Lawyer turned toward the employees.

- Océanie ... what have you seen?

All the eyes turned toward the help Cook of the grand Mansion, Océanie Shell.

The young girl of thin allure, and dark curly chestnut hair, was wearing her usual white work apron. Her large curious eyes and a pointed scrutinizer nose were noticed by afar. Océanie didn't seem in the slightest, intimidated by the situation, but rather displayed a proud smile.

- Sunday of last week ... I saw this little girl coming down the stairs of the grand Mansion hall ... and she was holding an object that belonged to Mr. Iskander Balthazar.

In a second, Dalya was thunderstruck. She had always left the grand Mansion in quiet steps. Yet, that day, Dalya wasn't careful enough, she was in a hurry. Mr. Ernest turned to Dalya and he asked in an arrogant tone:

- So ... who allowed you to enter this Mansion?

Dalya replied straightaway:

- No one.

Mr. Ernest Laszlo wasn't convinced with this answer:

- I repeat my question ... who allowed you to enter this Mansion?
- No one, Mons...
- WRONG!! YOU ARE LYING!!

Dalya remained silent. Mr. Ernest Laszlo yelled:

- WHO ALLOWED YOU TO COME INSIDE??!!

Dalya tried to keep her calm:

- I assure you that no one helped me to get inside, Monsieur.
- So then, you entered this house ... alone ... without anyone's help?
- Yes, Monsieur.

None of the employees dared to move or say a word. Mr. Ernest Laszlo got up from his chair and he came close to Dalya with slow steps, while staring at her:

- And ... may I know what you were doing inside this house?

Dalya hesitated a few seconds, and then she answered in the most confident voice possible:

- I ... I was visiting the grand Mansion, Monsieur. I was curious to see what was inside this place.

Mr. Ernest displayed a strange smile that gave Dalya chills. He continued to question her:

- And what is this object that you took during your … visit of this house?

This time, Dalya had no other answer to give but the truth. She replied calmly:

- I found a tiny ball, Monsieur.

Mr. Ernest Laszlo looked at Dalya for a moment, and then he laughed aloud. Neither the employees nor Dalya could understand Mr. Ernest's reaction, even less the reason for his laugh. Besides, no one has ever seen or heard the Lawyer laugh. He always displayed a marble face and an arrogant bad mood. But on that day, his laugh invaded the living room of the grand Mansion.

When suddenly, brutally and out of nowhere, Dalya received a slap. The movement was so violent and brusque that Dalya spun around, she lost her balance and she fell to the ground instantly. Her cheek inflated and became red, a small drop of blood appeared at the end of her lips.

- DON'T YOU EVER TREAT ME LIKE AN IDIOT!! NO ONE LIES TO ME!!

The Lawyer's eyes displayed a devil look.

The other employees were all shocked to witness Mr. Ernest Laszlo giving a slap to Dalya Bouvard. Cristelle hardly refrained a scream, without daring to intervene. Océanie seemed proud to have uncovered the little girl. The Cook, the head of the Mansion and the server, they all exchanged a worried look, disturbed by what happened in front of them.

Mr. Ernest Laszlo came close to Dalya; he knelt before her, and he said in a calm menacing tone:

- Listen to me, little vermin!! ... I will not repeat my orders a second time ... if I learn again that you have crossed the door of this house without my permission, you will get more than a slap from me. Is that clear enough to you?

Still immobile on the floor, Dalya replied with a trembling voice:

- Yes … Monsieur.

That night, the employees' dinner was held in a tense silence. And it was the first time that all the employees of the grand Mansion were mute. Cristelle's smile disappeared for the first time in many years; she stirred the spoon in her soup bowl, for the 100th times.

The server Igor served himself some bread. He broke the tense silence, and wondered aloud:

- Why did she lie?

None of the employees of the grand Mansion had an exact answer to this question. The server Igor continued:

- Why didn't she just tell him the truth? … quite simply …

Cristelle put her spoon on the table, she lay back on the chair and she answered the question:

- Because she protected me.

All the eyes turned toward her. Igor asked:

- Protect you, Cristelle ... But why?

Cristelle replied with a crushed voice and a tightened throat:

- Because ... I am the one who allowed her inside the grand Mansion.

All the employees were surprised to hear this confidence. The Cook Mr. Ferrero exclaimed:

- Da quando ... since when, Cristelle?

Cristelle explained without daring to raise her eyes:

- Since many months now. I showed her Mr. Iskander Balthazar's Library, one day. This little girl loves reading books. Sometimes, she comes in by the garden's door of the living room, and she spends a few hours in the Library, reading books.

Cristelle took a long breath before continuing:

- She is … different.

The server Igor was curious, like all the other employees as well:

- Different how?

Cristelle looked at him and she smiled sadly:

- Just as she helps the Gardener in the gardening work ... she offers to help me clean the rooms ... she even picked up the ashes of the fireplace in the living room, one day. She is different from all the other owners that I know.

The head of the servers, Mr. Bûchebois asked in a serious tone:

- And what happened the other day, Cristelle?

Cristelle's throat tightened:

- That day, I saw her outside in the garden ... I asked her to join me inside. She wanted to help me clean Mr. Iskander's bedroom. When noticed the pressure tiny balls of the Late Mr. Governor, she asked if she could have one … I didn't see any problem in her taking a tiny ball ... after all, she is the Heiress of the Late Mr. Governor.
- So then … she didn't lie about the tiny ball? Exclaimed the Cook.

Cristelle answered with a confident voice:

- No, she didn't lie about it. She took the tiny ball after asking me permission. Since I know this little girl, she never took anything from the grand Mansion!!

The head of the servers, Mr. Bûchebois thought aloud:

- So … if she had revealed to the Lawyer, that you allowed her to come inside the grand Mansion ...

Cristelle finished Mr. Bûchebois' sentence:

- ... I would have lost my job, and I wouldn't be sitting at this table, on this moment, dinning with you.

At this moment, all the employees had the same idea in their minds. Cristelle affirmed:

- This little girl swallowed a slap to protect a house maid.

A heavy silence invaded the kitchen. The employees needed some time to understand and accept these new revelations. Océanie who had remained silent throughout the entire discussion, she finally said with an arrogant tone:

- You shouldn't have allowed her to come inside the grand Mansion, Cristelle. She is just a poor little veggy seller at the market.

Cristelle turned toward Océanie; and she observed her with an angry stare. All the employees knew that Océanie had many faults. Except that, Cristelle never thought that Océanie could dare to do such a mean thing. Cristelle replied with a defiant angry voice:

- Yes ... this girl may be just a poor little veggy seller at the market ... she may be strange with her worn poor clothes and spontaneous manners ... however, this little girl endured a slap for me, today ... the slap she swallowed because of me, it makes her much more than an Heiress ... and today, I am sure and certain of one thing … this little girl is a Lady!!

All the employees watched Cristelle, and no one dared to interrupt or contradict her, while she repeated with a strong firm voice:

- Lady Dalya Bouvard!!

The same night.

In a narrow street on the South side of Georgetown city, silence ruled. Inside one of the many houses, there was a large square garden with an opened roof. That night, the sky was ornamented with thousands of bright stars. And the garden was also decorated with hundreds candles of a musk scent. The air was fresh, cold wind breezes caressed the leaves and the garden plants.

Master Fong Ka-Ho was sitting on the wood floor since many hours; he was observing the magnificent and calm garden. He closed his eyes for several minutes to marvel at the nature's sounds.

When suddenly, he heard a noise approaching him. Master Fong Ka-Ho didn't move. He waited for the noise getting close to him, to open his eyes.

The Snow Panther looked much scarier at night than on the daylight. Her big sapphire blue eyes were piercing. Her clear gray tattooed fur was formidable. Her large legs gave her a powerful stance. When the Snow Panther was only steps away from him, she stopped and looked at the old man. At this moment, Master Fong Ka-Ho bowed his head toward the Panther in a respectful way.

- Huanying *(welcome).*

The Snow Panther moved closer and she sat near the old man, while facing the large square garden. After several minutes of silence, the Snow Panther looked up toward the full moon, and she let out a long meowing. It was a sad sound. And Master Fong Ka-Ho understood it:

- As Noble as our intention may be ... we unfortunately cannot always protect her.

The Snow Panther looked at the old man. It was as if Séraphine understood Master Fong Ka-Ho's words, but she didn't seem convinced of his answer. The Snow Panther seemed disappointed of herself. The old man caressed the animal's back fur, in a delicate slow gesture.

- Some lessons are hard and difficult to learn … yet necessary for a change to the better.

Master Fong Ka-Ho and the Snow Panther observed the beautiful opened roof garden, for several minutes, in a total silence.

Chapter 26

A payback

Thursday, September 24th, 1891. At the Royal Georgetown College.

The classes were well advanced at school. And despite the pile of homework and the new lessons, Dalya was delighted to learn new things every day. When the Mathematics class ended that day, Dalya spent a few minutes in the school Library. She borrowed a few books before greeting Miss Guendolyn, and she headed toward the school exit. The Concierge Dadès stood near the main stairs, wearing thick gloves in his hands. He greeted Dalya with a joyful smile:

- Hello Lalla Dalya!
- Hello Dadès ... What are you doing?

Dadès showed her a small glass bottle, with a prudent move:

- That ... dangerous ... is to stop growth of grass on stairs ... so that stairs remains nice and clean ...
- Oh ... I understand. That's why you are wearing glov…

When Dalya was called by a voice, in an arrogant tone:

- Fortunately, I told them that it was you!! I was right!!

Lakita Fleuritel was sitting alone on the last step of the school stairs. She was brushing her long straight black hair, which she was always proud of. On a stair next to her, there was a comb and a small hair oil glass bottle. And although Dalya only knew Lakita from afar, Dalya couldn't understand how someone can be proud of their meanness. Dalya asked her:

- Was it necessary?

Lakita Fleuritel seemed surprised by this question. Dalya repeated in a serious voice:

- Was it necessary to uncover what I had done? Telling the other students that I've teached the Concierge our language? Was it necessary?

Lakita Fleuritel became pale in a second. Yet, she answered Dalya with an arrogant voice:

- You shouldn't have helped him!

Dalya replied immediately:

- You shouldn't have uncovered me to the other students!

Lakita laughed:

- He is only a poor Concierge!

Dalya hardly retained her anger, she completed Lakita's sentence:

- A poor Concierge to help ... not to humiliate!

Lakita fell silent; she lost her words, not knowing what to say to defend her meanness. And Dalya didn't wait for an answer to her comment. She turned around to Dadès and she smiled at him before leaving school:

- Good day Dadès!

Dadès put the glass bottle on the last step of the stairs and he replied:

- Good day Lalla Dalya!

Lakita Fleuritel continued brushing her hair. Dadès continued his work. And Dalya continued her way out.

Except that one small thing swapped without anyone noticing it. Two identical glass bottles were exchanged by an innocent mistake. A bottle filled with oil to stimulate hair growth. The other bottle filled with oil to stop once indefinitely the grass growth.

Lakita Fleuritel poured several drops on her comb, and she brushed her long straight black hair with a slow and an arrogant move.

If there is one thing you need to be assured and certain of ... is that for those who unjustly expose ... their wickedness will always be paid back!

Chapter 27

Stubborn

Friday, October 02nd, 1891.

The maid, Cristelle was sitting on a garden bench, near the front door of the grand Mansion. Usually brave, Cristelle was nervous for the first time in her life; she didn't know what words to say. It had been several nights now, since Cristelle couldn't even sleep.

When she noticed a little silhouette approaching the grand Mansion, Cristelle stood up at once, her heart tightened and her throat choked. When the little girl noticed Cristelle, she addressed her with a natural smile:

- Hello Cristelle!!

Cristelle murmured in a small trembling voice:

- Good ... Good evening Mademoiselle. You are coming back from school?

Dalya sighed:

- Yes ... and it was a long day!! The classes are accelerated. All the teachers charged us with tons of homework for the weekend. I don't even know where to star...

Suddenly, Dalya stopped speaking. She noticed Cristelle's discomfort. The maid of the grand Mansion displayed a gray face, dark under-eyes circles, her usual smile had faded away and she looked nervous.

- Cristelle ... is something wrong?

The maid wanted to speak, but words failed to come out of her mouth.

- What is it, Cristelle?

Dalya guessed that Cristelle was not feeling well. Never Dalya has seen her in such a state. Cristelle was always smiling and alive. It was the first time that she was so stressed. The maid of the grand Mansion didn't dare to look Dalya in the eyes, Cristelle murmured:

- It's just ... I wanted to ... I should have intervened ... I didn't do ... the other day … he …

Although her words were incoherent, Dalya Bouvard had a little clue of what was bothering Cristelle. Dalya said in a regretful voice:

- About the other day, Cristelle, I'm so sorry if I've put you in trouble with Mr. Ernest Laszlo. Even if the Lawyer insisted to know, I would have never revealed you to anyone!!

You were very kind to allow me to enter the Governor's Library ... I will always be grateful to you about that, Cristelle!

Given the silent and motionless attitude of Cristelle, Dalya continued:

- And I promise to never go inside the grand Mansion again. I certainly don't want you to have worries because of me ... I'm sorry for what happened the other day.

Cristelle couldn't believe what she was hearing. She looked at the little girl for a while with a confused and a surprised look. Cristelle was always fascinated by the spontaneous manners of the little girl. But this time, Cristelle was seduced by the kindness and goodness of Dalya.

When suddenly, her eyes in tears, Cristelle interrupted Dalya and she screamed:

- But ... Mademoiselle!! I am the one who should apologize for putting you in this situation!! I never thought that the Lawyer would be capable of such cruelty toward you!! I never liked this Ernest Laszlo anyway!! And I never thought he would dare to hurt you!! I'm so sorry Mademoiselle!! Sincerely sorry!!

And even if the maid of the grand Mansion was difficult to reassure and convince, Dalya did her best to calm her down and relieve her guilt.

- It's nothing serious, Cristelle!! And it was your fault ... I shouldn't have entered the grand Mansion, without the permission of Mr. Erne...

Cristelle exclaimed:

- But you have done nothing wrong, Mademoiselle!! You didn't deserve to be treated this way!! It was only a little worthless tiny ball!!

On that moment, Dalya couldn't repress an innocent laugh. Cristelle froze in her place, not understanding what had made the little girl laugh.

- Oh, Cristelle ... believe me, it was more than a little worthless tiny ball!

Walking both toward the huge garden of the grand Mansion, Dalya was proud and amused to tell Cristelle how this little worthless tiny ball ... has made 2 people dance!

Because if the little girl had stopped and given up, none of this would have been. It is often true, that the best thing to do, facing up the mocker, the cruel and the rude, is to continue your way up. Never stop, and never give up. And luckily, Dalya Bouvard was a stubborn little girl.

Chapter 28

Only a feeling

10 years before. In 1881.

The Library of the grand Mansion was a huge oval place, build in 3 floors. The books filled the shelves up to the ceiling. Countless books of all types, shapes, and colors. The place was refined by a splendid golden fireplace, armchairs and luxurious sofas, and white polished marble on the floor. The huge oval ceiling was a transparent glass in multi colored patterns, reflecting beautiful glow on the floor of the grand Mansion's Library.

Iskander Balthazar worked quietly for several hours. When he felt a presence in front of his desk. Without looking up, he could guess in front of him 3 little heads barely exceeding the height of his desk. Two little boys and a little girl, stood motionless observing Iskander Balthazar working. The man said in a calm voice, without even looking up from his file:

- Hello little intruders.

The 3 little children giggled. The boy asked, all curious:

- What do you do, Sir?

Iskander Balthazar finally raised his head to see the 3 children. The little ones were about 7-8 years old, and they wore humble clothes. Iskander Balthazar answered the child's curiosity:

- I am working on a new project … the expansion of the 12 bridges surrounding our city.

Facing the confused expression of the 3 children, Iskander Balthazar explained:

- It's a project that will benefit the residents of this city. If we increase the capacity of the 12 bridges connecting the city of Georgetown to the other side, we can facilitate the transport of goods and the flow of people, which will benefit the economy of the city. The expansion of these bridges is an important project!

One of the boys asked:

- So then ... you build bridges?

Iskander Balthazar replied:

- Yes and no. I don't build bridges, but I make the work easier for architects, workers, bankers ... to build bridges.
- And so, what is your occupation, Sir? Asked the second boy.
- I am the Governor of Washington State.

Seconds after, the little girl asked curiously:

- What does Governor mean?

Iskander Balthazar was a very patient and tolerant man:

- Being a Governor ... is caring for the people living in a specific territory.

The little girl jumped joyfully:

- So you're like my Aunt Touti, she is Governess too!! She looks after the children of a Noble Monsieur; she puts them to bed, she prepares them food and she takes them to parks!!

Iskander was struck by the comparison of the little girl; he hardly refrained his amused laugh:

- Well ... in some ways, yes ... I'm a bit like your Aunt Touti ... Governess ... except that I'm the Governess of many many people ...

At the door of the Library, someone could hold a laugh:

- I admit that it is not such a different job ... Governor and Governess!!

Irea Senderlson was a beautiful woman. Her long curly golden hair reflected the sunlight. Pink cheeks, large bright hazel eyes, and a wonderful kind smile, displayed her natural charm. The young woman walked toward her husband's desk, and she knelt in front of the 3 little children:

- The afternoon snacks are ready in the dining room ... there are peaches and chocolate pies, milk flavored with strawberry, caramel lollipops, and macarons of all colors ... go ahead!!

One of the boys asked:

- Can we play in the garden after that, Lady?

Irea smiled:

- Certainly!! ... But now, we must let the Governor work.

The three children greeted Iskander Balthazar with a smile, and they left the Library. Irea Senderlson approached her husband, she patted his shoulder in a thoughtful gesture, and she laughed:

- Governess Touti!! it is a nice nickname ...

Iskander Balthazar was amused by this comparison:

- The little girl is clever!! ... I never thought to link the two jobs ... Governess and Governor!!

Irea Senderlson moved toward the Library windows, to check on something. And while Iskander returned to his files, he was curious:

- How is their day going on?

In the vast garden of the grand Mansion, several inflatables toys were settled; a giant swing, a large swimming pool, a huge trampoline, a dozen balloons inflated. Thirty children of all ages were running, laughing and playing in the garden. Some swayed on inflatable games, others had fun lifting kites up to the sky, and others chased inflated balloons.

While watching the scene in the garden through the Library windows, Irea smiled:

- They are having fun like crazy!!

Iskander asked in an amused tone:

- Are there any material damages?

Irea laughed aloud:

- An upside down garden vase ... 4 broken plates ... a peach pie landed on the white carpet of the entrance ... the handle of the main door broke ... there are traces of shoes full of mud around the big lounge ... and one or two panes of windows broken by a ball ...

Iskander exclaimed jokingly:

- That's all?

Irea smiled:

- They are children ... they are just having fun!!
- I hope our employees are not too bothered by the visits of these children ...

Ira laughed:

- Cristelle loves the kids ... I even saw her going down the swing with them. The head of the Mansion, Mr. Bûchebois observes them with a very serious look. Océanie won't approach a child; she remains all day locked up in the kitchen ... Igor is dizzy to serve all the children at the same time ... The Gardener, Mr. Rosenwald barely held his anger when his flowers and vases have been touched ... Séraphine hates being locked up all day in a room ... but she has to be!
- And the Cook?
- Mr. Ferrero is delighted to be able to cook his favorite dishes!! The kids love his pasta with Italian cheeses and they keep asking for more!!
- So I guess he is happy today ... just like you are!

Iskander opened a new folder on his desk:

- Any way, if all the Noble women were benevolent like you, and they would open their homes to invite humble children ... our world would be a better place!

His wife let out a little laugh:

- I do not belong to the nobility, Iskander.

The Governor looked up at his wife, with an amused look:

- Fortunately!!

She smiled back at her husband. It is true that Irea Senderlson was the daughter of a well-known and wealthy businessman. And yet, she never felt comfortable among the Noble people. Her ideas and attitudes were very different from the social class she belonged to. Irea never tried to fit into the nobility. And that's what attracted Iskander Balthazar, the first time he met Irea Senderlson.

Iskander got up to get a book on a shelf. While his wife was staring through the large windows. Her mind went astray. After a moment of silence, Irea said:

- Iskander ...

Her husband was busy looking for a paragraph he needed, to complete his project. And yet, without raising his eyes from a folder, Iskander lent an ear to his beloved wife:

- Yes, my light?

While observing the garden, Irea said in a strangely convinced voice:

- If we have had a child ... if we have had a successor ... he would have pursued our duty and kindness ... he would have done great things.

Iskander Balthazar froze standing in his place, holding the book in his hands. He raised his eyes toward his wife. It was a strange comment coming from her.

Although he and his wife couldn't have children, they had never felt regret or sadness for this absence. They were both well aware that some things are beyond the human control. Irea occupied her time with charities and volunteering, and her husband firmly supported all her works. Irea Senderlson affirmed with a sure and certain voice:

- He would have pursued our duty ... he would have done great things ...

Iskander put his book down on his desk and he approached his wife. He could see the children playing in the garden through the windows of the Library. After a few hesitant seconds, Iskander asked in a curious voice:

- What makes you say that, my light?

At that moment, Irea turned around toward her husband. And Iskander could clearly see a bright strange glow in his wife's eyes. Irea Senderlson smiled:

- Only a feeling ...

Chapter 29

A bet

Saturday, November 14th, 1891.

Mr. Ferrero Lutché, the Cook of the grand Mansion, always wore his white apron that glamorized his big belly, a large hat on his bald head, and a checkered red and white scarf around his neck. The Cook of the grand Mansion tasted his dish with a wood spoon.

- Manca qualcosa! *(Something is missing)*

He tasted again, thinking aloud:

- Pepper ... ginger ... white beans ...

At this moment, Mr. Benjamin Bûchebois, the head of the Mansion, came into the kitchen. Mr. Bûchebois asked in a curious voice:

- What is for dinner, tonight?

Without even turning around, the Cook Mr. Ferrero replied proudly:

- A soup Minestrone italiano!!

Mr. Bûchebois didn't know what that means, he whispered in a small voice:

- I hope it's edible!

The Cook didn't hear the comment of Mr. Bûchebois; he was busy to find out what was missing in his recipe:

- Ho aggiunto parsley ... cilantro ... zucchini ...

The head of the Mansion, Mr. Bûchebois sat around the large rectangular dining table, and he started sewing a button of his jacket. When two silhouettes entered the kitchen.

- I loaded the chimney's wood 2 times this week! Wondered Igor, the server of the grand Mansion.
- Well ... load it for the 3rd time. Océanie replied with a mean smile.
- But I don't work for you!! Igor said, while he served himself some bread and butter, before he sat around the dining table.
- You work in this grand Mansion ... and you're responsible for loading wood in all the rooms. Océanie replied before sitting, and she continued:
- Last night, I didn't sleep well ... it was so cold in my room!!

Between two bites of bread, Igor murmured:

- Cover yourself well!!

Océanie gave him a menacing look:

- Wood ... in my room ... tonight!!

Igor rolled his eyes up to the sky and sighed:

- Alright … alright …

The server Igor opened a newspaper, while eating buttered bread. Océanie took out plates and cutlery; she prepared the dinner table. While the Cook, Mr. Ferrero was still seeking the missing ingredient in his recipe.

After a few minutes, Cristelle joined the employees of the grand Mansion in the kitchen. Since the incident of the little Dalya Bouvard and the Lawyer Mr. Ernest Laszlo, the maid Cristelle was a little quieter than usual. None of the employees dared to talk about this incident with Cristelle. And mostly, Cristelle was distant and cold with Océanie. After all, it was Océanie who reported to Mr. Ernest that Dalya entered the grand Mansion. And without her attitude, Dalya Bouvard would have not received a slap.

Océanie repeatedly told everyone that she had no regrets for what she has done. Yet, Océanie couldn't dare to look Cristelle in the eyes, nor speak to her.

- I've cleaned the living room and the Library, Mr. Bûchebois. Tomorrow, I will do the stairs of the hall and the entry. Cristelle said.

The head of the house smiled back at her, before continuing to sew his button. Cristelle sat next to Igor who was reading the newspaper; she took on to repair a hole in a straw basket.

- Yet, I added garlic … carrots chop ... but the gusto is not perfetto ... I miss something?

The Cook thought aloud, while peeling an onion. The dinner was almost ready. The employees of the grand Mansion were all busy at their tasks around the kitchen table. When Océanie broke the silence:

- I hope we'll have a good turkey this year for the Thanksgiving holiday!

Mr. Bûchebois replied:

- Mr. Gaultier assured me that he will give us his best turkey at a good price! I will visit him tomorrow!

Océanie polished forks and spoons:

- Mr. Gaultier have the best turkey of all town ... I heard he feed them wheat and corn.

Igor laughed without taking his eyes from his newspaper:

- The problem is not in the turkey ... the problem is in the cooking of the turkey!!

Barely had he finished his sentence, Igor received several hits from a wood spoon on the head. The Cook, Mr. Ferrero yelled furiously:

- IF YOU NOT LIKE MY TURKEY, CUCINO TURKEY YOURSELF!! LITTLE INGRATO!! YOU ALWAYS FINISCI TUO PLATE IL PRIMO!!

The Gardener, Mr. Rosenwald entered the kitchen at that moment. He didn't need to ask why the Cook was upset at Igor. This scene was usually repeated in the grand Mansion. The Gardener sat on a chair around the large table where everyone was already gathered. He put on the table a large bouquet of green herbs, and announced:

- Here are chives ... oregano … and basil.

The Cook Mr. Ferrero gathered himself of his anger, and he replied to the Gardener:

- Thank you Mr. Rosenwald ... I've just needed these, to prepare the marinade for the Thanksgiving turkey.

The Gardener used a knife, and he took care to arrange the plants he had picked, removing damaged leaves, stems and roots. And as usual, Océanie just couldn't filter her words:

- By the way ... after the Thanksgiving holiday, the little girl will pass the Challenge.

A heavy silence filled the kitchen of the grand Mansion. No one dared to mention the little Dalya Bouvard. Cristelle kept her silence and focus on repairing the straw basket. Mr. Bûchebois and Mr. Ferrero exchanged an awkward look. The Gardener took care of his herbs, without paying attention to the upcoming discussion. Only Igor asked:

- It will be the Second test, right?

Océanie sighed:

- And the last Challenge, hopefully!! ... it's time to have an employer worthy of managing the grand Mansion ...
- An employer who won't force us to load the wood more than 3 times! Igor exclaimed.
- Don't fool yourself, dear Igor ... With or without employers, you will still load wood in my bedroom! Océanie laughed.

When she placed the plates on the dining table, Océanie affirmed in an arrogant voice:

- Anyway … I bet 10 dollars she will fail to answer the Second Question!

Igor folded his newspaper and laughed:

- I bet 15 bucks that she won't be able to even READ the Second Question!

Cristelle remained silent and busy. Mr. Bûchebois had almost finished sewing his button. Mr. Ferrero was stirring his soup. Only Igor and Océanie animated the conversation. Océanie chuckled:

- Imagine if this strange box doesn't work on the Challenge, that night!!

Igor seemed very interested in the money to bet:

- So ... how exactly do you bet on it?

After a few seconds of reflection, Océanie answered:

- I bet 20 $ that she cannot answer this Question!

Igor seemed enthusiastic:

- I bet 30 $ that the box will not work that night!

Océanie exclaimed:

- The bet is open then!! Going for 30 dolla...

Suddenly, a quiet voice interrupted Océanie:

- 150 $.

All the employees of the grand Mansion froze in their movements. Océanie and Igor went silent. Mr. Bûchebois and Cristelle raised their heads from their occupations. The Cook, Mr. Ferrero turned around, unsure of what he may have heard. Everyone looked at the Gardener, in a shocked and an uncertain stare.

Since his hiring, the Gardener never joined the conversations of the other employees, during the meals. Mr. Rosenwald was always silent and discreet. Except this time, the Gardener, who was arranging oregano herbs in a basket, and without even raising his eyes, he repeated for the 2nd time in a calm strong voice:

- 150 $

Océanie let out a mocking laugh:

- This is your salary for several months ... it's not worth losing it for a little veggy seller.

The head of the house, Mr. Bûchebois asked the Gardener:

- You bet 150 $ ... that this strange box wouldn't work?

The Cook, Mr. Ferrero Lutché also joined the conversation:

- Or that the girl will not be able to rispondere domanda ... to the Question?

Igor was also curious:

- Or that she won't even manage to know what the Second Challenge is about?

The Gardener looked up, he stared at all the employees of the grand Mansion, for some long tense seconds. It was rare to see the Gardener interested in the employees' conversations. And the amount of the money bet, was so great that it aroused the employees' curiosity. The Gardener, Mr. Rosenwald smiled and replied with a defiant voice:

- 150 $ ... that she will live in the grand Mansion.

Chapter 30

Thanksgiving

Friday, November 27th, 1891. The Thanksgiving holiday.

A few days earlier, Dalya's father, Antman Bouvard announced to his family that his six brothers and only sister will join them for the Thanksgiving holiday of this year, which will be held at Mr. Pierrefonds house, the herbs' Merchant at the Saturday market.

Besides Uncle Giorgi Bouvard who lived in the same city, Dalya had an Aunt and 6 other paternal Uncles, living and working in the grandfather Bouvard's farm, in the North of the country.

The 6 Uncles and Aunt came once to visit them in Georgetown city, a very long time ago. Dalya had very few memories of them because she was still a baby, her twin sisters weren't even born. At this news announced by her father, Dalya was happy to meet the rest of her family during Thanksgiving.

The day of the festivity, Dalya wore her best clothes; a long pink dress that Uncle Giorgi created for her last year, she put on her black shoes, and she tied her hair in a chignon. Dalya helped her little sisters wear pink dresses and white hats. And then, all three of them went downstairs to the kitchen.

Her mother had already prepared 10 large pear pies and she was busy spreading honey on top of the pies. Meanwhile, her father was busy adjusting the bow tie he borrowed from a friend. When he noticed the little twins, Mr. Antman raised them both up to the sky in a strong move while exclaiming:

- Ah!! My little Ari and Adi!! How cute you are today!!
- Ant!! Ant!! Ant!! Yelled the twins simultaneously.

Mr. Antman gave a cold stare to his daughter Dalya, without speaking to her. Since many months now, her father had a cold attitude toward her, and Dalya didn't dare to ask him why.

When suddenly, a voice was heard at the entrance door of the house:

- Are we really in the Bouvard's house?

Mr. Antman turned around to the front door, and exclaimed joyfully:

- Welcome home, Scott!! ...Welcome everybody!! ... Please come inside!!
- Well well ... this is a beautiful house!! Wondered a second man.
- Good to see you, Alex!!
- Hello. Said a man in a calm, cold voice.

- Come on in, Adam!! Welcome!!
- So when will you leave this house? There is still only 2 months for you to stay here, isn't it? Asked a man.
- Happy holidays, Charles!! Mr. Antman greeted.
- It is too warm here. Complained a man.
- Far from the cold North, Jaafar, isn't it? laughed Mr. Antman
- There is no doubt that you will return to your old house!! laughed a man
- I'm not so sure about that, Fazio!
- Why didn't you invites us here, before? Asked a woman.
- It's good to see you with us in this celebration, dear sister Reeda.

The last man to enter the Annex house was Uncle Giorgi that Dalya knew very well. He greeted Dalya with a smile, before sitting in the living room with his siblings. Mr. Antman introduced his wife and his little girls in the living room, in a proud and happy voice:

- And of course ... you all remember my wife ... Augustine.

Mrs. Augustine greeted them all with a head sign and a forced smile. She seemed upset to see several men get her house into a mess. Mr. Antman moved his little twins Ari and Adi toward their Uncles:

- And here are my little jewels, Adi and Ari!!

The twins were always very friendly and natural with everyone. Except on that day, Ari and Adi firmly gripped their father's legs without letting it go. And always very talkative, Ari and Adi didn't speak a word, and they stared at the visitors, in a shy and fearful look. And at the sight of the little twins, the 6 Uncles and Aunt exclaimed:

- They are so skinny!! ... But what do you feed them?
- They walk already? ... I thought they will be slow to walk ...
- Where did they get this hair from?! ... They look like no one in the family!
- In a few years from now, they will be strong enough to work with us in the farm!
- I always thought that twins were an oddity of nature ...
- It must be tiring to take care of these two!
- These are ugly dresses! They had nothing better to wear?!

Mr. Antman couldn't place a single word between the comments of his many brothers and sister. He just smiled nervously. Apparently, and because of the distance and the absence, Mr. Antman had somehow forgotten the character of his brothers and sister.

A moment later, Antman turned toward Dalya, and he introduced her in a much less enthusiastic voice:

- And ... here is Dalya.

The 6 Uncles and Aunt stared at Dalya for a moment. The 6 brothers and sister could be clearly differentiated from one another, with very different characteristics.

Scott was brown skin, Adam was skeletal, Fazio was a very long man, Jaafar had marble facial features, Charles was short and fat, Alex had black dark hair, and Aunt Reeda had small eyes and a small mouth.

- Go ahead and say hello to your Uncles and Aunt! Antman ordered his daughter, in a voice that was forced to be nice.

Although intimidated by the new visitors, Dalya complied and she stepped inside the living room. Coming close to him, her Uncle Scott took off 2 little softdolls from his jacket, and he gave them to his niece:

- Here ... I bought these for your sisters ...

Dalya was pleasantly surprised by this nice gift to her sisters. She took them and smiled back at him:

- Thank you, Uncle Scott.

It was 2 small rag dolls, with wool hair arranged in a braid, white cotton dresses and little wood shoes.

Then, Dalya shook hands with her Uncle Adam. She could almost feel every bone in his hand. He looked at her for a moment and he said:

- You have grown up ...

Dalya just smiled. She turned toward the next. When she came near him, Uncle Fazio laughed in a loud voice:

- I'm pretty sure you won't fail the Challenges, to get this fortune!

Dalya was a little confused by this comment. She appreciated the encouragement of her Uncle, but she didn't understand his strange laugh.

When Dalya came close to her Uncle Jaafar, he shook her hand without pronouncing a word; neither displaying a clear expression on his face. Dalya didn't know if he was happy or upset to be here.

When she walked to her Uncle Charles, the short and fat Uncle stood up from his chair to shake her hand. He looked at her face and said:

- This is an unfortunate situation for you ... the school won't be useful to you ... you would have been better working with us on the farm ... you would have had a stronger and robust handshake!

It was the first time in her life that someone proposed to Dalya to work on a farm instead of attending classes at school. Dalya didn't know how to answer this advice. She merely kept her smile.

By being closer, Dalya noticed that her Uncle Alex had the blackest dark hair she had ever seen. And despite the scrutinizing gaze of her Uncle Alex, Dalya tried to smile and shake his hand. He asked in a serious tone:

- How much is this fortune? ... How much money you'll have exactly?

Dalya was surprised by this question. Although she was always curious, Dalya have never thought about this question before. She didn't know what to answer, so Dalya continued to smile nervously.

When she arrived near the only paternal Aunt she had, Dalya was curious to meet her as much as her other 6 Uncles. Before she would even shake hands with her niece, Aunt Reeda exclaimed in an annoyed tone:

- Are these good manners to welcome us without drinks or refreshments?

Dalya smiled, intimidated and nervous. It was not the perfect first contact that the little girl hoped to have with her 6 Uncles and Aunt. However, Dalya was happy to have visiting members of her family for the holiday. And it was going to be a very happy holiday...

While Mrs. Augustine was getting prepared in her bedroom, Dalya kept her little twin sisters in the kitchen. The twins were sitting on their usual chairs and Dalya arranged their hats. When two of her Uncles, Adam and Fazio came into the kitchen. Fazio exclaimed cheerfully, while discovering what was beneath the white lace napkin:

- Well ... well ... these are some delicious pear tarts you have here!!

Dalya explained:

- These are the desserts that mother prepared for Mr. Pierrefonds' party. Every year, the thanksgiving party takes place at someone's house, and everyone brings di...

But before Dalya could even finish her sentence, her Uncle Fazio took a spoon and he tasted one of the pear pies. Dalya replied in a terrified and intimidated voice:

- But ... Uncle ... these are the pies that we must bring to the thanksgiving party ...

Her Uncle Adam was drinking milk, observing the scene without saying a word. Uncle Fazio looked at Dalya and he replied joyfully, before putting back the white napkin on the pie:

- There will be plenty of desserts at the party ... don't worry, kid!

Dalya was not so sure about what to do or say at that moment. But she was certain that her mother would be furious to discover that the pies were tasted before the party. A few seconds later, Mrs. Augustine entered the kitchen and she exclaimed in an annoyed voice:

- We are already late! We must take the road now, if we want to arrive before the end of the party!

Mrs. Augustine asked her two brothers-in-laws:

- Pick up 7 pies, please ... and let 3 for us tomorrow ... I'll put on my hat and follow you.

Uncle Adam and Uncle Fazio executed immediately. They placed 7 pear tarts in a basket and they left the kitchen to join their brothers. Dalya noticed that the pie tasted by her Uncle Fazio, remained still on the kitchen table. Dalya didn't dare to tell and upset her mother that day. She held her little twin sisters, and they all left to the Thanksgiving party at Mr. Pierrefonds' house.

At Mr. Pierrefonds' house.

This holiday was an opportunity for all the Merchants of the Saturday market, to meet and celebrate with friends and family. Dalya's father had lent to Mr. Pierrefonds the tent he used in the last year's party in the Annex house. Dalya's mother was eager to show off her 7 pear pies to her friends. The Uncles and Aunt followed Antman toward Mr. Pierrefonds' house, in the East side of the city, while observing the landscape of Dumbarton Oaks Park.

After a while, they all stopped in front of a small two floors house, with tiny windows, red plaques roof, and a large door barely holding rightly. A small green garden appeared on the left side of the house. All the herbs were maintained by long stems. A large white tent was set up in the courtyard, on the right side of the house. It was a modest but cozy home.

The Bouvard family was greeted by a joyfully smiling Mr. Pierrefonds:

- Welcome Antman ... welcome to you and your entire family!!!

Dalya liked Mr. Pierrefonds very much. Whenever she bought herbs from him, Mr. Pierrefonds would always add to her basket more herbs for free. Mr. Pierrefonds was always smiling, polite and kind to everyone, including Dalya. Antman Bouvard greeted his friend warmly:

- Thank you for hosting us this year, Pierrefonds ... here are my brothers and my sister ... they came from the North specifically to spend the holidays with us!
- Welcome in my modest home!! Proudly exclaimed Mr. Pierrefonds.

Fazio asked, with a mean laugh:

- So, you are also a Merchant in the market? Just like Antman? That's all you do for a living?

Charles murmured while examining the house:

- You are right ... it's a very modest home ...

Alex wondered aloud:

- And what's there to eat?

Adam replied immediately:

- With all the road we have traveled ... there better be good food!

Scott chuckled:

- Antman, your plans are never right! It is obvious that we will stay hungry today!!

Reeda ordered:

- Enough talk! ... Find me a place to sit!!

Only Jaafar remained silent, a marble and a still face behind his brothers. And he was not the only one motionless. Mr. Pierrefonds seemed paralyzed by the comments of his friend's brothers; his smile was confused. Antman Bouvard felt the embarrassment of Mr. Pierrefonds; he hurried to lead his siblings inside the place.

Dalya came close to Mr. Pierrefonds, while holding her little sister by their hands. She greeted him with a smile:

- Thank you for inviting us this year, Mr. Pierrefonds. I'm sure this will be a successful party. Especially if Mrs. Pierrefonds has prepared her famous lemon pie. My sisters love it!

Ari and Adi were excited, tightly holding their stuffed softdolls, and jumping:

- LEMON PIE!! LEMON PIE!! LEMON PIE!!

Mr. Pierrefonds pulled himself together, and he smiled at the 3 little girls:

- Yes ... yes ... of course ... there will be plenty of lemon pies, at the desserts' corner ... don't forget to serve yourself ... and have fun!!

Dalya took her little sisters by their hands and she led them inside the installed tent.

The backyard was very large. Several rectangular tables with long benches were installed in a corner of the place. A small stage with 4 steps in front was set in another corner. Many wood empty crates were used as chairs. A long rectangular table was covered by white tablecloth. This table was filled gradually by the visitors' dishes and plates, of many types and sizes. At the end of the buffet table, a huge pot of soup was installed under a soft wood fire.

Dalya noticed the little children all gathered in a corner of the backyard, around Mr. Cosco, who was blowing and offering them inflated balloons. The little Adi and Ari left their big sister's hands, and they ran toward the children's gathering. The little twins held firmly their softdolls, while observing the extraordinary moves of Mr. Cosco. When the man finished blowing into the balloon, he tied it and made it either a flower or a dog shape, under the admiring eyes and exclamations of children surrounding him. Dalya was also admiring the work of Mr. Cosco, when a man's voice called her:

- What do you think of the softdolls that I gave you?

Dalya turned around to find her Uncle Scott near her.

- They are very pretty ... thank you.
- I bought them specifically for your sisters! Scott replied proudly, before leaving to join his brothers and sister at the other end of the courtyard.

Dalya was somehow confused by this strange conversation. But she was interrupted in her thoughts by her little sister's admiration screams, about the last balloon trick of Mr. Cosco.

Several minutes later, Dalya noticed her friends, Alfie Jaq and Maurice Gus.

- Hello Alfie ... Hello Maurice ... happy holiday to you!
- Happy thanksgiving to you, Dalya. Said Maurice, approaching her.
- You think that there will be Mrs. Pierrefonds' lemon pies, on the menu tonight? Alfie asked while staring at the long rectangular buffet table.

Maurice slapped Alfie's stomach, with an angry look:

- Happy holiday to you too, Alfie!!

With great difficulty, Alfie took off his eyes from the buffet table, and he turned to Dalya:

- Sorry ... joyful Thanksgiving, Dalya!!
- Thank you. Dalya laughed, before adding:
- And I assure you Alfie ... there will be many lemon pies for dessert tonight. Mr. Pierrefonds confirmed it to me.

Alfie's face lit up in an instant. Maurice asked her:

- It seems that you have some guests this year.
- Yes, my father's family. An Aunt and 6 Uncles. They are visiting us for the holidays.
- That's cool!! Exclaimed Alfie.

When Dalya noticed some little white papers in the hands of her friends, she asked what it was. Alfie and Maurice proudly answered:

- These are our brochures for our Snow cleaning service in winter.
- At the first Snow fall, we will be ready to take on appointments to remove Snow in front of the houses and shops.
- And to not waste the cost of renting a local ... Our office is the 3rd light pole to the right of the Toscana Restaurant.
- Open daily from 8:00 AM to noon.
- Our Secretary is Tom … the son of Mr. Cosco ... he will handle all our appointments.

Dalya was always amazed by the genius ideas of her friends, in order to earn more money, without losing their will and energy. And Dalya was always very proud of her friends:

- You are geniuses! I am sure you will succeed and get enough money to open your sto...

When suddenly, Dalya was interrupted by a familiar voice behind her:

- There you are! I was looking for you!

When Uncle Charles appeared behind her, Dalya smiled and she introduced her friends:

- These are my friends, Uncle Charles. Alfie and Maur...

Uncle Charles interrupted his niece and he spoke to the shortest of her friends:

- You, kid! Go get me a glass of lemonade!

Maurice hesitated for a moment, and then he turned and walked to the buffet table. Dalya was embarrassed that her Uncle ordered Maurice in a rude tone. Yet, she was still polite to her Uncle, who was examining the place with a disapproving look. Dalya explained:

- It will be a successful party. I am sure of it! Mr. Pierrefonds and his family are very nice people, everyone loves them. Nobody would have refused to come here today.

Her Uncle sighed bored, while observing the place. Alfie continued:

- And the buffet looks delicious. Everyone loves the famous lemon pie of Mrs. Pierrefonds. It is the best pie in the entire city.

While Uncle Charles observed Alfie from head to toe, Dalya proudly informed her Uncle:

- Alfie is a newspaper boy ... and Maurice is a shoeshiner. They work every day in downtown.
- Couldn't you have better friends that a Newspaper Seller and a Shoeshiner?! Uncle Charles exclaimed with a mocking arrogant voice.

Dalya and Alfie exchanged a confused look; they didn't understand the last comment of the Uncle. When Alfie proudly presented a small paper to Dalya's Uncle:

- This winter, we will go on our own business!
- Your business? ... But you are just little children? Said Uncle Charles naturally.

Alfie was surprised by this remark. And when Uncle Charles read the paper, he let out a sudden loud laugh. Dalya and Alfie stood motionless and confused about the man's laugh and attitude. Uncle Charles finally said:

- And you think you are strong enough to clear the Snow?
- Yes, Monsieur. Alfie spontaneously replied.

Uncle Charles was curious to know:

- And with what tools?

Alfie explained:

- With shovels, Monsieur. Maurice and I, we have several sizes. We also bought a big broom, and a little carr…

Uncle Charles laughed louder than before:

- With shovels! Really?! ... You think you'll clean it that easily? ... You are dreaming, kid!! It is clear you have never done any manual work before!! You should work in a farm before starting projects out of your reach!!

Alfie didn't understand why his idea seemed funny to Dalya's Uncle. Alfie and Maurice had already appointments of Mr. Pierrefonds and Mrs. Vannière, to clean the Snow off their front homes.
When Maurice returned with a goblet of lemonade, Uncle Charles took it and drank it, in one gulp. Maurice whispered:

- You are welcomed, Monsieur.

When he finished drinking, Uncle Charles asked curiously:

- And... How will you collect the Snow and get rid of it?

Despite the incomprehensible laughs of the man, Alfie replied with clear confidence:

- We will collect the Snow in bags, and we will transport them in a carriage.

Maurice proudly continued:

- We will move the Snow bags to another place.

Uncle Charles looked at Alfie and Maurice, with a bored gaze. Dalya said:

- It's a great idea! ... If I didn't have classes at school, I would have helped you with th...
- It's a stupid idea!! Laughed Uncle Charles. How can two children like you carry bags filled with Snow!

Uncles Charles handed the empty Goblet to Maurice, and then he joined his brothers and sister, while laughing aloud. Alfie and Dalya remained motionless and silent. Maurice wondered aloud:

- Isn't he supposed to encourage us and advise us, rather than demean and demoralize us?

Dalya lead her little sisters toward the buffet table, to serve them some lemonade. While her friends, Alfie and Maurice continued to give their business cards to the guests at the party, without losing a grain of enthusiasm or will. Ari and Adi were enjoying their drinks when Dalya noticed her Uncle Scott coming close to the buffet table too.

- Would you like a lemonade Goblet, Uncle Scott?
- Yes, please!

Dalya put down her sisters' softdolls, before filling a Goblet. When she handed him the juice, her Uncle Scott smiled:

- Do they like their softdolls?

Dalya hesitated for a moment to answer:

- Yes ... Yes ... thank you. Ari and Adi really like these softdolls ...
- That I've offered. Uncle Scott finished his niece's sentence, while observing the little twins, with a proud smile before leaving.

Dalya was slightly confused; she didn't understand her Uncle's comments. It was the 3rd time since his arrival that her Uncle Scott spoke and asked her about these softdolls. Yet, Dalya didn't forget to thank him. Was there anything else she should have done or said to him?

After her little sisters finished their drinks, they settled all three of them, near the table where her parents and her family were reunited.

Her Uncle Jaafar seemed the calmest of all her Uncles. He watched the crowded place, with a silent stare. Dalya came near him:

- My father told me you live far, in the North of the country. How many days of travel is it?

Uncle Jaafar looked at Dalya for a moment without saying a word. Usually, people's faces are clear and transparent of their emotions, either upset or delighted. Except this time, Dalya failed to understand the facial features of her Uncle Jaafar. A marble face. Yet, Dalya continued in a polite voice:

- Do you spend Thanksgiving holiday the same way, in the city where you live?

Uncle Jaafar didn't react. He ignored the conversation and stared ahead. Dalya persisted:

- Uncle Giorgi told me you all work in grandfather's farm ... do you have animals in the farm?

Uncle Jaafar didn't display any move or word.

- Or is it an agricultural farm only?

Dalya didn't understand this man's attitude.

- Do you want me to bring you some lemonade? ... It's delicious and refreshing.

Ari and Adi cheered when a balloon burst. Dalya continued to speak to her Uncle Jaafar:

- It will be a good party this year. Mr. Pierrefonds and his family invited all the Merchants of the Saturday market. It's the place where father and I used to work. It's right in front of the Toscana restaurant. It is the most … popular … market … in the …

Dalya stopped. Her Uncle Jaafar was a statue. He stared at the crowd with an emotionless cold look. Dalya was convinced now, that her Uncle Jaafar was really ... a marble.

The party under the tent was becoming noisier. Almost all the guests had arrived, some were standing, laughing and whispering, others sat to rest from their trips, the children were nearly all gathered around Mr. Cosco, admiring his balloons. The buffet table gathered several women who were arranging the dishes and cutlery. The party promised to be fun and joyful.

Moments later, a great man entered the tent. The Dean of Merchants Mr. Kenan Einsenberg could be clearly differentiated by his large size, white hair, his big coppery beard, his usual large green coat, but above all ... his crutch on which he leaned to walk.

The Dean of Merchants, Mr. Kenan Einsenberg greeted people on his way. And as it was the custom, the Dean of Merchants was about to pronounce the Thanksgiving speech. Mr. Kenan Einsenberg came up on the stage with a quick movement, and he addressed the crowd with a clear and strong voice:

- First, we thank Mr. Pierrefonds and his lovely family for welcoming us into his home for the thanksgiving party this year. And I hope everyone will have a beautiful day!!

  I know that most of you have had a difficult year because of the bad weather that affected the harvest and the trade. But on this blessed day, I would like to remind you that we thank God for his kindness, and also for his storms. Because the difficulties make us more humble, more grateful, more empathetic, and certainly more resistant. Difficulties reveal and amplify our strengths and qualities. And it is thanks to the difficulties that we recognize our best friends and allies. So we are grateful to God for all his generosities toward us, no matter what they are.

  I also would like to remind you that ... often, while facing a storm, the best thing to do, is to go on and do our best. No storm lasts forever. The sun always eventually works its way through the clouds, as dense as they can be!!

When the Dean of Merchants finished, everyone applauded warmly. Mr. Dean's speech had a motivating effect on every present person. Seconds later, Mr. Pierrefonds spoke to the guests:

- Ladies and gentlemen, I wish you again and again a warm welcome in my humble and modest home. It is a great honor for me and my family to welcome you on the Thanksgiving holiday this year. And I would like to reassure everyone that my wife had prepared enough lemon pies to feed half Georgetown city!!

A great laugh arose among the crowd of people. Mr. Pierrefonds continued:

- I am pleased to announce a surprise, which I and some friends have prepared for you all. The Thanksgiving feast this year will start with an exciting show of 4 artists. I'll let you discover the first one: Mr. Romane!

People cheered. Mr. Romane appeared among the crowd and he climbed the steps into the stage, while Mr. Pierrefonds vanished. Mr. Roman was a long very thin man. He had a big white mustache and a bald head.

- Hello ... hello ... hello!! He exclaimed with an enthusiastic tone. Today, I'll show you the element I handle well ... fire!

Mr. Roman took a long stick. The ends were surrounded by a fabric ball. He lit the ends of the stick with a fire match. And in a flash, Mr. Romane made moves, wrapping and lifting up the burning stick. All the children sitting in the front rows of the crowd, let out a scream of admiration whenever Mr. Romane launched the fire stick up in the air. Ari and Adi were jumping with joy and fear holding tightly their softdolls. Everyone had their eyes glued on the spectacle of the fire movements. Mr. Roman was so talented and fast.

At the end of the show, Mr. Romane greeted the crowd with a bow. And everyone applauded him warmly.

After that, it was Miss Elsa's turn. A girl in her twenties, very small size, with long braids of blond hair and a radiant smile. She climbed on the stage and greeted the crowd in a confident and cheerful voice:

- Ladies and gentlemen ... young and old ... tonight, I present to you my specialty ...

Miss Elsa took out of her bag 7 small balls. And even before the crowd could finish applauding, the girl juggled the balls in her hands at a rapid rate. All the children were amazed by her movements, and they tried to keep track with the balls. Men and women enjoyed the beautiful show that the girl gave. The crowd strongly applauded when she finished her show.

A moment later, a funny Monsieur made his way through the crowd. He wore a huge purple wig; he had a round red nose, very large brown shoes and a big fat belly. He wore green pants with suspenders that held barely on his shoulders. The man had a funny look. He went up on stage, and was followed by a poodle dog, small, cute and in a sandy color. The man announced to the crowd:

- Well ... well ... I shall introduce myself ... I am Mr. Leo, and this is my loyal companion, my dog Teo ... applauses for my companion, please!!

Everyone, old and young warmly applauded, and the dog immediately bowed to the crowd. Mr. Leo continued:

- Thank you ... thank you ... and now, I'll show you how my dog is very smart and obedient! ... Teo ... sit!

The dog raised his head and looked up at the sky, ignoring his Master. The children laughed at this reaction.

- Teo ... bring me the water bucket, next to you.

This time, the dog obeyed, he headed toward the bucket filled with water, he pulled it up with his teeth, and then slowly walked toward his Master. Except that, a few steps away, the dog made a sudden moves, and the water in the bucket splashed on the big pants of the man. A wave of laughs invaded the place.
Moments later, the clown had turned his back to the crowd to dry his pants; the dog jumped and took down the pants' suspenders of his Master. When the pants fell off on the stage floor, Mr. Leo found himself in huge short pants with drawings of yellow ducks and soap bubbles. The children had laugh tears in their eyes, all the people attending laughed aloud of this funny scene between Master Leo and his dog Teo.

The show lasted several minutes, during which the dog did many fooleries, making the crowd laugh every time. At the end of their show, the clown and the dog both bowed to the crowd, and they received warm applauses.

The last show was of Mr. Aymeric. Dalya knew the man very well; he was the milk and cheese Merchants at the Saturday market. He had a small farm with 4 cows and 5 goats, just outside the city of Georgetown. And his milk and cheese were the best of the entire city, many distinguished people even ordered from him. He was a small man, always cheerful. And on this festive day, he had abandoned his long white apron for a modest suit with a big bow tie. Mr. Aymeric went up on the small stage, and he faced the crowd. And everyone was curious to know what he will present to them. Mr. Aymeric announced his show:

- Ladies and gentlemen ... young and old ... I will charm you today with my guessing game ... 3 short and simple riddles ... Whoever finds them all, I offer him a portion of my best soft cheese!

The entire crowd applauded and was eager to participate in the game. Mr. Aymeric began:

- My first riddle is ... What has sugar and is never sweet?

Everyone went quiet, young and old. Everyone thought well and hard about the answer. Yet, it was a simple riddle. When suddenly, a voice said:

- Sugar cane!
- Sorry ... wrong answer! announced Mr. Aymeric

A second voice said:

- The sugar bowl!

Mr. Aymeric jumped:

- It's correct my boy!! What's your name?
- Maurice Gus, Sir.
- Well done boy!

The entire crowd applauded. Mr. Aymeric continued:

- So ... listen carefully and think hard ... My second riddle is ... the more it's hot, the more it's fresh, what is it?

The room plunged in total silence. Everyone thought.

- Fire! said a woman
- Sorry Madam, it's wrong ...
- Wrought iron! exclaimed a voice
- Missed Mr. Cosco! said Mr. Aymeric
- The sun! announced a boy
- Wrong ...

The silence reigned in the room for a few seconds, when a voice said:

- The bread!
- Yes!! Yes!! Yes!! Correct!! It's again our little Maurice Gus who found the right answer to the second riddle!! Bravo my boy!!

The entire audience warmly applauded Dalya's friend.

- Now listen carefully ... open your ears ... my third and final riddle is ... I'm before last in morning, the first in the night, in the middle of journey, missing in midday.

This time, again, silence filled the room.

- The stars! Said Mr. Kenan Einsenberg, the Dean of Merchants.

Mr. Aymeric asked:

- If I say it's the right answer, will that exempt me from the taxes this year?
- No. Mr. Einsenberg replied, laughing.

The entire crowd laughed at Mr. Aymeric, and his funny request. Mr. Aymeric also couldn't hold his laugh too:

- Well then ... so sorry, Mr. Dean ... incorrect answer.

The silence remained for several long minutes. Mr. Aymeric tried to motivate his crowd:

- Come on!! ... It's simple ... think about it ... I'm before last in morning, the first in the night, in the middle of journey, missing in midday.

After several long minutes of silence, Mr. Aymeric announced:

- Well then ... since the last riddle seems so difficult to uncover, I inform you that the answ....

When suddenly a little voice interrupted him:

- The letter N.

Dalya turned around to her friend Maurice who was standing a few feet away from her. He appeared calm as always. Mr. Aymeric asked him:

- Are you sure of the answer, young boy?
- Yes, Monsieur. The alphabet letter N.

Mr. Aymeric faced the crowd and yelled:

- CORRECT!!! WE HAVE A WINNER OF THE GUESSING GAME!!

While Mr. Aymeric invited Maurice to come into the stage, the crowd applauded very warmly and many voices screamed:

- Well done!
- Bravo son!
- What a smart kid!

Alfie and Dalya screamed simultaneously:

- Congratulations Maurice!!
- You're the best!!

Even the little twins, Ari and Adi applauded their sister's friend, exclaiming joyfully:

- Bavo Mauice!! Bavo Mauice!!

For the first time in his life, Maurice Gus blushed, under the applauses and people congratulating him. Mr. Aymeric gave him a big basket filled with soft cheese, with a proud smile:

- Here is your prize, son ... a well-deserved award!

Maurice thanked him with a smile before coming down the stage, holding his large portion of soft cheese in his hands.

Except that in an imprudent moment, Maurice missed to see the last step of the stairs ... and he stumbled. In a second, Maurice landed on the ground floor, and the entire cheese portion was spread all over his face!

Immediately, some men helped Maurice to get up. Mr. Aymeric jumped off the stage to check if the little boy was unharmed. Mrs. Pierrefonds handed a small towel to Maurice to wipe his face. A girl handed him a water bucket. Dalya and Alfie rushed to their friend. Two women picked up the rest of the scattered cheese and they cleaned the floor.

- I'm fine ... I didn't see the last step ... I'm fine ... thank you ...

Besides a little blue on his knees, Dalya was reassured that Maurice was alright.

However ... something very strange happened on that moment. While people were helping Maurice, Dalya heard a strange laugh behind her. And when she turned around, she was surprised to see a few steps away, her Uncle Fazio laughing aloud:

- He fell ... like a brick!! ... But what a fall!! ... He fell ... and received the award ... in the face!!

Of all the people present in this gathering ... children and adults ... nobody laughed at the fall of Maurice Gus. Except one person; Uncle Fazio Bouvard.

Dalya thought that her Uncle's reaction was weird. Maurice's fall wasn't like the show of Mr. Leo and his dog Teo, who voluntarily worked to make the crowd laugh. Maurice's fall was indeed a sad incident. Yet, Uncle Fazio seemed to find this incident somehow funny and he rejoiced of this fall. Dalya couldn't understand why.

Maurice joined Alfie, Dalya and her twin sisters, and they all sat down on a bench. Ari and Adi played with their new little softdolls.

- No one was as smart as you were, Maurice. Said Dalya.
- Yes!!! Exclaimed Alfie enthusiastic. How did you find the last riddle?

Maurice explained:

- It was tricky ... but when Mr. Aymeric said that it wasn't in midday, the only thing I noticed was the letter N. And in the other words, the letter N was present in different places.

Moments later, after Maurice had recovered from his fall, Mr. Pierrefonds announced in a proud and happy voice:

- Ladies and gentlemen ... I invite you to the buffet table. And please honor me and my family, by serving yourself large portions!!
- You can count on us!! Exclaimed Mr. Leo and his dog Teo immediately gave a barking noise, which triggered a wave of laughs that rejoiced the mood.

Instantly, People formed a long queue. They got plates and forks. And they served themselves at the buffet table. The menu of this year was much abundant, with typical American recipes and very delicious meals:

- 30 roasted turkeys. Several men were stirring them to complete their cooking, buttering them every minute with a sweet sauce

- A huge oatmeal soup cauldron
- 9 mashed potato pots with butter, garlic and herbs
- 14 large baskets filled with sweet corn bread
- 17 pans of baked vegetables; carrots, peas, potatoes, broccoli, zucchini
- 5 large cramberries sauce containers
- 19 pie of pumpkins, walnuts, pears and raspberries
- 25 lemon meringue pies.

Mrs. Augustine charged her daughter Dalya to watch over her little sisters throughout the evening. So then, Dalya asked her younger sisters to follow her. She served them turkey with cramberries sauce, corn bread, peas and broccoli. Then, Dalya settled her little sisters on a bench near the large buffet table. The little Ari and Adi were very hungry; they abandoned the forks and they ate spontaneously with their hands. A few moments later, Alfie and Maurice settled near Dalya, on the long wood bench.

- It's ... too ... very ... well ... this ... is ... meat ... never … tasted … such....

The words had trouble getting out of Alfie's full mouth.

- BREATHE!! BREATHE!! YOU'LL STRANGLE YOURSELF!! Yelled Maurice while tapping on Alfie's back to evacuate some air.

Dalya confirmed Alfie's opinion, while giggling:

- It's true that the turkey meat is delicious this year! Mrs. Pierrefonds made sure to cook all the turkeys herself. And she used her famous recipe for turkey stuffing ... a mixture of breadcrumbs, onions, garlic, herbs, chopped pieces of turkey ...
- Super ... good ... turkey ... very ... never ... tasted … great. Alfie continued talking while filling his mouth with meat.

Dalya turned toward her little sisters:

- Do you want me to serve you more turkey? Ari? Adi?
- Yes!! Turkey!! More!! More!!

The little twins handed their empty plates to their big sister, who walked toward the buffet. Several men were busy cutting the turkey meat for the guests. Dalya was happy to meet again Mr. Kenan Einsenberg, the Dean of Merchants. The great man was sitting in front of a huge turkey, a large fork and knife in each hand. And when he noticed Dalya, Mr. Kenan Einsenberg displayed a delighted smile:

- It's nice to see you, Demoiselle Dalya Bouvard!!
- I am delighted to see you too, Mr. Kenan Einsenberg. Dalya replied.

Since she could remember, Dalya always felt the attentive stares of Mr. Kenan Einsenberg toward her. He was always caring and kind to her. The Dean of Merchants even helped her to uncover a clue of the First Question.

Mr. Kenan Einsenberg filled the 3 plates that Dalya gave him:

- Here you go, Demoiselle ... the best turkey for you!!
- Thank you, Sir.

Before Dalya would leave him, Mr. Kenan Einsenberg said in a thoughtful tone:

- I hope you will finish all your turkey meat, Demoiselle ... you sure need strength and energy for next month!

Dalya guessed what Mr. Kenan Einsenberg meant by his words. The next month, Dalya will have to pass the Second Challenge. The Dean of Merchants had attended the First Challenge, last December. Dalya never dared to ask him why he was present there, that night. But she was always delighted with the encouragements of Mr. Kenan Einsenberg.

- I will, Sir. Thank you.

Dalya smiled back at him. She added some baked vegetables and sauce to the 3 plates, before returning back to her table. The little twins were happy to receive back their filled plates. Alfie and Maurice had served themselves some soup.

- Super ... good ... oatmeal soup ... of ... delicious ... try. Alfie muttered between mouthfuls.
- BREATHE!! YOU'LL STRANGLE YOURSELF WITH THE SOUP!! REMEMBER THAT YOUR BRAIN NEEDS OXYGEN!! Yelled Maurice all upset and worried about his friend.
- Soup ... deli ... good ... try the ... Dalya ...

Dalya asked her sisters if they wanted some soup too. Ari and Adi never ever refused any good food. Dalya then walked toward the large container where Mrs. Pierrefonds was serving people.

- Hello my dear ... would you like some soup?
- Yes. 2 bowls for my little sisters, please.

Mrs. Pierrefonds filled two bowls, and before handing them to Dalya, a little boy interrupted her:

- Mrs. Pierrefonds ... Mrs. Pierrefonds ... you are needed in the kitchen ... they lack the sauce to roast the turkey ... Mrs. Cosco don't know the ingredients she should mix!!
- But, I am serving soup to people ... I cannot leave now! Mrs. Pierrefonds said.
-

While taking the 2 bowls of soup from the woman's hand, Dalya proposed:

- I can handle it, Mrs. Pierrefonds ... I will bring the soup to my little sisters and I will replace you behind the cauldron, while you mix the sauce in the kitchen.
- Thank you, my dear!! I will be quick! Mrs. Pierrefonds smiled.

Dalya put the 2 soup bowls on the table, in front of her little sisters:

- Ari and Adi ... Here is your soup. Finish all your vegetables and I will let you pick desserts later. I will help serve the soup for a few minutes, and then I will come back.

Dalya asked Alfie and Maurice to keep an eye on her little sisters. Once Dalya stood behind the cauldron, the girl who juggled balls earlier, was her first client. Dalya filled a bowl and she handed it to her:

- It was a great show earlier on!! Congratulations!!

Miss Elsa blushed:

- Thank you, I almost dropped the balls twice because of stress.

Mr. Romane was the second in line. He giggled:

- This soup is so good ... I cannot help but take a second bowl!!
- You can take as many as you wish!! ... You impressed us with your movements with the stick of fire!! ... My little sisters were amazed by your movements!! Dalya smiled.
- The pleasure was all mine, my dear! Mr. Romane took his second bowl of soup and went all pleased with the compliment.

Mr. Leo and his dog Teo appeared in front of Dalya.

- Your scene was well done, Mr. Leo. We have never laughed as much as today!!
- Thank you Mademoiselle. We repeated for weeks. Replied Mr. Leo proudly.
- Here's your bowl Mr. Leo ... and ... here is a bowl for your dog, too. He deserves it for his great work today!

When Mr. Leo approached the bowl to his dog, the dog shivered his tail and his tongue.

- Thank you, Mademoiselle!! The soup will certainly please him!!

Dalya added 2 woods to burn under the cauldron to keep the soup warm. When she stood up, Dalya's uncle was in front of her.

- Would you like some soup, Uncle Adam? Dalya asked with a smile
- You've changed jobs? You're not a vegetable Merchant anymore, but a soup waitress now? Uncle Adam said with an arrogant smile.

Dalya was shocked by this remark. Yet, she pulled herself together quickly, and she handed him a full bowl, trying to keep her smile:

- I am replacing Mrs. Pierrefonds for a while. She is preparing the sauce to roast turkey in the kitchen ...

Uncle Adam stared at his niece from head to toe, with a mean look. Then, he went away. Uncle Jaafar followed. Dalya seized this opportunity to talk to her Uncle again, and make him speak:

- I hope you are having a good time and you are enjoying this party?

Uncle Jaafar looked at her, without a change in his face. Dalya filled a bowl, asking him:

- Do you also cook this soup at home, in the North?

Uncle Jaafar remained motionless and marble. Dalya gave him the bowl, trying for the last time:

- Have you tasted the stuffed turkey, Uncle Jaafar? Would you like me to get it for you?

Uncle Jaafar took his bowl of soup, and he just left, without looking at his niece, without a word, without a thank you. Dalya watched him go, until a voice interrupted her thoughts.

- Was he your friend, the kid who stumbled?

Uncle Fazio was in front of Dalya. He displayed a wide happy smile:

- He received his cheese on the face!! Did you see that?! ... On the face!!... He fall on his cheese!! Like a brick ... He received his prize on the face!

Dalya didn't think her friend Maurice's incident was funny, as Uncle Fazio did. She didn't understand her Uncle's reaction and didn't dare to ask him. She filled a bowl of soup in silence and she handed it to him. Uncle Fazio didn't stop laughing aloud:

- It was funny when he landed on his prize!! ... It was hilarious!! He had a very funny fall!!

For some long seconds, Dalya observed her Uncle Fazio walking toward the table where her family was settled. Moments after that, while she was arranging the bowls on the buffet table; Dalya received the visit of her Uncle Charles. After the strange comments of Uncle Charles toward her friends Alfie and Maurice, Dalya decided to weigh on her words. She smiled:

- Would you like a bowl of soup, Uncle Charles?
- What is it? He asked, taking a scrutinizing glance at the content of the cauldron.
- This is a great oatmeal soup, with vegetables, herbs, and gar...
- Oats? her Uncle exclaimed in shock
- Yes, it's very good. Mrs. Pierrefonds cooked it and she is a great Co...

Uncle Charles interrupted her in a scandalized and mocking voice:

- What are you talking about?! ... We give the oats to the sheep ... this thing is for animals to eat and not for us?! And I thought the people of the city were civilized!

Dalya didn't know what to answer to that. And before she could make a move, Uncle Charles disappeared among the crowd without tasting the soup. Dalya thought aloud:

- But ... the soup is really good ... Even Ari and Adi love it ...

She was interrupted by the enthusiastic voice of her Uncle Scott:

- Well ... this looks delicious!! I would like to have a bowl!! And fill it well as it should be!!
- Immediately, Uncle Scott. Said Dalya hurried.

When she handed him the bowl of soup, Uncle Scott asked her:

- I hope you will not lose the softdolls, you and your little sisters!

Dalya murmured all confused:

- No ... Uncle Scott ... certainly not ...
- It's good!! He exclaimed proudly, before continuing:
- Always remember that it is I who has offered them to you!!
- Yes ... thank you ...
- It's the good Uncle Scott who gave you these softdolls!! Keep them preciously!! Said Dalya's Uncle, before leaving to join his brothers.

Dalya didn't understand the remarks of her Uncle Scott. It has been the 4th time now in one day, since her Uncle told her about the softdolls. She didn't know what to do and what more to say, except to thank him for his gift.

- But ... why is Uncle Scott reminding me of his gift, at every moment?

Alfie joined Dalya near the cauldron, where she was stirring the soup with a large wood spoon. He put on the buffet table a full plate of bread slices buttered with garlic and some green herbs.

- Mrs. Pierrefonds will come back near the cauldron, in a minute. She handed me this plate to replace the one that was emptied.
- Ari and Adi? asked Dalya
- They are with Maurice. They have almost finished their plates.

Dalya added 2 woods underneath the cauldron, while Alfie was serving himself soup. When a man appeared in front of them. Uncle Alex asked in a serious and cold tone:

- Fill me a bowl of soup.

Dalya obeyed immediately. When she handed him the full soup bowl, her Uncle Alex took it without another word. And at that moment, Uncle Alex made an unusual move. Under the shocked stares of Dalya and Alfie, Uncle Alex lifted with one hand, the entire full plate of buttered bread, that Alfie had just brought there a few seconds ago, and then Uncle Alex just left.

Usually, people take many portions of the buffet meal, and they generously filled their plates. However, no one ever took with him the entire dish, all for himself. Dalya and Alfie remained motionless and stunned, because of Uncle Alex's selfish move. After some long seconds of silence and confusion, Alfie finally asked Dalya:

- Your Uncle ... is he aware that it's a sharing holiday?

Moments later, Mrs. Pierrefonds took her place back behind the cauldron and Dalya walked her little sisters toward the desserts corner. When they returned back on the bench, Maurice noticed that Dalya was lost in her thoughts:

- All is well Dalya?

She pulled herself together and smiled:

- Yes, Maurice … all is well.

This is what Dalya tried to believe. It was not the Thanksgiving holiday that Dalya had hoped for. Yet, the food was excellent, the shows on the stage were fun and amazing, the place was well organized, Mr. Pierrefonds and his family were very welcoming and friendly, the mood was joyful, everyone was laughing.

However ... something was bothering Dalya's mind. The words and attitudes of her Uncles were far from what the little Dalya Bouvard had hoped for.

Chapter 31

A family lunch

The next morning. Saturday, November 28th, 1891. In the Annex house of the grand Mansion.

Dalya helped her mother prepare the lunch table for their new guests. Dalya put the plates and cutlery, while her mother cut sliced bread and buttered it with garlic and herbs. Dalya's father undertook to place the big vegetable soup pot on the dining table. The little twins were already installed on their chairs in front of the table.

The 6 Uncles and Aunt came inside the kitchen, on the right time for lunch. Since this morning, they went on a tour in downtown, to buy some special supplies and tools they needed for their work in the farm.

The brothers and sister, settled all around the big lunch table that Antman had expanded. The only missing person was Uncle Giorgi; he had a stomach ache, because of too much turkey the day before.

When everyone was gathered around the table, Uncle Charles said aloud:

- I hope it will be good this time!! ... Not so poor and ordinary as your friend's meal of the Thanksgiving holiday!! ... I still can't believe that you people eat oats! ... Animal food?!

Dalya noticed that her Uncle Charles didn't filter his words, at all. His comments were often hurtful and mean. Dalya's father smiled nervously:

- My wife has prepared an excellent roasted chicken ... with a vegetable soup and some br...

Fazio screamed outraged:

- Soup again?! Don't you eat anything chewable, in this house! Are you on a diet?

Mrs. Augustine put down her plate of buttered bread with a sudden move, and she stared angrily at Fazio. Dalya put the big green salad plate on the table and she sat immediately near her little sisters to serve them.

- Antman ... should I wait an hour for you to serve me? The Aunt Reeda asked in an authoritarian tone.

Dalya's father hurried to fill his sister's plate of green salad and chicken. All the Uncles served themselves. The family lunch began.

- When are you returning to your old 2 rooms' house? Asked Charles in a natural tone between bites of salad.

Antman almost suffocated on his bite, he drank some water and answered:

- Never!
- How come never? Charles insisted in astonishment.

Antman relaxed on his chair and he said with a confident and assured tone:

- Because my daughter will manage to succeed at the Challenges ... and I will have this heritage money.

His brother Adam asked in a mocking tone:

- How can you be so sure? She cannot even read and write!

Dalya's mother Mrs. Augustine Bouvard served herself vegetable soup and said:

- That's what I keep telling him since the beginning, but your brother is stubborn. It's my daughter and I know her well; she is just an idiot and an ignorant!
- She is an illiterate. Charles continued

Dalya, who was sitting on the other end of the table, she dared to answer proudly:

- I am studying at the Royal Georgetown College. It is the most prestigious school in the entire East Coast of the United States.

The 6 Uncles, Aunt and Dalya's parents, all looked at her in surprise. It seems that they all forgot that this little girl was attending school since many months now. And yet, Dalya proudly continued:

- I took classes in Mathematics, Geography, History and Music. I got 16/20 in Mathematics. Professor Wyatt said it was a very good grade.
- And how the course of History or Geography can help a veggy seller, like you? Uncle Charles wondered aloud.

Dalya was about to answer her Uncle Charles, when her father surpassed her:

- History or Geography or Music or whatever ... my only goal is that she succeeds these Challenges and that I have this fortune!!

Since long ago, her father had set his goal on this fortune, and it was useless to dissuade him. The conversation continued with Antman asking his brothers:

- Did you find the ropes you needed?
- Yes, and it was not an easy search. Alex replied. The Merchant had only one in stock; he wanted us to pay a much higher price for it.
- Fortunately, Reeda was with us ... our beloved sister always helps us with her persuasive character. Said Scott.

Dalya discreetly observed her Aunt Reeda. Despite her quietness most of the time, unlike her brothers too talkative, Aunt Reeda inspired no trust or kindness to Dalya, nor to her little sisters. Ari and Adi were always friendly toward everyone; yet the little twins didn't get close an inch to their aunt. Her coldness and authority were intimidating.

Uncle Charles laughed in a mean way, in the middle of a conversation between his brothers Alex and Antman:

- A veggy seller ... studying Music! I cannot believe what I'm hearing!

Dalya replied in a spontaneous tone:

- And why not? ... My friend Maurice knows how to play the flute, and it's magnif...

The mean laugh of Uncle Fazio interrupted Dalya and it made her little sisters jump:

- Your friend Maurice!! ... The one who received the cheese on his face!! What a fall!! He received his prize right where it should be!! ... Did you see his fall? Did you see how he fell from the stairs? It was just like a brick!!

The brothers laughed aloud. Dalya still couldn't understand what was funny in the incident fall of her friend Maurice.

- Are you going to plant corn this year? asked Antman
- We thought about it, yes. Especially with the good rain we had last year, the land is fertile. Charles replied.

Dalya chose to ignore the conversation and focus on cutting a piece of roasted chicken for her little sisters. She served some chicken to her sister Adi.

When suddenly ... a left hand held the chicken on one side, and a right hand cut the chicken in half, with a knife. Under the astonished stares of Dalya, Uncle Alex didn't take one piece of the chicken ... he took half the chicken into his plate, and he ate it with appetite, without caring about anyone else.

It was the first time in her life that the little Dalya Bouvard understood the meaning of the word selfishness.

Dalya cut some chicken for her sister Ari. She served her sisters some sauce on top of the chicken, and then she continued her soup.

- Do you plan to buy a cow next month? asked Antman
- Maybe even a little earlier … we need help with the harvest. Adam replied.
- And we can also produce more milk! Continued Charles.
- My friend Aymeric has made a good deal out of his farm. Antman explained. He sells up to 40 liters of milk per day, thanks to his 4 cows and 5 goats!!
- What type does he have? Scott wondered

Antman served himself some of the remaining chicken, while explaining:

- If I remember well ... he has 2 Brown Swiss cows, since 5 years now. And he bought two Holstein cows, 3 years ago.
- Are they used for the harvest? asked Charles
- No, I don't think so. Antman said, pouring the sauce on his chicken before continuing:
- Aymeric uses his cows only to produce milk and cheese. He has other cattle to harvest his land. But I admit that he has well invested his money in cows. They produce the best cheese in the entire city!! ... I even heard that a Senator orders cheese from him!!

Dalya was cutting bread and butter into small pieces for her sisters, when a voice asked her:

- Your little sisters eat all their meals by themselves?

Uncle Scott got up to pour himself some water from a jug on the kitchen counter, near Dalya. She answered her Uncle Scott:

- Yes, they mastered the fork and spoon since some time now, but when they are too hungry they eat with their hands.

Before Uncle Scott returned to his seat, he asked Dalya in a curious tone:

- Where are the softdolls that I have given you?

Dalya froze and stared at her Uncle Scott, in a puzzled look:

- The ... softdolls are in my sisters' bedroom ... so as not to get them dirty at lunch ...
- That's good!! Yes!! You must not stain these gifts that I have offered you!!

Uncle Scott sat back on his chair and he continued his lunch, participating in the conversation among his brothers. But Dalya still couldn't understand the attention of her Uncle toward these softdolls. She stopped counting the number of times that her Uncle Scott spoke about them.

And it was not the only thing that preoccupied the little girl's mind. Dalya was sitting across the table in front of her Uncle Jaafar. During the meal, her Uncle didn't say a single word. He ate his meal without hearing his brothers' discussion. After she had failed several times to make him talk, Dalya didn't try to speak to her Uncle Jaafar anymore. His calm was unfazed, indifferent and cold.

- And what will you do after your daughter fails next month? Charles asked his brother Antman, in an amused arrogant voice.

Dalya let out a discreet sigh, unquestionably her Uncle Charles spoke only hurtful and crushing comments. Her father Antman answered his brother, in a confident voice:

- Oh no!! She will not fail ... I assure you of that, Charles!!
- If you say so ... Charles replied, displaying a mocking smile.

- In my opinion, I think you shouldn't count on your little girl that much! It is obvious to everyone that she will fail! Said Adam.

At that moment, Uncle Fazio let out a loud laugh:

- And it will be a great failure!! Can you imagine that? She will freeze when answering the Challenge ... And the very next day, you will return to live in your old 2 rooms' house!! ... She will fail ... sure and certain!! ... A beautiful failure!!

Dalya observed her Uncle Fazio for a long second. She had met many coldest and meanest people. But throughout her life, Dalya had never met anyone who laughed and rejoiced of people's failures ... And it was a villain vicious flaw!

Dalya was happy to receive visits from her paternal family before the holidays. But sometimes, it happens that the people we hope to meet, disappoint us. Dalya's appetite vanished; she put her spoon down on the table, and she watched her little sisters Adi and Ari finishing their meals. Uncle Fazio continued his mockery:

- She won't succeed at this Challenge!! She will be a great disappointment!! We'll laugh very well! A great fall!

For the first time since the beginning of the meal, the Aunt Reeda spoke. Her voice was icy and imposing:

- It's a pity you didn't have boys, Antman.

Dalya's father choked on a bite of bread. Dalya's mother became pale with anger. None of the six brothers dared to say a word. The Aunt Reeda continued her statement, while slowly cutting her piece of chicken, with a firm move:

- A boy would have served you better than a girl.

No one has ever dared to say such a thing to Dalya ... in all her life! At that moment, Dalya couldn't hold back her anger:

- And exactly, in what would a boy be better than me?

Instantly, a heavy silence fell in the room. Everyone turned around and looked at Dalya. Nobody ever dared to answer Reeda Bouvard before. The Aunt Reeda looked at her niece with an arrogant smile, and she replied in a calm cold voice:

- A boy would be better than you ... in everything. In the farm work, in the sale of vegetables and fruits, in the work of renov...

For the first time ever, Dalya lost her good manners, and she dared to interrupt her Aunt:

- But I already do all of this work! I helped my father at the Saturday market, I sold my potato bags, I helped my parents to renovate this house, I even painted my own room, I help mother in all the housework, I take care of the garden, I wash the carriage and organize the garage, I can perfectly work at the farm! I can do all the work by myself!

The Aunt Reeda didn't appreciate the audacity of Dalya. And Dalya didn't appreciate the inappropriate comments of her Aunt Reeda.

- It's good. But nonetheless ... it's a shame that you're just a girl.
- And why is that? Dalya asked in a shocked tone.
- Because ... it would have been better if you had been a boy.
- I don't understand your point, Aunt Reeda.

The Aunt Reeda put down her knife and fork, she stared at her niece with an arrogant look, and she explained in a calm cruel voice:

- Well, it's obvious ... a boy is always best in everything, than a girl ... a boy is always helpful to his family than a girl ... a boy will always be more valuable than a girl ... a boy always has a better future than a girl ... This is how it is.

Dalya was paralyzed by what she had just heard. She endured nasty comments all her life, she dealt with the worst insults, she received the worst attitudes, she met the worst evils ... but never ... really never Dalya heard such a mean comment. Even Dalya's parents who mistreated her, they never told her such a cruel thing. Though Dalya has always been calm, on that moment, she felt her ears burning; fever came up to her forehead, her lips trembling and her heart beating at fast speed. Never Dalya Bouvard had been so angry!

The Aunt Reeda continued to cut her chicken slowly and with great satisfaction. None of the 6 Uncles dared to place a word. Dalya's parents exchanged an embarrassed look, but they were forced not to upset Reeda Bouvard. The Aunt seemed to have an intimidating and imposing character. The lunch ended in a heavy and dense silence.

It certainly was not the best family reunion that Dalya imagined. She repressed her anger, and forced herself to stay calm.

Several minutes later, at the end of the lunch, Mrs. Augustine asked Dalya to bring the 3 pear pies that she had prepared the day before. Dalya complied. When Mrs. Augustine pulled the white napkins off the pies, she screamed:

- BUT WHAT IS THAT??!!

Dalya remembered yesterday's incident. Her Uncle Fazio had tasted the pie. And her Uncle Adam watched him without saying a word. Dalya knew that her mother would be so upset by finding the half-eaten pie. Suddenly, Mrs. Augustine pinched Dalya's cheek with a violent move:

- WHY DID YOU EAT THIS PIE??!!

Dalya jumped, but she dared to answer anyway:

- It's not ... I ... I did ... nothing!

Mrs. Augustine dropped her daughter's cheek with a sudden move and she yelled:

- AND WHO ELSE HAS DONE THIS?! BESIDES YOU, LITTLE VERMIN!!

Dalya fell to the floor. Her cheek burned and was all red. Dalya immediately answered, pointing out her finger:

- I didn't do anything!! It's him ... he ate the pie!! I tried to stop him but he wouldn't listen!!

All the eyes headed toward Fazio Bouvard. He let out a nervous laugh:

- I didn't eat anything ... come on!

Dalya didn't believe her ears, she stood up quickly:

- But this is not true!!! He ate the pie before we left for the Thanksgiving party, to Mr. Pierrefonds house!!
- Your little girl has a lot of imagination. Fazio laughed.

But Dalya insisted:

- I am not imagining anything!! Uncle Fazio ate the pie!! And Uncle Adam can confirm what I say; he was present in the kitchen on that moment!!

Uncle Adam answered in calm cold voice:

- I don't know what she's talking about.

Dalya was shocked by his answer. She couldn't believe what she was hearing. Dalya jumped:

- But it is unfair!! You were there and you saw him eating the pie!! Why would you lie? Why would you hide the truth?

Uncle Charles laughed aloud:

- Well well ... here's Antman education!! ... Your daughter is not as well educated as you pretend she is!!

Aunt Reeda added her opinion too:

- This girl has an audacious tongue ... We visit you for some days, and we are treated as liars ... it's a funny welcoming, Antman ... disappointing ... very disappointing!!

Dalya's father stood up brutally and he yelled:

- HOW DARE YOU TREAT YOUR UNCLE AS A LIAR!

Dalya defended herself as best as she could:

- But ... it's Uncle Fazio who ate the pie!! I am telling the truth!! And Uncle Adam was present and he saw it!!

At this moment, Dalya's father made a head sign to his wife. Mrs. Augustine caught Dalya by the arm in a sudden brusque move, and she dragged her to the garage under Dalya's begs:

- I didn't do anything ... I swear it's not me ... I didn't do anything ...

Chapter 32

Advices

Sunday, November 29th, 1891. The Annex house of the grand Mansion. The evening.

The November nights were colder and longer. The naked sky was decorated with stars, competing with each other to who shines brighter. The air was dry and cooler, announcing a close winter coming to the city of Georgetown.

Dalya had homework of the Mathematics course, due next week. Sitting in front of her desk, she tried to write her answers on the paper. But Dalya couldn't bend or move her fingers. Although she knew the answers to her homework, Dalya was unable to write a single word.

After several minutes of trying in vain, Dalya put down her pen, and she lay back on her chair. Dalya endured a cruel injustice. No matter how much she defended herself and spoke, no one listened. Feeling weak and powerless in front of the cruelty, Dalya buried her face in her hands wrapped in lace beige gloves and she let her tears flow down. The little girl cried silently and painfully.

A few moments later, Dalya heard her name called downstairs by her mother. She dried her eyes and she went down to the living room. Inside, Dalya found her 6 Uncles, her Aunt and her parents, seated on the chairs, enjoying a hot tea.

- So just like that, a box gives you clues to answer this Challenge? Uncle Charles Exclaimed.

While standing motionless, Dalya didn't speak, she didn't look at anyone, and she kept her head down.

- That's as silly requirement ... why didn't he simply give her the inheritance money? Uncle Alex asked.

Uncle Charles served himself some sugar, thinking aloud:

- It shows how much this Governor is crazy!! What an idiot!!

Dalya's mother laughed in an arrogant tone:

- And he wants to give his entire fortune to an idiot who will never succeed!!
- Probably because he was not sane. Uncle Adam joined the conversation.
- The entire town will know about her failure!! Uncle Fazio laughed.

Clearly, Dalya didn't expect her Uncles to be such people. She remained standing immobile, not daring to say a word, her head down. She hoped to return back to her bedroom and be away from her Uncles. When suddenly, Uncle Charles straightened up on his chair and he asked Dalya:

- Show us a clue!

Dalya hesitated:

- It's just that ... I only have two clues left ... And I prefer to ask for a clue, only when I need it ...
- GO GET THIS DAMN BOX! AND ASK FOR A CLUE! Yelled Dalya's father with a menacing tone.

Dalya turned around unwillingly, and she came down a few seconds later holding the small box. Dalya placed it on the little table in the center of the living room. All eyes were amazed by this strange box.

A shiny and powerful metal. A small rectangular opening on the edge. The top side of the box opened, and a cage of transparent and bright glass, in an oval form, straightened up in a slow and confident movement. The cage was welded after a few seconds by four cylinders in yellow gold forged and shaped as vine plant. A round clock arose within the transparent cage. A small needle attached to December 12, 1891. A big needle was between this night, on 29th and 30th November 1981.

The 6 Uncles and Aunt had wide big eyes and opened mouths, facing such a wonderful and unique object. Dalya's father insisted:

- Request a clue!

Dalya hesitated for a moment, then she took a little paper and wrote:

What is the 4th clue?

She introduced the paper into the rectangular opening of the strange box. Instantly, the 6 Uncles and Aunt jumped off their chairs and stepped back brusquely, because of the blinding light that crossed the oval glass cage. Seconds later, a small paper came out of the Excelbox.

Dalya was used to receive incomprehensible clues. She always needed days and weeks to uncover the meaning of a single sentence of this strange box. Except that this time, the moment Dalya read the clue, she couldn't believe her eyes. She reread it several times quickly. The clue was ... crystal clear.

- So? ... What does it say? Asked Uncle Charles impatient.
- Because you think she understands anything of it? Uncle Adam replied.
- She is an idiot; I am telling you. She never understands anything! Dalya's mother relaxed back on her chair.

- The failure is announced much earlier than expected!! Uncle Fazio laughed.
- That girl is really disappointing, Antman. The Aunt Reeda took back her tea.
- It's true!! Disappointing!! I shouldn't have lost my money to offer you and your sisters the softdolls!! Said Uncle Scott.

Dalya didn't dare to move or say a word. She held the paper of the clue in her hands, standing in front of her parents, her 6 Uncles and her aunt. Because of her silence, Dalya's father yelled:

- What is the matter with you?! Did you become mute?! Talk you idiot!!

Dalya obeyed. She turned toward her six Uncles and aunt, and then read aloud:

We continue to uncover, to learn, and to grow.
We continue to awaken, educate and dazzle.

Dalya looked at her Uncle Scott:

To the first constantly reminding his charities,
One could learn from the bee, offering goods and honey, for free.

Dalya addressed her Uncle Fazio:

To the second having fun of others' trips and falls,
One wonders, who's a lizard to laugh about a wolf?

Dalya turned to her Uncle Alex:

To the third who thinks only of himself,
One can assure you, as smart as the fox may be, he always end up lonely

Dalya observed her Uncle Charles:

To the fourth who filters no moves or words,
One could learn from the Owl, her politeness and silence make you bow

Dalya looked at her Uncle Adam:

To the fifth who hid the truth,
One guarantee, the monkey may jump well, but it will not escape a fall

Dalya faced her Uncle Jaafar:

To the sixth who is an austere cold,

One is amazed, how can bears live in winter, yet their hearts are warm.

Dalya looked at her Aunt Reeda:

To the last who only speaks venom,

One gladly reminds you, whatever the skunk releases, it sticks on it too.

And to all the befores and all the upcomings,

Our advices are only to keep or to let go.

A heavy tense silence reigned in the living room. No one dared to speak or move. Everyone was stunned and in shock.

After some long seconds, only Dalya decided to act. Without a word, she picked up the Excelbox and she went back to her bedroom, leaving her parents, her Aunt and her 6 Uncles, behind her.

Dalya gently placed the Excelbox on her desk and she sat in front of it, watching the transparent glass cage, the beautiful vine curves encircling the cage, and the luxurious clock inside of it.

During their stay, Dalya couldn't defend herself from the meanness and cruelty of her 6 Uncles and her Aunt. The little girl couldn't make her voice be heard.

Oh however ... when this strange little box lit up ... when the Excelbox speaks up ... trust what I say ... by fair means or fouls … you will hear very clearly her voice!

Chapter 33

Free generosity

Monday, November 30th, 1891.

Dalya woke up early. A sweet ray of sunshine crossed the window of her bedroom. Some clouds decorated the blue sky, and a light winter wind blew gently. Dalya put on her boy's overalls and her large cap, and then she went down to have breakfast with her family.

The 6 Uncles and Aunt had left well before dawn. Despite their characters, Dalya would have politely greeted them before their departure. Except that after reading the 4th clue, the day before, Dalya didn't dare to add another word and she didn't know what to tell her 6 Uncles and Aunt.

In the kitchen, her little sisters were already awake, sitting on their chairs in front of the table, enjoying mashed sweetened bread with milk. Dalya's father had left home earlier, for some work. When Mrs. Augustine noticed Dalya, she ordered her daughter:

- I need you to take your sisters outside; I have to clean the house today.
- Alright.

Dalya was happy she didn't have to stay to help her mother in the housework, for once. And after some the hard last days, Dalya needed a break. She served herself bread and jam, before asking her little sisters:

- How about a walk in downtown city, today?

The little twins straightened up on their chairs, they agreed right away:

- Downtown!! Yes!! Yes!! Yes!! Downtown!!
- We will visit Uncle Giorgi before ... but only if you both behave well!! Dalya threatened them with a serious look.
- Yes!! Behave ... Behave!!

Even though the little Ari and Adi didn't know what this word meant, they were happy to go outside with their older sister.

After they finished breakfast, Dalya dressed her little sisters in their little pink winter coats and white hats. Ari and Adi took their softdolls in their hands, and they left the Annex house. The Snow Panther quietly watched the 3 girls through the large living room windows of the grand Mansion. Séraphine sat motionless in her place, until the 3 silhouettes disappeared from the grand Mansion.

The Dumbarton Oaks Park path was peaceful. The spacious gardens were neatly trimmed. The lake welcomed ducks and white swans, to the delight of the little twins that watched them for a moment.

Several minutes of walk later, Dalya and her little sisters came close to the French neighbor's home, Les Poirier. The housekeeper, Mrs. Glorina was sweeping the house entrance.

- Good morning, Mademoiselle Dalya!! How nice to see you!!

Dalya paused in front of the entrance door of the garden.

- How are you Mrs. Glorina?

The woman approached and she opened the garden's door:

- Getting ready for winter ... I hope it will be Snowing for the December holidays.
- I hope so too ... my little sisters love to play in the Snow.

Mrs. Glorina knelt down in front of the little twins and she smiled at them. It was the first time that Mrs. Glorina met Dalya's little sisters.

- Hello Mesdemoiselles ... you are very beautiful with your hats and winter coats!!
- Thank you!! Thank you!! Murmured the little twins with a smile.

Mrs. Glorina stood up:

- Your sisters are lovely, Mademoiselle!!
- It depends on the day, Mrs. Glorina. Dalya sighed.
- Are you going somewhere? Asked the woman.
- Yes, mother is cleaning the house today. So I am in charge of keeping my sisters busy. We will visit my Uncle Giorgi, and we'll go for a walk downtown.
- It's a very beautiful day for a walk, Mademoiselle!! You have done very well to go outside for some fresh air!!

The little twins let off their sister's hands and they followed a butterfly inside the garden of les Poirier, while their big sister was talking to Mrs. Glorina.

- And how is Madame these days?
- She is well ... the weather is cold this month, so she doesn't leave the house.
- Yes, I understand.
- But currently, Mrs. Marianne spends more time in the living room than in her bedroom. I lit the fireplace all day for her.

The little twins were running near the bird's nest in the center of the garden, they giggled while chasing a butterfly.

- At least, she doesn't stay all day in her bedroom. said Dalya

- Yes, for sure!! And Mr. Richard sends her the newspaper every day for the guessing words game ... she loves it as much as I do!! Mrs. Glorina laughed.

The little twins walked in the garden, near the planted roses, leaving the lucky butterfly that had escaped their hunt.

- And how are your classes at school?
- It's well, Mrs. Glorina. I got good grades in Mathematics and even in Music, despite my delay compared to the other students! Dalya announced proudly.
- Because you are studious, Mademoiselle!! I was so sure of that!!
- We had a lot of homework for this Thanksgiving holiday. I still have some questions in History that I have to finish this aftern...

Dalya stopped and watched from afar, her little twin sisters who had their back turned. She couldn't see what Ari and Adi were doing, but their silence didn't announce anything good.

- Excuse me ... Mrs. Glorina ... I have to check on what my sisters are doing.

Dalya crossed the garden and she approached her little sisters. And when she found out what the twins had done!! ... Ari and Adi had picked the roses of Mrs. Marianne Poirier and they each held a small bouquet of flowers in their hands. Dalya was shocked.

- But ... what is ... why did you ... it's ... Madam's roses!!

The little twins displayed a joyful smile, and they showed their little bouquets of roses to their big sister:

- Zoli flowers!! Looky Dindin!! Very Zoli flowers!! You want zoli flowers too?

Dalya trembled with anger. Mrs. Glorina joined the 3 sisters and she laughed:

- They've made a nice bouquet of flowers!!
- But ... it's ... it's Madam's roses!! I ... I'm so sorry ... Madame will be upset to know she doesn't have any more rose in her garden ... they picked almost all the roses ... she will be upset ... I'm so sorry!!
- It's nothing really, Mademoiselle!! Mrs. Glorina tried to calm down Dalya. Mrs. Marianne will understand. And besides, the roses will grow up again ... there will be more and more...

The little twins approached Mrs. Glorina and they offered her their bouquets to see:

- You want zoli flowers too? ... Looky ... zoli flowers!!

Mrs. Glorina knelt in front of the little twins:

- You are adorable, Mesdemoiselles!!

Dalya couldn't contain her anger:

- Adorable?! I leave them free for one minute and they find a way to make fooleries!! Madame will be very upset to know that she doesn't have any more roses in her garden!! AND THIS IS BECAUSE OF TWO LITTLE PESTS!! GIVE ME BACK THE FLOWERS RIGHT NOW!!

The two little twins yelled no with one voice, before running each in an opposite side.

- COME HERE YOU!! LET GO OF THESE FLOWERS!! STOP RUNNING!!

Dalya tried to catch her little sisters, but in vain. Ari and Adi ran around the garden, giggling innocently and loudly, happy to escape their big sister's anger.

Mrs. Glorina was not the only one laughing while watching this scene. The shadow of Mrs. Marianne Poirier appeared on the large window of her bedroom. The great woman was curious to hear yells and laughs in her garden. She didn't understand what was happening, but at the sight of Dalya Bouvard running in all directions to catch two little girls amused by escaping from her, Mrs. Marianne laughed too.

- STOP RUNNING, I AM TALKING TO YOU!! LET GO OF THESE FLOWERS!! NO, THIS IS NOT A GAME!! YOU COME HERE!!

After several minutes of running and hunting, Dalya finally could catch her little sisters. She insisted on giving back the roses bouquets to Mrs. Glorina, despite the woman's refusal.

- Will you tell Madame that I'm sorry for her roses ... the next weekend I will bring you roses to plant here in the garden ... and I'm sorry for my sisters' foolery ...
- It's nothing really, Mademoiselle. Mrs. Glorina couldn't hold her amused laugh.

The woman knelt before the little twins and she smiled:

- It was a great pleasure to meet you ... Mesdemoiselles. You are welcomed here anytime!!

Ari and Adi smiled back at her:

- And we'll have zoli bouquet flowers?

Mrs. Glorina laughed aloud and she hugged them in her arms. Dalya left the house of the French neighbors, les Poirier, firmly holding her little sisters' hands.

The scenery on the road gradually changed from luxurious big houses to smaller and modest houses. Once the home of Uncle Giorgi appeared at the end of the road, the little twins broke away from the hands of their big sister and they ran yelling:

- Ogi!! Ogi!! Ogi!! Ogi!!

Uncle Giorgi's workshop was a big bazaar, where objects, gadgets and machines were piled on each other. It was difficult to discern the front door and the windows of the house.

A long thin man, with peppery curly hair and a large charcoal mustache, wearing a long apron with thousand pockets, came out to welcome his little nieces with open arms.

- My little mouses!!

Ari and Adi kissed their Uncle, before running toward the inside of his workshop. If there is one place that the little twins adored, it was the workshop of their Uncle, where they discovered so many bizarre items they played with.

- Mouses who do fooleries all day long and then escape!! Dalya sighed.
- Hello Biggo!! Uncle Giorgi laughed.
- Hello Uncle Giorgi.

Dalya settled on a chair inside the workshop:

- Mother needed me to occupy them today, while she cleans the house. We were going for a walk downtown, and I thought to stop by and see you.
- Your visit gives me great pleasure!!

While sitting on his big old chair, Uncle Giorgi was curious:

- I wanted to ask about the clue that you brought me the other day ...

The Excelbox clues fascinated Dalya's Uncle. Handyman and talented at solving problems, Giorgi Bouvard was always curious to understand the Excelbox clues. And Dalya enjoyed discussing the clues with him. She straightened up from her chair and informed him:

- So ... do you remember the first sentence? ... At JV-20-89, breath will be found ... the number was the coordinates of a book in the National Georgetown Library!
- Fascinating!! ... And what book was it?
- Memoirs of underwater diving! … And I can assure you, Uncle Giorgi … this book was very useful!

Uncle Giorgi was surprised:

- I always knew that the Excelbox is special! … And the second number? What was it?
- 17-HR-08 ... it was a time … 17:08!!

Uncle Giorgi exclaimed:

- I never thought it would be a time, Biggo ... very clever ... very very clever ...
- Me neither ... it was only by pure luck that I found out!!... And by the way, Uncle Giorgi … you never told me how you found the 3rd number … between the 69th and the 59th?

At this question, Uncle Giorgi laughed:

- Well … it was by pure luck too! … I needed a special spiral for a machine that I was making. I visited the Merchant from whom I usually buy, but he didn't have the size that I needed. And at the door, before I could leave his shop, the Merchant said to me: check the auto parts salesman; he may have the spiral you are looking for. When I asked him the address, he said: between 69th and 59th Street!!

- It's incredible!! Dalya was amazed.

Uncle Giorgi continued:

- And when as soon as I knew it, I ran straightaway to the grand Mansion to tell you!!
- And what about the spiral?
- I completely forgot to buy it, since that day!!

Uncle Giorgi and Dalya laughed aloud and amused, for a long minute. Uncle Giorgi got up from his chair and he came near a little weird Machine placed on his desk; he tightened the nails one by one, asking always in a curious tone:

- And have you found what the number 1703 meant, Biggo?
- Yes, and it was a quite strange discovery!!
- How?
- 1703 ... it's the postcode of the grand Mansion!

Uncle Giorgi thought aloud:

- Really?! ... The postcode? ... This box is smarter than we have thought ... It's a genius!

After a few moments of silence, the Uncle had finished tightening all the nails, he took a small brush and cleaned the machine which he was working on.

- And the last number, Biggo? ... AV-07-90 ... did you discover what it was?
- Not yet. Between Thanksgiving and homework, I haven't had time to search for it.
- You'll find it Biggo!! I am sure of that!! I always thought you were smart and talented; my intuition is never wrong!!

It is true that Uncle Giorgi was very different from all his brothers and sister. Since very young, Dalya always felt the care and kindness of her Uncle. He was always patient to explain to her his bizarre inventions, he always helped her find solutions to her worries, he always called her Biggo and called her little sisters the Mouses. Uncle Giorgi was nothing like his other siblings, including Antman. Dalya watched her Uncle Giorgi working on his strange machine. After a moment, Dalya dared to say:

- Uncle Giorgi ... thank you for always being kind, polite and caring ... not only with me and my little sisters, but with everyone.

Uncle Giorgi was stunned and surprised by his niece's comment. Yet, he instantly understood that Dalya was disappointed by her 6 Uncles and Aunt. Giorgi Bouvard knew perfectly and sadly well that his family was difficult sometimes. And when he couldn't find any words to comfort his niece, Uncle Giorgi sincerely and sadly smiled at her:

- I ... it's ... Biggo …

When suddenly, a strong explosion shake the entire workshop. Uncle Giorgi and Dalya jumped at once and exclaimed simultaneously:

- THE TWINS!!!

Because these little pests never do things by half, they succeed in the worst imaginable foolery. How these two little Mouses managed to destroy a 2 meters long machine? Dalya and her uncle were confused. Dalya cleaned her little sisters from dust on their faces, under the amused laughs of her Uncle Giorgi.

Ari and Adi shouldn't be watched every minute… but every second!

Dalya and her little sisters continued their way on to downtown. And this time, the little twins walked silently and sagely near their big sister, firmly holding their softdolls. They were aware of having done enough fooleries for one day.

The city of Georgetown after the Thanksgiving holiday was empty. Downtown was not as busy and noisy as in the other days. Most people traveled to the other cities during the holidays, to spend time with their extended family.

Dalya thought about visiting her friends Alfie and Maurice at their usual corner between two streets, a few steps away from the luxurious Toscana restaurant. And as usual, they were present there.

- Hello Maurice... Hello Alfie!!

Maurice was repairing his shoe shine box. Without lifting his head, he greeted her:

- Hi Dalya!!

Alfie was arranging his newspapers in his backpack:

- Hello Dalya. Are you walking Downtown, all 3 of you?
- Yes, and we spent all the day doing fooleries too! Dalya sighed.

Her little twin sisters let go of an innocent giggle. Dalya settled her little sisters on a bench and she sat near them, she watched them closely, as she spoke to her friends, to avoid more fooleries. And we must admit that the little Ari and Adi have calmed down. Maurice took out of his bag 2 strawberry lollipops that his father sold in his shop, and he offered them to the twins. They adored sweets!! The little twins firmly held their softdolls in their hands and watched passersby and shops, while enjoying their lollipops.

- Did your 6 Uncles and Aunt go back? asked Alfie
- Yes, this morning at dawn. They have 2 to 3 days on the road.

- And I thought my Uncle was hard and difficult ... I appreciate him way more now since I've met your Uncles! Exclaimed Alfie.
- Yes, I too didn't expect my Uncles and Aunt to be like that. Dalya sighed.
- Well, we never stop discovering people! Maurice laughed. Fortunately they live 2 days away!! Even 10 days away will not be a bad thing!!

Dalya and Alfie laughed to their friend Maurice's comment. He took a small hammer from his pocket and he fixed a nail on his shine shoes box.

- Did you know that Mr. Aymeric gave a 2nd large portion of soft cheese to Maurice?
- Really!! Exclaimed Dalya all happy for her friend. When was that?

Maurice replied proudly:

- Yesterday afternoon. We were doing our usual tour me and Alfie, and we met him not so far away. He called me and told me to follow him to his farm to give me a 2nd serving of cheese.

Alfie continued:

- And he gave us eggs and milk too!!
- Mr. Aymeric is always friendly and caring. Dalya replied. Each time, he gives me extra eggs when I visit him.
- I never would have thought that Mr. Aymeric was good at the guessing words game!! Alfie thought aloud.
- But of course he is! Don't you remember the fair, two years ago, where Mr. Aymeric had a milk stand, and he offered an extra liter to the one who answered his riddles!! Dalya jumped.
- And how does he know all these riddles? asked Maurice
- Probably from a book ... or from someone. Alfie thought.
- Or he invents them. said Dalya
- How can we invent riddles? That must be hard! Alfie was surprised.

The lively conversation between the three friends went on. And the little twins Ari and Adi were enjoying their lollipops. The street was gradually filled by passersby who walked or did their shopping on this day. The air was a little softer because of the bright sun. The street had many small shops and kiosks of various types and kinds.

- So... if I use milk on an ink stain, it takes it away? Are you sure about that? asked Dalya
- Yes! Certain! Just a little drop of milk on a cloth. Said Maurice while arranging the box in his backpack.
- Sounds weird as a trick ... but I can confirm it works! Alfie exclaimed, while standing up.
- I'm going to try it. My shirt is all tainted with blue and black ink. Thank you, Maurice.

Her friend smiled proudly. Alfie and Maurice had to leave to begin their newspaper sales and shoeshine tour.

- Good day Dalya!! We'll see you next Saturday at the market!! Try to come a little early!!
- Good day Ari ... Good day Adi!!

Dalya turned toward her little sisters, sitting close to her on the bench:

- Shall we go home, little ones?

Dalya noticed something strange. Her little sisters were holding firmly their softdolls in one hand and holding their lollipops on the other hand, without eating them. They were motionless; their eyes were focused on the Merchant in front of them. Dalya followed their gaze to understand what held the attention of her little sisters that much.

The Merchant in front was wearing a white apron and a small white hat on the head. He was a man of about thirty years old. He was behind a small kiosk of wood with a roof covered with a white cloth, a small counter, and a large pot in front of him. He was a Seller of Bouillon. A famous soup of herbs, spices, onions and garlic. Dalya's mother cooked them this soup a few times at home, but it was never as good as the one sold by the Merchants in their kiosks. It was a hot and delicious Bouillon, especially in winter. A very popular soup in the city of Georgetown, especially among the poor and the less fortunate people who could afford it.

Dalya didn't understand her little sisters' stare toward the kiosk, she stood up:

- Let's go home. Come on.

Ari and Adi got up and they both exclaimed simultaneously pointing out at the kiosk in front, with their little fingers:

- Dindin!! Dindin!!

Dalya wasn't sure for a moment:

- What do you want?

Ari and Adi pointed their fingers toward the Merchant:

- Dindin!! Dindin!!
- Do you want herbs Bouillon?
- Dindin!! Dindin!!

Because of her little sisters' persistence, Dalya led them to the kiosk in front. The Bouillon Merchant received them with a welcoming smile:

- Hello young girls!! How many bowls would you like?

However ... before Dalya could speak a word, the little twins walked toward the left side of the kiosk. Dalya followed her little sisters, fearing further foolery from them. But on the side of the kiosk, Dalya was surprised to find a little girl, who was of the same age as the twins, with lovely blue eyes, brown curly hair, she wore a clumsily stitched wool sweater, bigger than her, a worn and rolled up pants, and boy's shoes. The little girl appeared poor, she was quiet sitting on a big wood crate, and she was playing with some leaves and wood branches.

And because of the big resemblance with the Bouillon Merchant, Dalya realized that the little girl was his daughter. Yet, Dalya didn't understand what her little sisters wanted to do.

The little twins approached the poor little girl. Then, they made a gesture that Dalya never thought to see. Ari and Adi offered their 2 softdolls to the poor little girl!!

The 2 softdolls that Uncle Scott offered them as a gift, and he didn't stop reminding it to Dalya ... These 2 softdolls belonged now to a poor little girl of a Bouillon Merchant. The poor little girl dropped her leaves and branches, she stood up suddenly from her crate and she received the 2 softdolls with an innocent scream of joy and surprise.

And even if the little twins were themselves poor and only had very few toys at the Annex house, they offered their softdolls with a big smile and a great pleasure. Ari and Adi hugged the poor little girl in their arms. And the 3 little girls giggled together, under the proud smile of their big sister Dalya and the touched smile of the Bouillon Merchant.

Because you think that lessons of generosity and empathy, come only from the grown-ups?

It is true that the little twins were talented in all kinds of fooleries ... But on that day, Dalya was delighted and proud to discover that her little sisters, Ari and Adi were also talented in free generosity.

Chapter 34

Wilfrid's Doubts

Tuesday, December 01st, 1891.

Mr. Ferdinand Edelmen, the nephew of Late Mr. Governor, seemed nervous. He was sitting on a chair in front of his friend's office desk, the Lawyer Mr. Ernest Laszlo. The Lawyer was reading some documents and he seemed calm and focused on his reading. Ferdinand was anxiously holding his luxurious wood cane, and he was impatient:

- Only 11 days remain, Ernest!

The Lawyer didn't even take his eyes off the document he was holding:

- Yes ... I am well aware of that.

This reply was not enough to calm Ferdinand Edelmen:

- And so? What will happen next?

Before the Lawyer could answer his friend's question, the door of his office opened. His right-hand man, Mr. Sloan Wilfrid entered. He greeted Mr. Ferdinand bowing his head. Mr. Ferdinand didn't return the greeting, and he didn't lose his anxiety.

- Did you bring me the defense speech of the tomorrow morning's case? Asked Mr. Ernest.

Mr. Wilfrid placed in front of his employer, a file of multiple papers.

- Yes, Monsieur. I've reviewed everything myself. It is complete. I still need your consent on only two points.
- Good, what are they? Said Mr. Ernest flipping the pages.
- Page 2 … paragraph 3 ... the terms of the contract termination.

Mr. Wilfrid waited while Mr. Ernest was reading the indicated notes. Mr. Wilfrid noticed that the nephew of the Late Mr. Governor, Mr. Ferdinand Edelmen seemed nervous, he clutched his cane with a firm movement, sweat appeared on his forehead, and his eyes were worried.

After a few minutes of silence, the Lawyer, Mr. Ernest finally raised his head toward his friend and he said in a calm voice:

- It is needless to stress and worry this time ... everything will go as planned.

Mr. Ferdinand Edelmen couldn't contain his anxiety:

- THAT'S WHAT YOU SAID THE FIRST TIME!! AND SHE ANSWERED THE QUESTION!!

The Lawyer, Mr. Ernest Laszlo relaxed back on his chair, and answered in a confident voice:

- I admit ... we have all underestimated her. But this time will be different. She will not succeed.

Mr. Sloan Wilfrid was waiting for the correction of his files, and he easily guessed the topic of the conversation between the two men. Mr. Ferdinand Edelmen didn't understand the confidence and the calm of the Lawyer. He asked in a distressed tone:

- And how can you be so sure of it?

Mr. Ernest Laszlo smiled, something that happened rarely. It was a confident and defiant smile. The Lawyer Mr. Ernest Laszlo looked at his friend and he replied in a peaceful cold voice:

- Because this time, I will make sure she doesn't answer the Question.

A few minutes later, Sloan Wilfrid went back to his office, and he sat on his desk chair, something preoccupied his mind. Seconds shortly, Mr. Wilfrid received a visitor.

- I noticed Mr. Ferdinand Edelmen coming out of the office.

Lyor Laszlo was curious. Wilfrid remained calm and motionless, sitting in front of his desk, without saying a word; his eyes focused on a file in front of him, but his mind was clearly away. Lyor sat on the chair in front of his mentor's desk:

- It's about her, isn't it?

Without any answer or reaction from his mentor, Lyor worried. He had never seen Wilfrid so calm and lost in his mind. Lyor asked with a hesitant voice:

- Do you think that ... she … she can succeed this time?

For the first time since the arrival of Lyor in his office, Wilfrid moved. He lay back on his chair, and he answered the question in a serious tone:

- Honestly ... I have no idea.

Sloan Wilfrid stood up from his chair, and he faced the windows of his office. Wilfrid thought aloud, in a decided voice:

- I cannot help her succeed ... I cannot help her answer correctly the Second Challenge ... however ... I can surely protect her right to pass the Second Challenge!

Lyor didn't understand his mentor's thoughts and words. It seems that Sloan Wilfrid had an idea in his mind, and he was determined to make it work!

The same day. At the Annex house of the grand Mansion.

This December afternoon promised to be cold. The wind blew an icy breeze. And despite the clear blue sky, the sun was not that much warm.

Dalya's little sisters were playing in the living room, with their fabricated dolls, while their mother prepared a pie. Dalya came back home early from school, she was sitting in the living room doing her homework. The Mathematics Professor gave them ten full pages of equations to solve. Dalya was focused on her homework, when she heard her mother calling her from the kitchen:

- Hey you!! Come over here!!

Dalya stood up and joined the kitchen. Her mother had peeled some apples. She ordered her:

- I'll hang the laundry outside, as long as the wind is present. Cut these apples into cubes and put them on the pan, and then add a spoon sugar and 2 spoons of butter to caramelize it. I have to fill the apple pie, for dinner tonight.

When Mrs. Augustine left the kitchen, Dalya hurried up to cut the apples that her mother had peeled, in order to go back to her Mathematics homework before dinner. As ordered, Dalya cut the apples, she put them on a pan, 1 spoon of sugar and 2 spoons of butter. Then, Dalya waited for the apples to caramelize, while stirring occasionally.

When suddenly and abruptly, a scream shake the kitchen windows.

- BUT WHAT IS THIS??!!

Dalya jumped at the piercing voice of her mother. Mrs. Augustine was furious watching the apples on the pan.

- I ASKED YOU TO CUT THEM INTO CUBES!!!

Dalya answered, all confused:

- That's what I did ...

Mrs. Augustine came near Dalya:

- ISN'T IT CLEAR ENOUGH?! TO CUT THEM INTO CUBES!!! YOU IDIOT!! NOT IN ROUNDS OR TRIANGLES!! JUST SQUARE CUBES!!

Dalya hesitated to answer for a second. And yet, she had only one explanation to give to her mother:

- I didn't know how to cut the apples in perfect cubes ...

Mrs. Augustine screamed with all her might:

- IDIOT!! MISERABLE VERMIN!! YOU WILL NEVER LEARN ANYTHING!! **EVERY YEAR YOU BECOME MORE IDIOT THAN BEFORE**!! LITTLE WITLESS!! STUPID!! IDIOT!!

At this moment, Dalya asked spontaneously:

- But ... why do you insult me?

Her mother paused for a moment, paralyzed by her daughter's question. Dalya continued in a natural and curious tone:

- Why do you insult me? Explain to me my mistake, correct me, show me how to do it ... but ... what's the point of yelling at me, insulting me and calling me names?

Mrs. Augustine stared at her daughter with an evil look. In hurried steps, Mrs. Augustine came near Dalya, she pinched her daughter's cheek so hard and with a violent move that Dalya turned all red and had tears in her eyes. Then, Mrs. Augustine pulled her daughter by the cheek, and she led her outside of the house … to the garage …

Will someday the little Dalya Bouvard forget what her mother did to her?

Never will Dalya forget the fear that her mother set up in her.

Never will Dalya forget how her mother pinched her cheeks so painfully hard.

Never will Dalya forget her mother's evil looks.

Never will Dalya forget the violent and unfair attitude of her mother.

Never will Dalya forget how her mother slammed doors, destroyed things, and screamed like a devil.

Never will Dalya forget her mother's sentence; **every year you become more idiot than before**.

Never will Dalya forget that her mother ... is a monster.

Wednesday, December 02nd, 1891.

At the end of her classes, Dalya walked to the Lawyer's office, Mr. Ernest Laszlo, to inform him of the 4th clue. When she met Mr. Wilfrid in the hallway, Dalya greeted him with a smile:

- Good evening, Monsieur Wilfrid!

Sloan Wilfrid looked busy holding records in his hands. He suddenly jumped at Dalya's voice and he dropped a few papers, which soon dispersed on the floor.

- How dizzy am I! ... Good evening Mademoiselle Bouvard ... I am sorry I didn't see you come in!
- I'm sorry to interrupt you, Mr. Wilfrid.
- No no... not at all ... I just have many urgent Law cases to present these days, my mind is busy… How are your classes, Mademoiselle?
- Very well, Monsieur. Dalya replied, while kneeling down to help pick up the papers from the floor.
- Did you come to meet Mr. Ernest Laszlo, I believe? Asked Mr. Wilfrid, while picking up a big file from the floor.
- Yes Monsieur, to deliver him the 4th clue. Dalya answered.

When she stood up, Dalya handed him the papers that she had picked from the floor. Except that, Mr. Wilfrid was thunderstruck and alarmed. The Lawyer's attention was not on the papers that Dalya handed him, but his eyes were focused on Dalya's little hands. Mr. Wilfrid couldn't believe his eyes. He asked her in a shocked serious voice:

- What ... what is that? ... Why are your hands in such a state?

It was only at that moment; that Dalya realized she had spontaneously removed a glove to pick up the fallen papers of Mr. Wilfrid. She didn't think that a simple little careless move will rise up such a shocked reaction from the Lawyer. And it was the first time ever that Sloan Wilfrid spoke to Dalya with a serious tone; he had completely lost his smile. Mr. Wilfrid repeated his question, while taking Dalya's hand to examine it closely:

- What is that? ... What happened to you?

Dalya's hands were swollen, her nails were blue, the palm of her hand was full of red bloody scars, her hands trembled, and certainly not because of the cold. The Lawyer's office was well heated though. But the hands of Dalya trembled of pain. She didn't dare to look at Mr. Wilfrid straight in the eyes; she hesitated for a few long seconds to find an adequate and convincing answer. Mr. Wilfrid was alarmed by Dalya's hands, he insisted in serious voice:

- Mademoiselle Dalya Bouvard ... Who did this to you?

Dalya jumped immediately. She hid her trembling voice the best she could:

- No one, Monsieur! I was doing ... I ... I hurt myself … while doing housework.

Mr. Wilfrid stared at Dalya for a long minute. The Lawyer wasn't convinced at all by her answer. Since several months now, Sloan Wilfrid noticed that Dalya was frequently wearing gloves, even in the hottest summer days; and this attitude seemed strange to him.

Dalya didn't dare to raise her eyes toward the Lawyer. Mr. Wilfrid took back his papers from the little girl's hands, and he thought aloud:

- Housework? … Really? … Just that!

Chapter 35

An innocent cheating

Thursday, December 03rd, 1891. History course. Classroom N° 309.

Nearly all the students arrived in the classroom of the History course. Dalya sitting in her usual desk, she was reviewing her previous lessons. Eriem Eyelord was surrounded by her court, as usual, close by the large windows of the classroom. Since the incident where Gael was pushed to the floor, Eriem and her court didn't come close to Dalya. And Dalya was happy to be left alone; she didn't want a second confrontation.

When Amira Mounier entered the classroom, she put down her schoolbag and she sat in her usual place, a few chairs away from Dalya. Amira didn't come near Eriem and her court, since a while now. Amira finally realized that despite all her efforts, the other students will never easily accept her into their narrow circle.

The History Professor, Mr. Ajanar slammed the door of the classroom with a sudden move. He seemed in a very bad mood, that day. All the students took their seats immediately.

- Close your books!!

The students obeyed. Professor Ajanar sat on his desk and he faced the students:

- Today, I will test your knowledge of our course, before deciding your homework for the Christmas holidays.

Professor Ajanar opened his book and he called a name:

- Miss Eriem Eyelord ... please answer my questions.

Eriem stood up.

- At what age Caesar heads for the politics?
- Since sixteen years old, the studies of young Caesar are politics oriented, so that he could follow the path of his father.
- Excellent answer, Miss Eriem!! Excellent answer!! ... And what are the studies he follows to this effect?
- Caesar studied rhetoric ... the art of mastering public speaking and mostly how to convince people on the forum.
- Great, Miss Eriem!! ... And in parallel, what other courses does he follow?
- Caesar also received a military training.
- Expand this idea ...

- Caesar learns the combat techniques, tactics and strategy. He will become a very talented athlete, practicing riding, athletics and swimming.

Professor Ajanar smiled:

- This is excellent, Miss Eriem. You are a perfect student. It's always a pleasure to hear your answers.

Eriem Eyelord sat back slowly, with a smile much arrogant and prouder than before. Professor Ajanar called out a second name in a cold voice:

- Amira Mounier!!

She got up from her chair.

- In what year did Julius Caesar's father died?

Amira didn't hesitate a second, she replied in a slow clear voice:

- In 86 B.C
- WRONG!!! Professor Ajanar yelled with a strong voice.

Amira turned all red and confused. And she was not the only one. Dalya was also surprised of the Professor's reaction. This same question was in the mid-exams just few months ago, and the answer was 86 B.C. Dalya was curious about the Professor's correction.

Professor Ajanar continued furiously:

- It was in 86 B.C!! ... YOU WITLESS!!

But ... this is what Amira has replied. Is it possible that the Professor didn't hear her well? Professor Ajanar continued:

- In what year Julius Caesar was elected Quaestor?

Amira breathed a long shot, and then she said in a loud voice:

- In 69 B.C
- WRONG!!!

It's impossible. Some whispers were heard in the classroom. Dalya was sure that this date was indeed correct. Professor Ajanar explained in an imposing voice:

- Toward the end of the year 69 B.C!! … You idiot!! How many years do you need to learn your lessons!!

Amira lowered her head and eyes toward her shoes. Despite the fact that she had well mastered her History lessons; Amira didn't understand her false answers. And Dalya was sure that the History textbook doesn't contain the concept of the end or the beginning of the year. The book said exactly the answer: Year 69 B.C only!!

- In which year Julius Caesar was elected consul?

This time, Amira hesitated for a moment, she doubted her answer. Then, she finally said with a shy voice:

- In ... 59 ...
- WRONG!! WRONG!! AND STILL WRONG!! IDIOT!!

Dalya couldn't resist it this time; she discreetly opened her History book, curious to know the answer. And on the book, it was written the date of 59!!

Amira couldn't understand her wrong answers. She had spent the entire holidays learning by heart her lessons. Yet, all her answers were wrong!

Professor Ajanar was delighted to reprimand his student:

- It is 59 B.C!! Idiot!! Or we'll think it's 1759 or 1659 or 1559!!

The Professor's argument seemed ridiculous to Dalya. All their courses since the beginning of the year, took place in B.C. So if Amira Mounier forgot to say it, it was not such a big mistake after all ... she had given the exact date anyway!!

Yet, Dalya had a bad feeling ... It seems that Professor Ajanar didn't appreciate his student answering correctly his questions. So then, he searched for any excuse to diminish and humiliate her.

Amira Mounier sat back on her chair, dejected and crushed under the laughs of all the students and the reprimands of the History Professor, Mr. Ajanar:

- Do you even know how to read? ... It's like I am teaching History lessons to an illiterate!! ... But how will you manage next year's class? It's tiring to teach a student so idiot and witless!! ... I wonder how did you manage to be admitted to this school?

Straightaway, after the end of the History course, Dalya ran to the Library, in hurried angry steps. That Amira Mounier gives a wrong answer, it was an acceptable thing. But that she gives a correct answer, and despite that, she get reprimanded, claiming that her answer is wrong ... that was unfair!

As soon as she arrived at the Library's assistant desk, Dalya said breathless:

- Miss Guendolyn ... I need your help!! It's urgent!!

The young woman dropped her pen and she looked at Dalya:

- Of course Mademoiselle! What can I do for you?

Dalya pulled out a piece of paper from her backpack and she showed it to the young woman:

- Is this number just like the one that I showed you, before?

Miss Guendolyn examined it for a second:

- Yes ... it is the same reference!

A few minutes later, Dalya and Miss Guendolyn came out of the Royal College and they headed to the National Georgetown Library. Dalya couldn't enter alone, and she needed to know the last enigma of the first clue:

In AV-07-90, the mirror will reveal a forgotten kind.

The prestigious place still intimidated the little Dalya Bouvard. Walking beside Miss Guendolyn, Dalya admired the huge windows in glass and wrought iron. The sun rays had invited themselves inside the enormous National Georgetown Library. Miss Guendolyn walked the aisles one after another, and she seemed to know her way. The luxurious long wood tables and chairs, installed in the middle of the immense Library, were filled with people focused on their readings.

When they arrived at the aisle AV, section 07 and the location 90, Miss Guendolyn pulled out a pink book and she proudly handed it to Dalya.

The Art of the French Bordeaux hairstyle
Author: Madame Sophie Fressange

Dalya lost her words. She overturned the book front and back, and then she said:

- There is a mistake, Miss Guendolyn. This is not the right book.

Miss Guendolyn went back to the beginning of the aisle and rechecked the references in the piece of paper that she was holding:

- AV-07-90 ... aisle AV ...

Miss Guendolyn walked back toward Dalya:

- Section 05 ... 06 ... 07

And she counted the books:

- Location ... 88 ... 89 ... 90

Miss Guendolyn looked at Dalya, with a confident look:

- No, Mademoiselle ... there are no mistakes, I can assure you. This is the book that was mentioned to you. And there is rarely a classification error at the National Library.

Dalya reread the book's title for a moment, thinking aloud:

- It's just … because ... but ... how can this book be useful to me? … It's silly ... this is not logical!

Miss Guendolyn also tried to understand the usefulness of this book:

- There may be a clue inside of it ...

After Miss Guendolyn borrowed the book and she gave it to Dalya, the little girl ran back to the Annex house of the grand Mansion. And the night was very long, Dalya spent hours and hours reading and rereading the book of hairstyles, without being able to find a clear and useful solution out of it.

Friday, December 04th, 1891.

The Secretary, Miss Uplerine Amana was writing notes in a large registry. Dalya greeted her with a friendly smile:

- Good morning, Miss Uplerine. I was called to the Director's office.

Miss Uplerine smiled back at her:

- Good morning, Mademoiselle. Please take a seat; he will receive you in a moment.

Dalya sat on the bench in front of the woman's office, who kept throwing discreet glances at the little girl. Dalya liked the Secretary Miss Uplerine, but she thought she was strange woman.

A few minutes later, Amira Mounier left the Headmaster's office. Her face was all red, and her eyes wet. Amira could never hide that she had been crying. The Secretary, Miss Uplerine handed her a tissue:

- Will you be alright, Miss Amira?

Amira took the tissue and she answered with a head sign. When Amira disappeared in the corridor with hurried steps, Miss Uplerine sighed:

- Poor thing ... yet she's so sweet ... she always do her best ... she works so hard ...

Dalya sitting in front of the woman, she stayed silent, watching her classmate from afar. Miss Uplerine went back to writing on the register. When suddenly, the woman looked up at Dalya and she said with an amused defiant voice:

- It happens that sometimes ... courage needs a little boost!

Dalya knew that Miss Uplerine Amana was speaking to her; there was no one else in the office. Except that, Dalya didn't know what the woman meant to say by her strange words. When Miss Uplerine deliberately dropped a paper on the floor. Dalya bent over and she discovered that it was a list on which some names were registered. Miss Uplerine Amana continued, displaying a wide defying smile:

- And ... I admit that, for once, it would be fun to disappoint people who think we're weak!

Then, Miss Uplerine Amana repeated her previous movement; she deliberately dropped a pen on the floor, under the confused watch of Dalya. Miss Uplerine immediately turned her back on Dalya; she started watering her plant and sighed aloud:

- How busy am I today!!

For a second, Dalya didn't believe her eyes and ears. Was Miss Uplerine Amana encouraging Dalya to ... cheat? Yet, this is what the woman meant by her words and attitude!

Dalya moved and she knelt down slowly. Dalya wrote a name on the paper thrown on the floor, and then she placed the paper back on the Secretary's desk. Miss Uplerine Amana turned toward Dalya and she smiled at her ... a proud and an accomplice smile. And as crazy as it may seem, Dalya was glad to have cheated and wrote a name on that paper! ... An innocent cheating!

When Director Darkfett asked Dalya to his office, she opened the door and entered. The Director said in a cheerful voice:

- Only a few days and I should not see you in my school anymore!!

Dalya stood motionless in front of Director Darkfett's office. The man was sitting behind his desk, relaxed on his big chair. He continued, this time in a cold, menacing voice:

- Listen to me very well, kid!! ... It's out of question that I accept you here, next semester! I intend to discuss this matter firmly with Mr. Ernest Laszlo, the Lawyer in charge of the Will!! ... The Late Mr. Governor had a very kind soul, I can understand that ... but I'm tired of seeing a veggy seller in my school!! The prestigious Royal Georgetown College!!

For some long minutes, Director Darkfett spoke and spoke, without Dalya interrupting him. He finally dismissed Dalya as usual, with threats:

- Seek yourself another school, the next semester!!

When she closed the door of the Director's office, the Secretary Miss Uplerine Amana greeted Dalya, with a bright confident smile:

- Good day to you, Mademoiselle Dalya Bouvard ... see you on Saturday!

Dalya smiled back nervously at Miss Uplerine, before leaving school. In fact, Dalya didn't hear a single word of Director Darkfett's threats. Only one thing occupied Dalya's mind ... the name she just wrote on that list. Dalya had cheated. And the consequences of her action would be either disastrous ... or by some miracle, a victory!

Chapter 36

The contest

Saturday, December 05th, 1891. The contest day. The morning.

Dalya couldn't sleep the previous night. It was the contest day at the Royal Georgetown College. But Dalya wasn't stressing because of this competition, yet! Something else was worrying her. The last sentence of the clue was a true enigma. Dalya discovered a hairstyle book from the National Georgetown Library. And although, she read the book almost a hundred times, Dalya could deduce only one idea out of it. She was not certain if her idea was correct or not, and if she had understood well the clue. Yet, Dalya had no other choice but to try.

Before classes began, Dalya arrived early to school, and she walked to the Library. Miss Guendolyn greeted her with an excited smile:

- It is today, Mademoiselle!!

Dalya answered in a worried voice:

- Yes ... it is today, Miss Guendolyn.
- Everything will be alright. The woman reassured her.
- I don't worry about the contest. Anyway, not yet. It's just that ... we still have the last part of the clue. How will we do it? I cannot approach her. It's impossible!

Miss Guendolyn was seriously motivated:

- We will find a way, Mademoiselle!

Except that Dalya was concerned:

- But we must act quickly, it starts in a few hours ... and I admit this is the first time that I lack of ideas.

Miss Guendolyn remained silent, for a brief moment. Then suddenly, the young woman jumped:

- FOUND IT!!
- How will we do it? Dalya asked all curious.
- So here's the plan ... explained Miss Guendolyn all enthusiastic.

After a few seconds of listening, Dalya understood Miss Guendolyn's plan. And having no other better idea, Dalya asked for the second time:

- Are you sure that this will work?

- Positive!!! Said Miss Guendolyn with a strong determination.

At lunch time, all the students went to the canteen. Since the apple sauce incident poured on her head, Amira Mounier preferred to spend her lunch break at the Library, away from the offensive attitudes and laughs of the other students. She sat in her usual place in the Library, a desk near the large windows looking into the school garden. Amira was quietly reading a book, when a joyful voice surprised her:

- Miss Amira Mounier!! How nice to see you here!!

Amira looked up at Miss Guendolyn. Amira replied hesitantly:

- He ... hello ...
- Aren't you having lunch with the other students of your class?

Amira buried her head in her book and she murmured:

- No.

Miss Guendolyn didn't lose her enthusiasm or determination:

- You chose the right moment to study at the Library!! It's very quiet and empty at this time of the day!!

Amira didn't answer, she continued reading her book. It was now or never. Miss Guendolyn had only seconds to act before the Library got filled up with students. The young woman let out a piercing scream, which made Amira jump and drop her book on the floor:

- OOOOHHH!! GOOD HEAVEN!! DON'T EVEN MOVE MISS AMIRA!!

Amira looked at Miss Guendolyn, in a panicked stare:

- What ... what is happening?

Miss Guendolyn approached her and she whispered:

- You have an ant in your hair!! Do not move!! I'll remove it right away!!

When Miss Guendolyn touched Amira's hair, a strange thing happened. Amira felt that Miss Guendolyn's hands detached the pink ribbon braid off her hair, in a quick move. The little girl didn't have time to protest, the ribbon of her second braid was also removed:

- But ... aie ... but what are you doing? ... aie ... why did you take off my ... aie ... ribbons?
- THIS ANT IS ESCAPING!!! ... SHE IS ESCAPING!!! Exclaimed Miss Guendolyn.

Amira felt that her braids were undone, and her hair getting more volume, she tried to escape from Miss Guendolyn's hands:

- But ... are you … insane ... what are ... aie aie ... what are you doing ... aie ... but why … stop ... undo my ... aie aie aie!!!

Amira fought as best as she could to get away from Miss Guendolyn's hands. And as strange as it may seem, Amira felt a pair of extra hands, others than Miss Guendolyn's, joining in to completely undo her braids with a very quick move.

- I'LL CATCH HER SOON!!! HERE SHE IS!!! IT'S ALMOST DONE!! Continued Miss Guendolyn in a loud and determined voice, still holding Amira's hair.
- Aie ... but … what is ... aie ... what is wrong with you ... you insane ... aie aie aie … crazy ... Miss Guend ... stop ... aie aie!!

After several minutes of chaos, Miss Guendolyn stopped and she stepped back. The young woman looked at Amira with a proud and a happy stare:

- There you go!! The bee is out of your hair!!

Because of her struggle to escape, and the agitation of Miss Guendolyn's hands in her hair, Amira felt dizzy for a second. After a brief moment, Amira recovered her normal breath; and she looked at Miss Guendolyn curiously:

- I thought ... I thought it was an ant?

Miss Guendolyn became all pale and hesitant, she smiled nervously:

- I ... I don't remember ... bee or ant ... it's the same ... anyway; your hair is safe now!!

Amira Mounier stared at Miss Guendolyn for a moment, trying to understand the strange behavior of the young woman. Miss Guendolyn greeted Amira with a happy proud smile and she retired instantly.

Before undergoing another attack, Amira preferred to leave the Library. She gathered her things with a quick and brusque move, muttering angrily:

- School of crazy people!! ... Everyone here is crazy!! ... Bee or Ant, she doesn't remember?! It's a school of crazy people!!

Amira walked to the girls' bathroom to brush her hair and arrange it in braids just like it was before. After Miss Guendolyn's attack, her hair was disheveled and all free. Amira placed her backpack on the edge of the sink; she searched in her bag for another ribbon or elastic to attach her hair. Suddenly, a gentle voice frightened Amira:

- It's pretty.

Amira lifted her head to find Assami Eyelord, Eriem Eyelord's younger sister, washing her hands in a levier near her. Amira froze and she didn't dare to move. Assami was in a class before than her older sister. She was small, thin, with a lighter skin than her sister, platinum blonde short and wavy hair, and beautiful clear brown eyes. Assami Eyelord was a girl of great beauty.

And although her older sister was arrogant and mean, Assami was very different; she was known to be kind, calm and polite.

For several seconds, Assami looked at Amira Mounier, and she smiled at her. Amira didn't believe her eyes or what she had just heard. Under the astonished and confused looks of Amira, Assami dried her hands, displaying an amused smile. Assami said to Amira, in a sincere tone:

- You should let your hair free a little more often. It's pretty that way.

And before leaving the girl's bathroom, Assami smiled at her one last time. Amira was struggling to understand what had just happened. It is true that Assami was very different from her sister Eriem. Yet, Assami never spoke to her or smiled at her. Until today!

Amira didn't understand Assami's comments on her hair; she continued looking for a ribbon in her backpack to tie her hair, while thinking aloud:

- Pretty? ... But ... what is she talking about?

After a few moments, Amira found a small ribbon at the bottom of her backpack. To reattach her hair, Amira raised her eyes toward the bathroom's mirror for the first time since her arrival, and she was thunderstruck by what she was seeing.

For several seconds, Amira was paralyzed before the image reflection in front of her. She didn't believe her eyes; she actually waved her hand to make sure the mirror was really reflecting her image and not someone else's. Yet, Amira was seeing a different person in front of her.

Since so long ago, Amira used to arrange her hair in two long braids. She never dared to release her hair free. And after the strange moves of Miss Guendolyn, Amira discovered a new head.

Her beautiful long hair was wavy, shiny, soft, and it completely changed the shape of her face.

For the first time in her life, Amira felt a strange emotion ... the mirror revealed a forgotten kind ... confidence in herself!

Amira looked into the mirror, amazed and shocked, and she laughed:

- It's ... really pretty!

The contest day. The afternoon.

It was the first time in her life, that Dalya Bouvard was attending an essay competition. And she was curious to see how the contest would be held.

Minutes before 3:00 PM, Dalya left the Library and walked toward the big reception room, at the other end of the school. The place was huge. Large windows illuminated the reception room. Two columns of chairs were set up in many well-ordered rows; an empty alley in the middle was separating the two columns. At a side of the room, there was a large wood stage, and 7 empty chairs were placed. A long table for the jury was put right in front of the stage, with only 3 chairs.

After a few minutes, the reception room gradually filled up. Students and teachers were seated on the chairs on the right side. Parents and visitors sat on chairs on the left side. Dalya settled on one of the chairs at the end of the room. A moment later, the school's Director, Mr. Darkfett entered the reception room. And Dalya was very surprised to see him greet the students' parents with a soft gentle voice, and an angelic smile.

Dalya watched Eriem Eyelord and her court, settle on the chairs in the front rows. The Music teacher Miss Haîyang, Professor Canfield and some other teachers, also settled in the front rows too. As soon as Miss Guendolyn sat close to Dalya, she whispered in a cheerful voice:

- It will be a good day, Mademoiselle!!
- I hope so. Dalya whispered, not as sure as Miss Guendolyn was.

Dalya was stressing for this contest, she had no idea what will happen, and how things will turn out. Yet, Dalya was determined to be present at the contest, that day

After the chairs were nearly all occupied, a great man made quite an entrance in the reception room, accompanied by three men walking behind him. Everyone turned around and watched the great man. He was wearing an elegant green emerald suit. He was tall, a big belly, and an intimidating allure. The three men who followed him, all wore identical black suits.

Noticing Dalya's stare on the great man, Miss Guendolyn whispered to her:

- He is the Congressman ... Yolan McKlain ...

The School Director, Mr. Darkfett hurried to welcome the great man and his three men. He led them to their chairs in the first row on the right side.

A moment later, the History Professor Mr. Ajanar and the Mathematics Professor Mr. Wyatt, they both settled in the jury table in front of the stage.

Director Darkfett faced the crowd and he announced in a strong loud voice:

- Ladies and gentlemen. I am pleased to welcome you today, into the 32nd edition of the prestigious essay contest of our school. As always, the Royal Georgetown College is distinguished by the excellence of its teaching and education. And this year, I have the great pleasure to welcome Congressman McKlain ... who kindly accepted our invitation today!

After some applause, Director Darkfett continued:

- The jury of this year is composed of myself ... the History Professor Mr. Ajanar ... and the Mathematics Professor Mr. Wyatt ... As in previous years, the History Professor Mr. Ajanar will announce the essay topic ... the Mathematics Professor Mr. Wyatt will call the students' names that have chosen to participate in the contest. The highest note that the jury awards, would win the contest.

Director Darkfett announced cheerfully:

- Now ... let the contest begin!

The History Professor stood up and he addressed all the attending people:

- Ladies and gentlemen ... the essay topic of this year is ... What role did the Senate hold toward the people, during the Roman Empire? ... Each student will have 15 minutes to discuss this subject.

When he sat down, the Mathematics Professor, Mr. Wyatt also stood up and he announced:

- The first student is ... Mr. Salman Elpacha.

A student stood up from the crowd, and walked to the stage. He was a big size boy, skinny, wearing large glasses. He began his essay with a clear, strong voice:

- The Roman Senate is one of the oldest political institutions of the ancient Rome. The role of the Senate is religious, legislative, financial and political. The influence of the Senate has evolved throughout the Roman History and ...

Several minutes later, when the student finished, people applauded him. Director Darkfett, the History and Mathematics Professors murmured a few moments, discussing the note that they would attribute to the student. After a moment, the Mathematics Professor stood up and he announced the name of the second participant student.

- Miss Rose Ludivine.

A student joined the stage, tiny, thin and wearing her hair in a long ponytail, she faced the crowd, and she presented her essay:

- The role of the Senate under the monarchy was to advise the king. And at the beginning of the Republic, the Senate remained with low power of influence. Magistrates accumulated almost all the power. It will take several generations before the Senate is powerful, and ahead of the Magistrates ...

Three other students followed in front of the stage. They presented their essays, the crowd applauded them, and both Professors and the Director discussed in private their rating.

The Mathematics Professor, Mr. Wyatt announced:

- Miss Eriem Eyelord

Dalya could see her classmate from afar. Eriem got up and she walked toward the stage in confident steps. She displayed an arrogant smile, and she replied in a calm confident voice:

- Under the monarchy, the Senate has an advisory role. Its most important function is to elect the new kings. The people being unable to choose a new monarch, it is up to the Senate to handle this task. The period between the death of the king and the election of his successor is called the interregnum ... this is the time when the real sovereign power of the Senate stands out. A candidate is appointed to the succession, and the Senate gives its final approval.

  It is clear that without the Senate, the people would have been unable to manage themselves alone. Gathered from the wealthiest families and most distinguished of the Roman nobility, the Senate enacts the laws, advises the sovereign, and ensures peace and order in the Roman Empire. The Senators were chosen for their prestige, their fortunes, their social status and ancestral lineages, and their excellent speeches and education.

  The nobility, who composes the Senate, existed to govern, and the lower class was to be governed and to contribute to the growth of the Roman Empire. The people would not have survived without the governance of the Senate, the educated and wealthy nobility. That is the role of the Senate in the period of the Roman Empire.

When Eriem finished, the entire audience applauded. Eriem Eyelord turned around and she sat down on one of the chairs on the stage, showing off a winner and cheerful attitude. Since 3 years now, Eriem Eyelord was the only one to win this contest. Her friend Gael Benoble and Eriem's court, they all arrogantly smiled and warmly applauded her. The History Professor Mr. Ajanar addressed the audience in an arrogant voice, proud of his student:

- Miss Eriem Eyelord is among our most distinguished and talented students. All her previous essays are an example for all the students of this school.

Mr. and Mrs. Eyelord displayed a cocky smile. Director Darkfett and the History Professor whispered a few seconds before the Director Darkfett stood up and announced to the crowd, in a confident voice:

- Ladies and gentlemen ... I am pleased to announce the winner of this conte...

When suddenly, the Mathematics Professor, Mr. Wyatt interrupted him spontaneously:

- There is still a name on the list.

Director Darkfett, the History Professor, and all the attending people, turned around toward the Mathematics Professor. Mr. Wyatt was holding a paper in his hand; he repeated his sentence calmly but fairly well heard:

- The contest is not over yet. There is still a last name on the list.
- Who? Asked Director Darkfett in an exasperated tone, because was interrupted while announcing the winner.

The Mathematics Professor Mr. Wyatt announced in a well proud voice this time:

- Miss Amira Mounier.

Instantly, a wave of whispers and exclamations invaded the entire reception room. No one expected to hear that name pronounced. Several teachers, including Professor Canfield himself, were surprised by this announcement. Gael and his friends were shocked. Eriem Eyelord lost her cocky smile and she seemed upset of Amira Mounier's audacity. All eyes were turned toward the student whose name was pronounced.

Sitting among the other students, Amira Mounier became pale, she murmured:

- But ... I ... how ... I didn't sign up for this contest!!

The History Professor let out a grotesque laugh:

- Oh ... but I doubt very much that a little stuttering girl can beat Miss Eriem Eyelord's prestigious performance!!

A wave of laughs overcame the reception room. The Mathematics Professor insisted in a loud voice:

- The contest's rules are very clear!! Anyone who wished to participate in this event, will have the chance to present himself!!

Since the Mathematics Professor will not give up the matter, Director Darkfett was forced to announce to the audience in a serious tone:

- Ladies and gentlemen ... it seems that we still have one last student to listen to, before announcing Miss Eriem Eyelord winner of this contest.

In a sarcastic and mocking tone, the History Professor added:

- After all ... a few minutes of laughs, will certainly entertain us.

The mocking laughs echoed throughout the reception room. Amira was petrified and paralyzed in her chair:

- I don't ... I can't ... I did not write my name on the list ... it's a joke ... it's ... Eriem and Gael ... their fault ... it's a joke from Eriem and Gael ... certainly ... to humiliate me in front of everyone ...

Except that Amira Mounier could clearly see the shock on Gael Benoble's face and the anger in Eriem Eyelord's eyes. And given their attitudes, Amira was confused:

- But ... who did ... if it's not them ... then who signed me in ... it's insane ... I can't ...

The Mathematics Professor turned around and he spoke to the student with an encouraging smile:

- Miss Amira Mounier ... it's your turn.

Amira nearly fainted. She had never thought to be in this situation, in front of all the teachers, students and parents. How did her name ended up in this list? Amira had no idea. But on that moment, that was the least of her worries. Amira was forced to stand up to tell her dissertation and be humiliated in front of a crowd of people. Her heart stopped beating.

- Come on, Miss Amira ... we are waiting for you. The Mathematics Professor repeated, in a nice tone.

Dalya, sitting a few chairs behind, was anxious; she straightened up from her seat to watch her classmate. It seemed that Amira had no choice but to participate in this contest.

After a few seconds of hesitation, Dalya noticed that Amira leaned forward; she took out a small bottle from her backpack, and she drank a few sips from it. Amira then decided to stand up and walk toward the stage, with slow and hesitant steps. Dalya observed Amira, noticing that she was stretching her legs and her arms discreetly.

Director Darkfett and the History Professor seemed upset. While the Mathematics Professor Mr. Wyatt was smiling and all joyful:

- It is nice to see you participate in this contest for the first time, Miss Amira Mounier. Please proceed.

When Amira stood in front of the crowd and the jury, many people were astonished, not only because of her audacity to participate in this contest, but because of her new look. Since the incident in the Library with Miss Guendolyn and Assami Eyelord's comments, Amira had kept her hair free. Teachers and students discovered for the first time, her long chestnut free hair. Amira was beautiful, and a glimmer of confidence emanated from her.

Dalya was a little worried, she stick out her head to better follow what will happen the next minutes. When a small object caught Dalya's attention. Amira firmly clutched a tiny sponge ball, barely visible, in her hand. There and Now, Dalya was certain and sure that Amira had well understood all the clues provided to her. Amira Mounier was ready!

Amira took a deep breath peacefully, and then she spoke slowly and clearly:

- The Senate at the beginning of the Roman royalty, was gathering 100 members ... The king appoints himself these advisors, among the first great Roman families ... The Senate is considered at that time a religious institution as much as a political institution.

Dalya could very well hear her classmate. And at this rate, Dalya was sure that Amira will succeed in her dissertation.

Except what Dalya had deeply feared, happened. The History Professor Mr. Ajanar was not only upset because Amira dared to participate in the contest, but he was also bothered that the student gave a good essay speech in a clear strong voice. And the idea that someone may eclipse his favorite student Eriem, the History teacher couldn't let it be.

Amira continued to speak clearly, pronouncing all her words, as slowly as possible:

- In addition to its counseling role ... the growing power of the Senate can guide the king's decisions ... and even question th ...

The History Professor interrupted Amira and he exclaimed:

- Are we going to spend the night here, Miss Amira Mounier?

The audience laughed. The Mathematics Professor Mr. Wyatt protested in a serious and horrified voice, that Dalya never heard from him before:

- Professor Ajanar!! You have no right to interrupt the student's dissertation!!

The History Professor didn't like that the Mathematics Professor put him back into his place. Mr. Ajanar shot the Mathematics Professor with a cold look, and he addressed Amira in a mocking tone:

- Continue ... Continue ...

The audience calmed down, the History Professor became serious. But what Dalya have feared, happened. Amira Mounier blushed, she trembled, her cheeks were swollen, sweat covered her forehead and her mouth became dry:

- The mission of the Senate is to ser ... serve as ... as a mediator between the monar ... monar ... monarchy and the nation's in ... in ... interests and therefore the interests of the p ... p ... people.

The History Professor didn't need to say anything, the audience laughed all by itself. Some women had a nonstop laugh hearing Amira stutter, other men imitated her like a mentally retarded girl, some wondered; but what is happening to her? Others were simply confused by what was going on. Amira Mounier had tears in her eyes, she lowered her head and tried to keep talking, pronouncing the words, with all her body's strength:

- The sen ... sen ... sen ... Senate ... is ... is ... def ... def ... def ...

But the more Amira tried, the more people laughed. Dalya realized that she had failed to help Amira Mounier. The Excelbox clues didn't help much eventually.

In front of this scene, Amira struggling to pronounce her words, and people laughing at the History Professor who imitated her; an angry feeling invaded Dalya at that moment, she stood up to defend Amira Mounier and stop this masquerade. But Miss Guendolyn's hand restrained her on her chair, and the young woman whispered imploringly:

- Wait Mademoiselle Dalya ... just wait a moment!!
- But ... it's unfair!! They are laughing at her, while she has worked so hard to get there!! If only I could stop them from laughing at her!! I know she can make it!! Dalya insisted angrily.

Miss Guendolyn held her:

- You can't stop them from laughing at her, Mademoiselle … Only she can!!

Dalya was forced to admit that Miss Guendolyn was right. Nobody could stop the laughs of all these people, except Amira Mounier herself.

When suddenly, the Mathematics Professor, angry as much as Dalya was, he turned toward the History Professor and he yelled:

- YOU HAVE NO RIGHT TO LAUGH AT HER IN THAT WAY!!

The History teacher laughed all proud of his achievement:

- She is funny with her stuttering ...

Director Darkfett wondered aloud:

- Shouldn't we announce the winner, by now?

The Mathematics Professor was angry:

- Her stuttering is not funny!! This is a physical condition that can happen to anyone!! You should help her to talk better instead of la...

The History Professor was not embarrassed to answer:

- I shouldn't be wasting my time with an idiot like her, who cannot even pronounce a sentence correctly!!

The Mathematics Professor looked at the History teacher with a menacing eye:

- She's not an idiot!! If you are unable to help a student in difficulty, what does that make you?

The History Professor straightened up from his chair and he yelled:

- ARE YOU INSULTING ME PROFES...

Suddenly, a loud noise silenced both the teachers and the laughs of the audience. Everyone turned toward the stage. When everyone in the reception room realized that Amira Mounier gave a foot kick to the stage wood floor!

And in that moment, everyone noticed that something strange was happening. Amira had no more red cheeks, her mouth wasn't dry anymore, she straightened her head to be well seen by everyone, and her eyes displayed a defiant look. Amira took a deep breath, and then she announced in a clear voice, a slow tone, but confident words:

- I would like to ... resume my dissertation from the beginning. If the jury allows it.

The Mathematics Professor, Mr. Wyatt replied immediately with a cheerful voice:

- Certainly, Miss Amira Mounier, go ahead!! And nobody will stop you this time!!

The History Professor, Mr. Ajanar didn't dare to say a word. Dalya and Miss Guendolyn straightened up from their chairs to better see and hear her. Amira closed her eyes a few seconds, she took a deep breath, and she imagined herself being in the empty high tower of the school, where she had spent months trying to strengthen her voice. Amira could even see with closed eyes, the huge triangular ceiling which amplified her words. Then, with eyes closed, imagining herself in the high tower, alone, Amira Mounier said her dissertation, slow clear words:

- The Senate at the beginning of the Roman royalty, was gathering 100 members. The king himself appointed these advisors, among the first great Roman families. The Senate is considered at that time a religious institution as much as a political institution.

  In addition to its counseling role, the growing power of the Senate can guide the king's decisions, and even question them. The mission of the Senate is to serve as a mediator between the monarchy and the nation's interests ... and therefore the interests of the people. The Senate is then defined as the defender, the protector, and it ensures the permanence of peace.

At this instant, Amira opened her eyes; she turned around and looked at her classmate Eriem Eyelord, sitting on a chair on the stage. Then, Amira faced the crowd, and she continued her dissertation, with eyes opened, always in a clear voice and a slow pronunciation:

- It is true that the Senate was composed of the Roman nobility, well-educated and wealthy. However, the Senate's role was not to govern the people, but to serve the people.

  I disagree with the opinion of Eriem Eyelord; when she said that the people would not have survived without the governance of the Nobility that forms the Senate.

  I would love to see the Nobility do the laundry, cook their own meals, fix their cars, or clean their houses. It is thanks to the vegetable Merchants and the Cooks that we eat, thanks to the maids that we live in clean homes, thanks to the drivers that we ride, thanks to the newspapers sellers that we are informed, and it is thanks to the people that we live.

What I understand is that the Nobility will not survive without the people. On the other hand, the people will very well survive without the nobility. And History had always proved that it is the people who govern, who elect the Senators, who bring down the kings, and who appoint the successors.

My answer to the essay question is … as influential and distinguished as the Senate could be, it is the people who make the Senate and not the opposite.

At the end of her speech, Amira Mounier turned around instantly and she joined the other 6 candidates of this contest, sitting on the stage chairs. Amira had no more strength in her legs to hold her any longer; she fell exhausted on the last 7th empty chair.

A total silence reigned in the reception room for some long heavy seconds; everyone was speechless and motionless. Except one man, he said in a strong imposing voice:

- It is not the best voice, nor the best elocution, nor the best pronunciation that I've ever heard. However ... this is the first time in my career that I listen to a speech as right and true!! ... And I admit ... being myself a baker's son, I can only applaud your speech, Mademoiselle.

Under the surprised stares of everyone, the man stood up and he warmly applauded. And no one believed their eyes. Because you see, this man was ... the Congressman Yolan McKlain, himself!!

And when the Congressman McKlain stood up to applaud, all the people present were forced to follow his move, out of respect. Even Eriem Eyelord's parents stood up displaying a less arrogant look than earlier. All the guests stood up one after another, and applauded. Gael Benoble, Salman Elpacha, Lakita Fleuritel and all Eriem's court got up and they applauded silently and slowly, still in shock of what they had just watched and heard. The History Professor stood up, without applauding. He seemed furious and thunderstruck. The Mathematics Professor, Mr. Wyatt screamed happily, jumping despite his chubby size:

- Bravo!! Bravo!! Bravo!!

Professor Canfield couldn't hold his delighted laugh, while applauding warmly. Professor Haîyang stood up to applaud too, and she smiled sincerely. Miss Guendolyn applauded intensely, murmuring with an emotional voice:

- She made it!! She made it!!

All the teachers, the parents and the students, they all stood up and applauded Amira Mounier. All ... except one person.

He was a man in his mid-thirties. He was wearing a brown suit and bow tie, although modest, but clean and well ironed. He was short, chubby, with light brown hair; large glasses hardly hid his dark eyes circles. Tears ran extensively on his chubby cheeks. Because when the teachers, the students, the parents, and the Congressman himself ... all these people applaud your little daughter, your legs can't hold you anymore, and you don't have the strength to get up, to applaud her too.

Never in his life, would Amira Mounier's father could have imagined to witness such a scene. Aware of the pronunciation difficulty of his only daughter, Mr. Jacob Mounier cheered her up and encouraged her with all his strength and energy. And on that day, the father was incredibly proud of his daughter's determination to overcome her stuttering.

Amira Mounier was immobile in her chair; she didn't believe her eyes and ears. It was the first time in her life that someone applauded her. The student that everyone ignored and laughed at, the student that everyone treated as invisible, the daughter of the poor accountant who tried to fit in and have friends among the students of the Noble families. Amira Mounier, the student who stuttered ... she finally found her voice!

The Mathematics Professor, Mr. Wyatt didn't even consult Director Darkfett or the History Professor, he announced the winner of the essay contest, with a big smile and a sincere happiness:

- I am very proud to announce Miss Amira Mounier ... winner of the prize for best dissertation of this year!!

Then, the Mathematics Professor, Mr. Wyatt turned toward the History Professor, and he said with an amused smile:

- I leave you willingly the honor of presenting her the award of this year!!

The History Professor, Mr. Ajanar seemed was still thunderstruck, he seemed about to chock with anger. But the Mathematics Professor didn't hold himself from provoking him:

- Come on Professor!! Don't be sad that your favorite student failed this year!!

The History Professor took the trophy from the Mathematics Professor, with a brutal move, and he went on stage. When he came close to Amira; the History Professor observed her from head to toe in an angry arrogant look. Mr. Ajanar whispered a mocking low voice:

- You just got lucky, little witless. Don't rejoice that much. You'll stutter tomorrow!!

Then the History teacher handed the award to Amira Mounier. Except on that moment, something unusual happened. Amira Mounier looked at the History Professor, and she spoke to him without stuttering, in a slow clear strong voice:

- Thank you, Professor Ajanar. But I have already won more than a trophy. You can keep this prize ... or give it to your favorite student Eriem.

People in the reception room couldn't believe what Amira had just done and said. Yet, she dared!

The History Professor Mr. Ajanar stood immobile in his place, still holding the trophy in his hand. Before she walked down the stage steps, Amira turned around to the History Professor, and she announced with a defiant smile:

- Perhaps I will still stutter, for the next few days ... but ... I reassure you, Professor ... it will not be for long!

It seemed that the History Professor was barely holding a rage explosion. Never in his life, was Mr. Ajanar humiliated that much. Eriem Eyelord became pale, without daring to step in and comfort her favorite Professor.

When Amira Mounier walked down the stage, she was immediately greeted by the Congressman. The great man shook her hand warmly, and he said in an admiring loud voice:

- I hope to live long enough to see Congresswomen in our dear Country!

Amira blushed at the Congressman's comment, and she politely thanked him with a smile. And then, Amira turned around and she walked through the audience. Having no friends in this school, everyone was curious about who Amira wanted to meet, and where Amira was heading.

When Amira stopped in front of a person of her same height, she did something unpredictable. Amira firmly hugged Dalya Bouvard in her arms, and she whispered in a trembling happy voice:

- Thank you ... thank you so much for your help!

Dalya was surprised by her classmate's gesture. Yet, Dalya answered with a sincere smile:

- You're welcome.

When she released Dalya, Amira had tears in her eyes, and rosy cheeks. And for once, Dalya was glad to see Amira's tears. Not tears of humiliation, but tears of pride. However, Dalya dared to ask her:

- But, how did you know it was me?

Amira laughed aloud:

- Because every time I found a trick, you were always around ... and I admit that Miss Guendolyn's interventions were not so discreet and skilled.

The Library's assistant, Miss Guendolyn, laughed at her wrong steps, Dalya and Amira giggled too. When Dalya remembered an item:

- The beige lace gloves ... it was you?

Amira smiled shyly:

- I thought it would be easier to write ... with thin lace gloves.

To face the challenges, the strange little box provided the best clues ... to continue and ahead move.

Was it difficult? … Yes

Was it painful? … Yes

Was it worth the effort? ... The Excelbox smiles.

Chapter 37

Menaces

Monday, December 07th, 1891.

When she finished her Mathematics class, Dalya left school. She stopped at the grocery store a few streets away, to get milk that her mother asked her to bring.

While the Merchant served her milk, Dalya noticed three men in the other side of the street, and they were staring at her. The three men were all big size, wearing black jackets and caps. One of the three men had a charcoal black beard.

Dalya took the milk handed to her by the Merchant, and she continued her way to Dumbarton Oaks Park. When she arrived at the French neighbors' home, les Poirier, Dalya decided to say a quick hello to Mrs. Glorina. She opened the garden door and walked to the back door of the kitchen. Once Dalya rang the doorbell, Mrs. Glorina greeted her with a joyful smile:

- It's always a great pleasure to see you, Mademoiselle!!
- You too, Mrs. Glorina.
- Are you coming back from school?
- Yes, and I had some groceries to do too.
- Come inside for a moment!! I've prepared an excellent Cramberries pie with a delicious meringue!!

Dalya followed Mrs. Glorina inside the kitchen. When Dalya sat on a chair, the woman served her a portion of the pie. And at her first bite, Dalya's eyes lit up.

- Very very delicious!! Exclaimed Dalya.
- I told you, Mademoiselle. Mrs. Glorina laughed.

The woman folded multiple towels, while Dalya ate her pie.

- How is Madame doing lately?
- Oh!! Winter is not her favorite season. Replied Mrs. Glorina before continuing:
- She must remain close to the fireplace, either in her bedroom or the living room. But I admit ... this winter is warmer than in previous years.
- Yes! I quite agree with you Mrs. Glorina. Even the temperatures are softer.

Dalya finished her Cramberries pie, and then she greeted Mrs. Glorina and promised to come back again soon. When Dalya closed the garden door of the French neighbors' house, she noticed a strange thing. The three men she had seen at the grocery store when she was buying milk, they were standing at the house exit of the neighbors, les Poirier. The man with the black beard was leaning on the garden wall, and the two other men standing around him. They looked as if they were waiting for something.

Dalya continued her path to the Annex house of the grand Mansion. She had to hurry up in order to help her mother prepare dinner.

Passing by the Bowman's family house, Dalya could admire the beautiful almond trees, covered with little white flowers. Winter was the blossoming season of these beautiful trees...

Suddenly, Dalya looked behind her, and she was surprised to find the same three men, walking at a slow speed, right behind her. A strange feeling invaded Dalya in that moment.

- Is it possible that these three men were following her, since she left school?

Dalya quickly chased that idea from her mind. There was no reason to worry about these three men and imagine things. Dalya continued her way toward the grand Mansion.

However, before reaching the big door of the grand Mansion, and all of a sudden, Dalya felt a hand holding her from behind. When she turned around, she was surprised to discover the three men surrounding her. Up close, the three men had a smile that inspired no trust.

- Hello little Bouvard. Said one of the men.

Dalya's fears were confirmed, these three men were following her indeed, since she left school, and now they surrounded her!! And even if the man said her name and seemed to know who she was, Dalya didn't know any of the 3 men, she has never met them before, and she didn't know what they wanted from her.

- Who are you? Asked Dalya, trying the best she could to hide her fear.

One man replied:

- This is a very pretty house where you live ... you and your little family ...

Dalya didn't know why these three men have been following her and what they wanted. And although Dalya was not of the same size as these three men, she decided to ignore them and continue her way to the grand Mansion.

Except that, when she turned around to leave, one of the men held her by the arm brusquely. The move was so sudden that Dalya tripped and she fell on the floor. Her milk bottle crashed to the ground, and all the milk dispersed instantly.

- What do you want? Dalya asked in an intimidated tone.

The man with the charcoal black beard knelt down to be at Dalya's level; he looked at her and he said in a calm cold voice:

- Your father, Antman ... he owes us money.

Of all the possibilities that Dalya would have thought about, she would have never believed that these three men were following her because of her father!! She was shocked to find it out. Still on the ground, Dalya dared to say in the bravest voice she had:

- This ... this is between you and him.

The man with the black beard, who was still kneeling in front of her, he stared at her with an amused look:

- You're his daughter, aren't you?
- Yes ... but I don't even know who you are ... it's between you and my father ... I have nothing to do with it ...

The 3 men had an evil laugh. The man with the scary look and black beard, continued in an icy voice:

- I'll explain something to you, kid ... your father owes us 4 500 $ ... the accumulation of his debts in the card game at the old port pub ...

Dalya could feel her blood heated in her entire body, her throat tightened, sweat appeared on her forehead. She knew that her father hadn't stopped playing, and he spent all the money from his work in the card game. But never Dalya imagined that her father would owe such a sum of money!! 4 500 $ ... It was a huge debt!!

Given Dalya's silence, the man kneeling in front of her, pulled out some little papers from his pocket. He showed them to Dalya, and asked:

- Do you know what these are, kid?

Dalya answered no by a head sign. The man explained to her in a cold tone:

- These are debts letters ... signed by your father ... if he doesn't pay us the full amount soon and once ... we'll take very good care of him, and his family!

At that moment, when the man pronounced the word family, Dalya had only a single image in her mind; her little twins sisters. Dalya dared to ask the man in front of her, in a terrified voice:

- Is it a menace?

The man displayed a devil smile that made Dalya tremble, and he replied in an icy voice:

- Yes ... it's a menace.

Dalya's heart stopped beating. Fear invaded her. Her throat choked. She was breathing with difficulty. Dalya had never experienced such a feeling of fear. She became pale, her lips all white, and she nearly fainted.

At that instant, a car coming out of the grand Mansion, stopped close to the 3 men and Dalya. And the little girl was relieved to recognize a familiar face coming out of the car. Mr. Sloan Wilfrid got out of the car, and he walked straight up to her with hurried steps and a worried look:

- Are you alright, Mademoiselle?

Mr. Wilfrid helped Dalya to get up from the ground, instantly. He picked Dalya's backpack and he repeated his question in a concerned tone:

- Are you alright, Mademoiselle?

Although Dalya has recovered her normal breathing, she answered in a trembling voice:

- Yes, Monsieur. Everything is fine.

Sloan Wilfrid wasn't convinced at all by this answer. The young Lawyer didn't understand how and why Dalya was on the ground, all pale and terrified, he noticed the milk bottle crashed on the floor, and the strangers who surrounded Dalya didn't inspire any trust.

The three men didn't seem at all intimidated by the arrival of Mr. Wilfrid. The man with the black beard spoke to Dalya, display a calm devil smile:

- Report the message to your father ... from Agadir ... if he does not pay, we will do what is necessary...

Mr. Wilfrid didn't like the tone and the threatening stares of the 3 men toward the little girl. Dalya kept her silence, not daring to answer or to move. As soon as the three men walked away, Mr. Wilfrid insisted in a serious voice:

- Are you sure everything is alright, Mademoiselle?

Dalya was relieved that Mr. Wilfrid saved her from the 3 men, by his unexpected presence. Except that she was so embarrassed that the Lawyer had witnessed the menaces scene that she went through. Dalya forced herself to smile:

- Yes, Monsieur. All is fine.

Mr. Sloan Wilfrid stared at the little girl for a moment. He didn't want to intervene in the Bouvard family's privacy; even less embarrass Dalya with delicate questions. After a few seconds, Mr. Wilfrid asked Dalya in a natural tone:

- I went to the grand Mansion to settle some business with Mr. Bûchebois, the head of the Mansion. Would you like me to give you a ride back home, Mademoiselle?
- Thank you, Monsieur. But I'll walk. It's very close.

Mr. Wilfrid smiled tenderly. But before leaving, the young Lawyer said in a serious tone:

- Mademoiselle Dalya ... if someone bothers you or something worries you, you should let me know. I am here to assist you in anything.

Dalya was always touched by the kindness and the attention that Mr. Wilfrid had toward her, since the first day she met him with the Late Mr. Governor. Dalya smiled back politely:

- Thank you, Monsieur Wilfrid.

The young Lawyer returned to his car and he left. Dalya went on her way toward the Annex house of the grand Mansion. When she surpassed the big door entrance of the Mansion, Dalya felt her heart tighten up, her throat choked, her cheeks heated, and her tears fall down. She continued to walk forward anyway.

Will someday the little Dalya Bouvard forget what her father made her go through?

Never will Dalya forget the menaces she received because of her father.

Never will Dalya forget that her father took her money of her sold handmade bags.

Never will Dalya forget the selfishness and the oppression of her father.

Never will Dalya forget the chores her father charged her of, careless of her fatigue and her classes at school.

Never will Dalya forget that her father banned her from having a life, a voice, and a freedom.

Never will Dalya forget the day she asked her father pity, and he ignored her.

Never will Dalya forget.

Chapter 38

A bronze blue shawl

Friday, December 11th, 1891. The afternoon. One day before Dalya's birthday.

Winter reigned as master over the city of Georgetown. The air was very cold. The trees stood firmly without any foliage. A few centimeters of Snow covered the ground. Bright white clouds invaded the sky.

At the end of her classes, Dalya came out of school, heading back home. When a familiar figure called her out from behind:

- Demoiselle Dalya. I did well to come here; I've been looking for you!!

Dalya turned to be in front of the Dean of Merchants; Mr. Kenan Einsenberg. He approached her limping on his crutch and his wood leg. Dalya greeted him with a surprised smile:

- Hello Mr. Einsenberg.

The Dean of Merchants stared at the huge building of the Royal Georgetown College, and he asked in a curious voice:

- So, this is where you attend your classes?
- Yes, Sir. For many months now.

The Dean of Merchants looked at Dalya and he smiled:

- I have no doubt that you are a studious student!!

Dalya blushed a little:

- Some courses are easier than others, Sir. I am doing my best.

The little girl wondered what brought the Dean of Merchants to her school:

- You were looking for me ... you needed me for anything, Sir?

Mr. Kenan Einsenberg hesitated for a moment, and he seemed nervous. Something that was quite unusual for a man of his strong imposing character. When finally, he took out an item from his big coat pocket.

- Well yes ... this is for you, Demoiselle.

Dalya took the item from the Dean's hands. It was a very nice stitched shawl in soft cotton, with stripes of blue and bronze colors, and at each end of the shawl was sewed a flying eagle.

- For ... for me?

The big man seemed a bit shy and messy:

- Yes! ... it's ... just ... a small birthday gift … a little in advance ...

Never Dalya had received a birthday gift, neither from her parents, nor from anyone else. She was shocked and pleased by the Dean's gesture. She immediately wore the soft shawl around her neck. And in a spontaneous move, Dalya hugged the great man with her little arms:

- Thank you Sir!! … Thank you very much!! … It's really very pretty!! It's a wonderful gift!! … Thank you very much!!

Although strong imposing character, the Dean of Merchants had always been caring and kind toward Dalya. Mr. Kenan Einsenberg was somewhat surprised by the little girl's hug, but he was very happy that his gift pleased her that much. When Dalya released him, The Dean smiled in an amused tone:

- It's the shawls season, right now ... it will be useful to you in this cold weather!
- Yes Sir!! ... I'll always keep it!! … Thank you Sir!! … Thank you very much!!

Dalya greeted the Dean of Merchants and she went on her way toward the Annex house. She was thrilled with her birthday present, as modest as it was, a soft shawl made of cotton, in blue bronze colors, with a flying eagle designed at each end of the shawl.

In fact, the Dean of Merchants wasn't searching for Dalya only to offer her a birthday gift. The great man was well aware that Dalya's birthday was also the day of the 2nd Challenge that she should undergo. Tomorrow, this little girl's fate was certainly about to change ... for the better or for the worse, no one can predict it.

The Dean of Merchants observed the little silhouette disappearing in the street. His mind was occupied with a thought. Mr. Kenan Einsenberg murmured in a reflective tone:

- The voice they are trying to repress ... Oh ... she will be heard by thousands of millions!

Chapter 39

The day will come

On Friday evening, December 11th, 1891. At the Annex house of the grand Mansion.

Dalya and her parents were well aware that it could be their last meal in the Annex house of the grand Mansion. The very next day, Dalya will have to answer to the Second Challenge.

The little twins took their dinner earlier, and they were sleeping upstairs in their bedroom.

That night, dinner in the Annex house took place in a heavy dense silence. Dalya's mother placed the potatoes and carrots soup on the table, before sitting and serve herself. And for once, Augustine was silent. Dalya didn't hear her mother scream or insult, the entire day, which was quite unusual. Although eating her dinner in silence, Augustine observed her daughter with an evil and menacing look.

Dalya's father, Antman also was very quiet since few days now. And he stared at his daughter in a cold look.

The little girl didn't expect encouragements from her parents for the Challenge that awaits her, next day. In fact, since long ago, Dalya didn't expect anything from her parents.

When dinner was over, Dalya stood to pick up the plates and wash the dishes, like every night. But before making one more step, a hand firmly hold her arm. Dalya's father said in a menacing voice:

- I hope you have learned something useful in this stupid school, to answer this damn Question tomorrow!!

Dalya naturally replied:

- It's that ... the First Question wasn't about anything I studied in school. And I doubt that the Second Question will be ab...
- I DON'T CARE WHAT YOU THINK!! IF YOU FAIL TO ANSWER THIS SECOND QUESTION, YOU'LL HAVE TO DEAL WITH ME!! UNDERSTOOD?!

Dalya didn't dare to add a word. Antman tightened so hard his fist on his daughter's arm; that Dalya's cheeks became all red, and he screamed:

- AND DON'T THINK THAT I FORGOT YOUR INSOLENCE TOWARD ME AND YOUR MOTHER, WHEN YOU ANSWERED THE FIRST QUESTION!! THIS TIME, ANSWER ONLY THE DAMN QUESTION, WITHOUT EXPLANATIONS!! IS THAT CLEAR ENOUGH?!

- Yes. Dalya whispered bowing her head.

Her father continued in an icy tone:

- And after your answer ... you'll ask money from this Lawyer, so that I can pay my debts!! ... And this time, you'd better convince him to give you that money!!

Dalya couldn't move, because her father was tightly holding her arm. Yet, she answered spontaneously:

- But ... Why should I pay for your debts, father?

Antman Bouvard didn't expect this question from his little girl. He stood up from his chair and he exploded with rage, while tightening his fist on Dalya's arm:

- YOU DARE TO ANSWER ME!! YOU DARE TO DEFY ME!! LITTLE VERMIN!! YOU THINK YOU'RE STRONG ENOUGH TO DEFY AND ANSWER ME!!

With a sudden movement of rage, Antman Bouvard raised his right hand to slap his daughter. Dalya couldn't escape from her father, he held her by the arm very strongly. She closed her eyes, trembling from the slap that was falling on her.

Except that ... all of a sudden ... the hand of another man caught Antman's hand and it stopped him from slapping his daughter. When Dalya opened her eyes, she didn't believe what she was seeing ... Mr. Sloan Wilfrid, himself!!

The Lawyer dropped Antman's hand with a sudden move, and he asked him in a shocked voice:

- But ... What do you think you are doing?

Lyor Laszlo was behind Mr. Wilfrid, the young apprentice seemed surprised at what was happening in the Annex house. Antman Bouvard was shocked to see the two Lawyers in the kitchen, he replied in a confused voice:

- I ... I ... you are in my house Mr. Wilfrid!! ... You have no right to ask me this question!!

Antman was not a man to admit his mistakes. And Mr. Wilfrid was not a man to be easily intimidated:

- Sorry ... Did I hear right? ... Your house?

Antman was very stubborn in his defense:

- Yes!! My house that belongs to me!!

Mr. Wilfrid didn't believe what he had just heard:

- Belongs to you?! ... I think that you have forgotten that this house has been offered by the Late Mr. Governor to his Heiress ... to Dalya Bouvard only ... This house is hers!!

Antman had a different logic from the rest of the people. He naturally answered, with a strong conviction:

- My daughter belongs to me!! All that is hers belongs to me!! Her house belongs to me!! And her wealth also belongs to me!! I have debts and she'll pay them!!

Hearing these words, Wilfrid stepped toward Antman. The Lawyer tried to keep his calm and composure:

- I would like to clarify some things for you ... the fortune of Late Mr. Governor belongs unquestionably to Dalya Bouvard only, and to no one else. You won't touch any penny of the Heritage!

Since many years now, Dalya knew that her father was possessive and selfish. She could never forget how he took her money of the handmade bags she made and sold. Her father always reminded her that the money she earned was not hers. Her father's arguments were incomprehensible to Dalya; she is already housed and fed, therefore she didn't need the money she earned.

And as unfair as he could be, Antman never liked to be confronted; he answered the Lawyer in an angry tone:

- But she is my daughter!! She belongs to me!!

Mr. Wilfrid insisted to clarify the wrong convictions of Dalya's parents:

- She is your daughter, yes. But she is not yours. She belongs only to herself!!
- And so who will pay my debts? Antman said impatiently.

Mr. Wilfrid immediately replied, barely holding his amused laugh:

- But there are your debts ... your problems ... your mistakes ... It is up to you only, to pay them!!

Antman persisted in his selfish logic:

- So what's the use of having a daughter, if she doesn't pay my debts?

Mr. Wilfrid put him back into his place, in a cold firm voice:

- Your daughter should not assume your debts!! She is not supposed to receive threats from your creditors!! Your daughter is not supposed to spend her life correcting your mistakes!!

Antman didn't expect this answer; he didn't dare to add one more word, and he repressed with great difficulty his anger.

After a few seconds of a heavy silence in the kitchen of the Annex house, Mr. Wilfrid thought aloud:

- There is something ... that worried my mind, for some time now. And it is the reason of my visit, tonight.

Sloan Wilfrid approached Dalya, he took the little girl's hands in a delicate move, and he gently removed her lace gloves, without Dalya or anyone daring to stop him.

Swollen red fingers, bruises and broken blue nails, the palms of her hands were marked by bloody scars. Dalya trembled.

Lyor Laszlo stepped closer toward Dalya, not believing his eyes. He was shocked to see the little girl's hands condition. Lyor wondered how and why Dalya's hands were tortured. Sloan Wilfrid turned toward Dalya's parents, and he asked them in a curious tone:

- You did this to her, didn't you?

Augustine Bouvard didn't hesitate to answer in a defiant voice:

- I will beat my daughter as I like!! It is our right!!

Antman supported his wife and he exclaimed angrily:

- Yes ... Me and my wife will beat our daughter as we like!! It is our right, and nobody will stop us from doing it!! She belongs to us!!

Mr. Wilfrid let go of Dalya's hands gently. And while he walked toward the parents in slow steps, Mr. Wilfrid asked in a calm surprised voice:

- Your what? ... Your right? ... Beating your daughter is your right?!

Dalya's parents hesitated a few seconds to answer the Lawyer's question. When finally, Antman tried to sound threatening:

- Yes!! ... And we'll get no education lessons from you!! We have the right to do whatever we want with her!! We are her parents!! She belongs to us!!

At that moment, never Dalya imagined that she would witness Mr. Sloan Wilfrid's anger. And apparently, Lyor Laszlo never knew that hidden part of his mentor's personality. Sloan Wilfrid has always been a calm man, kind and courteous. Except that night.

In a second, the Lawyer walked toward Antman in quick steps. In a sudden move, Wilfrid threw the kitchen wood table that was on his way, it crashed to the ground in pieces. Everyone was shaken and surprised; Augustine let out a frightened scream, Dalya jumped, and Lyor yelled trying to calm down the Lawyer:

- Wilfrid!

Except that no one dared to intervene or stop him. Sloan Wilfrid nailed Dalya's father to the wall, with a violent unpredictable move. The Lawyer strangled Dalya's father with his hands, he looked straight into his eyes, and he said in a menacing cold voice:

- If you or your wife ... ever ... touch a single hair of the future Heiress of the Governor ... I swear to torture both of you, myself!! ... And believe me; I will have all the rights and the fun of doing it!!

Sloan Wilfrid released Dalya's father in such a brusque move, that Antman Bouvard stumbled to the floor, on the ruins of the kitchen wood table that Mr. Wilfrid demolished. Antman Bouvard was petrified by the Lawyer's violence; he didn't dare to get up from the floor.

Immediately, Sloan Wilfrid walked toward Dalya's mother. Augustine stepped back trembling. When he got close to her, Sloan Wilfrid addressed her in a threatening voice:

- And I allow myself to give you a lesson to remember ... people who beat their children don't deserve to be parents. You don't deserve this girl ... You don't deserve to be a mother!!

Augustine became all pale, her legs couldn't hold her anymore, she fell on a chair, and she didn't dare to raise her head up.

For some tense and long seconds, Mr. Wilfrid observed both parents in a disgusted look. The Lawyer knew that Dalya's parents were hard on her, but he never imagined that they would treat her with this much cruelty. In the kitchen of the Annex house, in front of everyone's silence and motionless, Sloan Wilfrid addressed the parents in a strong firm voice:

- As a Lawyer in charge of the future Heiress affairs, I inform you that if Dalya Bouvard succeeds to answer the Second Question ... I will personally make sure that she doesn't spend a single more second in this house ... with garbages like you two!!

Antman and Augustine Bouvard didn't dare to move or protest or even raise their eyes up. Mr. Wilfrid stepped back, and he pulled himself together for a second. He signaled to Lyor Laszlo, that they would be leaving. And before heading to the door exit, Mr. Sloan Wilfrid turned toward Dalya Bouvard, and he forced himself to smile at her:

- I shall see you tomorrow, Mademoiselle Dalya Bouvard.

Dalya didn't say a word; she just smiled back at the Lawyer.

After both Lawyers left the Annex house, Dalya went to her bedroom immediately, without taking care of the dinner dishes or the kitchen table debris. Her mother Augustine didn't speak a word, and she cleaned the kitchen herself, that night. While her father Antman took his coat and he left the house, in a tense silence.

Alone in her bedroom, it took Dalya several minutes to gather herself up, and understand what had just happened in front of her, in the kitchen. It is true that Mr. Wilfrid was always courteous and kind to her. But Dalya has never seen him in such anger, against the cruelty of her parents.

And it was not the only thing that occupied the little girl's mind, on that moment. For the first time in her life, Dalya wondered why her parents were so aggressive and violent with her. Dalya thought hard about this question, but she failed to find any answer to it.

Antman and Augustine Bouvard thought they possessed their daughter. Dalya was not supposed to have another life besides serving her parents, day and night. Antman and Augustine refused to let Dalya become independent from them. They wanted to keep her close to them and keep control on her, in any way possible, through violence, terror and injustice. Except that ... Dalya Bouvard will grow to understand that it is only the cowards and the weak that are aggressive and possessive.

The night seemed long. The cold of December was freezing. The sky was decorated with beautiful sparkling stars. The full moon was shining. Unable to sleep, Dalya sat on the edge of the large windows of her bedroom, watching the wonderful night landscape offered by the large garden.

When suddenly, an object placed on her small office table, moved. The Excelbox became alive. The top side of the box opened up, and a transparent oval glass cage gently straightened up. Four yellow gold cylinders in forged shaped vine plant, welded the transparent glass cage.

The round clock inside the cage stood up in a royal move. The small needle was set long ago on December 12th, 1891. The big needle was balancing between the night of 11th and 12th December 1891.

Dalya watched the Excelbox for some long minutes. It was a strange box, alive and smart, who always had the right answers in the most chaotic times...

A moment later, Dalya approached the Excelbox. She wrote on a paper:

What is the 5th clue?

As soon as Dalya placed the paper in the rectangular opening, the Excelbox took it. A shining light came out of the transparent cage, and a few seconds later, a little paper came out of the Excelbox.

The day when freedom will break its chains, will come.
The day when no more insolence will be swallowed, will come.
The day when respect will be continual, will come.
The day when injustice will bow, will come.
Because they thought burying a weak voice,
While they burry a seed that back will grow.

The same night.

The servant at the Toscana restaurant, Tudi, ran in an alley, on the South side of Georgetown city. She stopped at a small wood door. Scanning the street left and right to make sure no one followed her; Tudi opened the door and she entered inside.

The house had several rooms built around a large square garden with opened roof. The full moon illuminated the garden of a soft glow. Tudi followed the lit candles along a corridor, up to a door. She breathed a shot, and then she opened the door.

The room inside was impeccably refined. Instantly, a musk exquisite scent welcomed any visitor. Several paintings displaying Asian letters in black charcoal ink, were hung on the walls. Long rugs in soft colors, were placed to accommodate visitors. Ten lamps lit the place with a warm light.

Tudi bowed in front of an old man, and then she sat near Miss Haîyang. The woman seemed worried. Immediately, Master Fong Ka-Ho was the first to speak:

- Fāshēngle shénme shì? *(What happened?)*

Tudi replied right away:

- The man visited her home tonight ... When he found out the state of her hands by removing her gloves, he became very angry. He knocked the father to the ground and he threatened the mother.

Master Fong Ka-Ho asked:

- Hé nàgè nuhài? *(And the girl?)*
- She's alright, Master ... she was a bit shaken by what the man did to her parents. But it seems that the man is kind and caring toward her.

Master Fong Ka-Ho spoke to Miss Haîyang:

- Something is worrying you?

Miss Haîyang answered instantly:

- Yes Master. I don't understand! She has mastered the hand movement perfectly well, and she fought back at school. I saw her through the classroom door, that day. She threw down to the floor a boy; he was 3 times stronger than her! So then ... why didn't she defend herself from her parents?

After a few seconds of silence, Master Fong Ka-Ho replied:

- One does not defend itself from a sardine and a shark in the same way. Each offender requires a specific defense.

Miss Haîyang replied in an angry tone:

- But Master ... She endured the punishments for months, in silence, not daring to tell anyone! ... She failed to defend herself! ... She was not able to escape their punishments!

Tudi dared to say in a determined voice:

- We are ready to intervene, Master ... she cannot do it alone.

At this moment, Master Fong Ka-Ho smiled. Tudi and Miss Haîyang exchanged a confused look. Master Fong Ka-Ho explained:

- The jellyfish is a small sea creature ... an extremely delicate creature, gentle, peaceful, with a grace, and incomparable beauty ... without sharp teeth, no legs, no hands ... and yet, the jellyfish is the most frightening creature of the entire sea.

Miss Haîyang and Tudi didn't seem to understand the point of the old man. Master Fong Ka-Ho continued in a sure certain voice:

- Her endurance in front of violence, will be her greatest strength ... the injustice she has suffered, will fuel her determination ... her today's silence, is only a refill of energy … she might be soft and small as a jellyfish for now, but do not underestimate her … at the right time, she will defend herself!

Miss Haîyang asked:

- So then ... what can we do to help her, Master?

Master Fong Ka-Ho replied in a serene tone:

- We cannot prevent the challenges of our destiny ... we can only prepare for them … we observe, we prepare, and we wait ... the time to intervene has not yet come.

Addressing Miss Haîyang, Master Fong Ka-Ho ordered her:

- Let me know when Shang arrives.
- Yes, Master.

Then, Master Fong Ka-Ho turned toward Tudi:

- Tomorrow is an important day ... bàogào nin suo kàn dàa hé ting dào de yiqiè. *(Report everything you see and all you hear).*
- Shì Zhu. *(Yes, Master).*

Tudi bowed to Master Fong Ka-Ho and Miss Haîyang, and then she left the place with hurried steps.

Chapter 40

The Challenge

Saturday, December 12th, 1891. The day of her birthday. The morning.

What Dalya liked the most in her bedroom; it was the large windows that always invited sunlight into the room. Dalya woke up at the first rays of dawn. She went close to the windows and stared for a long moment at the beautiful Mansion's garden. A light fog slowly cleared up, and the greenery gradually appeared.

Dalya arranged her bed, she wore her school uniform and she went down to the kitchen. Her sisters and her parents were still asleep. And because of the difficult day ahead of her, Dalya didn't wish to hear her mother's reprimands, nor her father's threats. The little girl warmed some milk; she served herself buttered bread, and then she quietly ate her breakfast in the living room, next to the kitchen. The wood dining table was destroyed into pieces by Mr. Sloan Wilfrid, the night before.

After a few minutes, Dalya gently closed the door of the Annex house and she turned around to leave. Suddenly, Dalya was surprised to discover a visitor right in front of the Annex house ... the Snow Panther herself!!

Never had Séraphine been so close to the Annex house, except on that day. Séraphine was lying down on the grass, calm and peaceful. And when she noticed Dalya, Séraphine stood up immediately, her long tail straightened up, and she stared at the little girl with her sapphire blue sharp eyes. Dalya greeted her with a smile:

- It's good to see you Séraphine.

Once Dalya came down the few steps of the Annex house, and walked toward the garden, the Snow Panther followed the little girl, walking slowly by her side. The Snow Panther stopped at the exit door of the grand Mansion. Séraphine stared at the little girl until she disappeared from the road. Dalya continued her way to school.

The large stairs of the Royal Georgetown College were full of students. The start of classes wasn't until several minutes later. Some students were sitting on the edges of the large stairs, and others were standing talking at the front door. All the students were eager for their next Christmas Holidays in a few days. All the students were happy to leave school, except one.

The little Dalya Bouvard entered the school, with a pinch in the heart, and a tightened throat. At the stairs of the school entrance, all the eyes stared at Dalya and all the conversations stopped. Dalya made her way among the students, in a heavy tense silence.

In the Mathematics classroom, Eriem Eyelord, Gael Benoble and their court, were gathered near the big windows, laughing and sharing their plans for the Christmas holidays. When Dalya entered the classroom, she sat in her usual place; her legs couldn't hold her anymore. Immediately, the laughs and the conversations of Eriem and her court stopped and turned into whispers. And just like the other students at the front gate of the school, Dalya felt their scrutinizing eyes on her.

Seconds later, a student entered the classroom. She was easily known for her long braids light brown hair, and chubby cheeks. Amira Mounier sat on the chair right in front of Dalya, and she turned around toward her immediately:

- Hello!! Amira said displaying a radiant smile.

Dalya smiled back at her. Since the day she had won the essay contest, Amira Mounier and Dalya became best friends. Never someone had ever helped Amira as much as Dalya did.

- So ... it's tonight, isn't it? Amira asked in a nice tone.
- Yes, before midnight, in the living room of the grand Mansion. Dalya whispered.

Dalya tried all her best to hide her anxiety. But she failed. Amira could feel it, and she tried to support her friend:

- Is there anything I can do to help you answer the challenge?

Dalya replied no by a head sign. After a few seconds, Amira asked:

- And did you read well all the clues?
- Yes ... at least hundred times, last night ... the clues are supposed to help me pass the Challenge, but ... I don't know what it is about.

Amira fell silent for a moment, and then she jumped of her chair:

- Would you like to go to the Library after the Mathematics class? ... We could consult books ... I know by heart all the books' placements; I can help you find whatever you want!

Dalya thanked her with a smile. Amira tried to give back Dalya's kindness toward her, by helping her friend to succeed the Challenge.

When the Mathematics Professor, Mr. Wyatt entered the classroom, all the students joined their seats. Amira smiled at Dalya, and then she turned toward the Professor.

- Good morning ladies and gentlemen!!

Professor Wyatt was always cheerful during his class. His good humor and his excellent Mathematics course will be missed by Dalya.

- I am delighted that everyone is here today!! ... I will hand you your homework for the Christmas holidays ... and let me reassure you, even if it will seem like a mountain of homework ... climb it, one rock at a time!!

Professor Wyatt let out a little innocent joyful laugh, but he failed to reassure his students. They have hoped for no homework, in order to enjoy the festivities and the holidays.

- Come on ... come on ... Courage my children!! ... Homework is to improve your level and make your next semester easier ... Now open your notebooks and write down the notes!!

All the students opened their notebooks; they picked up their pens, and they noted what the Professor dictated. All the students wrote down their Christmas holiday homework. All the students were preparing for their next semester of the Mathematics course. All except one.

At the end of the Mathematics class, Dalya and Amira walked to the school Library. Dalya was delighted that the place was empty; most students had left school after class. Amira put her backpack on a desk, and then she turned toward Dalya, with a lively voice:

- So ... where do we start?
- I don't have the faintest idea. Dalya replied, before continuing:
- I don't even know what will the Second Challenge be ... will it be a question or a puzzle to solve, or something else ... and the First Question wasn't about my classes in this school ...

Despite the difficulty, Amira was a determined little girl:

- So then ... if you know nothing about the Second Challenge ... we'll read a new collection of stories! ... It will distract your brain for a minute, and allow it to breath!

Few steps away from Amira and Dalya, Miss Guendolyn had heard the entire conversation of the two students since their coming into the Library. Miss Guendolyn approached with her little book carriage, and she agreed with the idea:

- Well said, Miss Amira!! Nothing lifts your spirits and refreshes your mind better than a story!!
- I don't think it's useful for the Second Chall...

But before Dalya could complete her sentence, Amira had already disappeared in a Library aisle. She returned a few seconds later, holding a large big book in her hands. The two girls sat on the Library chairs, Miss Guendolyn choose a chair close to them, and Amira read in a slow, clear voice:

To run is nothing; we must timely start.
The hare and tortoise here shall teach the art.
"Let's bet," the tortoise said, "my clever spark
Which, you or I, the first shall gain that mark."

...

Oblivious of his bet, he sees
The tortoise the wished goal about to gain,
He sprang like lightning, but he sprang in vain:
The tortoise won just as the hare took flight.
"Well," she exclaimed, "good runner, was I right?"

After several minutes, Dalya and Miss Guendolyn applauded Amira warmly. It is true that Amira's pronunciation had greatly improved. She still stuttered a few times, but much less than before.

- It's a very funny story!! exclaimed Dalya
- Yes!! I found it a few months ago. And every time I read it, it makes me laugh. Amira explained.

Miss Guendolyn informed the two students:

- The Author is Monsieur de la Fontaine, a French famous poet ... he wrote several stories, as funny and clever ... almost all his characters are animals ... but I admit my favorite story is this one. The turtle is really smarter!!
- And fast too!! Amira laughed, before adding:
- By the way, Dalya ... don't you think that the rabbit looks like someone?

Dalya thought for a second:

- No ... who?
- Eriem Eyelord!!

Dalya and Amira burst out laughing.

- Yes! It's true! ... She is pretentious and arrogant, just like the rabbit.
- And especially white pale! ... Did you see Eriem's face when the price was offered to me?
- Yes!!! She became pale! Dalya laughed.
- And not just her, even her parents were shocked that their daughter lost the contest's prize ... for once!! Said Miss Guendolyn.

- And Gael who bragged about his friend? Did you see him? Asked Amira. He looked like a statue!! He didn't dare to move!!
- But one must admit that the person who was breathless that day, it was the History Professor, Mr. Ajanar. Miss Guendolyn laughed. Goodness, how happy I was to see that man furious and disappointed!
- You have disappointed many people Amira!! Dalya laughed.
- And for once, I'm glad I've disappointed!! Amira said.

The two little girls and the young woman laughed and giggled for several minutes. And luckily the Library was empty, that moment. When Miss Guendolyn stood up to push her book cart and continue her sorting, she said:

- Anyway, Miss Amira ... Thank you for amusing us with this story. And your pronunciation has become perfect!! Bravo!!
- It's true!... your speaking had improved so much! You've succeeded, Amira! Said Dalya in a proud voice.

Amira stood up, and she bowed in a theatrical way, with a serious voice:

- Thank you ... Thank you ... I may be slow, but I surely persevere just like the turtle!! Perseverance ... Ladies!! ... Perseverance!!

These few minutes of laughs, allowed Dalya to release her anxiety and breathe easier. Before Miss Guendolyn would leave them, the young woman turned and smiled at Dalya:

- I will accompany Professor Canfield, tonight to the grand Mansion ... if you don't mind of course, Mademoiselle.
- It will be my pleasure to see you, Miss Guendolyn. Dalya replied.

Amira and Dalya remained a few moments in the Library, to read a few stories by the same author, before deciding to leave. When they arrived at the school exit, Dalya turned toward Amira and she smiled at her:

- Well, Amira ... this is where we separate.

Amira stared at her for a moment, and then she hugged Dalya firmly in her arms, not daring to say goodbye, or any other word. The two girls separated with a sad smile and tears in their eyes. Amira remained motionless, watching her friend until she disappeared from the street.

Dumbarton Oaks Park was peaceful and quiet. Large trees stood all along the road. The cool December air cuddled the trees' branch. And despite the cold, Dumbarton Oaks Park was a welcoming place.

The lake that was on the way home, gathered some beautiful white swans. Dalya paused for a moment; she pulled out a small bag from her backpack, and threw to the birds some bread crumbs. Dalya got used to feed the migrant birds who settled on the lake, every time she passed on this road.

And while the little girl was feeding birds in the lake, a silhouette watched her from afar. The young French neighbor, Richard Poirier was working in his office, in his house across the lake. When he stood up to take a book, he noticed the little girl feeding the birds in the lake.

Since several months now, Richard Poirier curiously watched this strange new neighbor. He was a young man hard to impress. Except that ... how did a little girl help his mother to get out of her bed, and revived her life, despite her hopeless illness? How did a stubborn 13 years old girl succeeded, while talented and experienced Doctors had given up? For what reason did this little girl came into their lives? And how did she easily change their routine?

Questions that the young Richard Poirier wondered about each time he watched the silhouette of the little girl pass by this road.

When Dalya arrived to the Annex home, she noticed that all the windows shutters of the house were closed. It was barely 7:00 PM. When Dalya entered the house, the little twins ran toward their big sister, exclaiming all happy and excited:

- We go out to downtown!! We go out to downtown!!

Dalya's heart tightened. She understood that her parents have decided to return to their previous 2 rooms' home, in the East side of downtown. Augustine's mother appeared in the doorway, she was wearing her winter coat and her old hat.

- Are you going now? Dalya asked.

Augustine shot her daughter Dalya with a devil look. And for once, Augustine who enjoyed screaming and insulting, she remained silent. Augustine took the twins by their hands and she left the Annex house, walking toward the grand Mansion's exit, without saying a word. The little twins, too young to suspect anything, turned around to their big sister and waved at her:

- See you later Dindin!! See you later Dindin!!

Dalya remained motionless on the doorway of the Annex house; she watched her mother and her little sisters walk away. Dalya sad and sorry for her mother's reaction. When suddenly, a noise was heard from inside the Annex house. When Dalya turned around, her father was coming toward her; he was holding large bags in his hands. Dalya dared to ask him:

- You're not going to attend the Second Challenge, at the grand Mansion?

Antman Bouvard paused, he stared at his daughter in a dark and angry look, and he said in a cold tone:

- When you will fail in this damn Second Challenge ... join us in our old house.

Then, Antman left the Annex house. He loaded the bags into his carriage, and he drove it to the grand Mansion's exit, to join his wife and his twins.

Dalya stood still for a long moment, while observing her family leaving. Dalya never expected any support or encouragements. But she didn't also expect all this hardness from her parents. She didn't understand their reaction. Why leave so soon, without even attending the Challenge? Did they fear the presence of Mr. Wilfrid who threatened them the night before? Or were they ashamed of their cruelty toward their daughter during these last months? Had they no slight hope that their daughter can succeed?

As smart as the little Dalya Bouvard could be, she didn't know the answer to these questions. She went alone inside the Annex house, and walked up to her bedroom. Dalya changed her school uniform and she wore her usual clothes; faded blue overalls, an old shirt, a large hat that hid her hair, and black boy's shoes.

Dalya packed her few belongings, books and clothes. She went down. She put her bag on the doorsteps of the Annex house. She sat on the front stairs.

Then, Dalya Bouvard waited.

10:15 PM.

The landscape of the large garden of the grand Mansion darkened gradually. The night settled softly. And it promised to be a long night.

For several hours, Dalya sat on the steps of the Annex house; she waited for the time of the Second Challenge. She watched for the last time the large garden that separated the Annex house and the grand Mansion. The place where she had lived with her family, since many months now.

At a moment, two shadows from the grand Mansion approached Dalya. She could easily recognize them from afar. Mr. Sloan Wilfrid and the Snow Panther.

- Good evening, Mademoiselle!!

Mr. Wilfrid greeted her with his usual cheerful tone. The Snow Panther walked slowly beside him. Dalya stood up to greet him:

- Good evening, Mr. Wilfrid.

The young Lawyer looked up at the Annex house, he noticed that the windows shutters were all closed, and no light or human presence came from inside the house. Mr. Wilfrid asked all curious:

- Are you all alone, Mademoiselle?
- Yes, Monsieur.

- Where are your parents?

Dalya hesitated for a moment, but she had to give an answer to the Lawyer:

- They are ... my parents and my little sisters left to our old house, in the East side of downtown.

Mr. Wilfrid thought aloud:

- They won't attend the Challenge.

Dalya avoided Mr. Wilfrid's eyes. The young Lawyer noticed the little girl's discomfort, he continued in an encouraging tone:

- So then ... are you ready, Mademoiselle?

Dalya didn't know what to answer, she just smiled nervously. And Mr. Wilfrid understood. The young Lawyer spoke to Dalya, in a serious voice:

- Mademoiselle Dalya Bouvard ... I would like to assure you of something ... no matter what happens tonight, be sure that I will look after you!

Dalya was touched by the young Lawyer's help and kindness. Except that something worried her, Dalya said in a trembling tone:

- But, Sir... if I fail the Second Challenge, the Will is clear, you shouldn't defend me anym...

Mr. Wilfrid interrupted her with a determined strong voice:

- No matter what happens tonight, with or without a Will, I will look after you! ... Since the moment you have been chosen by the Late Mr. Governor Iskander Balthazar, protecting you had become my duty!

Dalya smiled back at him, grateful for his kindness. Séraphine was standing still and quiet, watching the two people with a serene look. Mr. Wilfrid continued with an amused laugh:

- And apparently ... I'm not the only one to insist in protecting you!

10:30 PM.

In the luxurious living room of the grand Mansion, many people were already present; some were standing chatting by the fireplace, others were sitting laughing.

The nephew of Late Mr. Governor, Mr. Ferdinand Edelmen was sitting, and firmly holding his wood cane with an anxious movement, Mr. Ferdinand didn't seem comfortable that night.

The previous First Challenge, nothing went as he has wished for. His sister, Mrs. Honoré Edelmen, beautiful and resplendent in her luxurious fur, was sitting quietly in a chair near her brother. Mrs. Honoré received the greetings of the guests, with a beautiful smile, before whispering softly to her brother:

- I hope your dear friend and Lawyer Ernest Laszlo will not disappoint us this time ...

Mr. Ferdinand was on his nerves, and the evening had not even started yet!

When the Lawyer Mr. Ernest Laszlo entered the living room, he went straight toward the Edelmen family. The Lawyer greeted them respectfully:

- Good evening Mr. Ferdinand Edelmen ... Mrs. Honoré Edelmen ...

When Mr. Ernest Laszlo sat near the nephew, the Lawyer murmured in a low voice:

- Everything will be fine, Ferdinand ... just as expected.

Mr. Ferdinand could not contain his anxiety:

- If she answers this damn Second Challenge, we will be ruined all of u...

Mr. Ernest Laszlo seemed to have an idea in his mind, he interrupted his friend:

- If she answers ... if she answers ...

The nephew was not reassured by the Lawyer's calm attitude:

- We cannot lose this fortune Ernest!! Not for the Second time!!

The Lawyer let out a discreet confident laugh:

- Don't worry, Ferdinand ... the first time was pure luck ... and tonight, I will make sure that luck will not be repeated a second time!!

Moments later, Dalya Bouvard and Mr. Sloan Wilfrid arrived at the living room of the grand Mansion. Escorted by the Snow Panther, which followed them from the Annex house, Dalya walked inside the living room, with slow hesitant steps. Mr. Wilfrid headed to greet some men. The Snow Panther walked in a sovereign attitude and she lay down in a corner of the living room, near a large window.

The first face Dalya noticed among the crowd, was Professor Canfield. He greeted her with his usual radiant smile. Sitting next to him was Miss Guendolyn. The young woman seemed intimidated to be in such a luxurious place. But when she noticed Dalya, Miss Guendolyn waved at her and smiled cheerfully.

And sitting next to Miss Guendolyn, Uncle Giorgi was patiently waiting for the start of the event. The clues that Dalya shared with him each time, kindled the man's curiosity. Uncle Giorgi insisted on being present with his niece during the Challenge, he displayed an encouraging smile.

Dalya walked a few steps toward the desk that was placed in a corner of the living room. The nephew and the niece of Late Mr. Governor were sitting on the chairs right next to the Lawyer, Mr. Ernest Laszlo. His son, Lyor Laszlo was standing near the living room windows; he observed the night landscape, without caring about what was happening inside the living room.

Barely two more steps forward, Dalya was surprised to find a familiar face: Amira Mounier and her father!! Amira stood up quickly and she approached Dalya:

- I hope you don't mind that I came ...
- On the contrary!! I'm glad to see you!!

Mr. Jacob Mounier, Amira's father stood up, and he greeted Dalya:

- Good luck tonight, Mademoiselle!!
- Thank you, Sir.

Amira hugged Dalya firmly in her arms. When Dalya arrived at the desk, she gently placed down the Excelbox on the table. And instantly, a little voice called her from behind:

- Mademoiselle Dalya Bouvard.

Never Dalya would have thought to see in the living room of the grand Mansion, Mrs. Glorina, the housekeeper of the French neighbors!! The woman was wearing her long beige coat, a small hat that showed off her red hair with silver reflections, and a small black bag. Dalya was overwhelmed by her presence:

- Mrs. Glorina!! ... It's a nice surprise to see you here!!

The woman hugged Dalya in her arms:

- I came for you, Mademoiselle!! You are very dear to our hearts!! Never a person has been so nice and polite with me as much as you were!! Mrs. Marianne would have wished to come too, but the cold stops her from leaving the house ...
- Yes, I understand. But I am delighted to see you here. Thank you very much for coming.

Mrs. Glorina sat next to Amira Mounier and her father. And just when Dalya was about to turn around and go back near the Desk, she noticed two silhouettes behind the opened door of the living room. The maid Cristelle and the Gardener Mr. Rosenwald. They were curious about the event happening that night. Cristelle waved cheerfully at Dalya, and the Gardener displayed an encouraging smile toward her.

Dalya Bouvard was very touched by the presence of all these people. And although her parents abstained from attending the event to support their own daughter, Dalya didn't feel the lack of support and encouragement when she observed the crowd of people present here tonight, coming only for her.

10:45 PM.

The Lawyer, Mr. Ernest Laszlo stood up and he walked toward the large desk. He faced the crowd of people attending and he announced in a calm serious voice:

- Ladies and gentlemen ... Good evening ... I am pleased to host this evening, the Second Challenge that will decide of the legitimacy of the Heir to Late Mr. Iskander Balthaz...
- Ah!! That dear Balthazar!! May he rest in peace!!

The voice that interrupted Mr. Ernest Laszlo was so strong and imposing, everyone turned around to locate the source of the voice. And everyone was surprised to find out who it was. On the doorstep of the living room, there was ... the Congressman Yolan McKlain himself!!

Amira and Dalya exchanged a surprised look; it was the same man who attended Amira's essay contest at the Royal Georgetown College, only a few days ago.

Without waiting to be invited in, the Congressman walked inside the living room, accompanied by three men behind him. The Congressman was wearing an elegant royal blue suit. And the 3 men were all in black and white shirt suit.

All the people stood up from their seats and armchairs to greet the Congressman, who shook hands with everyone, with a natural attitude and a sincere smile.

Mr. Ferdinand Edelmen and his sister Mrs. Honoré also stood up. Besides the anxiety of the Second Challenge, Mr. Ferdinand Edelmen didn't understand the presence of the Congressman Yolan McKlain, for this event. Mrs. Honoré was confused as well, she asked her brother in a whisper:

- Ferdinand ... what's happening? ... Why is the Congressman attending the Challenge?

Unable to understand what was going on, Ferdinand Edelmen turned toward his friend the Lawyer. And strangely, Mr. Ernest Laszlo became pale and he lost his confident smile. The nephew insisted upon his friend:

- Is it part of your plan, Ernest?

The Lawyer, Mr. Ernest Laszlo certainly had an idea in his mind to prevent Dalya from passing the Second Challenge. Except that, the presence of the Congressman was not part of his plan, at all!

Mr. Ernest Laszlo hurried toward the Congressman. He greeted him politely:

- Good evening, Congressman ... to what do we owe the honor of your visi...

The Congressman greeted Mr. Ernest Laszlo with a strong handshake:

- I gladly reply to your request, Mr. Ernest Laszlo!!
- My ... re ... request?

The Congressman continued spontaneously:

- Yes ... and I must admit that you were right, Ernest. The fortune of Dear Late Mr. Governor is an affair of state. The presence of a statesman is essential tonight. You have done well to remind me of that in your letter!
- My … letter?

Mr. Ernest Laszlo didn't understand what the Congressman McKlain was talking about. He stood in his place, confused and disoriented. The Congressman turned to the nephew, and he greeted him with a fairly robust handshake:

- I applaud your integrity Mr. Ferdinand Edelmen!! Your Uncle ... that Dear Balthazar … would have been proud of your honesty and integrity!

Mr. Ferdinand became red, and he murmured in confusion:

- My ... honest … and ... integr…

The Congressman walked forward and left behind him the Lawyer and the nephew. When he stopped in front of a little 13 years old girl, the Congressman said:

- Good evening, Mademoiselle.

Dalya Bouvard hesitated for a second, intimidated by the greatness of the man:

- G ... good evening, Sir.

Congressman Yolan McKlain shook Dalya's hand warmly:

- I am delighted to meet you, Mademoiselle. And I wish you good luck for tonight!!

Dalya murmured a surprised intimidated thank you. The Congressman and his men took place in the chairs right in front of the desk where Dalya was standing.

Everyone was shocked and confused by the presence of Congressman Yolan McKlain. Everyone, but one man ... Sloan Wilfrid. He displayed a proud and strangely joyful smile. No one knew how the Congressman was invited to this Second Challenge. Except...Sloan Wilfrid.

The young Lyor Laszlo also tried to understand what was happening in front of him. Sitting near his mentor Mr. Wilfrid, Lyor thought aloud:

- He said that he had received a letter from my father ... but my father doesn't seem to know what the Congressman was talking about ... how can a letter, which no one knows about, could have reached the Congressman?

Sloan Wilfrid couldn't hold a little discreet innocent laugh. Lyor turned toward his mentor, he stared at him for a second, and then Lyor jumped off his chair suddenly:

- It was not my father who sent the invitation ... it was you!!!

Sloan Wilfrid looked at his young apprentice:

- In the presence of the Congressman, no one will dare to attempt anything illegal ... no one can stop this little girl from her right to answer the Second Challenge ...

Lyor Laszlo didn't believe his ears; he was shocked by what he had just found out:

- But ... you ... how ... without my father knowing ... but ... his stamp?

Mr. Wilfrid displayed a proud smile:

- Lyor ... you will learn that sometimes, to avoid injustice, we have every right to cheat a little bit.

That moment, Sloan Wilfrid observed the little Dalya Bouvard who was still standing next to the Excelbox. And just as he had promised her, Mr. Wilfrid was determined to protect her.

11:05 PM.

The Lawyer, Mr. Ernest Laszlo had thought to end this Heritage case, once and for all, this evening. Except that the presence of the Congressman, turned his plan upside down. The Lawyer had better find a solution, and as quickly as possible. After a few seconds of reflection, Mr. Ernest faced the crowd of guests and he announced:

- Ladies and gentlemen ... I invite you to the next room, tea and pastries will be serv...

The Congressman, sitting in the front row, interrupted him with a natural tone:

- Dear Ernest ... although I appreciate your hospitality, isn't it time to pass this Challenge? ... I thought the limit of this Challenge is at Midnight ... it's only one hour away!!

Sloan Wilfrid smiled proudly:

- Nice try!

Mr. Wilfrid had long been a great admirer of the Congressman McKlain. And tonight, his admiration has only increased. Natural and spontaneous, the Congressman had just crushed the hopes of Mr. Ernest Laszlo. The Lawyer hoped to delay the Challenge, in order to waste Dalya more time to answer the question.

The Congressman continued in a friendlier tone:

- And besides ... with my big fat belly, I better stay away from pastries!!

The Congressman's comment sparked a laugh in the living room of the grand Mansion. Mr. Ernest Laszlo bit his lip and he repressed his anger with great difficulty. The Lawyer had planned this event since weeks, and now a statesman intervened with his business and was ruining his plan. Mr. Ernest Laszlo swallowed his anger, and he announced:

- Well ... let's start then.

The Lawyer made a sign to Dalya. She came close to the strange box, placed on the desk. She wrote on a small paper:

What is the 2nd Question?

Dalya placed the paper on the rectangular opening in one side of the box. And the paper disappeared inside instantly.

All the present people straightened up from their chairs, to watch the strange box which gathered all the attentions.

A strange energy came out of the little shining metal box. In a moment, the top side of the box opened, enabling a transparent and oval cage glass to form, with a royal and slow movement. Within seconds, the cage was complete and welded by 4 gold cylinders forged in the shape of a vine plant. A unique round clock arose within the bright cage. The big and small needles were both a few millimeters away, on December 12th, 1891 ... that same night.

None of the present people, including the Congressman, could hold back their amazement and admiration in front of such an object. The Excelbox fascinated.

Within seconds, the strange box emitted a small paper that Dalya took with a trembling hand. She read aloud:

The First helps to start
The Second helps to ahead walk
And the two are a might combined
My Second Question is
In a word, what it is?

Dalya Bouvard froze in her place. She was well aware that the Second Challenge would be as difficult and enigmatic as the first one. Some whispers were heard in the living room. Several people straightened up from their chairs, to better observe the little girl.

The nephew Mr. Ferdinand Edelmen and the Lawyer Mr. Ernest Laszlo, exchanged a worried look. The moment the Excelbox issued the Second Question, the two men couldn't control anything. The fate of this fortune was in the hands of this little 13 years old girl!

Dalya sat on the chair in front of the desk and she faced the crowd of people. Her head was dizzy, her throat tightened, and her heart was racing with all its might, Dalya seemed thunderstruck by the Second Question. Holding the paper emitted by the Excelbox in her hands, Dalya thought in a low voice:

- In a word, what it is? ... So then, the Second Question is the same as the first one ... the answer must be a single word ...

The living room of the grand Mansion plunged into a total silence and Dalya felt all eyes on her. However, she kept her head down and her eyes focused on the paper in her hand.

- The first helps to start … the first ... The First Question? ... The First Answer? ... Does it mean the Courage? ... Courage helps you to start ... ahead walk … walk forward … so what makes you walk forward? ... The Second Question is: what makes you move forward? ... In one word!

Several minutes later, Dalya used the full capacity of her brain to find an answer, but she was unable to see clearly through it. She wrote on a paper, all the clues that this box provided her for the Second Challenge.

When a strong voice interrupted her in her thoughts. The Congressman sitting in the front rows, asked in a kind polite voice:

- We would like to understand a little more about the way of this Second Challenge. If Mademoiselle don't mind to enlighten us.

Dalya Bouvard stood up to be seen and heard by everyone, and she explained:

- In the Will of the Late Mr. Governor, it was specified that I have to pass all the Challenges that this box submits to me. It is the one and only condition to be the legitimate Heiress of Late Mr. Governor. On my every birthday, this box emits a Challenge … it's a Question which I must answer correctly, before midnight. And previously, this box provides me with 5 clues to help me answer this Question.

The Congressman asked curiously:

- 5 clues ... and can we hear them, Mademoiselle?

Dalya took a paper in front of her, and she read aloud:

- The first clue was given to me on February 3rd :

Windows and doors can close in,
Forbid air and goodness to come in!
In JV-20-89, breath will be found,
In 17-HR-08, by a small key, fear will be released,
Between 69th and 59th, many things can be prepared,
In 1703, the pressure will be displaced,
In AV-07-90, the mirror will reveal a forgotten kind.
As dark and disturbing as the fog may appear,
It's only a weak cloud when we continue to walk.

The Congressman straightened up from his chair and he exclaimed:

- Well ... that's a mysterious clue ... and a difficult one to uncover!!

Amira Mounier was sitting a few steps in front of Dalya. She and her father, both seemed fascinated by the distinguished present people and the event happening in the living room. Amira insisted to support her friend Dalya and be there for her, tonight.

When Dalya looked at her friend Amira Mounier, in that instant, the two little girls exchanged an accomplice smile. They both understood the significance of the first clue and all its strange numbers. And they both achieved a triumph! If Dalya wasn't as stubborn and determined to help, Amira would have never had the confidence in herself to beat her stuttering.

Dalya continued reading:

- The second clue was given to me on June 16th :

26 lights illuminate our mind
From darkness to dawn
The blind comes out
No failure is infinite
When will and continuity are picked
Knowledge is, against cruelty, an ally
Knowledge is, against insolence, a dignity.

The Congressman was a curious man:

- And ... you've managed to find out what this clue means? ... I didn't even understand its first sentence!!

Nobody could hold their laughs. But everyone was convinced of one thing: as intimidating as the Congressman could have been, he was a very funny man, not filtering his words. And as strange as it may seem, his comic and innocent remarks, relaxed the atmosphere in the living room of the grand Mansion.

Dalya laughed too. On that moment, she remembered all the times she had helped the school Concierge, to learn new words. Throughout the summer holidays, Dalya wrote him a list of words, she helped him in pronunciation, and she explained to him the meaning of the words through drawings or translations that she found in the Library books. The Concierge Dadès was a good man, honest, kind and hardworking. He didn't deserve to be mocked by the pretentious students.

Dalya answered the Congressman:

- That is the only clue I understood from the first read, Mr. Congressman.

Congressman smiled:

- Well in that case, I understand why Iskander Balthazar chose you to pass these Challenges!

The Congressman's comment made Dalya blush. The Lawyer Mr. Sloan Wilfrid and Professor Canfield, who were following the event with all their attention and apprehension, the two men smiled proudly too.

Dalya resumed to her reading:

- The third clue ... I got it in September 9th:

For those who laugh
The calinours will giggle too
For those who demean down
The determination will rise up
For those who terrorize
Never will their cowardice overcome
For those who unjustly expose
Their wickedness will pay back
Facing up the mocker, the cruel and the rude
Stubborn, will continue our way up.

The Congressman seemed more and more fascinated by the words of this strange box. He murmured aloud:

- For those who demean down … the determination will rise up … that's very well said!

Dalya agreed with the Excelbox. For having faced mockeries, critics and attacks from Eriem Eyelord, Gael Benoble, Lakita Fleuritel and all their court, Dalya remembered that this clue had a reassuring and encouraging effect on her.

Dalya continued:

- The fourth clue was provided to me in November 29th:

We continue to uncover, to learn, and to grow.
We continue to awaken, educate and dazzle.

To the first constantly reminding his charities,
One could learn from the bee, offering goods and honey, for free.

To the second having fun of others' trips and falls,
One wonders, who's a lizard to laugh about a wolf?

To the third who thinks only of himself,
One can assure you, as smart as the fox may be, he always end up lonely

To the fourth who filters no moves or words,
One could learn from the Owl, her politeness and silence make you bow

To the fifth who hid the truth,
One guarantee, the monkey may jump well, but it will not escape a fall

To the sixth who is an austere cold,
One is amazed, how can bears live in winter, yet their hearts are warm.

To the last who only speaks venom,
One gladly reminds you, whatever the skunk releases, it sticks on it too.

And to all the befores and all the upcomings,
Our advices are only to keep or to let go.

Some whispers were heard in the living room. No one knew who the strange box was referring to in its 4th clue. Dalya looked up at her Uncle Giorgi. Sitting a few chairs away from his niece, Uncle Giorgi seemed to be the only one to understand Dalya's thoughts in that moment. This clue was referring to Dalya's 6 other Uncles and Aunt who visited them during the Thanksgiving holiday. Saddened and aware of the bad flaws of his brothers and sister, Giorgi Bouvard offered a comforting and kind smile to his niece. Although Dalya was disappointed of her 6 Uncles and Aunt, she was happy to have Uncle Giorgi Bouvard, an encouraging and kind Uncle.

Dalya looked at her paper for a moment, and then she read aloud:

- The fifth and final clue, I received from the Excelbox last night, December 11th :

The day when freedom will break its chains, will come.
The day when no more insolence will be swallowed, will come.
The day when respect will be continual, will come.
The day when injustice will bow, will come.
Because they thought burying a weak voice,
While they burry a seed that back will grow.

Silence reigned in the living room. Although some clues were incomprehensible, yet some clues were enough clear and made you tremble. The Congressman himself was impressed by this strange box, he murmured:

- Injustice will bow ... injustice will bow ...

11:20 PM.

Dalya Bouvard sat back in her chair. She read the clues in a low voice, many times. She wrote on a paper many sentences and words. She thought hard:

- I need one word ... Courage helps to start ... a single word helps to move forward ... But which one?

Dalya lay back on her chair for a moment:

- The 5 clues that I had, most often they refer to people ... how do these people help to move forward? ... and I had the clues during difficult situations ... Amira was mocked by Professors ... Dadès was mocked by Eriem and her court ... my Uncles were not the people I had hoped for ... how can I define these difficult situations in one word?

Several minutes later, Dalya was still unable to get an answer. The 5 clues were as much enigmatic and different from each other.

When suddenly, Dalya was interrupted by the Lawyer's voice, Mr. Ernest Laszlo announced:

- 20 minutes remain!!

Dalya was paralyzed in her chair. Her throat tightened, her heart choked, her face became all red and the anxiety conquered her. She looked up to see in front of her, the Lawyer, Mr. Ernest Laszlo who showed off a satisfied smile. After all, even if his original plan had failed, the Lawyer was sure that the little girl couldn't find the right answer. Luck played in the Lawyer's favor!

Despite all her efforts, the 5 clues were not sufficient to Dalya to answer this Second Challenge. She was a smart little girl, but she had absolutely no idea of the answer.

Mr. Ernest Laszlo was in hurry and determined to end this case, as soon as possible. The Lawyer stood up, he faced the crowd, and he announced with a calm voice:

- Ladies and gentlemen ... I inform you that, according to the Will, if this little girl doesn't provide any answer to the Second Question, in exactly 17 minutes ... the legitimate Heir will be announced tonight!

Then, the Lawyer Mr. Ernest Laszlo turned around, and he whispered to Dalya:

- It was useless to dream, little beggar ... tonight, you will return to your rat hole, I promise you that ... you have more in common with gutter rats, than with this Noble world!

At this precise moment, and although he was sitting away from her, Sloan Wilfrid decided to intervene. Standing up and coming near Mr. Ernest Laszlo, Sloan Wilfrid said in a loud voice:

- Mademoiselle still must provide an answer to this strange box. And if the answer is wrong, only then, the legitimate Heir can be announced.

The Congressman supported Mr. Wilfrid's idea :

- Law is law ... wrong or right answer ... the young girl must imperatively answer the question, before proclaiming the Heir of this fortune.
- Yes, you are right. Mr. Ernest Laszlo replied, without any objection, confident and sure of his luck tonight.

Mr. Ernest Laszlo went back to his seat. At that moment, Mr. Wilfrid turned around toward Dalya, and he whispered in a serious voice:

- Dalya!! ... You still have 16 minutes!!

Dalya trembled:

- But ... Sir ... I have no idea for any answer ... I don't know what it's abou...

Wilfrid insisted in a serious voice:

- Listen to me!! Reread the clues!! Remember all the details!! Focus and give the best answer you think is correct. I know it seems impossible. But this is your last chance!! ... You still have 16 minutes!! I implore you, Dalya ... do your best!!

Dalya was touched by Mr. Wilfrid's gesture and insistence. As soon as the young Lawyer returned to sit on a chair in front of her, Dalya reread her paper and she thought quietly:

- The first ... Courage makes you start ... what allows you to progress? ... 5 clues were all given to me in difficult times ... so ... difficult times can make you progress? ... difficult times, these are two words ... and it is not logical ...

Dalya lay back on her chair:

- I don't see through it, at all ... even with 5 clues, it's incomprehensible ... this Second Question is much more difficult than the first one ... I have not the slightest idea about the answer!!

Dalya looked up to notice the Lawyer Mr. Ernest Laszlo staring at her. The Lawyer displayed a devil grin. Since the first day she had met him, Dalya knew that Mr. Ernest Laszlo would do everything to prevent her from succeeding. Dalya thought:

- I may have failed to answer this Second Question ... yes ... but he is wrong! I have nothing in common with gutter rats and I w...

When all of a sudden, Dalya straightened up from her chair. She thought aloud:

- I have nothing in common with ... I have nothing in common ...

Dalya read her notes and she murmured:

- In common … in common ... ...

Dalya reread all the clues:

- There is only one word in common with all the clues ... one word is repeated ... continue ... continuity … will continue ... continual ... that is all that connects these five clues ...

Mr. Ernest Laszlo announced in a proud and strong voice:

- You have 13 minutes left!!

To this announcement, Dalya was paralyzed, and it seemed that Mr. Ernest Laszlo had a horrible pleasure to remind her that she lacked of time. In 13 minutes, she will have to find a correct answer. Her heart ran full speed, her throat choked, Dalya was about to faint. In 13 minutes, Dalya's life was about to change.

When she raised up her head, Dalya realized that she wasn't the only one stressing. Professor Canfield had a serious and grave allure. Mr. Wilfrid was cleaning his round glasses with an anxious movement. Cristelle and Mr. Gardener looked serious and stressed. Mrs. Glorina had lost her usual smile, and she seemed worried. Miss Guendolyn was biting her lips. Uncle Giorgi caressed his mustache with a trembling hand. Her friend Amira had red cheeks, she seemed about to choke.

And when Dalya observed her friend Amira for a moment, a strange idea settled in Dalya's mind:

- Continue ... continuity ... will continue ... continual ... the turtle and the rabbit ... the turtle … Monsieur de la Fontaine ... the Second helps to progress ... could it be that...?

The Lawyer, Mr. Ernest Laszlo stood up from his chair; he came near the desk and announced:

- 11 minutes!!

Dalya had one word in her mind, but she was not so sure about it. She couldn't connect the word to the 5 clues, which were very distinct from each other. She couldn't explain how this word is used to ahead walk. And she didn't understand the lesson of this Challenge. Yet, Dalya decided to get up and she announced in a little trembling voice:

- I ... I have an answer. The only answer I could find. Yet, I am not sure it's the right one.

A few whispers and exclamations arose in the living room of the grand Mansion. Mr. Wilfrid stood up suddenly and he approached Dalya. She wrote a note on a small paper, and she handed it to Mr. Wilfrid.

- I'm sorry, Mr. Wilfrid ... this is the only word that I could find ... I don't think it's the correct answer ... I couldn't understand what the 5 clues meant this time ... I'm so sorry ...

Mr. Wilfrid offered a sympathetic smile to Dalya, while taking her little paper:

- You have done your best, Mademoiselle. It's all that matters.

For the first time in years, Sloan Wilfrid was sad. It is true that he had tried to help Dalya and protect her from all the ruses of his employer, Mr. Ernest Laszlo. But the answer to the Second Question was of the sole control of the little girl.

Lyor Laszlo was somehow reassured that this entire affair had finally ended. From its beginning, Lyor had refused this responsibility that was forced on him. And tonight, Lyor felt relieved of a heavy burden.

Dalya walked toward the people present. The Congressman Yolan McKlain and his men got up. Addressing Dalya in a nice tone, the Congressman said:

- I'm sorry that it didn't go on as you wished, Mademoiselle. However, I am convinced that you are a smart little girl. And I have no doubt that life will offer you many pleasant surprises.

The Congressman's words were sincere and comforting, despite Dalya's difficult situation. She smiled back at him:

- Thank you, Mr. Congressman.

The Lawyer Mr. Ernest Laszlo, and the nephew Mr. Ferdinand Edelmen, looked at Dalya with an arrogant stare. The two men could barely contain their happiness and relief. Finally!! They finally managed to get rid of this little veggy seller!! The Fortune of Late Mr. Governor had finally returned to the legal Heir!!

After months of tension, this case was finally closed!!

Dalya turned toward another person. Professor Canfield always had encouraging words for her. Except that night, he seemed to have lost his words. Professor Canfield shook Dalya's hand and he smiled with a regretful look. Miss Guendolyn couldn't stop her tears from flowing. She squeezed Dalya tightly in her arms, without daring to say a word. Mrs. Glorina, the housekeeper of the French neighbors, appeared pale and overwhelmed. She kissed Dalya and she collapsed back into her chair, her legs held her no more.

Uncle Giorgi stood up and he smiled sadly to his niece:

- I'll walk you home ... Biggo.

Dalya was glad not to walk alone, all the way up to her old house, at the East side of downtown. She appreciated Uncle Giorgi's kindness and goodness toward her.

When Dalya walked to her friend, she noticed that Amira wanted to speak, but words didn't came out of her mouth, her throat was tightened, her cheeks were red, sweat appeared on her forehead. Amira made a considerable effort to pronounce her words. This time, Amira Mounier didn't stutter because of mockery or critics, but because of sadness:

- Ca ... ca … can't … y … y … you … st … st … stay in … school?
- I can't pay the school tuition. I must return to the market, to work and help my family.

Tears flowed from Amira's eyes, and she couldn't stop them:

- The m ... moment I succeed to … to have a friend ... is the same moment when I lose her.

The two little girls exchanged a sad smile. Amira had trouble releasing Dalya from her arms, she cried loudly. Dalya greeted Amira's father, before leaving the living room.

In the hall of the grand Mansion, before the exit door, Dalya met the maid Cristelle and the Gardener Mr. Rosenwald. They both seemed shocked by the turn of the event they had followed since the beginning, from the verge of the living room door. Cristelle had red wet eyes, swollen with tears that she painfully tried to hold, her smile was erased. When Dalya left the living room and approached her, Cristelle lowered her head and she bowed, murmuring in a sincerely sad voice:

- Lady Dalya Bouvard.

It was the first time that Cristelle called her that way. And it was the second employee of the grand Mansion to call her Lady. Dalya approached Cristelle and she hugged her tightly. Cristelle was as always, surprised by the spontaneous and the humble manners of the little girl. Dalya smiled:

- Goodbye, Cristelle. It was a pleasure to know you.

Dalya turned toward the Gardener. Mr. Rosenwald and Dalya exchanged a smile. The old man bowed his head and he affirmed in a sad voice:

- Lady Dalya Bouvard.

The little girl turned around and she left the house. The Snow Panther escorted the little girl outside the grand Mansion. At the big exit gate of the garden, Séraphine stopped and watched the little girl go on her way.

In the grand Mansion, some people were happy and relieved that this story was finally over. Some people were sad and disappointed that this story was unjustly over.

What is commonly known, is that luck happens only once in a life, never twice. The little girl had no chance to succeed in correctly answering the Second Question. Seriously ... no chance!

11:52 PM.

The Lawyer, Mr. Ernest Laszlo had regained his usual arrogant attitude. He asked his right-hand man Mr. Wilfrid, with an oddly happy voice:

- Wilfrid!! Put this paper inside this box ... so we can finally announce the legitimate Heir!!

Before Sloan Wilfrid could insert the little paper inside the strange box, he read the content of what Dalya had given him. Only one word:

Perseverance

It was the only word that the little girl could find. And even if it was the wrong answer, Mr. Wilfrid was forced to insert the paper into the Excelbox to legitimize the nomination of Mr. Ferdinand Edelmen as rightful Heir.

Reluctantly, and with a heavy heart, Mr. Wilfrid introduced the small paper on the open edge of the strange box, and the paper was swallowed immediately inside the Excelbox. Straightaway, the Lawyer Mr. Ernest Laszlo announced aloud proudly:

- Ladies and gentlemen ... I am pleased to appoint Mr. Ferdinand Edelmen ... legitimate Heir to the fortune of Late Mr. Iskander Balthazar!!

A wave of applause conquered the living room of the grand Mansion. The Congressman instantly turned to the nephew, Mr. Ferdinand Edelmen, and said:

- I understand that you are now the Heir to the fortune of your deceased Uncle. I hope that you will live up to his integrity and honesty ... Iskander Balthazar was a great man ... a great man!!

Mr. Ferdinand Edelmen smiled happily:

- Thank you for your presence tonight, Congressman McKlain.

The nephew and new Heir instantly received the congratulations of the attending people.

Meanwhile, Sloan Wilfrid turned toward the windows of the living room. With a heavy heart, he watched the silhouette of the poor 13 years old little girl leaving the grand Mansion, and returning to her old life.

Dalya Bouvard did the best she could to find an answer. And even if the little girl had failed this Second Challenge ... even if she was sad and crushed because she didn't succeed and help her family ... at that moment, a strange force invaded Dalya Bouvard.

On the road of Dumbarton Oaks Parks, the air was fresh. The silence of nature was imposed. The night was lit by the stars and a full moon. Some raindrops announced a storm coming ahead.

Dalya Bouvard slowly walked ahead ... invaded by a Perseverance facing the rain that wet her gradually...

A perseverance facing failure.

A perseverance facing sadness, confusion, and doubt.

A Perseverance facing abuse, violence, mockery and injustice.

A perseverance facing pain, exhaustion, and weakness.

A Perseverance facing dark days.

There and then ... A Perseverance was born.

Because if courage makes you start ... oh, well ... a different strength will make you ahead walk.

11:55 PM.

The Excelbox turned on.